RUTHLESS CROSS

Off the Grid: FBI Series #6

BARBARA FREETHY

BARBARA
FREETHY
—BOOKS—

Fog City Publishing

PRAISE FOR BARBARA FREETHY

"A fabulous, page-turning combination of romance and intrigue. Fans of Nora Roberts and Elizabeth Lowell will love this book." — *NYT Bestselling Author Kristin Hannah on Golden Lies*

"PERILOUS TRUST is a non-stop thriller that seamlessly melds jaw-dropping suspense with sizzling romance. Readers will be breathless in anticipation as this fast-paced and enthralling love story goes in unforeseeable directions." — *USA Today HEA Blog*

"Barbara Freethy's first book PERILOUS TRUST in her OFF THE GRID series is an emotional, action packed, crime drama that keeps you on the edge of your seat...I'm exhausted after reading this but in a good way. 5 Stars!" — *Booklovers Anonymous*

"Powerful and absorbing...sheer hold-your-breath suspense." — *NYT Bestselling Author Karen Robards on Don't Say A Word*

"I loved this story from start to finish. Right from the start of PERILOUS TRUST, the tension sets in. Goodness, my heart was starting to beat a little fast by the end of the prologue! I found myself staying up late finishing this book, and that is something I don't normally do." — *My Book Filled Life Blog*

"Freethy is at the top of her form. Fans of Nora Roberts will find a similar tone here, framed in Freethy's own spare, elegant style." — *Contra Costa Times on Summer Secrets*

"Freethy hits the ground running as she kicks off another winning romantic suspense series...Freethy is at her prime with a superb combo of engaging characters and gripping plot." — *Publishers' Weekly on Silent Run*

PRAISE FOR BARBARA FREETHY

"Barbara Freethy is a master storyteller with a gift for spinning tales about ordinary people in extraordinary situations and drawing readers into their lives." — *Romance Reviews Today*

"Freethy (Silent Fall) has a gift for creating complex, appealing characters and emotionally involving, often suspenseful, sometimes magical stories." — *Library Journal on Suddenly One Summer*

Freethy hits the ground running as she kicks off another winning romantic suspense series...Freethy is at her prime with a superb combo of engaging characters and gripping plot." — *Publishers' Weekly on Silent Run*

"Grab a drink, find a comfortable reading nook, and get immersed in this fast paced, realistic, romantic thriller! 5 STARS!" *Perrin – Goodreads on ELUSIVE PROMISE*

"If you love nail-biting suspense and heartbreaking emotion, Silent Run belongs on the top of your to-be-bought list. I could not turn the pages fast enough." — *NYT Bestselling Author Mariah Stewart*

"Words cannot explain how phenomenal this book was. The characters are so believable and relatable. The twists and turns keep you on the edge of your seat and flying through the pages. This is one book you should be desperate to read." *Caroline - Goodreads*

"Hooked me from the start and kept me turning pages throughout all the twists and turns. Silent Run is powerful romantic intrigue at its best." — *NYT Bestselling Author JoAnn Ross*

RUTHLESS CROSS
Off the Grid: FBI Series #6

© Copyright 2019 Barbara Freethy
All Rights Reserved
ISBN: 9781944417666

For more information on Barbara Freethy's books, visit her website:
www.barbarafreethy.com

CHAPTER ONE

BEAUTY, money, and art had brought all the pretty people together. FBI Agent Flynn MacKenzie accepted a glass of champagne as his gaze swept the grand hall of the elegant Piquard Art Museum, set on ten acres in the Santa Monica mountains with sweeping views of Los Angeles and the Pacific Ocean. He'd been at the Piquard many times. He knew almost every inch of the four-story architectural wonder that housed pre-twentieth-century European paintings, illuminated manuscripts, sculptures, and photographs from the 1830s through present day.

Today's exhibition by French painter Gerard Bissette was like so many other events he'd attended in his lifetime. But he hadn't come for the art; he'd come for an old friend, a man who had been a father figure to him at a time when he'd desperately needed one. Judge Arthur Corbyn had called him earlier that day, an urgent note in his voice, requesting that he meet him tonight at the museum. He'd said he needed a favor and would explain everything at the party. The call had given him a bad feeling. He hoped Arthur wasn't in trouble, but if he was, Flynn would do everything he could to help him.

As his gaze swept the magnificent hall, with its sleek marble floors and exquisitely ornate glass chandeliers, he saw titans of industry: the white-haired and regal Hamilton Augustyn, head of the Augustyn luxury hotel chain; Valerie Dare, the voluptuous copper-haired CEO of Dare Perfume; and Colin Chambers, the gregarious Brit, whose new electric cars were being hailed as the fleet of the future.

There were celebrities and film stars, athletes and social media influencers, and of course, there were the icons of the art world including Kyle Logan, who had recently taken over the Logan Gallery in New York City from his father Walter Logan. Flynn had met Kyle years ago when they'd both been bored young teenagers attending an art exhibit with their fathers. He smiled as he saw Kyle swing his arm around a beautiful woman. Kyle's dark, handsome looks had always made him attractive to the ladies.

As his gaze moved around Kyle's circle, he saw Pamela Smythe, a tall, haughty art critic, whose scathing reviews could destroy an artist's career in only a few words; the new Italian boy wonder, artist Marcus Vitelli, who was taking the art world by storm; Gretchen Vale, the attractive platinum blonde who had once been his father's most trusted assistant; and the short and stocky Gerard Bissette, the fifty-five-year-old French artist, whose work was being honored tonight.

And then there were the worker bees, the museum staff moving surreptitiously through the crowd in their conservative suits and dresses, making sure that the guests were having a good time. There were also security guards, some in uniform, others in plain clothes, keeping an eye on not only the central exhibition area, that was still hidden behind white curtains, but also the many other exhibits housed in various rooms throughout the building.

But where was Arthur?

That question had no sooner crossed his mind when Arthur entered the hall. It had been years since he'd seen him, but he hadn't changed much. He was of medium height with a lean build and a bit of gray in his brown hair. The woman at his side had short, dark-brown hair and a frame so thin that the enormous diamond on the third finger of her left hand seemed to weigh her down. He hadn't realized that Arthur had gotten married again, but he was happy for him.

Following Arthur and his wife was a beautiful, young woman, who, despite the January chill, was wearing a slim-fitting red mini dress that fell off her shoulders and showed off her legs. Her dark hair cascaded over her bare shoulders in shimmering waves. She would have been even more stunning if there had been a smile on her face, but the tight line of her lips indicated someone who'd rather be anywhere else.

As they moved into the room, Arthur's gaze connected with his. Relief flashed in his brown eyes. Arthur said something to his wife and then crossed the room to speak to him.

"I almost didn't recognize you without a surfboard under your arm, Flynn."

"I still hit the waves as often as I can." They exchanged a handshake and a brief hug. "It's good to see you."

"You, too. Thank you for coming. I'm sure this art museum is probably the last place you'd want to be after everything that happened with your father."

"What do you need from me?" he asked, not wanting to talk about his dad.

"A conversation, but the subject matter is..." Arthur glanced around their immediate vicinity to make sure they were alone. "Sensitive."

He could see the discomfort in Arthur's gaze. "Then perhaps we should meet another time. You could come by my office."

"No. This isn't FBI business. It's personal. It's private."

"Then I could come to your home."

"That might be noticed as well."

"By who?"

Arthur took a step closer, lowering his voice. "Someone is watching me. That's why I asked you to come here. After Gerard's talk, we'll find a moment, perhaps on the upstairs terrace. We'll just be two old friends catching up." He paused. "Did you bring a date as I requested?"

"She's on her way. Although, I don't know why I need a date."

"Our meeting must appear to be coincidental, social. No one comes to these events on their own."

With every word, Flynn's bad feeling got worse. "You're being very mysterious."

"I know." Arthur gave him an apologetic look. "I've gotten myself into a tricky situation. I'm hoping you can help me. I'm feeling a bit desperate."

"I'll certainly try to help you. You got me through some very dark times."

Relief filled Arthur's eyes. "I'm happy to see that you're doing well for yourself. I knew you would. You have a resiliency, a stubborn determination, that keeps you going no matter what gets in your way." He paused, his gaze moving to the woman approaching. "She doesn't know."

"Understood," he said quietly.

"Juliette, I'd like you to meet an old friend. This is Flynn MacKenzie, the young man I was telling you about."

"Olivia's friend," Juliette said. "It's lovely to meet you." While there was warmth in her eyes, her hand was ice cold, and he wanted to shove his own hand in his pocket just to heat it back up.

"You, too," he said.

"Juliette organized this exhibition," Arthur continued. "She's the events director here at the museum."

"It looks to be amazing," he said, giving her a smile.

"I hope so. There are always so many last-minute details to worry about. But Gerard is important to the museum, to us personally. He's a good friend of Arthur's, and I want everything to be perfect."

He could hear the strain in her voice. "I'm sure it will be."

"Juliette and I met at a similar party about eighteen months ago," Arthur said, sliding his arm around his wife's waist. "We were married six months later, and we celebrated our anniversary at Christmas."

"That's very fast."

"When it's right, you know it." Arthur gave his wife a loving smile.

Juliette smiled back, but there was something a little forced about it.

"Mom," the beautiful brunette interrupted. "Victoria Waltham is looking for you, and she has fire in her eyes. Apparently, there's a problem with someone's ticket."

"Oh, dear. I better take care of that," Juliette said, hurrying over to speak to the museum director, who was standing by the entrance with an elderly couple.

"Callie, this is Flynn MacKenzie," Arthur said. "My stepdaughter Callie Harper."

"Hello," she said.

He extended his hand, wondering if her touch would be as cold as her mother's, but it wasn't—it was red-hot. A fiery warmth spread through him as their gazes met. Her dark-brown eyes made it almost impossible to look away or to let go, but as a question entered her gaze, he released her hand.

She stepped back, her tongue swiping across her lower lip, a flush of pink spreading across her cheeks. "Excuse me," she said. "I have to…find someone."

He felt inexplicably disappointed by her abrupt departure.

"That's Callie—never eager to spend more than one minute in my company," Arthur said with annoyance.

"Arthur, my old friend, and my most loyal patron," Gerard Bissette interrupted.

Flynn stepped back as Arthur and Gerard embraced.

"You look well," Arthur told Gerard.

"As do you. Who is your friend?"

"Flynn MacKenzie, meet Gerard Bissette, one of the most important artists of our time."

"I'm honored," he said.

"You look familiar. Have we met before?" Gerard asked, a thoughtful gleam in his eyes.

"No," he said, having a feeling that Gerard might have met his father.

"Interesting. I rarely forget a face." Gerard turned back to

Arthur. "I hate to interrupt, but I'd like you to meet some of my friends from Paris before the show opens."

"I would love to. Will you excuse us, Flynn?"

"Of course." As they left, he let out a breath and took a sip of champagne. He had stopped hiding from his father's shame a long time ago. In fact, he'd turned that bad experience into an advantage. But sometimes the memory still stung.

"I'm here," Savannah Kane proclaimed.

"You're late," he grumbled.

"It takes time to get this pretty." She gave him a saucy, confident smile.

Savannah Kane was more than a little pretty. She was a former Miss Georgia, but her blonde hair and light-green eyes had never impressed him as much as her analytical skills and her ability to blend into any environment, which made her a valuable member of his FBI task force.

"Your time was well spent," he told her.

"You look pretty, too, Flynn. Although, you could have shaved."

"It's my look," he said with a grin.

"I get it. That sexy scruff charms all the girls," she drawled. "So, why am I here? Is there a threat to the exhibit?"

"No. This is a personal situation. I was asked to bring a date."

"And none of your thousand girlfriends were free?"

"Since I don't know exactly what this is about, or what I'm walking into, I thought you would be a better cover."

"All right. Then I need some champagne. For cover, of course," she added with a laugh.

He snagged a glass from the tray of a passing waiter. "Here you go."

She took a sip. "Nice and expensive, just the way I like it."

"Good. I hope I didn't pull you away from an actual date."

"No Friday night plans for me. I was going to catch up on paperwork. My boss likes to bend the rules during the investigation, but when it comes to the after-reports, he's a stickler for detail."

He smiled at her pointed comment. "That's because my boss gives me latitude until he has to justify everything that happened under his watch."

"Your boss is Damon now. I'm sure he'll cut you some slack. He's one of us. We came through Quantico together."

Savannah was right. Damon Wolfe was one of them, even though he now headed up the LA field office and oversaw many divisions, including Flynn's specialized task force.

"Damon is great, but he has a boss, too."

"The many layers of bureaucracy," she grumbled. "It's why I like working for you so much, Flynn. You cut through the red tape with a ruthless pair of scissors."

"I love wielding those scissors."

"I know you do. Can you tell me anything about tonight?"

He tipped his head toward Arthur, who had been joined by his wife, Juliette, and was now talking to not only Gerard Bissette, but also an older couple in their sixties, as well as Kyle Logan and his date, and the museum director Victoria Waltham, a sophisticated blonde in her early forties.

Victoria had been around the art scene since she was an eighteen-year-old intern at the Benedict Auction House and had worked her way through galleries and museums to get to her current position. He'd met her when he was about fifteen. She'd spent a month at his father's gallery. She'd been about twenty-two then. She'd been completely disinterested in him, but she'd been very flirty with his father, something that had made him uncomfortable. But despite other things his dad had eventually been found culpable for, cheating on his wife had never been one of them. Not that that meant it hadn't happened. His father had turned out to be a master of deception.

"Flynn?" Savannah pressed. "Are you still with me?"

"Sorry. The man in the gray suit is a federal judge—Arthur Corbyn," he explained. "Next to him is the featured artist for tonight's exhibit, Gerard Bissette; Victoria Waltham, the museum director; Kyle Logan a gallery owner out of New York and his date; and I don't know the other couple. Arthur called me earlier today and asked me to meet him here. He has something to discuss with me but wants to do it in a social setting where no one would think anything of him speaking to an FBI agent."

"Is this about a case then?"

"He said it's personal."

"How do you know him?"

"I dated his daughter, Olivia, my senior year in high school." He paused. "You've heard that story." At Quantico, exercises and tests had forced them to reveal their darkest secrets, their deepest sorrows, to strip them bare, to forge trust and to make them less vulnerable down the road. Olivia had been part of his reveal.

Savannah gave him a compassionate look. "Olivia died on vacation with her mom shortly after you graduated."

"Yes. And Arthur helped me get through it. And it wasn't the first time he did that. When I met him, I was still reeling from what had gone down with my dad. Arthur was like a second father to me. I owe him for that."

"Sounds like he wants to collect."

"He does want a favor. He told me that much. But he wouldn't say more. The last time I spoke to him was more than five years ago, right before I went to Quantico. We ran into each other at a restaurant, and that was a brief conversation. I have no idea what his life is about now, but he's in some kind of trouble. He said someone is watching him, another reason for the very public meeting."

"Makes sense. So, we'll help him, because he's important to you."

"Thanks." He liked how simple Savannah kept things. Loyalty and trust were what made them work so well together.

"It looks like the judge is headed somewhere," she murmured.

He nodded as Arthur slipped away from the group and down a hallway. "Maybe the restroom. I'll see if I can find him. I'd prefer to have our conversation sooner rather than later."

"Go. I'll wander around and see if I can learn something about art or maybe find an attractive, single, art collector."

He smiled, doubting she'd have any trouble doing that. He headed across the room but was almost immediately waylaid by his father's former assistant, Gretchen Vale.

"Flynn, is that you?" she asked, surprise in her eyes.

"Gretchen."

She gave him a confused look. "I can't believe you're here, at an art museum. I thought you had given up your love of art after your dad…"

"That was a long time ago. You look well. Are you still running the gallery in Laguna Beach?" After his father's departure, Gretchen had taken over his gallery, changing the name but keeping some of their customer base.

"Yes. I'm here with my husband, Stephen, although I don't know where he is at the moment. You remember Stephen."

"I do."

"How have you been, Flynn?"

"I'm good."

"What are you up to now?"

"I'd love to chat, but I have to meet someone. Excuse me."

"Of course. Maybe we can catch up later, Flynn. There are things we should talk about."

He couldn't imagine what those things could be. "That would be great," he lied. The last person he wanted to talk to was Gretchen. He didn't know what he really thought about her, but the one thing he did know was that he couldn't trust her.

Moving across the room, he turned down the hallway where he'd seen Arthur go. As he came around a corner, he ran smack into Arthur's stepdaughter, Callie Harper.

He caught her by the arm as she stumbled. "Sorry," he murmured. "I didn't see you."

"It's fine," she said quickly.

She glanced away, but not before he saw what looked like tears in her dark eyes.

His gut clenched at her beauty, at her inexplicable sorrow. Before he could ask her if she was all right, she slipped past him.

He thought about following her, but he needed to focus on finding Arthur. He checked the nearby restroom, but it was empty. He wandered down the hall, scanning the two nearby exhibit rooms for any sign of Arthur, but he was not among those admiring the work of German sculptor, Heinrich Schmidt, or in the crowd viewing the erotic art of Sylvia Plum.

When he stepped into the corridor, the museum speaker announced that the exhibit would be opening shortly in the grand hall. He joined the throng of guests making their way back to the center of the building.

He scanned the hall for Arthur, but there was no sign of him. Nor did he see Juliette or Callie. The absence of all three was somewhat disturbing.

Savannah came up next to him. "Did you find Judge Corbyn?"

"No. And I don't see him now."

"Neither do I. Maybe he's on one of the other floors. The entire museum is open tonight, right?"

"I believe so. But why wouldn't he be here now, supporting Gerard?" His bad feeling grew as Victoria Waltham stepped up to the microphone. After welcoming the guests, she directed their attention to a large screen for a short video of Gerard's life and work.

As the video ended, Callie came back into the hall. She took a glass of champagne from a waiter, her attention on the stage as Gerard stepped onto the stage. The artist thanked everyone for coming and talked about his inspiration for his latest collection.

Flynn barely heard what Gerard was saying, every nerve in his body on high alert. Something was wrong.

Where the hell was Arthur?

He heard a crashing noise overhead. It was so loud that Gerard paused, and the entire crowd looked upward just in time to see a body come over the fourth-floor railing.

A woman screamed. The guests scattered as the body crashed to the ground. People ran for the doors, diving for cover behind statues, not sure where the danger was coming from.

He pushed through the crowd, the first to run toward the body and not away.

When he saw the crumpled body of a man, his brown eyes wide open, his gaze fixed in disbelief, the breath left his chest.

It was Arthur Corbyn. And he was dead.

CHAPTER TWO

FLYNN SQUATTED DOWN NEXT to Arthur's body, wondering if there was anything he could do to help him, but it was clear from the positioning of his body that Arthur's neck was broken. There was a pool of blood gathering under his head, spreading across the stage in an alarming amount. Arthur's pants were halfway down his thighs, revealing white briefs. Only his face was unmarred by the violence that had taken his life.

Savannah came up behind him. He gave her a grim look. "He's gone."

"I'm sorry," she said, concern in her eyes.

He stood up, glancing overhead. "I'm going upstairs."

"I'll stay here."

He jogged over to the stairway, taking the steps three at a time, until he reached the top floor. A broken vase and a champagne glass were on the ground near the spot where Arthur had gone over the railing. As he looked over the rail, he could see the chaos in the grand hall. The small stage had emptied. There were broken champagne glasses on the floor, trays dropped haphazardly, some personal items strewn about in the rush toward the exits.

And there was Arthur's body in the middle of everything. Savannah and a security guard stood next to the body.

Then Juliette ran forward, screaming in anguish, her daughter, Callie, right behind her. The guard held her back to maintain the integrity of the crime scene, getting some help from the museum director Victoria Waltham, who was trying to comfort Juliette.

But he doubted Juliette could hear or see anyone but Arthur. He couldn't blame her for her hysterical screams. She'd just witnessed her husband's death.

Beyond the small circle surrounding Arthur, he could see that most of the guests had already fled the building, with probably the killer among them. Anger and frustration ran through him.

He should have pressed Arthur for more information. He should have insisted they talk immediately. But regrets would get him nowhere. He might not have been able to save Arthur, but he would find his killer. He would get him justice.

Pulling out his phone, he snapped several photos of the scene below, then did the same for the broken vase near his feet. He moved down the corridor. There were two exhibit rooms on this floor as well as two restrooms. He moved in and out of those rooms, but they were empty and there was no sign of a struggle or an additional crime scene. There were, however, security cameras, so hopefully there would be helpful footage.

He snapped several more photos and then made his way back into the hallway as Savannah came up the stairs, with a man in a dark suit, who was wearing an earpiece.

"Flynn, this is Rand Bentley, director of museum security," Savannah said.

"Mr. Bentley. I'm Agent MacKenzie."

"Did you find anything up here?" Rand asked.

"Just a shattered vase and a broken champagne glass. No obvious trace of blood on the railing. I'm hoping the cameras caught the judge's fall."

Rand's lips tightened in anger. "Unfortunately, the system went down several minutes before Judge Corbyn fell over the railing. My tech guy believes the system was hacked."

His stomach twisted at that piece of information. "Then this was planned. It was no accident."

"It doesn't appear to be. Can you tell me why you and Agent Kane were here at the event? Was there a concern I wasn't aware of?"

"We were simply here for the exhibit." He preferred to keep Arthur's request to himself for the moment. "But I do know the victim. He's a federal judge."

"I'm aware. Judge Corbyn has been a patron of the museum for many years. And with his wife, Juliette, working here, the judge is part of our family. This is a tragedy." Rand cleared his throat as emotion thickened his voice. "The police have arrived. I'm sure you'll want to speak to them."

"Yes." When he returned to the ground floor, he met up with Detective Miles Gage, a balding, dark-eyed man who appeared to be in his late forties.

"I'm Agent MacKenzie. This is Agent Kane," he said. "The victim is a federal judge, so we'll need to work together."

"Fine with me. I'm not into turf wars," the detective replied. "Can you tell me what happened?"

"All I know is that Judge Corbyn was thrown over the fourth-floor railing. There's a broken vase nearby. The security cameras were hacked and apparently off-line during the incident. But we'll need to look at the footage up until that point."

"You're sure he didn't just fall?" the detective asked. "Was he drinking?"

"He wasn't drunk, and he didn't fall."

"How did you happen to be here?"

"I'm an art lover."

"Both of you?" Gage asked, his sharp gaze drifting to Savannah.

She gave him a brief smile. "I came for the champagne."

The detective smiled at her, as most men did when Savannah turned on the charm. Flynn was more than happy to let her take the lead with Gage. She was great at forging relationships that could be helpful to the team.

"The medical examiner and forensics investigator are on their way," Gage added. "I've called in additional officers to take witness statements. There's a large crowd outside."

"Good. Because the killer could be among them."

"That's the family?" Gage tipped his head toward Juliette, who was weeping in her daughter's arms. Other museum staffers looked on with uncomfortable sympathy.

"Yes, the judge's wife, Juliette Corbyn, is the events director. Holding her is her daughter, Callie Harper."

As Callie wrapped her arms around her mother, she glanced over at Arthur's body, and her expression was not one of anger or sadness; it looked like relief. He frowned at that errant thought.

"I'll get their statements," Gage said. "Looks like it's going to be a long night."

"I'll be right with you," Flynn said, as Savannah and Gage moved toward Juliette.

He punched in Damon's number.

"What's up?" Damon asked.

"I just caught a murder case. It will be headed to your office, but I want it."

"What happened?"

"A federal judge was murdered at the Piquard Museum tonight —Judge Arthur Corbyn. He's someone I used to know. In fact, I was at the exhibition at his request. He said someone was watching him and he was in a tricky situation. He needed my help, but he didn't have a chance to tell me anything else before he was killed."

"I'm sorry. But if this is personal, Flynn, we should run with it. The murder of a federal judge is going to put a lot of eyes on this case."

"I'm aware. I'm also extremely motivated, and I'm already working the case. Savannah is here as well."

"Got it. I either get out of your way, or you'll be in mine," Damon said dryly.

"Then we understand each other."

"All right. You're in charge but keep me in the loop."

"Will do."

As he hung up, he saw Juliette, Callie, Detective Gage, and

Savannah walking toward the executive office suite. Juliette was still crying, but maybe she could pull herself a little more together when she didn't have to look at her husband's body.

While he wanted to join them, he headed first to the security center. Rand Bentley was there and was happy to pull up the camera footage.

"We picked up Judge Corbyn on the second floor approximately eight minutes before he fell," Rand said. "He walked into the Monet exhibit, as you can see."

He nodded, feeling a tightness in his chest as he watched some of Arthur's last moments. He moved around the exhibit without glancing at any of the paintings. There was no one else in the room, but he appeared to be looking for someone. He checked his watch and then a woman came into view—Juliette.

His gut clenched. Juliette looked angry. She was talking fast and waving her hand in the air. Arthur seemed to be trying to tell her to calm down. He put a hand on her shoulder, but she jerked away and left the room. Arthur glanced at his watch once more, waited for several seconds and then moved back into the hall. An elderly couple walked past him. Then Arthur headed toward the stairs, where he ran into Stephen Vale, Gretchen's husband.

He'd known Stephen a very long time ago, when he was a struggling painter and part-time delivery person. That was years ago, before he and Gretchen had gotten married and taken over his father's gallery. Stephen exchanged a few words with Arthur and then he went downstairs while Arthur headed up. A moment later, the footage stopped.

"That's it," Rand said. "We just got the cameras back online a few minutes ago."

"I'd like to get one of my techs over here to work with your guys, see if we can figure out where the hack might have come from."

"We'll take all the help we can get."

He texted his cyber expert, Lucas Raines, explaining what he needed and asking him to come down to the museum as soon as possible. Then he went to find Juliette.

She'd spoken to her husband only minutes before his death, and they'd argued about something. He needed to know what that was about.

Callie and Juliette were seated on a couch in the director's office, but there was no sign of Victoria. Savannah and Gage were on their feet in front of them.

Juliette was still crying, constantly rubbing a wad of tissues across her dripping eyes and nose.

"I need to see Arthur," Juliette sobbed. "I need to go to the hospital."

"Mom, he's gone," Callie said gently, her arm around her mom's fragile shoulders.

"He can't be. He just can't be."

"Are we done here?" Callie asked sharply. "We've told you everything we know, which is nothing. We didn't see who pushed Arthur over the railing. We don't know anything. I need to get my mom home. She needs time to process everything."

Before either Savannah or Gage could answer, he said, "One moment." Her gaze flew to his, and he could see the anger in her eyes.

"What?" she snapped.

"I have a question for Juliette," he returned.

Juliette gave him a teary look. "You're Arthur's old friend."

"Yes, and I want to help you."

"No one can help me. Arthur is...dead." She finished that sentence with a sob.

"You spoke to Arthur in the Monet room on the second floor a few minutes before he went upstairs. It looked like you were arguing. What was that conversation about?"

She gave him a blank look. "What?"

"You spoke to your husband shortly before he was killed. You seemed angry. I'd like to know what you were talking about."

Juliette glanced at her daughter, as if seeking help from her.

Callie lifted her chin as she faced him. "My mom is very upset. Can this wait?"

"It really can't. It's a simple question."

Callie's gaze moved back to her mother, then she said, "Were you and Arthur still arguing about your weekend plans?"

"Yes. That's right. I wanted Arthur to go to a party with me tomorrow night, but he wanted to head down to Palm Springs again. January is too cold in the desert. I didn't want to go. Is that what you wanted to know? I'm sorry if I'm not making sense. I'm so shocked. I feel like I'm in the middle of a nightmare. Is this a dream? Am I going to wake up?"

He wasn't sure what to think of Juliette. She was definitely a mess of emotion, her eyes bloodshot, her nose red. She seemed genuinely shattered, but his simple question had confused her, and Callie had led her mother to an answer. *Was there more going on than just runaway shock and grief?*

"My mother and I are happy to answer questions tomorrow," Callie said. "But I need to get her home now. Can we please leave?"

He glanced at Savannah and Gage. Gage shrugged, and Savannah gave him a subtle nod, as if to say there was nothing more to be gained at this moment.

"All right," he said. "We'll have a police officer take you home."

"That's not necessary. We hired a limo for the night. I'm sure it's outside," Callie said, pulling her mom to her feet.

"I'll make sure you find it," he said, leading them out of the room.

Callie tried to hurry her mother along, but as they entered the grand hall, Juliette hung back, her gaze returning to Arthur, although his body was surrounded by security and crime scene investigators.

"I still can't believe it," she said.

"Let's go, Mom," Callie said, determination in her gaze as she pushed her mom in the direction of the entrance.

He kept the crowd at bay as they made their way out to the circular drive. A few staff members offered condolences to Juliette, but Callie didn't seem inclined to let her mom stop and talk to anyone.

Finally, they got to the limo. The driver was standing next to the vehicle. He gave them a compassionate look as he opened the doors. He'd apparently heard the news.

Juliette got in first. Callie paused, glancing back at him. "Are you really Arthur's friend?"

"Yes, and I will do everything I can to find his killer." He didn't know if she took his words as a promise or a threat, because while Juliette was a ball of emotion, Callie was completely unreadable. There were dark shadows of worry in her eyes, but he didn't know if that worry was for Arthur or for her mother.

"I hope you succeed," she said.

"I will. No doubt about it."

"How do you know that my mom and Arthur were having an argument?"

"Because their discussion was caught on the security camera." He paused. "What are you worried about?"

"Right now? Everything. My mother's husband died right in front of me."

"Are you concerned for your mother's safety?"

"Should I be?" she countered.

"I don't know," he said honestly.

She frowned. "Arthur's house has a security system."

"Make sure to use it."

"I will."

"And Callie—"

"What?" she asked shortly.

"Why were you crying earlier tonight? When I ran into you in the hallway, there were tears in your eyes."

"I was having an allergy attack."

He gave her a hard look. "I don't believe you."

"I don't care if you believe me or not."

"You should care. I could be your best friend or your worst enemy. Think about that before we speak tomorrow."

"My mother and I have said everything there is to say. I'm not trying to be combative, but we spoke to the police detective and the other agent before you came into the room. You should check with them if you want more details. I don't have anything else to tell you."

"I'm sure you believe that, but this investigation is just beginning. Arthur was a federal judge, which means you'll have the FBI and the local police working on this case. Everyone will be digging deep into Arthur's life, and you and your mother are the two people who are closest to Arthur." He pulled out his card and handed it to her. "If you have any problems tonight, call me."

She reluctantly took his card, then stared back at him as if she wanted to say something, but eventually she shrugged and got in the car, slamming the door behind her.

As the limo pulled away, he had a feeling that digging into Arthur's life could turn up secrets that no one was ready for, including him.

CHAPTER THREE

SATURDAY MORNING, Flynn headed into the office a little before eight. After a long night spent interviewing witnesses, going over statements taken by other personnel, and dealing with the crime scene investigators and the medical examiner, he'd headed home for a few hours of rest. But sleep hadn't come easy. This wasn't a typical case for him. This was the murder of a man who had been not only a father figure to him, but the actual father of a girl he had once loved. He owed it to Arthur and to Olivia to bring his killer to justice.

Since his townhouse was only a few miles from his office, it was a quick drive, with an even quicker stop for coffee at the café next door. Then he pulled into the underground garage for a two-story, nondescript building in Santa Monica. There was no signage on the structure, but there was a code required for the elevator, from both the garage and the lobby, and another code required to enter the office suite on the second floor.

The suite contained a reception arca that was rarely used, and two offices, one of which was his. The other belonged to Beck, his second-in-command, who was currently working a case that had taken him to San Francisco. In addition to the offices, there was a conference room, a tech center, and a large room they called the bullpen, with eight desks and a wall of monitors.

There were currently twelve people working under his leadership on the task force: two cyber experts, two analysts, and eight agents, all of whom he had handpicked, and most of whom he'd gone through Quantico with.

When he walked into the bullpen, he found Savannah already at work. Today she was in black jeans, black boots, and a teal sweater. She'd swept her blonde hair into a ponytail and was seated in front of a computer screen. Since it was the weekend, most of the other agents were off or working other cases. But he was ready to call in more help as needed.

He sat down in the chair next to Savannah's desk. "Thanks for coming in today."

"Of course. Lucas is in the tech center. He's trying to get into Arthur's phone. Those damned passwords can be tricky. In the meantime, I've been looking into the judge's family."

"He doesn't have much in the way of family beyond his new wife and her daughter."

"And a sister in Sydney, Australia. She hasn't been back to the States in over a decade."

"They've been estranged for all of their adult lives. She won't be any help. I think the key to Arthur's life is probably Juliette."

"I wouldn't count on that," Savannah said grimly. "Juliette has a long history of depression and anxiety, including two hospital stays, one of them being a 5150 psychiatric hold after a suicide attempt."

His gut churned at that piece of information. "When did these hospital stays occur?"

"The first was eighteen years ago after the death of Juliette's first husband, Travis Harper. He was killed when their car hit a tree during a storm. Juliette was the driver."

"That's terrible. And the daughter—Callie—was she in the car?"

"No. She was ten years old at the time and at home with a babysitter. The second hospital admission was six years later, when

Juliette tried to kill herself with sleeping pills. I found no evidence of any other hospital admissions after that."

He was beginning to understand why Callie had been so protective of her mother last night. "What about the daughter? Any mental health issues?"

"Not that I've seen. Callie Harper is a twenty-eight-year-old chef. Her current employer is Bouffage, a French restaurant in Manhattan Beach."

"A chef, huh? Interesting."

"Getting back to Juliette," Savannah continued. "Her work history is spotty. She stayed home for a long time while Callie was young, then worked as an admin at an artist's cooperative in Venice Beach for a few years. After that, she moved on to a party-planning firm, which eventually led to her job at the Piquard Museum, where she has been for the last three years. She started there as an event coordinator and worked her way up to the director position last year, shortly after she married Arthur, who, as you know, was a major financial contributor to the museum."

"Yes. He has always been a collector and a supporter of the arts."

"It seems somewhat ironic that an art collector would be killed in an art museum."

"I agree. There has to be a tie. Although, Juliette's mental health adds a new dimension to the investigation."

"Especially in light of the heated conversation that went on between her and her husband shortly before he went over the railing. Juliette's answer to you last night didn't seem like the whole truth."

"No. I thought her daughter led her to that answer."

"But I can't imagine that frail woman being able to shove Judge Corbyn over the railing."

Savannah made a good point. "Maybe she had someone else do it," he suggested.

"Possibly."

"Well, keep digging." He got to his feet. "I'm heading over to Arthur's house now to see what other clues I can find."

"We don't have a warrant yet," Savannah reminded him.

"Hopefully, with my personal connection, I won't need one."

"From what I saw last night, I wouldn't be so sure. Juliette might not have found you to be a threat, but Callie certainly did, especially when you started questioning her mother."

"I understand her protective instinct, but I think I can win them both over."

"With your charm?" she teased.

He smiled. "That, too. But I was thinking more about my past relationship with Arthur. He introduced me to both of them as a friend. I just need to remind them that we're on the same side."

"Are you on the same side?" she challenged.

"I'm on the side of the truth. We'll see where we all end up when we get there."

It had been a hellishly long fourteen hours, Callie thought, as she took a seat on the couch in Arthur's study just before ten o'clock on Saturday morning. She'd managed to get a few hours of sleep, and after taking a long shower and changing into jeans and a sweater, she felt marginally better, but she was still weighed down with worry.

She hadn't wanted to go to the art exhibit the night before. She'd tried to beg off several times, but her mother had insisted. She knew how important it was to her mom to have support at her events, so she'd been the dutiful daughter and agreed to attend. She'd never imagined it would end up the way it had. She'd never been Arthur's biggest fan, but she couldn't believe someone had hated him enough to kill him.

She drew in a shaky breath at the memory. Arthur's murder had been so public, so undignified. He would have hated that. Appearances were everything to him.

Her gaze drifted to the life-sized painted portrait of Arthur on the opposite wall. He had been an extremely handsome and vain man. He'd also been a brilliant lawyer and judge. He was generous with his money, especially when it came to art and struggling artists, but he could be stingy when it came to leaving a tip after a good meal. In many ways, he was still an enigma to her. She'd sensed he had secrets, but she'd never thought those secrets were big enough to get him killed.

She'd been shocked when Flynn MacKenzie had asked her mother about a tense conversation she'd had with Arthur only a short time before Arthur was killed. Seeing her mother flounder in search of an answer had made her worry.

Fortunately, her mom had followed her lead, and the explanation was certainly plausible. They had, in fact, argued about their weekend plans when they'd picked her up in the limo on the way to the event. That hadn't been a lie. She just didn't know if that's what they'd been arguing about in the museum. She hadn't mentioned her mother's recent concerns about Arthur's fidelity to the police or the FBI agents, because they hadn't asked, and she really didn't know anything.

That was a question for her mother, but her mom had been in no condition to speak coherently about anything. Hopefully, today she would be better, but that might be a foolish hope. She'd seen her mother spiral downward too many times to count, and an event like this might trigger a complete breakdown. She'd already put in a call to her mother's doctor but had gotten his answering service. She'd asked for a call back as soon as possible, but she wasn't sure when that would happen, and she was dreading the next interrogation, especially if it was going to be done under the penetrating blue gaze of Agent Flynn MacKenzie.

The man was not only incredibly attractive, he also seemed to be unusually preoccupied with her and her mother. That was partly her fault. She'd let him see her tears earlier in the evening, and he thought those tears were a mystery he needed to unravel, particularly in light of what had happened. But her tears were completely irrelevant to Arthur's death. And her mother was innocent as well. She needed to make sure Flynn understood that.

Blowing out a sigh of frustration, she set down her coffee mug on the table in front of her and picked up a blank notepad and pen.

She needed to start making plans about what needed to be done. Making calls to Arthur's family and friends was at the top of the list, although the news of his death was already online and on the local news broadcasts. However, there might be some people her mother would want her to contact personally. She just didn't know exactly who they would be.

Arthur had very little family. He'd lost his first wife and daughter in a tragic accident years ago. His parents were long dead, and he had one sister, but she lived in Australia, and, according to Arthur, they hadn't spoken in years. Still, she would need to get word to her of Arthur's passing. She had no idea about Arthur's other friends. Her mom would know many of them, but she'd only been in Arthur's life a little over a year and a half. *What about his old friends from high school, from college, from the law firms where he'd worked before becoming a judge?*

And would her mother know about Arthur's wishes for a funeral? Had they talked about death and funeral options in the short time they'd been together? It seemed unlikely. Arthur was only sixty-five, and her mother was sixty-two. They had been planning on years together.

She jotted down questions: *Cremation or burial? Does he have a plot? Would he want a religious ceremony?* He'd been raised Catholic, but he never went to Mass. *Would he want one now?*

Tapping her pen against the paper, she wrote down what she knew he would want for sure—a big, splashy, newsworthy funeral. He would want an obituary detailing the amazing achievements in his life. He would want press conferences about his murder. He would want the world to be desperate to find his killer. *What else?*

She set down her pen, unable to move beyond her questions. She couldn't plan a funeral without her mom's input, not for a man she barely knew and didn't like all that much. What she wanted to do was take her mother somewhere far away and save her from what was about to come. But her mother couldn't leave, and neither could she. They would have to see this through.

Needing more coffee, she got to her feet, then froze as the doorbell rang.

Every muscle in her body tensed. The aftermath was starting, and she didn't know if she was ready. But she had to be, because her mother certainly wasn't up for anything.

She walked out of the den and down the hall to the front door. Checking the peephole, she saw Flynn MacKenzie on the porch. He'd changed out of his tuxedo, but he looked just as attractive in gray slacks and a button-down shirt with light-blue stripes. His blond hair was slicked back, and at the moment a pair of aviator glasses hid his very blue eyes.

She drew in a quick breath, quite sure she wasn't ready for him. But the doorbell rang once more, and she knew he wasn't going anywhere. She turned the knob and opened the door.

"Ms. Harper," he said, removing his glasses.

"Agent MacKenzie. My mother is sleeping."

"Then you and I can talk." He gave her a smile that was probably meant to reassure her, but it sent a tingle down her spine that screamed caution. "May I come in?"

"Can I say no?"

"It would be better if you didn't."

She stepped back, and he walked into the house, his curious gaze sweeping the entry, probably noting the slick marble floors, the impressive artwork, and the massive chandelier.

Arthur Corbyn had not only been born into an incredibly wealthy family, he'd also inherited a great deal of money after his first wife passed away, tripling his net worth.

"We can go into the living room," she said, waving him through the archway into the very formal room that overlooked the gardens of the Pacific Palisades mansion. The ornate sofas were not to her taste. Nor were they very comfortable, making this room the perfect place to put someone she didn't want to stay long.

Flynn's gaze swept the room. "It's very much like I remember," he murmured. "Not exactly the same, but close enough."

"When was the last time you were here?"

"About ten years ago, I think." He walked over to the grand piano, pausing in front of several framed photographs.

His expression grew somber the longer he stood there, his

profile hardening, his jaw setting into something that looked like anger.

"Do you want coffee?" she asked, feeling an inexplicable need to draw his attention away from the photographs of Arthur and his first family.

"What?" he asked sharply, giving her a sharp look that made her shiver.

"Coffee?" she repeated.

"Oh, no, thanks." He lifted his chin, his lips drawing into a taut line. "Did you like Arthur, Callie?"

She stiffened at the surprising question. "Of course. He was my mother's husband. She's devastated."

"But you're not," he said flatly. "Oh, and by the way, that wasn't a question."

She swallowed hard, not liking the look in his eyes. "I don't know what you're talking about. I need coffee."

She left him alone in the living room as she headed toward the kitchen. She didn't just need coffee; she needed to get her head together, because clearly his questions were going to be personal and probably a little terrifying.

Flynn let Callie go. He knew he'd rattled her, and maybe it would have been better to push her a little further, but he also knew he had to get a grip on his own emotions, so he didn't screw this case up before it got started.

Turning his gaze back to the photos, he felt a stabbing pain at the sight of Olivia's sweet face. The picture taken at her eighteenth birthday party had perfectly captured the optimism and innocence of the first girl he'd ever loved. The next day, she'd left on a graduation trip with her mother to Italy, Spain and France. A month later, she and her mother had died in a boating accident.

The agonizing grief had connected him and Arthur in a way that neither had expected, and for a few months, they'd leaned on each other to get through that terrible summer. But then it had been time for him to go to college. Arthur had encouraged him to do what he needed to do, to live his life in a way that would make Olivia proud.

He hadn't always done that, but he had found a way to go on. It had been fifteen years now since her death. He could hardly believe how much time had passed. He felt a little guilty that he hadn't thought about her all that much in recent years.

But she was in his head now. Her father was dead, and staring at her face, he knew she would want him to do everything he could to find her dad's killer.

That investigation had to start with Arthur's new wife and step-daughter.

Callie had been reticent the night before. Her mother had been almost incoherent. He needed one of them to start talking. But since they weren't inclined to do so at the moment, maybe he'd take a look around.

He turned away from the pictures and made his way down the hall. He hadn't been in this house in a long time, but he knew exactly where Arthur's study was. If there was a clue to be found, that would be the best place to find it.

Callie took her time making another pot of coffee. She was a little surprised that Flynn hadn't followed her into the kitchen. On the other hand, he was probably searching the house for clues. Maybe it had been a mistake to leave him alone in the living room, although she couldn't imagine what he would find there. She'd done her own research into Arthur when her mother had fallen madly in love on her first date with the man, and she'd found nothing negative. Although, her investigation had been amateurish at best.

She didn't know why she didn't trust Arthur. He'd always been perfectly polite, although a little too hands-on at times, but then he was an affectionate man. He liked to hug people, men as well as women. And he couldn't stop touching her mother. He was always holding her hand or putting his arm around her. Her mom had loved that.

Callie had never been a hugger or a toucher. She liked her personal space. She'd never dated anyone who had to hold her hand while she was eating dinner, and that was just fine with her. But she and her mother were very different people.

Her mom had an innocence, a naivete, a cluelessness about her that made her vulnerable to charmers and smooth talkers. Callie, on the other hand, was skeptical about everyone, always looking for what was wrong with them, instead of what was right with them. She couldn't help herself. After her father had died, she'd grown up in an unstable, unpredictable home, with lots of tears and raging emotions. Dealing with her mom's moods had made it almost impossible for her to have any of her own.

She felt a little like that now. With her mom falling apart, she had to be the one to hold it together. Which meant she really couldn't hide out in the kitchen any longer. She had to face Flynn. She had to tell him something that would make him look away from her and from her mom. *But what on earth would that be?*

She didn't want to lie. She didn't want to obstruct the investigation. But first she needed to talk to her mother when she was in her right mind. She had to make sure that her mom couldn't be hurt in any way by whatever was about to come. She'd been protecting her since she was ten years old; she wasn't going to stop now.

CHAPTER FOUR

ARTHUR'S DESK was extremely well organized. Flynn shook his head at the sight of a dozen pens, all the same color, and the same brand. There was nothing out of place. The files in the drawers all appeared to be related to household bills or personal items. He found a copy of Arthur's marriage license to Juliette, reminding him that they'd only been married a year. He was still a little surprised that Arthur had married again. He had told him a long time ago that he doubted he would ever walk down the aisle again, but he had, and to Juliette, a beautiful woman, no doubt, but also a woman who was emotionally messy. That didn't seem to fit Arthur's personality.

He was the kind of man who was always in charge, whether it was his courtroom or his home or his personal life. He didn't suffer fools. He was impatient with incompetence. He liked to control everything within his realm.

Juliette didn't seem that controllable, although maybe he was reading the situation incorrectly. Perhaps her personality, her issues with anxiety and depression, made her the kind of person that Arthur wanted to protect, because he'd always had a strong protective instinct as well.

He'd been very strict with Olivia when she was a teenager.

She'd had an early curfew. And if she was a minute late, she'd be grounded for a week. Olivia had railed against her father's rules, but she'd also respected the fact that he wanted to keep her safe. Olivia had told him once that she loved her father, but sometimes she didn't like him very much.

He frowned, wondering if that's how Callie felt about Arthur. *But why wouldn't she like him?* He needed to figure out the dynamics of Arthur's new family. He also needed to figure out why Arthur had wanted to talk to him.

He moved across the room to the wall of file cabinets. He did a quick, cursory search, noting copies of tax returns and more household files. He went a little slower through the drawer containing information and invoice forms related to the art Arthur had purchased during the past year. He'd been quite active, buying numerous paintings, sculptures, and some interesting historic trinkets, like a music box from the eighteen hundreds.

Arthur seemed to work mostly through two art dealers: Ray Hutchins, who had an office in New York, and Gretchen Vale, who had taken over his father's gallery. He frowned at the sight of her name. He hadn't spoken to Gretchen after Arthur's death last night, but he'd read Savannah's notes from their interview. Gretchen had been very upset but had appeared to be cooperative, although she'd provided no information of note.

"Find anything?" Callie asked.

He jerked at the sound of her voice.

She stood just inside the doorway and took a sip of her coffee, giving him a cool look. She was definitely more poised and in control than her mother. She was pale, and there were dark shadows under her eyes, but there was no sign of tears in her eyes —not today, anyway. He missed the clingy red dress from the night before, but even in dark jeans and a deep-purple sweater, she was strikingly pretty. He could not let that distract him.

"I'm just getting started," he said.

"Shouldn't you have my mother's permission before you continue searching? Unless you have a warrant?"

"Warrants take time. So does waiting for your mother to wake up. Every minute that passes makes it that much more difficult to find Arthur's killer."

"I understand, but my mother is shattered. She needs to rest. I'm not going to wake my mom up so you can interrogate her. I also don't think you're going to find a clue in this house. Arthur was super organized, a neat freak really. He would get angry if there was a cup left on the counter. I can't imagine you'll find anything that will tie to his killer."

"Maybe not, but I need to look. I assume Arthur has a housekeeper."

"Yes, Lois Garcia. She's been with him for a long time."

"Since before Francine and Olivia died," he said, his lips tightening. "She's still with him? She used to live here. Where is she now?"

"At her apartment in Silverlake. She moved out after my mom moved in. Since Arthur was no longer living alone, Lois wanted to give him and his new wife more privacy. She works every day from eight to five and cooks most of the meals, but I spoke to her this morning, and I told her not to come in. She was very upset, and there's nothing to be done today."

"Does anyone else work here in the house?"

"There's another woman who comes in to do a heavy cleaning once a week. I don't know her name. There's a gardener." She shrugged. "I'm not sure if there's anyone else."

"I'll need to ask your mother."

"You could also ask Lois."

"Oh, I will. Speaking of your mother…was she happy in her marriage to Arthur? Were they having problems?"

"No. They're practically newlyweds. They're crazy about each other." She drew in a breath, giving him a troubled look. "Why are you so focused on us? Is it just that you always look to the family?"

"That's partly it. But there was also a personal element to Arthur's murder. The killer wanted drama and shame. Arthur's pants didn't just fall down, Callie."

"Maybe when he fell, his clothing caught on something."

"That's not what happened, and you know it."

"Then what do you think occurred?"

"I don't have enough information to answer that question. But as I mentioned last night, I know that Juliette and Arthur argued shortly before his death."

"She explained that."

"I don't believe for one second it was regarding their weekend plans. You came up with that story, and your mother went along with it."

"They were arguing about their weekend plans in the limo. I assumed that's what they discussed at the museum. That's why I mentioned it."

"Nice hedge. Try again."

She frowned. "Look, I don't know any more than you do. She said that's what it was about, and as far as I'm concerned, that's it."

"Did she think Arthur was having an affair?"

Callie paled at his question, which told him a lot.

"Like I said, they were very much in love," she reiterated. "I can't imagine that he would have been having an affair. But if he was, there must be some evidence of it—some text on his phone, charges on his credit card, something…right?"

"I would think so."

"Then maybe you should spend your time on that. Because my mother is grief-stricken. She just lost her husband. She's not able to help you right now. She needs to get herself together."

"What about you? Are you grief-stricken?"

"You don't seem to believe me when I answer you, so why should I bother?"

"You do know that lying to the FBI is a felony, don't you?"

She squared her shoulders and gave him a stubborn look. "Yes. I also know that I don't have to talk to you."

"Actually, you do have to answer my questions. You're a witness to the murder of a federal judge." He paused. "What are you afraid of, Callie?"

She stared back at him, indecision in her eyes. Before she could answer, a scream rang through the house.

Callie bolted toward the door of the study. He followed close behind, jogging up the stairs behind her. More deep, gut-wrenching screams came as they ran down the hall.

She stopped abruptly in front of closed double doors. "Please go back downstairs."

"Not a chance."

"This is private."

"Open the door."

She gave him a tense look, but as another heartbreaking wail came from inside the room, she pushed open the door.

At first, he didn't know where the screams were coming from. The bed was empty. But then he saw Juliette on the balcony. She was dressed in a pink silky nightgown, her feet bare, her brown hair disheveled. She attempted to climb onto the railing, screaming Arthur's name with each wobbly attempt.

"Mom, no," Callie yelled, rushing forward. She grabbed her mom around the waist and pulled her backward. They tumbled onto the ground together.

"Let me go," Juliette pleaded. "Arthur is gone, and I'm alone again. I can't do it, Callie. I can't. I'm sorry."

"You're not alone. You have me."

"I'm a terrible mother. I can't start over. It's too hard. And this —this is my fault. I'm the reason Arthur is dead."

"Don't say that. It's not your fault. Let's get you back to bed. And then I'm going to call the doctor."

Callie helped her mom to her feet and walked her back into the bedroom. Juliette barely gave him a passing glance. She seemed completely unaware of his presence as she crawled under the covers, sobbing in grief.

Callie walked over to him. "You have to go," she hissed, pushing him toward the door. "Please, give her some time."

He stepped into the hall. "Why does she think Arthur's death is her fault?"

"She doesn't know what she's saying."

He saw the fierce, protective gleam in her brown eyes, and as she started to close the door, he said, "Now I know what you're afraid of."

She gave him a bleak, desperate look. "You really have no idea. Just go. Please."

He stepped back, and she shut the bedroom door.

He could hear Callie talking to her mother, pleading with her to calm down, to take a breath, to try to relax. He didn't think Juliette could hear her daughter. She was overwhelmed with pain, so much that she'd apparently thought about flinging herself over the balcony.

Was she just hysterical with sadness or had she had something to do with Arthur's death?

It took Callie twenty minutes to get her mother to stop crying. Finally, she ran out of tears.

"I'm going to call Dr. Clarke," she told her mom when she was calm enough to hear her.

"No. Please don't," her mother said, a new panic coming into her gaze.

"I have to, Mom. It will be okay. He'll know what to do, and we can trust him."

"I don't need a doctor; I need my husband."

"I wish Arthur was here." Arthur had not been her favorite person in the world, but he had taken care of her mother, and for the past year she hadn't had to be the person who was always there, always checking. In fact, Arthur had preferred she not be in such constant contact with her mother. At first, she'd rebelled against him trying to control how often she spoke to her mom. But she had to admit that she'd had more time to focus on her own life than she ever had before.

That was over now. She didn't know how far down her mother would spiral. But she would be there for her, as she'd always been.

"I can't believe he's dead," her mom said. "How can that be? I can still smell his cologne on these sheets."

She didn't really want to think about her mom and Arthur in bed together. "I'm so sorry, Mom."

"What am I going to do?"

"We'll figure it out. I'm here for you."

"You haven't been around as much lately."

Her mother's comment tweaked her guilt. "You and Arthur were busy."

"He was just trying to help you, Callie. You were so mean to him last night."

She frowned. "It wasn't that bad."

"I was mean to him, too." Her mom's bottom lip began to tremble once more. "I let my insecurities get away from me. My imagination—it's too big. Arthur always told me that. He said I just made stuff up in my head. But it seemed so real."

She didn't know what her mother was talking about, but she didn't like what she was hearing. "What kind of stuff?"

"I thought… It doesn't matter anymore."

"What did you think?"

"I'm tired. I don't know what I'm saying."

"You should sleep. No more going out on the balcony."

"What?" she asked in confusion. "Was I on the balcony? I thought I was dreaming. Is that why my feet are so cold?"

"You'll warm up soon. Close your eyes and think about something happy."

"Arthur made me happy."

"Going to the beach makes you happy, too," she reminded her. "Remember when we'd drive up to Santa Barbara and walk on Butterfly Beach? You loved the feel of the sand between your toes. It was warm, too. We'd stretch out on the ground, the sun on our faces, and we'd hear music playing from the nearby hotels. It was so pretty."

Her mother's eyes closed as she talked in gentle, soothing tones, telling her a story she'd told her a hundred times before. And when her chest rose and fell with peaceful quiet, Callie got to her feet.

She walked over to the balcony doors and made sure the lock at the top was on. Then she grabbed the desk by the window and pulled it over to block the doors. At least, if her mom tried to get out, she'd hear her.

Then she walked down the hall to the guest room where she stayed when she was there. She pulled out her phone and called her mother's doctor again. The service put her through this time, and he agreed to come over to the house to determine whether or not her mother needed to be admitted to the hospital.

The thought of that possibility made her nauseous. Her mom had been doing well for a long time. She didn't want to see her hospitalized again. But she also knew that sometimes that had to happen to get her mother back on track.

She frowned as she heard a clatter from downstairs. She'd thought Flynn had left. But he had probably decided to take advantage of her mom's breakdown to search the house. She headed down the hall, wondering if she had any legal ability to make him leave.

But that would mean calling the police, and would they really throw an FBI agent out of the house? Even if they did, wouldn't that only cause more problems in the long run?

She hurried down the stairs, pausing by the window on the landing as the outside crowd drew her attention. There was a crush of people in front of the house, and her heart sank at the sight of a news van and a reporter setting up their shot on the sidewalk. Thankfully, no one had come into the yard, and the house was set back from the street, but the media still felt too close.

This was the last thing her mom needed, and she mentally kicked herself for not anticipating the arrival of the press. She should have never brought her mother home. Although, in reality, she doubted she would have been able to get her mother to go to her apartment. She'd wanted to be close to Arthur and their life was here.

But now her mother was living in a fishbowl and the arrival of her psychiatrist might raise questions—questions that she didn't want her mother to have to answer. She knew she could count on

Dr. Clarke to be discreet, but a smart reporter might still figure out who he was and why he was there.

Looking away from the window, she drew in a breath and then wrinkled her nose in confusion. It smelled like bacon. Moving into the kitchen, she was shocked to see Flynn standing at the stove, scrambling eggs.

"What the hell are you doing?" she asked in amazement.

"Cooking breakfast," he replied, as if it was the most normal thing in the world. "I didn't eat earlier, and I have a feeling you didn't, either. How's your mother doing?"

"She's…look, you need to leave. I told you to go."

"I know, and I thought about it, but I didn't want to leave you alone to deal with everything."

"I've been alone, dealing with everything, for most of my life." Even as she said the words, she immediately regretted them. She didn't need to give Flynn any more ammunition to go after her mother. He'd already seen far too much.

"Well, today, you're not alone. You need to eat, because things may get worse before they get better."

"That's a dire prediction."

"Do you disagree?"

"I wish I could. Just so you know, my mom didn't even realize she was on the balcony. She was sleepwalking. She wasn't trying to…kill herself." It was hard to get the words out, because they made the past few moments seem more real.

Flynn gave her an even look. "Okay. Why don't you sit down?" He tipped his head toward the place setting at the island counter across from the stovetop. "I poured you a juice. I'm guessing you've already had a lot of coffee."

She stared at him in bewilderment. "What is wrong with you? You can't just come in here and start cooking. What are you thinking?"

"It's breakfast, Callie. I'm not a chef like you, but I am known for my scrambled eggs, and the refrigerator provided quite a few fresh vegetables for the scramble. There's also bacon, English muffins, and fruit. There's plenty if you think your mother might want something to eat."

"She's sleeping again."

"Good." He filled a plate with eggs and slid it across the island, as she sat down. Then he made one for himself and came around the corner to sit adjacent to her.

"I don't get you," she said warily.

"You don't have to get me—just eat."

She felt torn between making a stand and trying his eggs, because they did look delicious, with tomatoes, onions, and green peppers mixed in. Finally, she decided to be pragmatic and eat. Clearly Flynn wasn't going anywhere, and she was actually starting to feel hungry.

"Did you reach your mother's doctor?" he asked, as she picked up her fork.

"He's on his way." She took a bite, and the savory flavor was rather amazing. "These are actually good."

"I told you—eggs are my specialty," he said with a smile.

She found his charming smile to be almost as unnerving as his serious demeanor, because she didn't know what to think or how to feel. He was acting like a friend, but he could also be her enemy. He'd said as much the night before.

While she wanted to know who had killed Arthur, she was afraid of what the answer would be, which didn't put her and Flynn on the same side. He would have no restraint when it came to tracking down the person who had murdered Arthur. He wanted justice for the man who had helped him get through the loss of his first love. He wouldn't let anything or anyone get in the way of that.

Thinking about Flynn and Olivia raised a few other questions in her head. She'd heard Arthur speak about his daughter on a number of occasions. Even though she'd been dead for fifteen years, she was still very much on his mind. He always referred to her as his flower girl, because she'd loved nothing more than playing in the garden or tucking flowers into her hair. He'd had the gardens in the back designed in her honor. There was even a bench with her name on it.

Arthur had talked far more often about Olivia than about his first wife Francine, but perhaps that was out of respect for Juliette. He hadn't wanted her to feel like she was second.

"Do you want more eggs?" Flynn asked, drawing her attention back to him.

Her stomach clenched as their eyes met. He really was an attractive man. He must have loved a lot of other women since Olivia. He wasn't wearing a ring, but that didn't necessarily mean anything. Still, she wished she knew as much about him as he apparently knew about her. But then, she didn't have the resources of the FBI to investigate. She could do an internet search, but she doubted an agent would ever leave information online that wasn't completely meaningless.

"Callie?"

She realized she had yet to answer his question. "No, I'm fine. Thank you for cooking."

"I was being selfish. I was hungry."

"Do you always make meals for yourself when you're interrogating a witness?"

"I made an exception for you."

There was that sexy smile again. She had to fight the impulse to smile back, reminding herself she had nothing to smile about.

"Now that I know what you're afraid of, why don't you let me help you?" he suggested. "Talk to me about your concerns."

"I'm concerned that my mother is overwhelmed with grief."

"You're concerned," he said pointedly, "that your mother might have had something to do with Arthur's death."

Her breath caught in her chest at his blunt words. "My mom is the sweetest, kindest, nicest person you could ever meet. If anything, she's a pushover. She's not a killer."

"But she has problems with depression and anxiety."

"Half the people in the world suffer with similar problems. She's been fine the last few years. She has been happy." That was partly why she'd been against her mom's whirlwind love affair with

Arthur. When her mom was in love, she tended to lose grip on her other emotions. She became less interested in her own mental health and more interested in making a man feel good.

"She was first hospitalized after your father died, right?"

"I can't believe that there's an FBI file on my mother," said, amazed by that fact.

"My team worked all night compiling information on the people most closely connected to Arthur. Your mom is at the top of that list. And you didn't answer the question."

"Yes. She had a breakdown after my father died. She felt responsible because she was driving the car when they skidded in the rain and crashed into a tree."

"I'm sorry."

"It was a very difficult time. My dad was a great guy. He was always smiling and laughing. He was my biggest cheerleader. I used to play softball, and I'd hear his voice over everyone else's. He'd always shout, 'You can do it, Callie.' It's been eighteen years, but I can still hear him saying that." She felt a wave of sadness, because she hadn't just lost her father that day; she'd lost her mother, too, for a very long time.

"He sounds like a great dad."

"He was the center of our family universe, our anchor. He grounded us, especially my mother. She's very creative, very dreamy. She has big ideas but often no practical application. When I was young, she'd get lost in whatever new project had caught her interest, whether it was crocheting a blanket, or painting a vase of flowers, or practicing yoga. My dad would come home from work and have to run to the store to get us food for dinner. He always did what had to be done, and after he died, my mom fell apart. She'd always been fragile, but without her anchor, she was lost."

"So, you stepped up—at the age of ten."

"I tried. I instinctively knew that she needed me to do what my dad used to do. My aunt was around then, too. My mom's sister, Diane, helped us a lot, especially the first several years. But then she got a job in New York and had to move away when I was thirteen. My mom was better for the next few years. She'd still have some depression every now and then, but she was significantly improved."

"How long did that last?"

"She had a bad spell when I was in high school. But then she recovered. She's a fragile person. But she's not a killer."

"Then why are you worried?"

"Because she was arguing with Arthur right before he died. And when people hear that she's had some mental health issues, they look at her differently. You've been suspicious of her from the start, and now I'm sure you're even more so after what you just saw upstairs."

"And from what I heard. She said she's responsible for his death."

"She didn't mean that she killed him. She probably just feels guilty because she argued with him." She took a breath. "You asked me about an affair. I don't believe he was having one, but my mom did say a few times that she didn't like the way he flirted with other women, but I think it was just his manner. I told her that, but she didn't seem convinced. She has a high level of anxiety that takes her to the worst-case scenario in ten seconds flat. Arthur could have smiled at someone, and my mother would have assumed the worst. She's not an easy person to love sometimes."

He gave her a long, thoughtful look. "You're having a rough day, aren't you, Callie?"

For some reason, his kind words brought an unexpected rush of tears to her eyes. She hadn't cried at all since Arthur had plummeted to his death, but now she felt a tidal wave coming. "Don't be nice," she said, shaking her head, grimly hanging on to her emotions. "I can't take it."

"I think you need someone to be nice."

"Well, not you. I can't trust you."

"You actually can."

"I need to know more about you. Tell me about your relationship with Arthur. I know you dated Olivia, but what's the bigger story?"

Flynn frowned at her question, and she liked the fact that he was suddenly the one who didn't want to talk.

"If you want me to trust you, then you need to open up," she added.

"All right." He wiped his mouth with a napkin, then pushed his empty plate away as he rested his arms on the counter. "I met Olivia my senior year of high school. We had our first date at the winter formal and we spent almost every minute together from January to June. After graduation, we planned on moving to Santa Barbara. She'd gotten into the university there, and I, well, I didn't have the best GPA, so I was going to go to the community college. But, as you know, she and her mom went on a trip. It was Olivia's graduation present. On a ferry crossing in the Greek islands, there was an accident, and five people drowned. Olivia and Francine were two of them."

His voice was stoic, but she could see the pain in his eyes. "I am sorry."

"Olivia had so much potential, so much promise. She was smart and ambitious and wanted to be independent. She railed against Arthur's controlling personality. That's one reason why she wanted to move away to school. She wanted a little distance from him, but she loved him, too."

"He loved her as well. When he told me about her, he got choked up. And he made it clear to me that her room was off-limits. He said he goes in there sometimes because it's the only place where he still feels close to her." She paused. "Did you go upstairs while I was dealing with my mother? Did you look in Olivia's room?"

Flynn's expression tightened. "No. I didn't check her room."

"Why not?" she challenged.

He stared back at her, his blue eyes darkening. "I don't know."

She was surprised by his answer. "You don't?"

"Maybe it was one door too many for me to open," he admitted.

She almost felt bad for challenging him, because there was no denying the hurt in his gaze.

"But I need to get in there," he said quickly. "And in every other room in this house. You asked about my relationship to Arthur. He was good to me when I was dating Olivia, and after she died, he basically helped me keep my head above water. He was there for me in a way that no one else was."

"What about your own parents?"

"My mom was working. My dad wasn't around. But Arthur was there. He was in pain, too. We supported each other, but it went beyond that. Arthur convinced me to go to college, to make something of my life. If he hadn't been around, I probably could have ruined my life in a lot of different ways. That's why I owe him, why I need to find his killer."

"That makes sense. I am surprised, though, given your relationship, why I've never heard of you before. You weren't at Arthur's wedding or his sixty-fifth birthday last month. Yet, you were there last night. Was that a coincidence?"

"No," he said, surprising her once more. "Arthur asked me to meet him. He said he needed some help, a favor."

"What did he want you to do?"

"I don't know. He wanted to speak to me after the exhibit opened."

"I wonder what he wanted."

"It's driving me crazy," Flynn admitted.

Looking at him now, he didn't seem so much like a terrifying FBI agent who could put her mother in jail but more like a man with his own guilt to assuage, his own demons to battle. And she found herself wanting to trust him, because she needed to trust someone.

"For the police, the other agents, this is just a case," he continued. "It's more than that for me. I'll be honest with you; your mother is a target right now. The video is concerning, her behavior is alarming, and you need to help me find a clue that takes this investigation in another direction."

"I would like to do that; I just don't know as much as you think I do."

"Or you might know more than you realize. Sometimes a detail seems insignificant, but it's part of a bigger picture. Will you help me?"

Before she could answer, the doorbell rang. "That must be Dr. Clarke. I need to deal with my mother's situation first."

"I understand. We'll talk again. I'm not going anywhere."

His promises always sounded threatening, but she couldn't worry about Flynn. She couldn't help him, until she helped her mother.

CHAPTER FIVE

CALLIE HELD her breath as Dr. Clarke examined her mother. While he was able to rouse her from sleep, she was still very confused as to what was going on. She did remember that Arthur was dead. But she couldn't remember going out on the balcony and trying to climb over the railing. She also had no idea what day or time it was.

With each bewildered, rambling answer, Callie's concern grew. This was just like the last time. Her mom was losing her grip on reality, lost in a sea of pain, and she was going to need professional help to get out of it. Or she could spiral away to a place that no one else would be able to get to.

She hated Arthur's killer even more now. Because that person hadn't just taken Arthur's life; he might have also taken her mother's.

Unless her mother had been the one to somehow shove Arthur over that railing?

She hadn't seen her mom in the grand hall when the exhibition started, and she'd wondered where she was, but she'd assumed she was tending to some other aspect of the event.

She also couldn't see how her mother could have gotten Arthur over the railing. She wasn't very strong. And she wouldn't have been able to hide what she'd done so well. She couldn't be guilty of killing him.

When Dr. Clarke finished his examination, he motioned for Callie to follow him into the hall. The somber light in his eyes didn't give her much confidence for an optimistic diagnosis.

"Your mother needs to be hospitalized, Callie. Based on her current state and what you told me happened earlier, I'd like to take her in now."

"She won't want to go."

"She's so confused I'm not sure she'll know where she's going. We can hold her for seventy-two hours without her permission since she's a danger to herself."

"I know, but I can keep an eye on her."

"Twenty-four hours a day?" he challenged. "I understand that this isn't your choice, Callie, but it's the best thing you can do for your mother."

"She's been so good the past several years."

"Which gives me hope we can get her back on track, but the shock of Arthur's death has overwhelmed her. She's not thinking rationally."

"She hates being in the hospital. The drugs turn her into a zombie."

He gave her a compassionate smile. "She needs medical treatment and she needs to be safe. We'll take her to St. Mark's. You've been there before. You know the patients are made to feel as comfortable as possible."

Her mother had gone to St. Mark's the last time, and it had been a good place. She didn't want to put her back there, but what choice did she have? She couldn't watch her mother every second, and she did want her to be safe. "I know you're right. I just wish there was another alternative."

"Do you want me to tell Juliette?"

She thought about that. "She's been asking to go to the hospital to see Arthur. She's trying to convince herself he's not dead. I can probably get her dressed if she thinks that's the reason we're going to St. Mark's. I hate to deceive her, though. She might never forgive me."

"She'll forgive you when she's better, when she understands that you have her best interests at heart."

"I hope so." She took a breath. "The FBI wants to talk to her again. She gave an initial statement last night, but they want more details. Will this hospitalization prevent that from happening?"

He gave her a thoughtful look. "I can prohibit any contact with law enforcement until I feel she's lucid and understands what she's being asked. At this moment in time, I don't believe she is in the right state of mind to speak to the police or the FBI."

She was relieved to hear that. Maybe the hospital was the best possible place for her mom to be, so she couldn't incriminate herself in some way. "I'll help her get dressed," she told him.

"I'll wait for you downstairs."

"All right. Just so you know, there is an FBI agent in the house, Agent Flynn MacKenzie. He may try to speak to you about my mother's condition. He was in the room when she tried to throw herself over the balcony, so he's aware that she's having mental health problems, but I'd prefer that you don't share any information with him."

"I never speak about my patients. You don't have to worry about that."

"Thanks."

As Dr. Clarke stepped out of the room, she walked over to the bed. Her mom was more awake now, but she was a mess: her eyes red, her nose raw, and dark shadows under her eyes that made her look beaten down, defeated. She hadn't looked this bad in a very long time.

"Mom," she said, drawing her mother's attention. "You said you wanted to go to the hospital."

"Will you take me to see Arthur?" her mom asked, a gleam of hope entering her eyes.

She felt awful for lying, but she had no choice. She had to be strong enough to do what needed to be done. "I'll take you to the hospital, but we need to get you dressed. Do you think you can get up?"

Her mom nodded and sat up, swinging her legs over the side of the bed, the idea of seeing Arthur giving her new energy. Callie helped her up, but she needed to keep her arm around her waist to keep her mother upright. They made their way into the walk-in closet. Her mom sat down on a bench while she pulled out a sweater and pants, keeping things as simple as she could. It still took a few minutes to get her into her clothes, and then brush her hair, but eventually she looked halfway decent. At least, she wouldn't be leaving the house in her nightgown.

"Do you think Arthur will be mad?" her mom asked.

"About what?"

"He didn't like it when I asked him about Gretchen. He said I was crazy to be jealous. I hate when people think I'm crazy."

"Who's Gretchen?"

"She owns a gallery. She was at the event. Didn't you see her?"

"I don't know. Maybe I did. I don't know who she is."

"She's married, too, but she and Arthur have been talking all the time. And whenever I come into the room, he says he has to go, and he abruptly hangs up. Do you think I'm being paranoid and jealous, Callie?"

She saw the earnest, worried light in her mom's eyes, and she did what she always did—she tried to protect her. "I know Arthur loved you. That's all you need to think about."

"He did love me," Juliette said, nodding as if to reassure herself. "He still loves me. Why did you say he *used* to love me?"

"I just meant he has loved you from the first day you met." She was disappointed to realize that her mom was no longer accepting the fact that Arthur was dead.

"I was lucky to find him. I hope I didn't mess it up. I always do that, don't I, Callie? I always mess things up with men. I did it with your father. And now with Arthur. Why can't I be better?"

"You're great, Mom. Don't ever think you're not."

"I love you, Callie. You're the only one I can really trust."

Her mother's words twisted the knife of guilt in her heart. "I love you, too. I just want what's best for you. You know that, right?"

Her mom gave her a vacant smile. "You're a sweet girl. I just wish you'd come and spend more time with me and Arthur. Maybe next week."

She didn't answer; she just helped her mom to her feet and led her down the stairs.

Flynn and Dr. Clarke were standing in the entryway. Whatever conversation they'd been having ended when she and her mother came down the stairs.

"The police will keep the press away from your vehicle," Flynn told her.

"Why is the press outside?" her mom asked. "Are they here for Arthur?"

"Yes," she said, keeping it simple.

"You're Arthur's friend," her mother said, her gaze focusing on Flynn. "We spoke last night, didn't we?"

"We did," Flynn replied.

"You used to date Olivia. It was so sad what happened to her. Did you find another girl to love?"

Callie couldn't help but wonder how Flynn would answer that question. *Had he found another woman to love?*

"It was a long time ago," he said carefully.

"I'm going to see Arthur now," her mother told him.

Flynn nodded, his gaze concerned.

"I'll meet you there, Callie," Dr. Clarke said.

"Yes." She looked at Flynn. "We'll have to talk later."

"I understand. Good luck," he murmured.

She waited for Flynn and the doctor to leave the house. Then she locked the door behind them and took her mom down the hall and into the garage. She opened the door to her mom's car, got her into the passenger seat and then moved around behind the wheel. As she drove out of the garage and down the drive, she could see dozens of people, not only the press, but also some of the neighbors.

She had a moment of panic when the crowd appeared to be

blocking the driveway. She saw some photographers rushing forward to take photos and was really glad she'd managed to get her mother looking halfway presentable.

Thankfully, the police intervened, moving the crowd back. When she reached the street and pulled away from the house, she let out a sigh of relief. One hurdle down. Unfortunately, the next one would be a lot more challenging.

Getting her mother to the hospital was easy; leaving her there would be really difficult.

———

Flynn moved through the crowd outside of Arthur's house, happy not to be in a uniform and therefore able to leave without being questioned. Dr. Clarke had not stopped to speak to anyone, either, so hopefully his visit to the house would not be noted in any media reports. Flynn didn't want the media coming up with stories that could create obstacles in the investigation.

He got into his black SUV and punched in Savannah's number. She'd texted him an hour earlier that they'd gotten a search warrant for Arthur's office at the courthouse, and she was taking Diego and Lucas with her.

"How's it going?" he asked. "Did you find anything in Arthur's office?"

"I'm not sure yet. We just got back to the bullpen with boxes of files and paperwork plus a hard drive containing everything on Arthur's work computer. It will take some time to go through it all. Arthur did keep a calendar on his desk. He was old school when it came to appointments, lunches, and meetings. He had a lunch meeting with the museum director, Victoria Waltham, on Thursday, the day before the exhibit. I interviewed Ms. Waltham last night, and she made no mention of that lunch, although she did tell me that she had a personal friendship with Arthur and that he was very involved at the museum. He was a major donor and used his connections in the art world to help them attain pieces that they wanted."

"That makes sense."

"The other interesting name from the art scene was Gretchen Vale. Arthur had noted a show at a gallery in Laguna Beach two weeks ago. The gallery is owned by the Vales. I'm assuming you'll want follow-up interviews with both Ms. Waltham and the Vales."

The last people he wanted to talk to were the Vales. He didn't like how this case was taking him back in time, and he was beginning to worry if that's why Arthur had wanted his help.

"Also, Lucas was able to get into Arthur's phone," Savannah continued. "Gretchen Vale's personal phone number was listed several times, and there were a half-dozen calls to an artist named Marcus Vitelli in the last two weeks. Mr. Vitelli resides in New York but was in LA for the event."

"Yes, I saw him there."

"Detective Gage took his statement. I reviewed it, and, like everyone else, he knew nothing and had seen nothing. But he's staying at the Halcyon Hotel in Beverly Hills. He checked in last Monday, and he has not yet checked out."

Flynn changed lanes. "That's not far from me. I'll head to the hotel now and see if I can catch him."

"Do you have any information for me from the family? Have you been able to speak to Juliette yet?"

"Only briefly. She's having a rough time. She became so confused in her grief that she tried to jump off the balcony."

"What? Are you serious?"

"Yes. Her daughter called in Juliette's psychiatrist. They're taking her to the hospital now. She's going to be admitted and held for at least seventy-two hours."

"That's both good and bad. She'll get help, but we won't be able to speak to her."

"Honestly, right now she's in no condition to tell us anything. She needs to get her head together if we're going to be able to get any insight from her."

"What about the daughter? Have you charmed her into helping you yet?"

He smiled to himself at that question. "Still working on it, but I think she sees the benefit of cooperating with me. She just needs to get her mother into a safe place first."

"I can understand that."

"Callie did tell me that her mother was worried Arthur was having an affair. But she also said that her mom often imagines things that aren't true. So, take that for whatever it's worth."

"Well, by the time we're through, we're going to know everything there is to know about Arthur's life."

"Yes, we will," he said heavily, a little afraid of what might be revealed.

Marcus Vitelli was having lunch in the restaurant at the Halcyon Hotel in Beverly Hills when Flynn arrived just before two o'clock. He was seated at a table with two beautiful young women, who were both blonde, sleek, and sophisticated, the perfect bookends for Marcus's dark Italian looks.

Flynn had first heard about Marcus's success three years earlier when he'd been working undercover in the New York art scene. Marcus had been only twenty-one years old then and had sold his first painting to the CEO of a Silicon Valley tech company for half a million dollars. His good looks and young, brash, arrogant charm had brought him a lot of media coverage as well.

He'd met artists like Marcus before. They rose fast but sometimes they fell just as quickly. Only time would tell if Marcus had staying power when it came to relevance and popularity.

He stopped by the table, pulling out his badge. "Mr. Vitelli? I'm Agent Flynn MacKenzie. May I speak to you for a moment?"

Marcus's gaze darkened. There was not only surprise in his eyes but also wariness. "I spoke to the police last night."

"I understand that. I'm doing follow-up. It would be best if we spoke alone. Unless you'd rather come down to my office or the police station?"

"No. I have a few minutes." He got up from his chair. "Order dessert, ladies. I'll be right back."

Marcus walked out of the restaurant and onto an adjacent patio. Since it was a cool January day, the tables were empty, and they were completely alone.

"What do you need from me?" Marcus asked. "I didn't see anything last night. I told the detective that. I was completely shocked and saddened by what happened. I still can't believe it."

"How well did you know Judge Corbyn?"

"He was a fan of mine. He bought one of my paintings last year and has been very interested in buying more."

"Is that why he called you a dozen times in the last two weeks? To buy a painting?"

Marcus's gaze shifted. He cleared his throat. "He's been waiting for me to complete a painting for him, and he made his impatience quite clear to me, but I told him I couldn't sell it to him until it was perfect."

"That's interesting. I've never known Judge Corbyn to be particularly impatient, not when it comes to art."

"Then perhaps you know him better than I do. Beyond his interest in my art, I know nothing about him. I have met his wife, of course. She's a very nice woman. I feel terrible for her. I wish I could help you. I just don't know who would want to kill him. He was a huge supporter of artists and art. We all loved him." He paused. "I should get back to my friends. Are we done?"

"For the moment," he murmured.

Flynn followed Marcus back into the restaurant, watching as he joined his female friends. He was about to leave the dining room when another woman entered the restaurant—Victoria Waltham. That couldn't be a coincidence. She had to be here to see Marcus.

It wasn't unusual for a museum director to meet with an artist, but there was something about the way she checked her smile when she saw Marcus with the women that made him wonder about their relationship.

As she approached his table, Marcus got up. He said something to Victoria and her head turned in his direction. She looked a bit startled to see him, but she left Marcus and made her way over to the bar.

"Do you remember me, Flynn? From your father's gallery, a very long time ago?"

"I do," he said with a nod.

"I thought you looked familiar last night, but I heard the other agent say your last name was MacKenzie, and I got confused. And there was no time to ask. Everything was so chaotic and upsetting. When did you change your name?"

"A long time ago."

"I guess that's understandable. You didn't want to live under the shadow of your father's name."

"No, I didn't."

"I can't believe you're an FBI agent. That's awfully ironic. Have you been searching for your father?"

"Right now, I'm focused on figuring out who killed Arthur Corbyn."

"Why are you here?"

"I came to speak to Mr. Vitelli."

"Is he a suspect?"

"He's a witness, as are you."

She gave him a rueful look. "I wish I'd seen more. I wish the cameras hadn't gone out and that our security had been better. I feel responsible for not providing a safe environment for all the guests. This happened on my watch, and that's unacceptable. I thought we had set everything up so well, but I was wrong." She shook her head, self-directed anger in her eyes. "The Piquard family is also extremely upset, as is every member on our board of directors. I hope you know we'll cooperate in every way that we can."

"I'm glad to hear it."

Her gaze darkened. "I still can't believe it happened. Arthur almost hit me when he landed. I was right by the stage. I didn't know what was falling at first. I thought it was a light. But someone pushed him over the rail, right?"

"It appears that way."

"And you don't have any suspects? Arthur was a judge. I imagine he made people angry in his line of work."

"That's possible. But whoever killed him was at the event last night, and they had an invitation. There was no sign of forced entry anywhere. They came through the front door and probably left the same way. Do you know if Arthur had any problems with anyone at the museum or with anyone in the art world?"

"No, I don't." She cast a quick look at Marcus, who wasn't paying them any attention. He was quite wrapped up in his friends. "You don't think Marcus had anything to do with this, do you?"

"Like I said, I'm just following up on witness statements. How well did you know Arthur, Victoria?"

"Very well. He was a generous contributor to the museum. I also know him personally, because his wife, Juliette, works for me. We've been to many social events together. He's practically family. His death is tragic."

While her words were appropriate, he didn't quite feel the emotion behind them, but then Victoria had always hidden her emotions.

"Was there something else?" he asked as she lingered, giving him a somewhat awkward look.

"I probably shouldn't say this, but I heard a rumor recently that your father might be back in business."

His gut tightened. "Who told you that?"

"Arthur. He mentioned it last week."

"What exactly did he say?"

"That when he was in Paris last month, he heard Sam might be stealing and selling again. He wanted to know if I knew anything, but, of course, I didn't. I haven't spoken to your father in almost twenty years."

He didn't know what to make of her statement. *Why had Arthur been talking about Sam at all?* They didn't know each other. They weren't old friends. Whatever Arthur knew about his father had come from him, and that had been a very long time ago. *So, why bring up Sam now? Was his father the real reason Arthur had sought him out?*

"I should get to my meeting with Marcus," Victoria said. "The museum wants to buy one of his pieces. His work is amazing. Have you seen any of it?"

"I haven't, but I heard he's good."

"He's a true artist. He paints with every emotion. His work is provocative and intellectually intense. He's going to be one of the biggest artists of his generation. Anyway, let me know if I can help, Flynn. Juliette is not just my employee; she's my friend."

"I'll do that."

As Victoria joined Marcus and his female friends, he thought about what she'd told him. She'd deliberately tried to point him in the direction of his father. *Was that because she honestly believed Sam had been involved, or because she had another motive, perhaps a desire to protect someone else? But who would she be protecting, and why would she want Arthur dead?*

He couldn't turn her into a liar just because he hadn't liked her when he'd first met her. But he could do a little more digging into her life and into her relationship with Arthur.

CHAPTER SIX

CALLIE SUFFERED through hours of her mother's bewilderment, followed by anger, tears, crying, shouting, and finally a sedative. Then she'd sat next to her mother's bedside for another hour, reliving every painful, guilty moment of what had just transpired. Her mother had called her a traitor when she'd finally figured out that she wasn't going to see Arthur, that she was going to be hospitalized for her mental issues.

She'd felt like a traitor, too. When her mother's anger had turned to desperate pleas, she'd wanted to run out of the hospital and take her mother with her. But she couldn't do that. And she hadn't needed the doctor or the nurses to tell her that, even though they had. She'd been down this road before. While the hospital freaked her out, her mom had always gotten better after treatment, and she needed her mother to be well. She couldn't stand the thought of her trying to hurt herself because she'd lost Arthur. She had to leave her here, where she would hopefully get better. What happened after that, she had no idea.

Would her mother forgive her when her brain cleared? She had in the past, but was this one time too many? Would the loss of Arthur completely break her mom down?

The door opened, and she got to her feet as Dr. Clarke walked in. He gave her a compassionate look, having been with her most of the past few hours. "She's going to be sleeping for a long time, Callie. You should go home. You've been here all day."

"I hate to leave her here alone. She gets so scared when she wakes up."

"We're going to take care of her. She won't be alone."

"But she needs me." As she said the words, she felt the heavy weight of that need pushing toward the floor; it was all she could do to stay upright.

"She needs treatment. And we can give her that. We can help her get through this crisis. She'll also be safe here. She can't hurt herself."

"I just hate seeing her like this again. She was so good for so long. I had started thinking it would last."

"What happened last night was extremely traumatic for anyone, but for your mother, it was especially so."

"I know. She had to see another husband die. Two completely different events, but the result was the same."

Dr. Clarke nodded. He might have only been working with her mom for a year, but he was well educated on her mother's history. "She will have to work through all those emotions again. But she can do it."

"Do you really think so?"

"I'm not saying it will be overnight, but I will do everything I can to help her get back to herself. Now, go home. Get some rest. You must be exhausted."

"I am, but there's so much to do, and no one to do it but me."

"You have to take care of yourself, too."

"I don't think that's on the to-do list."

"Put it there. It's important."

"Thanks."

He walked her to the door, and with one last look at her mom, who was now sleeping peacefully, she left the room.

Feeling completely drained, she took the elevator downstairs. She couldn't believe it was four. The day was flying by, and she'd accomplished very little.

When she got to the lobby, she was surprised and dismayed to find Flynn MacKenzie waiting for her. "What are you doing here?"

"I came to check on your mom. How is she?"

"Terrible," she said, feeling way too many emotions. "When she realized that I'd brought her here to be admitted, she went wild. She pleaded with me to take her home. She called me a traitor. They had to restrain her and then sedate her. It was awful."

"That must have been rough," he said, a somber gleam in his blue eyes. "I'm sorry, Callie. You might not believe that, but I am. I had to get my mom through some rough times. It wasn't as bad as what you're dealing with, but I know what it feels like to watch your parent struggle, to be strong for them, when you feel weak as hell."

His understanding was the last straw. Tears gathered in her eyes. She had been feeling so alone, but Flynn was here. And he was stable, strong. He was also absolutely the last person she should lean on, the last person she should trust. But he was being so kind.

Somehow, she found herself moving forward. Flynn's arms came around her, and his chest was just as solid as she'd expected. She rested her head on his shoulder, closing her eyes for just a moment, savoring the feeling of being supported. It drove the tears away. She no longer felt like she was about to collapse, because he was holding her.

She wanted to soak in his strength, to stay in this safe place for a very long time. But she had to pull away. He wasn't her friend. He was an FBI agent. If anything, he was her enemy.

But he didn't feel like her enemy; he felt too good for that. And as she stayed in his embrace, her body began to tingle for reasons that had nothing to do with comfort. It was that scary feeling that finally made her step back. She couldn't be attracted to this man. That was crazy.

Flynn's blue gaze locked with hers, and she felt even more unnerved.

"I—I'm sorry," she said. "I don't know why I did that."

"You don't have to apologize, Callie."

"You must think I'm weak."

"I think you're incredibly strong."

She shook her head in confusion. "I really don't know what to make of you."

He gave her a small smile. "I feel exactly the same way about you."

She shivered as they shared a look that was far too personal and intimate. She sucked in a breath and cleared her throat. "Anyway...you can't talk to my mom, if that's why you came. She won't be awake for hours."

"Are you headed home?"

"I wish. I'd like to be in my apartment, to feel like things are normal. But I need to do what my mom is not capable of doing. I just don't know exactly what that is. Am I going to plan Arthur's funeral by myself? Will my mother even be able to attend? How long should I wait? And what would Arthur want? I'm sure his friends will be expecting some kind of service. I know he was Catholic, but would he want a rosary, a Mass, a burial somewhere?"

"I don't know if this helps, but his daughter and first wife are buried at Holy Cross Cemetery. I'm sure he has a plot there."

"I guess that's something."

"You have some time, Callie. I doubt his body will be released by the medical examiner's office for at least another day."

"They're doing an autopsy?"

"Yes."

"I thought he was pushed over the railing."

"That's still to be determined." He paused. "I also happened to notice a large binder containing information about Arthur's trust while I was looking through his study earlier. I suspect that has at least some of the information you need."

Flynn was being logical and pragmatic, and it actually helped cut through the tidal wave of feelings she'd been experiencing. "Of course. I'm sure all his wishes are outlined in great detail. Arthur never left anything up in the air. It's probably all in his study and very clearly marked. I should have thought about that before."

"Why don't we get out of here?"

She was more than a little happy to follow him out of the stifling, medicinal air of the hospital.

"I'll go with you to Arthur's house," Flynn said.

"So you can continue searching it?"

"Yes. I want to look in every room, every closet, every drawer. I want to sit down with you and go over every single person you can think of who has had any contact or business with Arthur, especially any women who might have had a personal relationship with him."

"That's a lot," she said, feeling the weight on her shoulders getting heavier again.

"The funeral can wait a few days, even a week. But we need to find Arthur's killer as fast as possible."

"All right." She didn't have the energy to fight him.

As they moved toward the parking lot, Flynn added, "Did Arthur ever mention Marcus Vitelli to you?"

"He's a young artist, right? I think Arthur bought one of his paintings. He said he was really good. He had a fresh perspective."

"That's Marcus. He exchanged quite a few calls with Arthur this past week. He said Arthur wanted to buy a painting from him, but it wasn't finished yet, and Arthur kept nagging him about it. He was practically begging him to finish."

She frowned at that comment. "That doesn't sound right. Arthur doesn't beg; he commands. He also knows how to negotiate. He wouldn't let an artist think he was desperate to make a purchase. I know that for sure. He gave me quite a lecture about learning how to negotiate for myself about two weeks ago."

"What were you negotiating?"

"I had an offer for a job as an executive chef at a popular vegan restaurant. I considered the opportunity, but the salary was low, and I don't particularly like cooking only vegan. Nor did I think I would have enough autonomy. The owner is known to be a micro-manager. I made the mistake of telling Arthur about it, and he got all over me, telling me I needed to fight for what I wanted, demand more money, more freedom, and not just walk away. I then found out that the offer had only come my way because Arthur had used his connections to get the owner to hire me. I was furious. I had told him several times before not to get involved in my business. But he didn't listen."

She paused by her car, impulsively deciding to tell him the rest. "Last night, Arthur made a snide comment about my decision. That's why I had tears in my eyes. I had run into him in the hallway, and he told me that not only had I let myself down, but I'd also embarrassed him. He'd called in a favor for me, and I'd blown it off. He was really harsh. He said, 'You're a quitter, Callie. All you know how to do is walk away. You need to learn how to fight.'"

"That sounds like Arthur," Flynn admitted, an odd look in his eyes. "I'd forgotten he could be like that."

"Very judgmental? I guess it was part of his being a judge. He believed he knew what was best in every situation. He was used to people doing what he told them to do." She took a breath. "But he wasn't completely wrong. I haven't always fought when it comes to my career. I've never felt like I could give a hundred percent to a job—or two hundred percent, as most restaurant owners demand from their chefs."

"Because of your mother," he said quietly.

She was surprised that he'd realized that so quickly. "Yes. It's funny that you get it, but Arthur never did."

"I don't know why he didn't think you were a fighter, because when it comes to your mom, you're a warrior."

"Am I? Or did I just walk away from her, too?" As the tears gathered in her eyes again, she said, "Dammit. I'm not usually a crier."

He gave her a smile. "I believe you. And you didn't walk away from your mom. You're getting her help."

"You said your mother went through hard times, too. What happened?"

"That's a long story."

"I could use a story that has nothing to do with me. I could also use a coffee and maybe something to eat. I know you're eager to get back into Arthur's house, but I need a little break. Maybe I can meet you there later."

"Or we could have a late lunch/early dinner. I'm hungry, too. It has been a long time since breakfast. I can tell you my story while we eat."

As much as she wanted to put some distance between herself and Flynn, she was also interested in learning more about him. "All right. Where do you want to go?"

"You're the chef. You pick."

"One of my favorite restaurants is not far from here. Do you like seafood?"

"Love it. Where's the restaurant?"

"It's in Malibu. Is that too far?"

"Not at all. Why don't I drive? We can pick up your car on our way back to Arthur's house."

"That's fine. And this is my mother's car. She and Arthur picked me up in the limo last night. I haven't been to my apartment since then."

"Where's your place?"

"Manhattan Beach."

"Not too far from me. I'm in Santa Monica."

"I guess we both like being near the water."

"I love it. I surf three times a week."

"You're a surfer and an FBI agent? That's an interesting combination."

He flashed her a smile that warmed her like a blast of sunlight. "I like being a contradiction. Predictability can be boring."

"Then you're going to have a boring dinner, because I'm pretty much the poster child for predictability."

"Somehow I doubt that," he said, opening the car door for her. "I have a feeling you have hidden depths, Callie Harper."

As she slid into the passenger seat, she thought he might be right, but she'd buried parts of herself so deep, she didn't think they were ever coming back to light.

CHAPTER SEVEN

THEY DIDN'T TALK MUCH on the way to Malibu. Despite asking him to share his story, Callie seemed more interested in looking out the window. Clearly, she needed time to decompress after leaving her mother at the hospital. Even though she was torn up inside about lying to her mom, he believed she'd done exactly the right thing.

He'd witnessed firsthand Juliette's attempt to throw herself off the balcony. While her efforts had been clumsy and confused, she might have succeeded if Callie hadn't pulled her to the ground. And worse than leaving her mom at the hospital would be having to deal with her killing herself. Hopefully, Juliette would get the help she needed. But he had a feeling he would have to solve this case without Juliette's input, because he had no doubt that she was having a breakdown. She wasn't faking anything to get out of questions. She was truly out of her mind at the moment.

Not that that meant she was innocent. Her breakdown could be because she felt guilty for having Arthur killed. There was no way she could have done it herself. But she could have paid someone else to do it. She had a history of instability. Who knew to what lengths she would have gone if she thought Arthur was cheating on her?

But that was all speculation. And he dealt in facts. He just needed to find some.

When they arrived at the restaurant, he turned his car over to the valet and ushered Callie into the restaurant. It was a little before five and there were only three couples in the room, all over the age of seventy.

"Are you feeling old?" Callie asked with a light smile as they sat at a beautiful table overlooking the water.

"We're definitely in the early-bird-special crowd tonight," he said, smiling back at her, thinking once again how pretty she was, even exhausted and overwhelmed. There was still a beauty to her features, to her big, dark eyes, to her unblemished skin and sweet pink lips. He cleared his throat, directing his attention to his menu before his thoughts got the better of him.

"Callie, oh my God, I was just thinking about you," a woman said, as she approached the table. She wore a white chef's coat, her brown hair pulled up in a high ponytail. "Veronica told me you were here. I couldn't believe it. I heard about what happened to your stepfather on the news this morning. I was going to text you, but I didn't want to bother you."

"Thanks. It's been a rough day." As the chef's gaze darted to his, Callie added, "This is Flynn MacKenzie. My good friend Melissa Haven. She's the chef here."

"Nice to meet you," he said, noting that Callie had omitted the fact that he was an FBI agent.

"You, too." Melissa turned back to Callie. "Is there anything I can do for you?"

"No, but thanks."

"How is your mother?"

"She's having a hard time, but she'll be all right."

"Do they know who killed Judge Corbyn?"

"Not yet."

"It's unbelievable."

"It feels surreal to me, too," Callie admitted.

"Well, the least I can do is cook you a good meal. Do you both like salmon?"

"You know I do," Callie replied.

"I love salmon," he said, at Melissa's enquiring gaze.

"Then if you'll leave it to me, I'd love to make you both something special, and it will be on the house."

"We'd love to leave our meal in your hands," Flynn said. "But we'll definitely pay."

"Absolutely not," Melissa said. "Callie helped me move last month, so I owe her a meal anyway, and if you're helping her get through this terrible situation, I'm grateful to you. No arguing."

"Thanks, Melissa," Callie said, handing over their menus.

Melissa headed back to the kitchen, and a moment later, a waiter came over with a bottle of wine and poured them each a glass. As he moved away, Callie took a sip and then sat back in her seat, her gaze moving toward the crashing waves below. Then she looked back at him.

"Would you surf these waves?" she asked.

"Probably not, since they're very close to the rocks. I'm not as young and reckless as I used to be."

"I've never surfed, even though I've spent my entire life in Southern California. I'm more of a sunbather."

He wouldn't mind seeing her in a bikini, soaking up the sun, but that kind of moment felt very far away.

"So, it's story time," she continued, a gleam in her eyes. "The Flynn MacKenzie story. Start talking."

"Where do you want me to begin?"

"At the beginning. Did you grow up in California? Because it seems like you have a faint British accent at times."

"My mother is British. I was born here in the US, but we lived in England from the time I was about one to six. Then we moved back to the States, settling in Laguna Beach, home to many art galleries. My father was an art dealer and he eventually took over a gallery there."

"What did your mom do?"

"She taught English literature at the community college a few nights a week. The rest of the time, she was home with me."

"Sounds like a nice life. Laguna is beautiful."

"It is. We had a big house on a cliff, ocean views from every window, but it turns out my father's money was not all gained by legal means."

Her expression changed at his words, surprise entering her eyes. "What did he do?"

"He bought and sold stolen art, and some of that art he actually stole himself. He was what you might have called a cat burglar."

"Seriously?"

"Yes. He stole from rich people while he was a guest at their parties, or he'd come back to the house in the middle of the night after casing the place. He was a very good thief. Eventually, he expanded his skills, breaking into museums and galleries. After stealing the art, he'd sell it for big bucks. I'm sure he thought he was invincible, but the law caught up to him."

"Well, that's not a story I was expecting to hear. What happened to him? Did he go to jail?"

"He would have gone to jail, if he hadn't run. He disappeared in the dark of the night. He left my mother and me to fend for ourselves, which turned out to be more difficult than we imagined. The government froze all of my dad's assets. We lost the house. We lost everything."

"That's what you meant when you said your mom had gone through a dark time."

"She didn't fall apart, but she was struggling. We moved in with friends of hers in Pacific Palisades. I started a new high school in my senior year, but I was actually happy about that, because I was away from all the rumors, all the chatter about my dad. I met Olivia at the new school, and she brought some real light into my life. I was in a bad place, but she made it so much better. She took me home and introduced me to her family. Francine and Arthur were stable people, and Arthur had just become a judge. He knew what was right and what was wrong. There was no moral ambiguity with him. I felt like I'd found my compass."

"Maybe there was moral ambiguity, but you just didn't see it."

"I'm beginning to think you're right, but I need to know the truth, whatever it is."

"The truth can hurt, Flynn. I don't think it's all it's cracked up to be."

He could see why she would feel that way, but for him truth was all that mattered now. "Having grown up with someone who turned out to be a complete liar, who was not even close to who he appeared to be, I value honesty more than anything else."

She gazed at him, dark shadows in her eyes. "Do you still think I'm holding something back?"

"I think," he said, choosing his words carefully, "that you're afraid your mother had something to do with Arthur's death. You don't want to believe that, but you're just not one-hundred percent positive, so your go-to move is to defend her, to protect her."

"She doesn't have anyone else to do that for her but me."

He noticed she hadn't denied his point.

"Let's get back to you," Callie said. "What happened after Olivia died?"

"I went off the rails. I was drinking. I was surfing dangerous waves. I was almost daring the world to take me, too. But Judge Corbyn pulled me out of it. He physically dragged me out of a bar one night. He gave me a harsh lecture. It was a few months after Olivia died. He told me I was wasting my life and that was the last thing Olivia would want to see me doing. His words woke me up, because he was right. About that time, my mother had decided to move back to England to be near her parents, who were aging and in ill health. I went with her. I went to university there and when I graduated, I decided I would use my knowledge of the art world in a more positive way. I'd grown up in the gallery. I knew a lot about art and even more about the players, my dad's old buddies. But I knew I wouldn't get far using my dad's name, so I changed my name to mother's maiden name."

"So MacKenzie is not your dad's name?"

"No. His last name was Beringer—Sam Beringer. He was half

French, half Russian. His father was a well-known artist in Moscow. He died of cancer before I was born. I'm sure he would have hated the direction my father took." He cleared his throat and took a sip of his wine, then continued. "I took a job in a gallery in London and I decided to look for my father. I wanted to make him pay for what he'd done. I made a lot of trips around Europe, hoping to find him. Along the way, I stumbled upon a counterfeit art network. It wasn't tied to my dad, but I wound up going to the FBI, to the person who had actually arrested my father. I told him I wanted to even out the scales. He used me to make a case, and after that, he suggested I come and work for the bureau."

"It's so strange that you would work for the people who nailed your dad. But I guess there's a kind of dark poetic justice to that. You're more complicated than you appear, aren't you?"

"Maybe, but then most people are."

"That's true. Do you mostly work on art crimes then?"

"I did for the first two and a half years after I went through Quantico. I managed to bring down a terror network that was using art to fund their terrorism efforts. It was a big coup for the bureau. At that point, I was done with art and thought I might be done with the bureau. I couldn't spend the rest of my life chasing my father's ghost."

"That makes sense."

"But the higher-ups wanted to keep me on board, so they offered me my own task force to work on whatever needs to be done."

"You run a task force? That sounds impressive. You're not that old, are you?"

"No, but I'm that good," he said with a cocky smile. "And I'm better when I can move outside the layers of bureaucracy. I was able to prove that to my bosses and they rewarded me."

"But now you're investigating a murder that could be tied to the art world. You're back where you started."

"And it's my knowledge of that world that will hopefully help me solve the crime."

"Not if you keep looking at me and my mother as suspects," Callie said somewhat tartly, giving him a pointed look.

"I look at everyone as a suspect. But just so you know, you're off the list. I don't think you killed Arthur or that you know who did."

"I'm happy to hear that. But you still haven't cleared my mother."

"No, but I'm not trying to railroad her. I would love some other leads."

"I would, too, but I really don't know anything, Flynn."

"You might know more than you think. You said your mom mentioned being jealous. Did she give you a name?"

"Yes. Gretchen Vale. She was apparently at the event last night. My mom was annoyed by that and the fact that Gretchen and Arthur were constantly on the phone to each other. Apparently, Gretchen was getting a painting for him or something like that, so it could have been completely innocent."

"There were a number of calls between her and Arthur," he admitted.

"Then why are you talking to me instead of her?"

"Savannah spoke to her last night, but I'm planning to do a follow-up interview."

"Savannah is the agent you brought as your date. Are you two involved?"

"No. She works for me. Savannah was there because Arthur requested that I bring a date for cover. He wanted anyone who saw us talking to think we were just having a casual conversation."

"I wonder what he wanted to ask you."

"I wish I knew."

"You should talk to this Gretchen person. We should go find her after this. I'd like to know why she was calling my mother's husband, too."

He smiled at the new light in her eyes. "I don't know how Arthur could have ever thought you were not a fighter, Callie."

"I do fight for people I love."

"Is there someone else you love, besides your mother?" It probably wasn't a question he should have asked, but he was curious.

"I love my friends, but if you're asking about a boyfriend, I don't have one at the moment. Actually, I haven't had one in a while. I've been busy building my career. And when I'm not cooking, I'm usually dealing with my mom. Although, I have to admit that while I didn't want her to fall for Arthur and marry him so fast, her marriage did give me some freedom."

"Why didn't you want her to love Arthur?" he asked curiously. "He's a good man."

"He might be. He might not be. I'm not sure either of us knows anymore. But it wasn't just about that. When my mom falls in love, her emotions run wild. It's like the love endorphins make her crazy. And that's when her mental health starts to fall apart. Her romance with Arthur was a whirlwind; it felt chaotic. I didn't believe she was thinking things through, but when it comes to love, nothing can stop her."

He thought about her comments. "Was she that way with your dad, too?"

"They met when they were young, so it wasn't as fast. They dated for four or five years before they got married. But she was very much in love with him. And she could get a little obsessive about it."

"In what way?"

She hesitated. "It doesn't matter."

"I'm not going to use it against her," he said, hoping that he was telling the truth.

"I'm not sure I believe you."

"Did she think your dad was cheating on her, too?"

She stared back at him, a troubled gleam in her eyes. "Yes, she did. It's what she thinks when she feels insecure, and she often feels that way. She had a difficult childhood. Her father left the family when she was eight, and I think she always felt abandoned by him. That feeling extended to other men. At least, that's what one of her doctors told me."

"Her first breakdown came after your dad's death. What about the second one, when you were in high school?"

"That was after a bad breakup. She'd been seeing this man, Martin, for almost a year when he decided to end it. She went off the deep end. It took her over a year to get back to herself. Now, Arthur is dead, and she's alone again. I just don't know how many times I can bring her back from the brink."

"I know you think that's your job, but it's really not."

"It is. I'm the only one she has."

"What about her sister?"

"She lives far away, and she's finally in remission after a battle with breast cancer. I can't dump any more on her. To be honest, after the last time my mom fell apart, my aunt pretty much told me she just couldn't do it anymore. She felt like she'd been taking care of my mom her whole life. I was really angry with her, but there was a part of me that could understand her feeling."

Juliette had certainly had problems with the men in her life. He sipped his wine as he contemplated what he wanted to say next, something he was sure would bring the tension back between them, but the words were bouncing around inside his head, begging to come out.

"What?" she asked. "I can see the wheels turning, Flynn. You want to say something. Say it."

"You won't like it."

"I haven't liked a lot of what you've said; that hasn't stopped you. Go ahead. I can take it."

"All right. Have you ever wondered if the car accident was just an accident?"

She sucked in a quick breath, her gaze darkening. "I read the police report. It was determined to be a skid caused by the rain."

"When did you read that? You were ten years old when your dad died."

"I read it when I was sixteen, after my mom went to the hospital for the second time."

"You were afraid." He could see the truth in her eyes.

"After the way she reacted to Martin leaving, it made me

wonder," she said, a defensive note in her voice. "My mom was saying the same things to me that she'd said about my dad—that he didn't love her enough, that she was sure he was cheating, and that people always left her. I not only read the report, I also talked to the patrol officer who had been the first one on the scene. He reassured me that my mother was completely sober at the time, that the rain was bad, that there was simply no evidence that she'd deliberately run into the tree. There were signs that she attempted to brake. If she'd done it on purpose, she wouldn't have tried to stop."

"Well, good," he said, hoping she was right. "Then we don't need to discuss that."

"We don't. I'm not blind, Flynn."

She looked him straight in the eye, and he felt something twist inside him. She was defiantly beautiful, and he didn't think he ever wanted to stop looking at her. Not that she was thinking about him. She was fired up over her mom.

"I know who my mother is," she continued, "faults and all, but she's not a killer. She didn't kill my dad, and she didn't kill Arthur. I know her better than anyone, Flynn. You have to believe me."

"I want to," he said.

"What else can I say?"

"You've said enough—for now. And I want you to know that I heard you."

"Okay." She paused as the waiter brought over their salads. When he left, she said, "Since we're done with my mom, let's get back to the woman my mother was concerned about most recently —Gretchen Vale. What do you know about her?"

"More than I want to know."

"What does that mean?"

"Gretchen was my father's assistant for several years before he disappeared. Even though my dad was running his stolen art through the gallery, somehow, Gretchen came away with clean hands. I thought she might have turned him in or bargained for immunity, but I found no trace of that in the FBI files. At any rate, she and her husband Stephen now run the gallery. They've changed the name and the style, but it's the same place I used to go after school, where I used to work, where my father had some of his best moments and some of his worst."

"What is your relationship with her now?"

"I don't have one. Until last night, I hadn't seen her since my dad left. At that time, I was sixteen, and she was probably about thirty. Back then, she felt like a big sister to me. She was nice to me when I was in the gallery. We had some good talks, but I never heard from her after my dad took off."

"What about her husband?"

"I was never a fan of Stephen, who was her boyfriend when I knew her. He was a wannabe artist, but he wasn't any good. My dad then hired him to do pickups and deliveries for the gallery. I think Stephen was probably involved in my dad's schemes, but there was no evidence to prove that."

"It seems strange that no one in your dad's circle was involved. He was a one-man operation. Seems unbelievable."

"I've always thought so."

"Maybe they were both just clever enough to hide their crimes. You've asked me a number of times why I don't seem to like Arthur. There was something about him I just didn't trust, but I also had no facts to back up my instincts. I know you liked him and respected him. In fact, everyone I know feels that way about him, so maybe I was wrong."

"Or he was also very clever. We should eat. This salad looks good."

"I'm sure it's delicious," she said, picking up her fork. "Melissa is an incredible chef. We met in cooking school and became instant friends. We've worked in some of the same restaurants and followed each other's careers. She became the executive chef here six months ago, and the crowds have doubled since then. She's really great with seafood. She brings out unbelievable flavor."

"When did you decide you wanted to be a chef?" he asked curiously, taking a forkful of salad that was bursting with flavor.

"I started cooking a long time ago. My mom, even on her good days, was not great in the kitchen, so I took over that job. I was making all our meals from about age twelve on. It was a good distraction for me. It also made me feel like I was in control of a small part of my life. Cooking became my stress reducer, my escape, my passion, and I was good at it. When my mom ate well, she was less erratic. I felt like if I could get some good meals into her every day, our lives would be better. It probably wasn't ever about that, but it made me feel good to think so."

"You mentioned you have an apartment. When did you stop living with your mom?"

"I moved out three years ago, after she started working at the Piquard Museum. She was really happy and riding a wave of good health and sanity. It felt like she was normal, and I could leave her. But I didn't move too far away. I still saw her a lot, at least until she met Arthur, and then it was all about him. She has always been a person who needs a lot of love. I think she had that…for a while, anyway."

He saw the sad glimmer in her eyes and wanted to chase it away. "Let's get back to food. What's your specialty?"

"Well, I work at Bouffage, which is a French restaurant, and I'm very good at classical French dishes."

"But…"

"How did you know there was a but?"

"Because I'm starting to know you. So, continue…"

"I'd like to have my own restaurant one day, and not the vegan restaurant Arthur was trying to get me into. If I was going to run my own kitchen, it would be a mix of California and Italy."

"What does that mean exactly?"

"I fell in love with Italian cooking when I spent a month in Italy. But I also love California and its devotion to farm-to-table, fresh, organic ingredients. I want to blend the two. I can see my restaurant in my head. It will have a magnificent pizza oven in an open kitchen and the dining room will be lined with brick and wood. On the menu will be incredible pasta, of course. But I'll contrast the earthy dishes with fresh, light, seafood entrees."

"It sounds amazing. When can I go?"

"Right now, it's just a dream. Maybe it always will be. I probably should have taken the offer I had."

"No. You have to stick to your dreams."

"That's what I think, too. Maybe one day I'll be more willing to settle, but not yet."

"You'll never settle, Callie. It's not who you are."

"You've known me for a day."

"And yet I'm right, aren't I?" he challenged.

She gave a helpless shrug. "I guess I'll find out."

CHAPTER EIGHT

THE SALMON HAD BEEN JUST as delicious as she'd expected, and with her stomach full, Callie felt a lot better than when she'd left the hospital. She could always count on a good meal to change her mood, even one she hadn't cooked herself. But it wasn't just the food that had lessened her stress; it was Flynn.

He was an interesting man, far more complicated than his blond good looks and charming smile might imply. He'd been abandoned by his father and suffered tragedy in the loss of his girlfriend. Those were two horrific events that she wouldn't wish on anyone. But Flynn had taken control of his life. He'd turned his father's bad deeds into his own good ones. And then he'd found a way to let go of the past.

But now he was back in the art world and she had a feeling his respect for Arthur was also going to take a big hit. She hated that the man who had been a second father figure to Flynn might disappoint him, too, but she couldn't stop whatever revelations were coming. In fact, she needed to bring those revelations to light so they could find Arthur's killer and get her mother off the suspect list.

She sipped the last of her wine as she shook off thoughts of her mother alone in the hospital room. She was safe. And she was probably asleep.

Flynn had certainly asked her some brutal questions about her mother. No one had ever dared to question the accident that had taken her dad's life. Maybe some had thought it, but certainly no one had ever asked her point blank the way Flynn had.

She should hate him for that. She should be angry with him for a lot of his assumptions. But, oddly, she found herself liking him.

For all his tough questions, he'd also been incredibly kind. And he respected her for her fight. It was warming to have someone see how hard she was battling to keep her mom sane.

Not that she let many people see the private war she'd been engaged in for her entire life. She'd built a wall around her very small family and no one saw over that wall. She didn't think even Arthur had really understood the depth of her mom's problems.

But Flynn had battered through her wall and there was no kicking him out now. She just needed to remember that no matter how nice he was being, if her mother had had anything to do with Arthur's death, Flynn would make her pay.

So, she had to stay close to Flynn and help him find a lead to somewhere else. Fighting him, trying to keep him away from him, was the wrong approach.

"I'm going to help you," she said aloud.

"Is that what you've been thinking about the last fifteen minutes? You've been very quiet," he commented.

"I was also enjoying my salmon, but, yes, I have been thinking about our rather odd relationship."

He smiled. "I've never been in an odd relationship before."

"It's a first for me, too." She paused and then took the plunge. "On that note, I've also been pondering what I might know that could be helpful, and I think there might be something."

"What's that?"

"There was a barbecue at Arthur's house a few weeks ago. My mom sent me to look for him, because their guests were arriving, and he was nowhere to be found. He was in Olivia's room. The door was partly ajar, and he was talking on the phone. I didn't hear him say anything that strange. But when he ended the call, I pushed the door open and I saw him put his phone in his pocket. He gave me a startled, angry look and told me I was never to come in there. I apologized, and then he immediately backed down and said he was sorry for snapping at me."

"Okay," Flynn said, his brows knitting together. "Why is that helpful? What am I missing?"

"I haven't gotten to the helpful part yet. When Arthur and I walked downstairs, my mom met us on the landing. She handed Arthur a phone and said it had been ringing for the last fifteen minutes."

A light entered his eyes. "Arthur had two phones."

"Yes. I don't know if that matters."

"We need to find that other phone. There wasn't another line registered to his name. It might have been a prepaid phone."

"It did look cheap and small, not like his other smartphone. I didn't think that much about it at the time, because I know he liked to keep work separate from his personal life. He rarely spoke about the cases in his court. He said that it was his duty to maintain confidentiality, and, frankly, I didn't care that much, so I never pressed him about his job or what cases he was overseeing." She paused. "Are you sure his death doesn't have to do with a case? Don't judges get threatened all the time?"

"Savannah is looking into that angle. I'm focused on the art, because that's the world I know well. I didn't see a second phone in the study. Where would Arthur have kept it?"

"Maybe Olivia's room. It was the one room in the house that no one ever went into but him." Discomfort entered Flynn's eyes. "Looks like you might have to open that door after all," she said. "Or I can look."

"I can do it. Thanks for telling me about the phone. Are you ready to go?"

"I'll just pop my head in the kitchen and say goodbye to Melissa."

"I'll meet you out front."

After driving Callie back to the hospital parking lot so she could get her mother's car, Flynn followed her to Arthur's house. He was happy to have a few minutes alone. He'd enjoyed having dinner with Callie. Talking to her had been surprisingly easy. When she wasn't on guard about her mother, she was very forthcoming. He'd found himself sharing far more than he usually did about his father and his past and even about Olivia.

He'd wanted to open up to get Callie to trust him, and he'd succeeded. But through their very personal conversation, he had also begun to trust her. And he felt a very strong emotional connection to her. He was more than a little impressed at her strength in dealing with her mother, and not just now, but since she was ten years old. He could imagine her as a little girl taking charge of the house and the kitchen. She stepped up when she had to. Her mom might be a fragile flower, but Callie was sweet steel.

He knew it was probably a mistake to get so close to her, but he couldn't stop himself. She'd caught his eye the first second he'd seen her, and since then he hadn't really been able to look away. He kept wanting to see her again, to know more about her, to keep talking to her for as long as he could.

But he couldn't afford that kind of distraction.

He needed to find Arthur's killer. That should be his only focus. And his only interest in Callie should be to further that goal.

Turning the corner, he drove down Arthur's street, happy to see that the press had disappeared. It was almost seven now and completely dark. There wasn't one light on in the house, and for some reason it felt a little foreboding, maybe because he knew Arthur would never come back to the home he'd lived in for forty plus years.

Callie drove into the garage, while he stopped on the circular drive in front of the house. As he got out of the car, he realized that the porch was filled with not only floral arrangements but also boxes of chocolates, gourmet cookies, fruit baskets, and even bottles of wine. Arthur's friends were showing their love to his family.

When Callie opened the front door, she stared at the offerings in astonishment. "Wow, I wasn't expecting this."

"A lot of people cared about Arthur," he said, feeling a heaviness in his heart. He wasn't sure what he was going to find out about Arthur, but at the moment he still had love for the man. And he was incredibly saddened that he was gone. "I'll help you bring this stuff in." He grabbed a bottle of wine and the nearest bouquet.

It took them about ten minutes to clear the porch. They put everything on the very sleek and polished table in the formal dining room. Callie looked through the cards and tags. "Some of these are addressed to my mom."

"I'm sure they're all for her, even if they've been sent in honor of Arthur's memory."

"She'd be touched to see all this. I wish she could see it now. It might make her feel better."

"She'll see it when she's better."

She drew in a breath and let it out. "All right. What's next? It feels weird being here at night. It feels lonelier than it did earlier. Maybe that's because my mom is gone, too."

"I want to check out Olivia's room first. I don't think it will take that long."

"While you do that, I'm going to look in the study and see if I can find the trust information."

"It was in the bottom drawer of the first file cabinet. A large binder. You can't miss it."

"Okay. Good luck, Flynn."

He knew she was purposefully letting him go into Olivia's room on his own, and he appreciated that. "Thanks."

He moved up the stairs, feeling more trepidation with each step. At the second-floor landing, he switched on the lights and paused. He'd opened a lot of doors in his life, and behind those doors, he'd confronted danger, bullets, criminals, and terrorists, and he'd never felt the kind of fear he felt now. He'd locked his feelings for Olivia away. All the pain, the anger, had been banished to some distant part of his brain that he never accessed. But now he had to face the past.

His hand moved to the knob, but he couldn't seem to turn it.

He was being ridiculous. The room had surely been cleared out after so many years. He was probably going to see nothing but a bed and a dresser, same as the guest rooms on the first floor.

Pushing past his paralysis, he opened the door, stepping inside and back in time.

The room wasn't exactly the same, but there were more memories than he'd anticipated. The walls were no longer adorned with Olivia's favorite posters, but her favorite books were still on the bookshelves over the white desk where she'd once done her homework. The bedding had been changed from young and girlish and very yellow, Olivia's favorite color, to more neutral pastels, but still with a feminine edge.

He walked over to the closet and opened the door. Thank God her clothes weren't there. That would have been too much. There were a couple of raincoats and down jackets hanging in the closet, but he suspected they were just overflow from one of the other rooms, because he didn't recognize them.

On the shelf of the closet were several boxes, two of them marked with Olivia's name, and one with the added word—*photos.*

He told himself to leave the box alone. This search wasn't about Olivia; it was about her father. But he couldn't stop himself from grabbing the box and setting it on the desk. Opening the lid, he found a pile of loose photos, and he was suddenly seeing Olivia again—beautiful, young, full of life.

His breath caught in his chest.

Pain rocked through him. He hadn't actually looked at her face in a very long time, but here she was, with blonde hair and hazel eyes that had often seemed amazed by life. Her smile was sweet and a little shy. He'd been taken in by that smile the first time he'd seen her. He'd been the new kid in high school, and as a senior, it was not the best position to be in. Everyone else had known each other, many from kindergarten, and he'd had to power his way through, hoping to find a few friends to hang with. When he'd met

Olivia, he'd been immediately accepted by her group, and he'd been able to start over.

He moved on to another photo, one of Olivia with her parents. The Corbyn family that he'd known—Olivia, Francine, and now Arthur—was gone. It was hard to get his head around that fact. An entire family gone too soon.

As Olivia's face stared back at him, he could almost hear her pleading with him to find her father's killer. He really didn't want to let her down.

"Flynn?"

Callie's questioning voice brought his head around.

"Did you find the phone?" she asked from the doorway.

"Not yet. I got a little sidetracked."

Callie crossed the room and looked into the box of photos. She pulled out a shot of Olivia and him at Zuma Beach. He had one arm around Olivia and the other around a surfboard. Olivia had on a bright-yellow bikini and he was bare-chested, wearing his favorite board shorts. His hair was longer and blonder. He didn't look like he had a care in the world, and neither did she. It was a perfect moment in time. And it hurt.

"You both look young," Callie murmured. "And tan." She lifted her gaze to his. "Olivia was a surfer, too?"

"No. She'd paddleboard, but she didn't like deep water. Another reason why her dying at sea seemed so wrong. She must have been terrified when she went overboard. It's hard to even think about it."

She gave him a compassionate look and put the photo back in the box. "Maybe you should keep some of these. I don't know anyone else who would want them."

"I was thinking about that. There's no one left from the Corbyn family that I knew. I never would have thought they'd all be gone so young." He cleared his throat. "But I need to look for the phone."

"There's not really much in here. I thought by the way Arthur treated this room that there would be more of Olivia."

"I would have thought so, too," he agreed. "On the other hand,

Arthur didn't like clutter. And even though they had a housekeeper, he was always on Olivia to clean things up or give things away. He was very rigid when it came to mess."

"He was the same way with my mom. I don't know how she managed to live up to his neat-freak standards."

"Olivia used to hide stuff away so he wouldn't find it and then get rid of it when she left the house." He stopped abruptly, his gaze moving to the floorboards by the window. "Dammit. Why didn't I think of that sooner?" He walked across the room and squatted down, pushing on the end of a floorboard. It popped right up.

"What's that?" Callie asked in surprise.

"It was her secret hiding place. And it looks like it was Arthur's too." He pulled out a flip phone and set it on the ground. Then he took out an envelope, his heart starting to race at the thought of what might be inside.

There were six photos, each one of a different painting.

"What are those?" Callie asked.

"I'm not sure. I don't recognize the pieces. I don't think I've seen them in this house. Have you?" He grabbed the phone and stood up, handing her the pictures as he did so.

"They don't look familiar. Why would he hide pictures of paintings in the floorboard?"

Only one answer ran through his head and his jaw tightened. "My guess is that the paintings are stolen."

"You think Arthur stole them?" she asked in amazement.

"No, I think he bought them. But we're getting ahead of ourselves. We first need to determine if these paintings were stolen. If they were, they could be the reason he's dead. I need to find out what the history is on each one, who owned it last, where it is now." He opened the flip phone, the kind of prepaid phone one might buy at any electronics store. It was locked by a password. "I'll get this to my tech, see if he can pull up the call history."

"This could be the clue you were looking for, the one that leads you away from my mom."

"I hope it is," he said, meaning his words. "But your mom does work in the art world."

"She plans events at the museum. She doesn't buy and sell artwork."

"She could still be a connection to someone else. I'm not trying to hang onto her as a suspect; I just don't want to lie to you." He was surprised by his own words, and he could see that Callie was startled too.

"You wouldn't lie to me if you thought it might get you to the truth?" she challenged.

"Last night I would have said that I'd have no problem lying to you, but tonight, I feel differently. I like you, Callie. I admire the way you protect your mother, and I feel for what you're going through. I'd like to be honest with you, and I hope you'll return the favor."

"I've told you everything I know."

"Good. Did you find the trust?"

"I did. I'll take it home with me. I don't want to stay here any longer. The house feels creepy."

"I don't blame you. I'll give you a ride home, so you can leave your mom's car here."

"Thanks. I want to put together a small bag for my mom, some familiar things to ground her in her life while she's at the hospital."

"Good idea. I wouldn't mind looking in your mother's room, either. I haven't been in there yet, except for the few moments when she was on the balcony."

Callie frowned at that reminder, then said, "That's fine. But I doubt Arthur would have left anything damning in their room. Not with the way my mom kept an eye on him."

He still wanted to take a look.

When they entered the master bedroom, a blast of cool air hit them in the face. Callie stopped abruptly, her gaze on the open door leading onto thc balcony.

"That was closed," she said. "Locked. And I pushed the desk in front of it in case my mom woke up and tried to get out there again. I never moved it back."

His gaze moved to the desk that was a few feet from the wall and at an odd angle, as if someone had shoved it out of the way. Some of the drawers were open as well.

He put a hand on Callie's arm, as she started forward. "Wait," he said. "Don't touch anything."

She gave him a wide, scared look. "Why not?"

"Someone was in here. Do you notice anything else that's different?"

Her gaze swept the room. "The drawers in the bedside table are open. One has my mother's medication in it."

"Someone was in here."

"Maybe it was Lois. She might have come over to check on my mom even though I told her not to."

"And left the door and the drawers open? Do you have her number in your phone?"

"It's in my mom's phone, which is downstairs in my bag." Callie gave him a worried look. "You think someone came in here?"

"Yes. But we'll call Lois to rule her out. What do you want to get for your mom?"

"I don't know. I can't think," she said, panic in her voice. "This is too much, Flynn."

He put his hands on her shoulders, feeling the tight knots in her muscles. "One step at a time. Let's get a bag for your mom. Where would that be?"

"In the closet," she murmured, her gaze fixed on his. "You don't think they're still in the house, do you? It's such a big place. Someone could be hiding." She dropped her voice. "Maybe in the closet."

He let go of her shoulders and moved over to the closet. The door was ajar. He slowly pushed it open, and then he saw the chaos. The drawers had been ripped apart, clothes pulled off hangers, shoes thrown around on the floor. But there was no one inside.

"If Arthur wasn't dead, this would have killed him," Callie said, coming up behind him. "Sorry. That was thoughtless."

"No, you're right. He would have had a heart attack if he'd walked into this."

"I don't understand, Flynn. I didn't notice a mess like this in the study. Why wouldn't they have gone through that room?"

"I don't know, but I'd prefer if you touched as few things as possible. I'll get my team over here to go through the house, with your permission, of course."

"Do whatever you need to do." She grabbed a tote bag off a shelf and then packed a small bag for her mom.

While she was doing that, he stepped back into the bedroom, his thoughts running a mile a minute. *Why hadn't the intruder gone through the study?* It seemed like an obvious place to hide something like a phone. And, clearly, they hadn't tried to make it look like this room had been untouched. *Or had they gotten frustrated by the time they arrived in the bedroom? And just started ripping things apart?*

"I'm done," Callie said, coming out of the closet.

"Let's go back downstairs."

When they reached the study, he moved into the room. As Callie had said, it was neat, but…

He walked around the desk and noted some of the drawers were still partly open. "Did you open these?"

"No. I just opened the filing cabinet and took out the big binder and then I went back into the living room, because, to be honest, I just didn't want to look at Arthur's portrait." She paused. "They did come in here, didn't they? But they weren't as clumsy and ruthless."

"Maybe they ran out of time when we arrived. It could explain why the door was open to the balcony. They might have taken off when we got here."

"It would be on the security cameras, right?"

He nodded, as they headed back into the living room. Callie grabbed her purse and pulled out her mom's phone. "Arthur put the camera app on her phone in case she was here alone." She opened the app and handed him the phone.

It took him only a second to realize the cameras had been turned off. "They were able to turn off the system. It could have been a hack or was done on-site. This system is not particularly complicated." As he looked at the phone, he couldn't help noticing that Juliette had received voicemails and messages. "People have been calling and texting your mom."

"I know. It's been buzzing all day, but I haven't had a chance to look through it."

"Why don't you let me do that?"

"No," she said abruptly. "I need to hang onto the phone. May I have it, please?"

He handed it back to her, not wanting to break the trust they were starting to build. Plus, he thought he could probably get her to go through the messages and voicemails with him.

"Thanks." Callie put the phone in her pocket and then wrapped her arms around her waist. "I feel cold."

It wasn't all that chilly, but he suspected the events of the last twenty-four hours were catching up to her.

"I'll take you home now."

"I probably should say no and just drive myself."

"Why should you say no?" he challenged.

"Because…" Her voice drifted away, but her gaze clung to his. "I'm feeling too connected to you, Flynn. And it scares me. You seem like you could be a friend, but you could also be an enemy. I don't want to like you, but I do. And there's this really strong connection between us that I don't understand and that I'm not sure I want."

He should lie and say he didn't know what she was talking about, but he'd already promised her honesty. "I feel the connection, too, Callie."

"It's weird, right?"

"Weird and not so bad at the same time," he said lightly. "I noticed you the first moment I saw you. When you walked into the museum last night in that spectacular red dress, my heart stopped."

She flushed at his words. "I borrowed the dress from a friend. I thought it was a little too much, but she said I should go for it. I didn't have time to argue."

"It wasn't too much. It was…nice. Really nice."

"Thank you. I have to say a part of me thinks there's a hidden agenda behind your flirting."

"I told you I was going to tell you the truth."

"I'm trying to believe that. I just can't quite figure you out."

"Good. I prefer to be more interesting than predictable. Now, why don't we get out of here?"

"Before someone else arrives?" she murmured.

He met her gaze. "I wasn't going to say that, but yes."

"Do you think they were looking for the phone or the photos or something else entirely?"

"That's what we need to figure out."

CHAPTER NINE

WHEN THEY ARRIVED at her apartment and took the stairs to her third-floor apartment, Callie was more than happy to have Flynn at her side. She was rattled from the scene at Arthur's house and not sure what to expect in her own home. She felt like she hadn't been home in days, even though it had only been twenty-four hours. So much had happened since she'd met her mother and Arthur in the limo for what was supposed to have been a fun evening of art and champagne.

She inserted her key in the lock and held her breath as she opened the door. Stepping inside, her gaze moved across the open space living area that included the living room, kitchen and dining area. Relief ran through her as it appeared that nothing had been touched.

She wasn't nearly as neat as Arthur, but there was only one used coffee mug on the kitchen counter since she had loaded the dishwasher yesterday before she'd gone to the museum. Her laptop sat open on the coffee table next to a bottle of roasted peanuts, one of her favorite snacks, and the book she'd been reading was on the table by the couch.

"No one has been in here," she said, turning to Flynn.

"Mind if I check the bedroom?"

"Go ahead."

She followed him down the short hallway into the bedroom and attached bath. She hadn't made her bed, and her robe had been tossed haphazardly across the bottom of the bed, but she hadn't been expecting company.

Flynn stuck his head in the bathroom and then said, "Looks fine."

"I wish I'd made my bed now."

He smiled. "Mine isn't made, either. Sometimes I don't see the point."

"Right? You're just going to get back into bed at the end of the day."

"Exactly. And I would really love to know what it is with women and pillows." He tipped his head toward the pile of blue and white throw pillows on the floor next to the bed. "That's where they always end up—on the floor."

"But they look great when the bed is made. I'm just a little lazy. We don't have to stay in here," she added, thinking that getting Flynn out of her bedroom was probably a good idea.

As they walked down the hall, he said, "I like your place. You're lucky to be beachfront."

"I am lucky. A friend of my mother's owns this building; she gave me a break on the rent." When they reached the living room, she said, "Do you want some coffee?"

"That would be great."

As she started the coffeemaker, Flynn wandered around the apartment, stopping in front of her floor-to-ceiling bookshelves, which were not only stuffed with books but also with record albums.

"What is all this?" he asked in surprise. "You have the Beatles' White Album? My mother must have played that a million times."

"My dad did, too. That's my father's collection. He was a huge Beatles fan. All their records are there."

"And you can still play them. Amazing." He moved over to the record player on the adjacent table. "I haven't seen one of these in fifteen years."

"It was also my dad's, but it still works. You can play something if you want."

He took a record out of its sleeve and put it on the player. After fiddling around with the buttons, the song *Revolution* blared across the small speakers attached to the player.

"It sounds great," Flynn said, as he came over to the island. "Old school."

She smiled. "Yes. It's a different experience to play a record than to stream music over headphones, which is usually how I listen. But the records always take me back to the past, to the music of my parents, and it's nice. Sometimes, it's a little sad, too, but not in a bad way. That probably doesn't make sense."

"It makes perfect sense. This takes me back, too, and not in a bad way." He paused. "It actually surprises me to say that, but this song makes me remember my mom dancing around the house as she picked up clutter and dusted off the furniture. She made cleaning look fun. I'm sure it was a ruse to get me to help, and it worked."

"My father used to play his records when he was making dinner. It was a happy time for us. We were usually cooking together. Sometimes, in between taking something in and out of the oven, he'd grab my hands and spin me around like we were dancing." A wave of sadness followed her words. "It's funny how some moments in our lives stand out forever, while others disappear so quickly."

Flynn nodded in agreement. "You never know what will stick."

"Do you have a favorite memory with one or both of your parents?"

"My mom was a puzzle fiend. She liked the gigantic 2,000-piece puzzles. She always said it wasn't fun if it wasn't a challenge. My father would say get something easier, something you can finish faster. But she liked the battle."

"I have a suspicion that you might take after her."

"I do like a good puzzle. Mine just aren't jigsaws anymore. The stakes are much higher."

"Like Arthur's puzzling death."

"Yes. I wish there was a box with a picture on it so I would know where I'm heading. Right now, all I see are random pieces that don't go together."

"Speaking of random pieces…how long do you think it will take to figure out whether those pictures of paintings we found in Olivia's room are important?"

"Probably not long. I can check the FBI database of stolen art. In fact, I can get that going now." He pulled out his phone and spread the pictures across the island counter, then snapped a photo of each one of them. "I'll upload these to the database when I get back to my computer."

"It's Saturday night. Don't you ever take a minute off?" She had to admit she was impressed with his devotion to duty.

"Not in the middle of a case." He looked back at the photos. "I do know that this painting was stolen four years ago from a museum in Madrid. I was involved with art crimes at the time. It's an abstract by Miguel DeRosa, a Spanish painter. This piece is entitled *A Winter Garden*. It was originally purchased for over five million dollars and then donated to the museum after the owner passed away."

"That's a garden?" she asked, moving to the island to take a closer look. She squinted at the blobs of dark green mixed with white and gray. "It doesn't look like anything to me."

He smiled. "Abstract art is not my favorite, either, but to some it's the ultimate form of expression. The painting can be seen in an infinite number of ways by whoever is looking at it."

"I guess," she said doubtfully. "If this painting was stolen, and this picture was sent to Arthur, what do you take away from that?"

"I'm not sure. The fact that he hid the pictures in the floor-board tells me that they're important and probably not in a good way."

"I know you don't want to believe Arthur is a criminal."

"I don't. Arthur spent so much of his life discharging justice to criminals. It seems unimaginable that he could be one himself. But then, I've been fooled before."

She was sorry to have reminded him of that fact. She suspected

Flynn had kicked himself around the block a million times for not seeing his father for who he was.

Flynn's gaze moved to the other photos spread across the counter. "I don't recognize these paintings, but I suspect they're stolen, too."

"What would they be worth?"

"Millions of dollars. Someone spent twenty-seven million dollars last year for a painting by Stanley Warinsky, a Russian painter."

She shook her head in amazement. "That's a lot of cash. I know Arthur is rich, but is he that wealthy?"

"His current net worth is about sixty million dollars."

"Seriously?" She was shocked at that figure.

"Arthur inherited money from his parents and also from Francine's estate. He might not spend twenty-seven million for a painting, but he has enough to play on the black market."

"Now I know why he had my mother sign a prenup."

"How did that go over?"

"She didn't like it at first, but she was madly in love. And she's never been about money. She was lucky enough to have inherited enough money and real estate from my dad's estate that she has been able to either not work or just work part-time for most of her life. She's not rich, but she's okay." She paused. "You probably already knew that."

"I did. Have you ever asked your mother to invest in your dream restaurant?"

"No. My mother needs to keep her money. These hospital stays are not cheap, and insurance doesn't cover everything. I would never risk her nest egg on my dream."

"I'm sure she'll inherit something from Arthur."

Her gaze drifted to the large binder she'd set on the counter. "I need to go through that tomorrow. I also need to go through my mom's phone and listen to her voicemails and read her messages. There could be something urgent I have to deal with." She moved back to the coffeemaker, filling two mugs with coffee. She had a feeling she was going to need it.

"Let's go through the phone now," he suggested, as she handed him a mug. "Do you have her password?"

"I do." She grabbed her mom's phone, put in the code, and then hesitated. "I probably should look at them myself first."

"In case she has said something incriminating?" he asked. "I can get a warrant for her phone, Callie. Even if you erased the messages or voicemails, my tech would be able to retrieve them."

"You're saying you'll know everything eventually anyway."

"Yes," he said, meeting her gaze.

As she stared down at the large number by the message icon, she realized she just wasn't up to going through them all. She handed the phone to Flynn, silently praying that there wouldn't be anything damning on the phone. She didn't believe her mother was guilty. She really hoped she was right.

"She has about twenty messages," Flynn muttered. "And eight voicemails."

"Start with the messages. You can read them aloud if they're important."

Flynn skimmed for a minute. "There are a lot of one liners—hope you're okay, thinking of you kind of stuff—from Elaine, Shari, and Rose Baker, and some phone numbers that don't have names attached."

"Elaine and Shari work at the museum. Rose is her hair stylist."

"Here's one that's a little longer and much more intriguing. It's from Moira Shanahan."

"That's Arthur's administrative assistant. What does she say?" she asked curiously.

"Juliette, I can't believe what's happened," he read aloud. "I keep thinking it's a nightmare, and I'll wake up. You must feel the same way. I know how much you loved Arthur. I feel so terrible. I want to help in any way I can. Please call me or text me and let me know what I can do."

"Moira must be devastated. She's been with Arthur for almost ten years."

Flynn frowned as he looked down at the phone once more. "This message is odd."

"What does it say?"

"I think you should know your husband was cheating on you," he read. "He was in love with me. And he was going to leave you. I have this terrible feeling you already know that, and that's why you killed him. Arthur said you would go crazy if you knew. But I think you're already crazy. Arthur was too good for you and now he's dead. You should be careful you don't end up the same way."

Her stomach tightened and her pulse began to race. "Can you trace that phone number? This woman is threatening to hurt my mother."

"She's also suggesting your mom killed Arthur because she found out about the affair."

"But that didn't happen. And I don't like that she says my mother might end up dead, too."

"No one can get to your mom right now. She's safe."

"I hope so."

"There's a chance this text is also not true," he said.

She was surprised by his words. "Why wouldn't it be?"

"Any number of reasons. Someone could be trying to set your mother up, but we'll know more when we trace the number."

"How long will that take?"

"At least until tomorrow."

She knew that Flynn and his team were working around the clock, but it still didn't seem fast enough. "I have to know who sent that text."

"We'll figure it out."

"I wonder if Moira would know about an affair. She handled his work schedule, which sometimes overlapped with his personal schedule. Hand me my mom's phone. I want to call Moira."

He hesitated.

"What?" she demanded.

"I don't want you in the middle of this investigation, Callie. I'll talk to Moira."

"She's much more likely to tell me the truth than to tell you. She was fiercely loyal to Arthur. She will want to protect his reputation."

"She might not want you or your mother to know about an affair."

"I still think I'll get further than you," she argued.

His lips tightened, and he didn't look happy with her suggestion, but he did hand her the phone.

"All right," he said. "Just remember to ask more questions than you answer. We want to find out what Moira knows without telling her what we know."

"Got it."

"And put the call on speaker."

"I will." She punched in Moira's number, which was already programmed into her mother's phone. It rang twice and then Moira picked up.

"Juliette? Are you all right?"

"It's actually Callie, Moira."

"Oh, Callie, I'm so sorry. I can't believe this. I've been crying all day. I just don't want it to be true."

"I know. I feel the same way."

"How is your mother?"

"She's resting. I didn't want you to think she didn't appreciate your text. She just can't talk to anyone right now."

"Oh, I wasn't expecting an answer. I'm sure she's very upset." Moira paused. "I know a little about her problems, Callie, so if I can help, please ask."

"Actually, you can help. I don't know how to say this, so I'm just going to say it. My mom is getting a lot of questions about Arthur and other women. I know you want to protect his reputation, and so do I, but I need to know the truth so that I can also protect my mother. I think, together, we can figure out a way to keep private what needs to be private."

"Oh, Callie. I'm not sure what to tell you."

"Was Arthur having an affair, Moira?"

There was a long silence at the other end of the phone. Then Moira said, "I never thought he would cheat on your mom. He was madly in love with her. But the last two months, he was different. He was tense and out of sorts. He didn't want to take the call sometimes when your mom was on the phone. And about three weeks ago, he asked me to make him a dinner reservation for two in Palm Springs. When I asked him if he was taking Juliette, he said that she was busy and that he'd be going with a friend."

"Do you know who he took?"

"I'm assuming it was someone named Layana, because he got on the phone with her right after I told him the details of the reservation. I just heard him say her name. I didn't hear anything else. That's all I know, Callie. It could have been innocent. She could have been a colleague, although I hadn't heard the name before."

"Have you given the FBI this information?"

"Not yet. I don't know for sure that there was anything going on romantically. I would hate to say Arthur was having an affair when I'm not certain. Your mother would be devastated. And Arthur's reputation would be damaged. But if you or your mother knows who this Layana is, you might want to get in front of this."

"I definitely want to do that. Thanks for telling me."

"Do you know if there are any suspects?"

"I don't."

"Is there anything I can do to help you and your mom with funeral arrangements?"

"We're talking about all that. I'll let you know when we know."

"All right. Take care."

"You, too."

She ended the call and looked at Flynn, feeling unsettled by Moira's words. "She tried really hard not to say Arthur was having an affair, but she obviously thought that he was."

"I would agree."

"My mother's instincts were right. Arthur was having an affair. And the woman who sent my mother that threatening message is probably his lover."

"Possibly."

"She wants to make it look like my mom found out about them and killed Arthur. But maybe that's to hide the fact that she killed Arthur. What if he wasn't going to leave my mom? What if his lover thought she was losing him to his wife?"

"It's a theory," he said carefully. "But you're making a lot of leaps."

"We need to figure out who Layana is. Can you run that name through some FBI database?"

"Yes, although, it would be helpful to have a last name. But it is an unusual first name, so we might get lucky. I'm also wondering about Palm Springs. This is the second time it has come up. You said Arthur and your mother were fighting about going down there this week."

"That's true. Maybe that's where he had his affair."

"Where did Arthur and your mother stay when they went down there?"

"At the house Arthur bought last year."

His gaze narrowed. "I have a list of Arthur's assets, which includes his real estate holdings, and I didn't see a house in the desert. There's a condo in Maui but nothing in Palm Springs."

"I don't know why it wouldn't be on there; he bought it about six months ago."

"Have you been there?"

"Once for the weekend. It's a beautiful place, like everything else Arthur owns."

"Do you have a key?"

"I know the code. Unless Arthur changed it."

"I'm going to need the address and the code. I'll head down there tomorrow."

"Why don't I go with you?" she suggested.

"I don't think so."

"Why not?"

"Because this is an FBI investigation and you're not an agent."

"But I'm helping you. You wouldn't even know about Palm Springs if it wasn't for me," she argued. "And I want to be there if you find any clues. Also, the property technically belongs to my mom, so I feel a need to protect her interests. If you want the code, you have to take me with you."

"I can find the house without you."

"As fast as you want to find it?" she challenged. "Wouldn't it be easier if I went along for the ride? Or, I could just go on my own."

He gave her an annoyed look. "Fine, you can come."

"Good. What time?"

"I'll be free around noon. I have a brunch in the morning."

"That's perfect. I'll want to check on my mom in the morning." She sipped her coffee. "What else should we be doing?"

The smile returned to his lips. "You should probably be thinking about getting some sleep. I'm sure you didn't get much rest last night."

"Only a few hours, but I don't feel sleepy. I'm too wired. There are so many questions running around my head. Was Arthur having an affair? Was he buying stolen artwork? And who is Layana?"

"All good questions. Unfortunately, we don't have any answers. And it's been a long day. I should probably get going."

"Right now?" she asked, realizing she sounded a little desperate, but the thought of being by herself made her uncomfortable.

"Do you want me to stay longer?" he asked, a gleam in his eyes.

"Yes. But you don't have to. I'm just a little spooked. I keep thinking about someone going through Arthur's house. It feels like something more is coming. Or maybe that's just my imagination. It can get the better of me. You know what? You should go. I'm fine on my own. And I'm sure you're tired, too. You haven't had much of a weekend."

"I'm not in a hurry to leave."

Relief flooded through her. "We could go out on the deck. I have a heat lamp. The waves are always calming."

"Sold."

She felt a rush of warmth as his smile washed over her. She had a feeling she probably wouldn't need a heat lamp with Flynn around. She also had the feeling she was probably making a big mistake by inviting him to stay. But it was too late now.

CHAPTER TEN

HANGING out with Callie might not be the best decision Flynn had ever made, but he was enjoying her company too much to care. "I'm extremely jealous of your deck," he said, as Callie switched on the heat lamp, and they settled on a loveseat overlooking the water.

It was cold, but he didn't give a damn. The crashing waves, the starry sky, and the beautiful woman next to him were an irresistible combination.

Callie pulled a blanket off the back of the couch. "Do you want to share?"

"I'm okay." He needed to use a little restraint when it came to Callie and snuggling under a blanket with her might be a bridge too far. There was a small, cynical voice in his head that kept popping up with reminders that while he didn't believe Callie had anything to do with Arthur's death, she could be trying to get close to him to protect her mother.

Frowning at that thought, he sipped his coffee and looked out at the water. There was a full moon tonight, illuminating the crashing white water.

"You're quiet," Callie commented.

He gazed back at her. "Just enjoying the endless and relentless pounding of the waves on the beach. It's like a heartbeat. It keeps going no matter what else is happening."

"It can be a comforting beat," she agreed. "I often sleep with the windows open. But I have to admit that I like watching the water more than I like being in it."

"You're missing out. Being farther away from the shore gives you a new perspective."

"But it's deep and there could be sharks. Have you ever run into one?"

"No."

"And you're not scared that you will?"

"Terrible things have happened in my life that I never expected, that I never worried about. Those events taught me not to try to predict the future. I just deal with what's in front of me."

"That's a good philosophy. Is it really that easy?"

He smiled. "No. But it's a goal I keep going after."

She nodded, falling silent for a moment. Then she said, "It's not that cold out, even for January."

"The benefit of living in Southern California."

"I bet London was a lot colder."

"It was also grayer and wetter."

"Does your mom still live in England?"

"Yes. She lives in Bath now, a cottage very near to where Jane Austen lived as a teenager. She's written a couple of novels that she managed to get published by a small press. They aren't bestsellers, but they found their way onto some bookstore shelves, including the place where she works part-time. She met a new man last year and they've been dating for a few months. I haven't met him yet, but she told me he's a good man. I hope that's true."

"She sounds happy."

"She is now. It took a while for her to get there. My dad's betrayal was very painful. She had no idea she'd fallen in love with a criminal. It wasn't even that he was a thief; it was that he left us to save himself. She couldn't forgive that."

"How did she feel about you going into the FBI to look for your father?"

"She didn't like it at all. She was afraid I was going to find him and afraid I wouldn't. She didn't want me to spend my life chasing his ghost or being caught up in the same world that had ripped apart our family. Of course, I didn't listen to her. I was obsessed when I was younger. I wanted to see his face again. I wanted to confront him for everything he'd done. I wanted him to have to see me, to have to hear what he did to us. And there was a part of me that wanted to put him in jail, to make him pay." He could still feel that fiery anger.

"I'm a little surprised you haven't been able to find him, given your connections."

"He went deep underground, somewhere far away from here. I'm sure he changed his name. And I suspect he had enough connections in the black market that he was able to find enough money to start over."

"Do you think he's still doing what he was doing?"

"I don't even know if he's alive, so speculating about anything else is pointless."

"Well, I'm glad your mom was able to get her life back together, and that she might have a new love now. Trusting another man wouldn't be easy for her." Callie paused, tilting her head as she gave him a thoughtful look. "What about you? I know you've moved past your father's betrayal, but what about Olivia. Have you moved past her death, too?"

"Both events happened a long time ago, Callie."

"That's not an answer. Have you had any other long-term, serious relationships since Olivia?"

"First of all, Olivia and I only dated about six months before she died, so long-term wasn't that long. We were kids. We were crazy about each other, but we were young."

"And after she died…who came next?"

He frowned at her pressing question. "I had one relationship in my twenties that lasted about a year but wasn't meant for forever. Since then, I've been busy with work. I travel a lot. I work unpredictable hours. I get obsessed with a case and I can't think of anything else until it's solved. None of those things make me a good boyfriend. Believe me, I've been told that a lot by the women I have dated."

She laughed. "I'll bet."

"So, I prefer to keep things light, easy."

"In other words, you're like most guys I know," she said dryly.

"I hope not. I'd rather be one of a kind."

"Sorry, but I've heard this song before. Everyone uses work as a reason not to commit, but that's never the reason. It's always about the person. When you find someone that you want to see every single day of the week, then work doesn't matter. That's my opinion, anyway."

"Didn't you tell me earlier that you've been too busy to date, too, that you've been building your career?"

"Well, I didn't say I wasn't like everyone else," she admitted.

He appreciated her candor. Callie was not a woman who played games, and that was refreshing. Although, they weren't dating, so perhaps that's why they could be more honest with each other.

"Love scares me," she continued. "I've seen what love has done to my mom. All those emotions can be overwhelming and exhausting. I'm not sure I need that in my life."

"You're not your mother."

"I've always been a little afraid that I could be like her. When I was younger, if I started to cry, I'd immediately force myself to stop. I thought if I broke down even a little bit, I might fall completely apart. I did everything I could not to let myself get too involved, too caught up in anything or anyone."

"Because if you didn't allow yourself to care, you couldn't be hurt." He thought that was a rather sad way to live, but he completely understood her fears.

"And there would be no tears," she added. "No endless harangue of whining and crying and feeling like I was in a black hole that I couldn't get out of."

"That kind of isolation can prevent you from living a full, rich life," he said, not liking the way she'd put her emotions on ice.

"But I won't end up in a psych ward."

"You wouldn't end up there even if you did let go a little. Your core is steel, Callie. Beautiful, determined, stubborn steel."

Her gaze widened in surprise. "No one has ever described me that way."

"Maybe you've never let anyone see you that way. But I see you."

Their gazes clung together as the air between them sizzled. He felt an irresistible pull in her direction, and he shut down all instincts warning caution. He'd always liked to live dangerously, and tonight was no exception.

He slid his hand around the back of her neck. She didn't say no or push him away, so he leaned over and covered her mouth with his.

It was a hot kiss on a cold, dark night, and it felt incredibly close to perfect. As he deepened the kiss, they moved closer together, their arms coming around each other in complete accord. There was something so right about kissing her. It was new and exciting, but it also felt completely familiar, as if they'd been kissing each other forever with a hunger that would never go away.

The crashing of the waves perfectly reflected the turmoil of desire building inside of him. But just like the ocean, there was danger within the beauty of the moment. He didn't want to hurt her. He didn't want to get hurt.

They'd both been fleeing the possibility of that kind of pain for a long time, and now they had crossed a line that they probably couldn't cross back. They'd opened the gates to something amazing and possibly terrifying.

Callie pulled away first, her breath curling up like hot clouds in the chilly air. Her lips were parted, as she drew in a shaky breath, and he wanted back in that warm cavern of heat. He wanted to kiss her again. He wanted to strip away all the layers between them, get even closer to this beautiful woman who'd stolen the breath out of his chest from the first second he'd seen her.

But Callie was sliding away from him, wrapping the blanket around her like a suit of armor.

He watched her for a long minute, not sure what he wanted to say. She seemed to be suffering from the same lack of words.

"You should probably go," she said finally. "It's getting late."

He nodded, disappointed by the words she'd eventually come up with. On the other hand, they were dancing dangerously close to a precipice. It would be wiser to back away from the edge before things got too complicated. Although, he had a feeling it was already too late for caution.

As she stood up, he also got to his feet, then followed her into the apartment. The bright lights of her home reinforced their return to reality. But it also gave him another chance to look at her, to see the desire still glittering in her eyes.

"Callie," he began.

She shook her head, giving him a warning look. "Let's not talk about it."

"Why not?"

"Because some things should just be what they are in the moment. Tomorrow we have to get back to finding Arthur's killer and proving my mother's innocence. That's what we should focus on. You said noon tomorrow for Palm Springs?"

He was impressed with her immediate return to focus, something he usually excelled at. "Yes. That should work."

"Then I'll see you tomorrow."

"Are you going to be all right here by yourself?"

"I'll be fine."

"You can call me any time," he said, even though he knew she wouldn't call.

"I have your number, but I'm just going to go to bed and hopefully catch up on the sleep I missed last night." She crossed the room and opened the door.

He paused in front of her. "Just for the record—that moment we had was amazing."

"But it shouldn't happen again."

"Maybe it shouldn't," he said, as he walked into the hallway. "But, somehow, I think it will."

Flynn didn't sleep well, tossing and turning with both thoughts of Callie and questions about Arthur. He got up around seven on Sunday morning and did what he always did when he needed to make sense of his life; he went surfing. He wasn't alone on the ocean. There were dozens of weekend surfers in wetsuits paddling their boards out to the break, but he kept his distance from the crowd, wanting to be on his own.

As he sat on his board, looking for just the right wave, he couldn't help thinking that it wasn't a wave he needed, but some hard leads. He had a few clues: Arthur's second phone, the pictures of the paintings, the mysterious Layana, the Palm Springs property that hadn't come up on the list of Arthur's assets, the calls between Arthur and Gretchen, and Arthur and Marcus Vitelli. There was also Victoria Waltham's suggestion that his father might be back in business, that piece of info allegedly having come from Arthur.

He didn't want his dad in the middle of this. His relationship to Arthur was enough of a conflict of interest. If his father was involved, he'd have to take himself off the case, and even though his team was good, he wanted to lead the investigation.

There was also the issue of the break-in at Arthur's house. *Had that person been looking for the phone and the photos or something else entirely? Did they know about the house in Palm Springs? Would it be cleaned out by the time he arrived?*

And then there was Callie. Her beautiful face had been in his head all night.

He'd kissed women before to get what he needed in the pursuit of justice. But all he'd wanted last night was her. He didn't know if she believed that. Deep down, she still didn't trust him, and he couldn't completely blame her. He was sending her mixed messages, because he had mixed emotions. Getting personal with her had enabled him to learn things more quickly, but it had also made him vulnerable, because she knew things about him, too. And vulnerability was a weakness in any investigation.

Actually, he considered it a weakness in every part of his life, which was why he so rarely shared his past with anyone. No one outside his friends from Quantico knew about his father. His high school friends, who had been around at the time of his father's disappearance had disappeared long ago. In his present-day life, discussion of his dad never came up. If someone asked, which was rare, he simply said his parents were divorced and his father was out of his life. They never pressed for more details.

But he and Callie had gotten very deep very fast. Maybe it was knowing what she was dealing with that had made it easier to open up. They'd both revealed parts of themselves that rarely saw the light. He didn't want to abuse the trust she'd put in him, and he hoped she felt the same way.

He thought she did. She was a good person. She wasn't just pretty on the outside; she had a beautiful spirit. She loved deeply, especially when it came to her mother. But that depth of love scared her. She'd admitted that last night. She couldn't handle anyone else needing her in such a profound way. It was too much, so she stayed away from relationships.

He stayed away from relationships, too, but not for the same reason. Well, maybe it was partly the same reason, he silently admitted. Although in his case, it was more about avoiding pain than need. The anger he'd felt when his father had abandoned them had been overpowering. He'd literally put his fist through a wall. And the grief he'd felt when Olivia had died had almost driven him mad.

Both events had happened a long time ago, and he had moved on. He had cared about other women. He had grown up. He had become his own man. But now the door to the past had been thrown wide open, and he was being forced to step through it.

"What are you waiting for—an invitation?" Wyatt asked, as he paddled over to him.

Wyatt Tanner had joined his task force a year ago, and while they'd been rivals during their Quantico days, now they were tight. He had great respect for Wyatt's undercover skills. He was a chameleon: he could go into any situation, any environment, and own it. It was a true talent. Although, that talent had almost gotten him killed a few times.

Beyond the job, he'd always felt a kinship to Wyatt, because Wyatt's father, an investment banker, had gotten himself and his clients and even his older son into serious financial trouble and legal trouble by playing fast and loose with the law. But unlike his father, Wyatt's dad had gone to jail, and his brother had as well. Wyatt had fortunately been too young to get caught up in the family business. He'd ended up working for the FBI, just as Flynn had.

He smiled into Wyatt's curious brown eyes. "I was thinking."

"That tends to happen when you're sitting on a surfboard. But did you come out here to think or to surf?"

"I came out here because it's where I go for answers."

"Find any?"

"Not yet. I thought you weren't supposed to be back until later today."

"Avery got an invitation to speak at UCLA tomorrow, and she wanted to take it, so we took an earlier flight and got in last night."

"Cutting the honeymoon short for work? That's no good."

"We had a great time. And two weeks was the longest I've ever gone without working in I can't remember how long." Wyatt paused. "I spoke to Savannah last night. She told me about your friend's death and the investigation. I'm happy to help. I have some time, unless you want me on something else?"

"Actually, I could use you on this. Beck and Jax are working a trafficking case that's taken them to San Francisco, Caitlyn had to go to DC for her brother's wedding, and Bree has been consulting on a kidnapping case. Savannah and Lucas have been helping me, but I could use your sharp eye as well. We're also coordinating with the police and Damon's office."

"Savannah said she and Lucas have been focusing on the judge's court cases while you've been concentrating on his connection to the art world."

"Which is where I think this investigation is headed. Arthur was a private collector, a patron of the arts, and hidden away in his home, I found a second phone and photos of paintings, at least one of which was stolen years ago."

"Where were they hidden?"

"Under a floorboard in the room belonging to his daughter who passed away years ago."

"So, not a place anyone would look."

"Only someone who knew that his daughter used to hide things there."

"Which was you. We're talking about the girl you lost."

"Yes. There's also the fact that Arthur asked me for help before he died. I hadn't spoken to him in over five years when I got a call out of the blue that he needed a favor. He told me he was in a delicate situation and that someone was watching him. That's, unfortunately, all I got before he was killed."

"His murder was dramatic and bold."

"It feels personal as well. How did you know I was out here, by the way?"

"I called you, and you didn't answer. Where else would you be on Sunday morning at seven a.m.?" Wyatt paused, his gaze thoughtful. "This case must be opening some old wounds, Flynn."

"I can handle it."

"Can you? The art world is tied to your father. The judge is tied to the tragic loss of your first love. That's a lot of the past for anyone to handle."

"It won't be a problem."

"Maybe you should step away. Let your team handle this."

"I believe I told you the same thing when you were falling for Avery while you were running for your lives. You didn't listen to me then."

"That was different." Wyatt smiled. "Or maybe it's not. Savannah says you've been concentrating on the judge's stepdaughter. I saw a photo of her. Very pretty."

"She is attractive," he agreed. "She's also helping me. So, it's all good. If at any time I think I'm losing my objectivity, I will bow out, because justice needs to be served."

"Then we're good. Are you going to Bree's for brunch today?"

"Yes, but I'm just going to drop in for a short time. I have a few leads I want to follow up on. In the meantime, let's see if your surfing skills have gotten any better."

"They're as good as yours any day," Wyatt snapped back.

"Prove it," he challenged.

"You're on."

They surfed for almost an hour, conversing only briefly during ocean lulls, but mostly just enjoying the challenges of the waves.

When they hit the beach, he headed home to change, as Wyatt did the same. He wanted to stop in at the office before he went to Bree's and do some work or at least get some balls in motion that could keep rolling after brunch and while he was driving down to Palm Springs.

He called Callie from the car, but she didn't answer. It was only eight. Hopefully, she was still sleeping. She needed to rest, because he had a feeling it would be another long day.

CHAPTER ELEVEN

CALLIE WOKE up around nine on Sunday, feeling much more ener-
gized than she'd felt the day before. She'd actually been able to
sleep without seeing Arthur's dead body or hearing her mother's
hysterical weeping.

After taking a shower and putting on faded, ripped jeans and a
soft, cozy blue sweater, she made herself breakfast, thinking about
Flynn's scrambled eggs from the day before, as she whipped up an
egg white omelet with tomatoes and mushrooms and mixed in
some roasted potatoes she had left over from a few days earlier.
Flynn had done a nice job with his scramble. The man clearly had
many talents besides being a federal agent. He was a good cook
and a really good kisser.

She smiled to herself at the memory. It had been a long time
since she'd felt so thoroughly wrapped up in a man's kiss where she
hadn't been thinking about anything except making it last as long
as possible. Usually, her mind was ahead of her emotions, warning
her not to go too fast or too slow, thinking about random things
like whether or not the guy was too tall or too short or if she had
time to go to the gym or for a run before she went to work in the
morning. But with Flynn, she'd been consumed by his taste and his
touch, the heat of his breath, the feel of his arms around her. She

hadn't been able to think of anything or anyone else. The only word going through her head had been *more*. She'd wanted more of him. More of everything.

But that couldn't—shouldn't—happen. He was too attractive, and she already liked him way too much. He was still in a position to hurt her mother. Until her mom was completely in the clear, she couldn't let herself forget that.

Today was a new day, and she was determined to help Flynn get leads that would move him off her mother. And maybe some new clues would also clear her own lingering doubts about her mom. She wanted that more than anything.

She drank two cups of coffee while she ate her breakfast. Her caffeine addiction was getting worse by the minute, but it was helping her focus.

Opening up the large binder that contained Arthur's trust, she read through the first several pages. What was most interesting was that the trust had been updated four weeks earlier. She wondered what had changed in this version. She could probably find out, but it would take a fair amount of reading and probably a call to the attorney.

What she could see was that the bulk of Arthur's estate was going to the family foundation, which had been put in place by his parents and distributed money to various charities. Arthur was also leaving money to several museums, one of which was the Piquard. There were several other businesses called out for endowments, including the Art Co-op of San Diego, and the Vazquez Studio. Arthur's love of art would continue after his death.

Moving on, she saw that her mother would receive a million-dollar flat payment as well as the condo in Hawaii. Her mother could remain in the Pacific Palisades home for one year and then it would be sold with the proceeds going back into the foundation. The management of the foundation would go to Arthur's sister in Australia.

There was no mention of the house in Palm Springs. *Why was that?* If the trust had been redone four weeks ago, that property should be in it somewhere.

As she continued to read, she saw mention of several LLCs and corporations where Arthur was apparently a member or an owner. She ran through the list of names, wondering what on earth all those companies did, but the names were very generic, like Brixton Holdings, JC Corporation, MMD Investments, and Haxton LLC. Maybe she should turn this binder over to Flynn so he could decipher all of Arthur's relationships, although she suspected they probably already had this information. But they hadn't known about Palm Springs. *Why? Because it wasn't listed under Arthur's name?* That begged the next question. *Who was on the deed to the house?* She could go back to Arthur's home and try to find the deed, but she didn't relish the idea of walking through that house again.

Putting the binder aside, she got on her computer. Thinking about the threatening text her mother had gotten on her phone made her wonder if there was anything going on in her mom's email. She'd had her mom's passwords memorized for years, so it was easy to open her mail account.

There were two or three dozen unopened emails. Most seemed to be spam. But one subject heading jumped out at her. It said: *How I See Arthur.*

Opening the email, she caught her breath at the photo of a woman painting what appeared to be Arthur's portrait, only he wasn't wearing clothes in the picture. The shot of the woman revealed her bare back, her long black hair pulled around to the front of her body, her tanned skin.

There was a brief message under the photo. *You need to let him go, Juliette. He's mine.*

As she stared at the picture for several long minutes, Callie's mind whirled with questions, but she also felt a nagging certainty that she might know this woman. She couldn't see her face, but her hair…

And then it clicked into place. The portrait of Arthur that hung in his study. The one she'd been looking at yesterday morning. A woman had painted that portrait. She'd caught a glimpse of her one day when she'd stopped by the house to see her mother; Arthur had been in the middle of posing for his painting. The woman had had her back to her, her long black hair falling to her waist.

The artist had to be Arthur's lover. *Was her name Layana?*

She clicked out of email and opened her mother's bank account. Her mom had actually paid for the portrait. It had been her birthday gift to Arthur. She searched back in time, looking for the transaction. There wasn't a tremendous amount of activity on the page, since Arthur had paid most of her mom's expenses after they married.

Her pulse leapt as she saw a check made out to Vazquez Studio, which was the studio also listed in Arthur's trust. Her heart beat faster as she went into search and found the website.

Suddenly, she was staring into the dark-brown eyes of Layana Vazquez, a stunning Latin beauty who appeared to be in her early thirties. Her portfolio of work was extensive for someone so young. No wonder her mother had hired her; she'd come with amazing credentials, including having done a recent portrait for the perfume billionaire Valerie Dare, who had been at the museum on Friday night.

The studio was located in Century City, only twenty minutes away. It probably wouldn't be open on a Sunday. But maybe…

She had to go to the hospital anyway and Century City wasn't much of a side trip. She could just drive by and see what she could see after she saw her mother. If nothing else, she had a great clue to give Flynn.

As she grabbed her keys and bag, she opened her phone to call Flynn and then realized she'd missed a call from him around eight. She punched in his number, excited to share the results of her amateur sleuthing, but, unfortunately, she got his voicemail.

She left a short message. "I know you're at breakfast, so call me later when you're done. Or I'll call you. I'm on my way to visit my mom, so I may not be able to answer my phone. But get this—I figured out who Layana is."

Flynn pulled up in front of Bree's townhouse. She was hosting brunch to celebrate her husband Nathan's birthday and had invited the whole team to share in the celebration. Flynn was more than happy to attend the party. Bree had saved his life on more than one occasion, and he was thrilled that she'd reconnected with her first love and found happiness. He was also happy she was now working for him.

Before he got out of his car, he checked his phone, realizing he'd somehow missed Callie's call back. It must have come in when he was putting gas in the car.

As he listened to her voicemail, his gut twisted with a variety of emotions. He'd been trying to temper his feelings about her, but her excited, proud voice sent a rush of warmth through his body. If just hearing her voice created such a strong reaction, he had a feeling seeing her again would be an even bigger test.

He was also more than a little intrigued by the fact that she'd figured out who Layana was. He called her back, but she didn't answer. She must be at the hospital. He would have to wait, and there was nothing he hated more than waiting.

As he got out of his car, he ran into Damon and Sophie and their adorable three-month-old daughter, Ciara, who had inherited her dark hair and blue eyes from her father.

"My favorite girl is getting big," he said, smiling at the very happy baby.

"I hope you're talking about Ciara," Sophie said dryly. Sophie was a professor of archaeology, who was currently on leave from her teaching job at UCLA.

"Of course I am. You look beautiful, Sophie."

"I can always count on you to be charming, Flynn."

"Why don't we meet you inside, Sophie?" Damon suggested.

"So you two can talk shop? Make it quick. Bree said she wanted this brunch to be about something other than work. You guys see enough of each other during the week."

"It will just be a minute," Damon promised. As Sophie took their daughter into the house, he turned back to Flynn. "Any updates?"

"Not since I texted you last night," he replied, having already filled both Damon and Savannah in on what he'd found at the house and the break-in. "But hopefully today will bring new clues. What about you?"

"I do have an update. The broken champagne glass found in the fourth-floor hallway tested positive for traces of atropine."

"Arthur was poisoned," he said, as another puzzle piece fell into place. "It makes perfect sense. I was wondering how anyone was able to throw him over that railing without there being more of a struggle. But atropine causes paralysis."

"He would have been incapacitated within seconds."

"This was meticulously planned out in advance, with the security hack to cut off visibility to that corridor."

"Yes. I also spoke to Lucas," Damon added. "He's syncing up with Stella in my office to see if they can trace the hack at the museum and also at Judge Corbyn's home. Do you need me to send a team through the house?"

"No. My team can handle it. I've already looked through the entire house, so I doubt there's more to find there. However, I'm going down to Palm Springs after this. Callie Harper, the judge's stepdaughter, told me that Arthur purchased a house down there several months ago, but it doesn't appear on his list of holdings."

"Did you trace the ownership?"

"I don't have the address yet, but I'll get it." He didn't mention to Damon that he would get it when he took Callie to Palm Springs. It wasn't his first choice but legally compelling her to reveal the address would take longer than letting her come along for the ride.

"Keep me posted. And don't forget to keep Detective Gage in the loop."

"Savannah is my liaison with the police department. You really don't have to worry, Damon. This isn't my first case."

"I know, but we're dealing with the murder of a federal judge, and you have a personal connection. That makes everyone nervous."

"I always get the job done. Trust me."

"I do trust you."

"Good."

He'd no sooner finished speaking when Bree stepped onto her porch and called them inside. Bree was dressed in a dark-green sweater dress that set off her light-green eyes and brown hair.

"Sorry to interrupt," she said, as she hugged them both. "Nathan is going a little crazy."

"Why is Nathan going crazy?" he asked curiously, as she led them into the house.

"Because he has something he wants to share with you all." She waved them into the living room where Sophie and Ciara, Savannah and Lucas, Wyatt and Avery, and Diego Rivera and his girlfriend Tara Powell, were already seated.

Bree walked over to Nathan, who was standing by the window. "Everyone who could be here is here. So, go for it."

"I think you should say it," Nathan told Bree.

"But you wanted to do it."

"Somebody say it," Savannah put in.

Bree grinned. "Fine. I'm pregnant." She let out a happy squeal at the end of her statement.

Congratulations came from every corner of the room.

"Ciara will have a playmate," Sophie said, as she and Damon hugged Nathan and Bree.

"And I will be asking you for plenty of advice, Sophie," Bree said.

"Truly happy for you," Savannah put in.

"Likewise," Lucas said.

"I'm so glad we came home early," Avery interjected, as she and Wyatt offered their best wishes. "This is the best news."

"We're very happy, and I'm sure you're all very hungry," Bree said. "Please hit the buffet and load up your plates."

As the others headed toward the dining room table, Flynn shook Nathan's hand and then gave Bree a long hug.

"I probably should have already told you, boss," Bree said, as her husband went to make mimosas. "I wanted to tell everyone at once, but I kept waiting for the right time and finally realized that while our team is tight, we are often scattered. I had to text Beck, Jax, and Caitlyn, but at least it's not a secret anymore."

"I'm very happy for you. I hope this doesn't mean you're quitting."

"Are you kidding? I'll probably be working up until the last minute. It's who I am," she said with a happy laugh. "Although, Nathan would prefer I spend more time in the office than the field."

"I'll use you wherever you feel comfortable."

"How are you doing, Flynn? I'm so sorry about your friend and that I wasn't able to help yesterday."

"It's all good. I heard you found the kid."

"I helped find the child," she corrected. "It's nice when there's a happy ending. It doesn't happen all that often."

"But this time you got a win."

"Yes. But tomorrow I am at your service."

"I will take you up on that."

"There have certainly been a lot of changes in our group," she said. "Marriages and babies. Don't you want to join us?"

He laughed. "I'm very happy being single."

"That's because you haven't met the right person, but you will. And when you do, that will be it. You won't be able to imagine your life without her."

Bree's words brought Callie's image into his head.

"Wait, have you met someone?" Bree asked, her speculative gaze narrowing.

"Let's get some food," he said, ignoring her question. "I'm starving."

"Fine, I won't press. At least not today," she added, with a gleam in her eyes. "Who knows what will happen tomorrow?"

"Who knows?" he agreed. Although, first he would have to get through today.

After watching her mother sleep for almost a half hour, Callie left her room, both disappointed that she hadn't been able to speak to her and relieved that she was apparently sleeping without sedation. The nurse also said she'd eaten a little yogurt for breakfast, which seemed like a good sign. Dr. Clarke would be in to see her that afternoon and would give Callie a call after that conversation.

Since there was nothing to do but wait, she decided to leave. She still had time before she was due to meet up with Flynn, and Layana's address was burning a hole in her pocket. After leaving the hospital, she headed to Century City.

The studio was located on the corner of a block filled with small retail stores, boutiques, and gift shops, two hair salons and a nail studio as well as a bagel shop and a Mexican restaurant. Callie parked and got out of the car, walking up to the studio window. There were some smaller portraits on display. None were of Arthur, but they were all very good.

Unfortunately, there was also a Closed sign on the door and while there seemed to be a light on at the back of the studio, there was no sign of life in the showroom.

She turned around, feeling deflated. The sign said the shop would open tomorrow at eleven, but she really didn't want to wait until then. Unfortunately, she didn't appear to have a choice.

She was about to return to her car when a woman came out of the bagel place with a coffee and a brown paper bag in her hand. Her focus was on her phone, her waist-long black hair flowing out behind her. She was a slender, curvy woman wearing skintight jeans and a loose tunic top with cutouts on the sleeves.

She didn't look up until she was a few feet from Callie, and then she stopped abruptly, surprise and wariness in her dark eyes.

"Layana?" Callie said, her heart starting to race.

"What do you want?"

"I'm Callie Harper."

"I know who you are."

Layana's mouth tightened, and the movement only made her face thinner and her expression bleaker. Her eyes were red. She'd been crying.

Faced with that genuine emotion, Callie didn't quite know what to say. She'd been thinking of Layana as a monster, a home-wrecker...but she was also apparently very sad.

"We need to talk about Arthur," she finally said.

"I don't have anything to say."

"I think you have a lot to say, and that you're dying to say it. That's why you've sent my mom a text and an email. You want her to know what was going on between you and Arthur."

"Well, you're not her."

"I'm her daughter. Arthur was my stepfather."

"He said you didn't like him much."

She ignored that. "You can talk to me, or you can talk to the FBI. I know what I would pick if I were you."

"Fine. You can come in."

As Layana unlocked her studio door, Callie had the sudden thought that going inside with this crazy woman might not be the smartest idea, but she'd come this far, and she didn't want to leave without knowing what was between Arthur and Layana.

The studio was beautiful, with Layana's portraits covering most of the wall space. In the back, she could see the workshop with easels and paints, but for now Layana seemed content to move behind the counter where she had her computer and phone.

Callie was fine with that. She was near the door. Escape was not that far away, if she needed it. But she wasn't really afraid of this woman hurting her. She was more afraid of what the truth would do to her mother.

"You were having an affair with Arthur," she said, not bothering to make it a question. "How did it start?"

"Arthur and I fell in love while I was painting his portrait. We didn't mean for it to happen, but it did."

"How long has it been going on?"

"Three months. He was going to leave your mother. He said he needed to be with an artist, someone creative, bold, rebellious and beautiful." Layana's hand shook as she sipped her coffee. "But now he's dead and that won't happen. Your mother got her revenge." She drew in a ragged breath. "It's my fault. I taunted her. I wanted her to leave him, not kill him. But he'd always said she'd lose it if she found out, and that he had to be careful what he said and when he said it. He didn't trust what she would do. I thought he was just making excuses. And I was angry."

"So you sent her the email. But she didn't open it. It was unread in her inbox."

Layana stared back at her. "She must have opened it. Because Arthur is dead. And he was really upset on Wednesday night, hours after I sent the email. He was supposed to see me when he got back from Palm Springs, but he called off our date. I think Juliette showed him my message. He said we had to talk, but it would have to wait until the weekend. Only the weekend never came." Layana's lips trembled as she struggled for composure. "Juliette pushed him over the railing. She punished him."

"She didn't do that, Layana."

"Are you sure? Were you with her when he died?"

"No, but I know her. She's not a killer."

"People I've talked to don't seem as sure."

"Who would those people be?"

"Art people. Rumors are flying. Don't you know that?"

"Those rumors aren't true."

"I don't think you're as sure as you're pretending to be," Layana said. "Where is your mother now? Why didn't she come here to confront me?"

"Because she's grief-stricken; she just lost her husband," Callie reminded her. "She loved him, Layana. Maybe he fell out of love with her, but her feelings didn't change." Pausing, she added, "My mother hired you to paint Arthur's portrait. Did you not ever have one moment of guilt, one second where you thought you were wrong to go after someone else's husband?"

"I loved him so much. I couldn't think. I couldn't see her. All I could see was him. We were soul mates. We would talk for hours. It wasn't just sex. We were like two parts of the same person. It was a great love story, the kind people paint."

She almost felt sorry for Layana, because she doubted Arthur had loved her the way she'd loved him. But then her compassion faded when she remembered the threatening message Layana had sent to her mother. "If you think trying to pin Arthur's murder on my mother is a good idea, you should keep thinking. Because she didn't do it. Which means someone else did. If you want that person to pay, then you need to start considering who else might have wanted him dead."

"No one wanted that. Everyone loved him."

"Was Arthur buying stolen art?"

Layana's gaze sharpened. "Why would you ask me that?"

"Because apparently you knew him really well, so tell me— was he purchasing art that had been stolen?"

"No. Arthur loved art. He spoke of how a certain brushstroke could sweep him away. I can't imagine that he would buy something that had been stolen. He had too much respect for art. We had that in common." Layana dabbed at her eyes with her fingers. "He was such a good man."

She frowned, wondering if Layana was right. It was difficult to believe that Arthur had been comfortable dealing in stolen art. *But what about the pictures, the second phone, the calls to Gretchen Vale?*

"Do you know Gretchen Vale?" she asked Layana. "She runs a gallery in Laguna Beach. She and Arthur exchanged quite a few calls before his death."

Layana frowned. "He was unhappy with her. They had an intense conversation last week. But I don't think she would have killed him, because I heard him say he wasn't going to pay her until she delivered. Why would she murder someone who owed her money?"

"What was she supposed to deliver?"

"I don't know. And that's all I have to say. No one in the art world would have killed Arthur. He was a benefactor, a patron of many struggling artists. No one had a reason to kill him, except your mother."

She frowned as Layana once again brought the conversation back to her mom. "Or you," she said impulsively. "Maybe he wasn't going to leave my mom. Maybe you finally figured that out."

Layana's jaw dropped, anger filling her eyes. "Get out."

"I'll go. But don't threaten my mother again."

Layana heaved the cup of coffee in her hand straight at her. Callie managed to jump to the side before it hit her and then she ran out of the gallery.

When she got into her car, she automatically flipped the locks, her heart pounding against her chest. Maybe she shouldn't have taunted Layana, but the words had come out before she could stop them.

And what if she was right? *Who better than to throw Arthur over the railing than a lover who'd suddenly realized he was never going to leave his wife?*

She needed to talk to Flynn. She pulled out of her spot and drove quickly back to her apartment.

CHAPTER TWELVE

"YOU DID WHAT?" Flynn asked, pulling the car over to the side of the road, as Callie's shocking words echoed through his head. He'd picked her up five minutes earlier and was only two blocks from her apartment, when she'd told him she'd gone to Layana's studio.

"Why are we stopping?" she asked nervously.

"Because I need to hear exactly what you did."

"I found Layana and I went to talk to her," she repeated.

"Why the hell would you do that?" He shifted in his seat so he was facing her.

She frowned at his words. "Why are you angry? This is a good thing. I know who she is."

"It's not a good thing. This is an investigation, and you might have just screwed it up."

"You didn't even know who she was or where she was. I figured it out, and you weren't available, so I acted on my own. Do you want to hear what I found out or not?"

He drew in a quick breath, knowing his anger wasn't so much about the fact that she'd acted on her own but that she could have put herself in a dangerous situation. The last thing he wanted was for her to get hurt. "All right, start at the beginning."

"I was going through my mom's email. We looked at her texts

last night, but I was curious what was going on in her emails, and there was one with a photo of a woman painting Arthur's portrait, only Arthur was nude in the portrait and the back of the woman was bare. All I could see was her black hair. I actually printed it out, so you can see it." She reached into her bag and pulled out a piece of paper and handed it to him.

He glanced at the photo. It was exactly as she'd described.

"In the email, the woman said that this was the way she saw Arthur, and I started thinking about the portrait. My mom paid for it to be done. It was her birthday gift to Arthur. He'd always said he wanted an oil portrait of himself. So, a few months into their marriage, she found who she considered to be the right artist, a woman named Layana."

"But you didn't recognize the name yesterday."

"No, because I never knew the name. But I went into my mother's bank account to see who she paid for the portrait and that's when I realized it was Layana Vazquez. Her studio is in Century City. I went by there, thinking it was probably closed, but while I was out front, Layana came out of the bagel shop next door and I recognized her hair from the photo. She's also the one who sent the text, by the way. We went into her studio to talk."

"You just went in, with no thought to your own safety?"

"I did have a thought," Callie admitted. "But she'd been crying, Flynn. She looked like hell. She felt like a very sad person, not a dangerous one."

"Even though she threatened your mother?"

"She was in love with Arthur. He allegedly told her he would leave my mother for her, but he had to pick the right time, because my mother had mental problems and she'd go crazy when she found out. Apparently, as time dragged on, Layana got impatient. She decided to spur things along last week when she sent my mom the photo. She assumed that my mother flipped out after she saw it and killed Arthur. That's why she sent the text yesterday. But here's the thing—my mother never opened that email. I don't think she saw it."

"You were looking at her mail from your computer. She might

have looked at it through an app on her phone and it didn't show as read."

"Well, we can check it from her phone, too. But I don't think she saw it. She didn't check her email every day."

"Okay." He thought about what she'd told him. "So Layana thinks your mother killed Arthur, but if she didn't, we still don't know who did."

"I asked her a few more questions, thinking the same thing, that we need more information about Arthur's life. Layana said that Arthur got very nervous on Wednesday night. He was supposed to meet up with her after he got back from Palm Springs, but then he bailed at the last minute. She thought it was because he'd found out about the photo she'd sent that morning."

"Interesting. Savannah got Arthur's work schedule, and he called in sick that day. But he didn't take Layana with him to the desert."

"Not that day anyway. I asked her who else Arthur might have been upset with. I even suggested that he was buying stolen art. She said she couldn't believe that, that he had too much respect for artists to do that. She did say that he was upset with Gretchen Vale, that he'd purchased some art from her, and it hadn't arrived."

"Gretchen's name comes back up," he murmured, feeling another tug on that old string. "Anything else?"

"No. That's it. I did good, right?"

Seeing the expectant smile on her face, he couldn't help but smile back. "You did good. But you shouldn't have done anything without me. I'm glad you're all right. This could have ended up differently. You don't confront people who are threatening you without at least some backup."

"I've always fought to protect my mom, and I never had any backup. I guess this felt like that."

"But it's not, because Arthur is dead. You can't forget that, Callie."

"I take your point, but it felt good to do something proactive. Yesterday, I felt like I was moving around in a daze, and this morning I felt so much more like myself. I'm not a victim. I'm a fixer. If something is broken, I try to fix it."

He nodded, understanding where that desire came from. She'd had to grow up on her own, with no one to fix her problems. He'd felt like that after his dad's crimes had come to light. He'd taken everything on himself. He'd known he had to be the man in the family, take care of his mom, take care of himself. He'd never let anyone else shoulder that burden. Callie hadn't, either. They'd each turned themselves into fortresses on their own private islands. He wondered if she ever felt as lonely as he did.

"Flynn?" she questioned.

"After the way you grew up, I understand why you need to fix what's broken. How is your mom?"

She let out a sigh. "She was asleep when I went there. The nurse claimed she's not as emotional as she was, that she actually ate a little something for breakfast, and that she was sleeping without sedation. I guess that's good. But why is she still so tired?"

"Because her brain and body are processing a horrific event."

"I suppose. I just wish we could have spoken. I hope she knows I've been checking on her. Dr. Clarke will see her this afternoon. He's supposed to call me with an update."

"So, after you left your mom's, you needed to do something. That's why you went to Layana's studio."

"I had already decided to go there before that, but I did have some energy to burn off after I left the hospital." She paused. "There is a little more."

He didn't like the guilty look in her eyes. "What else did you do?"

"Well, Layana kept saying how my mom killed Arthur, and I said I could think of someone else who might have been just as motivated."

"You didn't," he breathed, both impressed and alarmed by her audacity. "You accused her of killing Arthur. What did she do?"

"She threw her coffee at me and I ran."

"Oh, my God, Callie."

"That might not have been the best decision," she admitted. "The words just came out."

"Which is why you're not supposed to be doing these things on your own."

"Well, it's done. She didn't follow me or try to hurt me. Anyway, that's the whole story. I think we need to get down to Palm Springs."

"I'm tempted to turn around and take you home."

"You don't have the address for the Palm Springs house. You have to take me with you. We already discussed this. Time is of the essence. And you'll be with me, so I won't do anything stupid."

"No, you won't, and if you're coming, you need to follow my orders."

She raised an eyebrow. "I don't like orders, Flynn."

He wasn't quite sure what to make of this version of Callie. She was different today, and maybe even more beautiful with her fierce, stubborn, independent streak. And as their gazes clashed, all he could think about was how much he wanted to kiss her again.

Her gaze shifted as if she'd read his mind. Her lips parted ever so slightly.

"Damn," he murmured.

"Are you swearing at me now?"

"I'm swearing at how much I want to kiss you." He paused, looking deep into her eyes. "Do you want to stop me?"

She answered him by leaning over, putting her hands on both sides of his face, and pressing her mouth against his.

He slid one hand around the back of her neck, holding her close, taking the kiss she'd started to where he wanted it to go. He took his time exploring her mouth, savoring her taste, loving the way she met him kiss for kiss. She was in a reckless mood, and he was right there with her. They were nearing the edge of something, and he needed to make sure they didn't go off the cliff, but it was not easy to call a halt when everything inside him wanted to get even closer.

He didn't just want to take her home and leave her there anymore. He wanted to go there with her. He wanted to toss her into the middle of her soft, unmade bed and make love to her until their desire was completely sated. That could take hours or days, maybe even longer.

He was still thinking about that when Callie pulled away, her eyes sparkling, streaks of pink warming her cheeks.

He reluctantly let her go, amazed at how completely he'd just lost his mind right in the middle of a case. And not just any case— an investigation that was important and personal.

"So, that happened," she said.

"Yeah," he murmured. "You pack quite a punch."

"So do you. We should go." She sat back in her seat. "That's enough of that for today. We have work to do."

"I don't think it was nearly enough. But we can always come back to it."

She ran her tongue along the edge of her lips. "We'll have to see how the day goes."

He drew in a breath and let it out, taking a minute to settle his body and his emotions. And then he put the SUV into drive and headed for the freeway.

It took a good ten minutes for Callie's pulse to return to normal, and that only happened because she deliberately kept her gaze away from the man behind the wheel. Every time she looked at Flynn, she had all kinds of reckless thoughts, some of which she'd just acted out in a fairly spectacular fashion.

She didn't know what to make of the crazy attraction between them. It wasn't like they were dating. It wasn't like they were friends. She didn't know what they were, except that they were together, and when they kissed there were literally fireworks going off in her head. Maybe it was the shadow of danger surrounding them that heightened the emotions. Or perhaps the danger was just coming from the sparks that went off every time they got close.

It wasn't smart for her to fool around with Flynn, no matter how much she liked him. And she did like him. It wasn't just a physical attraction. They'd opened up to each other. She'd shared things with him she hadn't told anyone else, and he'd been forthcoming, too. Their childhoods were vastly different and yet they both understood what it was like to lose a parent, to feel like they had to be the strong one.

But Flynn was still an FBI agent, and her mother was still a suspect. She couldn't forget where their loyalties were—Flynn's was to Arthur, hers was to her mother. Hopefully, neither one of them would have to make a choice at the expense of the other.

She finally glanced over at him, and he met her gaze, giving her a faint smile. "Heart rate back to normal?"

"Getting there," she admitted. "How about you?"

"Same. We definitely seem to light each other up."

"We better put the matches away."

"For now." He paused. "I want to make a stop in Laguna Beach on the way to Palm Springs. Gretchen's name keeps coming up. I tried her earlier today and got her voicemail, but she'll probably have the gallery open for the Sunday Art Walk."

"That's a good idea. I'd like to meet this woman who posed a threat to my mother's marriage."

"It sounds like Layana was the real threat—to the marriage, anyway."

"Tell me more about Gretchen. I know she worked for your father, but what's she like? Is she pretty? Is she ambitious? Is she artsy?"

"She's attractive and ambitious. She's never been an artist; she has always been about the business of art. I liked Gretchen well enough when I was a kid. She was friendly and enjoyed gossiping, which was fairly entertaining. She didn't treat me like an idiot, which Stephen always did. I also thought Stephen was shady. I caught him in my father's office one day, and he gave me some lame excuse about why he was in there. I told my dad about it, and he just laughed and said, 'Trust me, Flynn, I know exactly who Stephen is.' I have no idea now if that meant he knew Stephen was as big a thief as he was. But he certainly wasn't worried about him."

"It sounds like he should have been worried about both Gretchen and Stephen. They probably sold him out to save themselves."

"That's what I thought, but like I said, I couldn't prove it."

"How did Gretchen and her husband come to own the gallery? I thought you said your dad's assets were frozen."

"They were. The government sold the gallery at auction. Gretchen and Stephen found a way to buy it. They own the building now, which also includes an upstairs apartment where they live."

"Where did they get the money for that?"

"I don't know. I haven't dug into it. Something else I need to do."

"Or you could have someone on your team do it."

"Maybe."

As Flynn drew in a breath and let it out, she could feel his tension, and that tension increased as they neared the exit for Laguna Beach. She didn't think talking to Gretchen was the reason for his stress; it was the gallery.

"Have you been to the gallery since your dad left?" she asked curiously.

"I drove by once—a long time ago. But I didn't go inside."

"So this would be the first time…"

"Since my dad left, yes," he said tightly.

"Are you ready to face your past?"

"I have to be," he replied, flinging her a quick look. "And I will be."

CHAPTER THIRTEEN

HE WASN'T EVEN CLOSE to ready, Flynn thought, as he parked the SUV near Gallery Row on the Coast Highway. He hadn't been to Laguna for the Sunday Art Walk in years. Seeing all the gallery doors open, the paintings displayed along the sidewalk, and the pop-up booths for wine tasting, brought back a lot of memories. He'd often helped out at the gallery on Sundays when tourists came to see the amazing art from both famous and local artists.

Art was as big an attraction in Laguna as the nearby beach, and there was tremendous competition between the galleries to have the best and most innovative artists showing their work.

"This looks fun," Callie murmured, as they got out of the car.

"We're not here for fun," he reminded her.

"I know. But it still looks like a nice event. I came here once a long time ago with my parents. I remember my dad bought this huge painting of a stormy sea and a ship battling the waves. In the far corner of the painting, the storm turns to sunshine. My dad said he liked the feeling of turbulence and then triumph. He thought it was a perfect representation of life. You fight your way through the storms, and on the other side, the sun is waiting for you. That painting hung in our living room for a very long time. I wonder what happened to it." She paused, giving him an apologetic look. "Sorry, that was my own little trip to the past."

"I like your trip better than mine."

"You'll get through this storm."

He grinned. "How long are we going to work that metaphor?"

"As long as we need to."

He barely heard her answer as they approached the gallery. There was a young woman on the sidewalk, talking to some customers. The front door was wide open. And inside he could see Gretchen's blonde hair.

"She's here," he murmured. "I need to do this alone, Callie. Maybe you should wander around, take a look at the art, have a glass of wine."

Disappointment filled her eyes. "I'd rather hear what Gretchen has to say."

"She'll be more forthcoming if I'm on my own."

"Fine, but I'm not going far, and I won't stay outside forever."

He didn't need forever; he just needed ten minutes. He had no interest in staying in the gallery any longer than necessary.

When he stepped over the threshold, Gretchen's gaze widened. She'd been talking to her husband, who was looking down at a computer on the desk. She grabbed his arm and tipped her head toward Flynn.

He moved across the room. "Hello, Gretchen—Stephen."

"I can't believe you're here, Flynn," Gretchen said, a wary light in her eyes.

"I can't quite believe it, either." His gaze swept the room, which still felt incredibly familiar.

While his father's gallery had focused on abstracts and impressionistic art, the paintings in front of him were modern and eclectic, including pop art and cubism. Despite the differences in the displays, he could still see his father wandering through the room, talking to customers, making sure every piece of art was displayed in the most perfect light. And when there was a sale, he'd include a bottle of champagne with the customer's new purchase, as if bringing a new painting home was a reason to celebrate.

"What do you want, Flynn?" Stephen asked, interrupting his thoughts.

He cleared his throat, bringing his mind back to the present. "I want to talk to you both about Arthur's murder."

"We already gave our statements to the other FBI agent," Stephen said.

"I have follow-up questions. Let's start with you, Stephen. You ran into Arthur in the stairwell ten or fifteen minutes before he went over the railing. You spoke to him. What did you say?"

Stephen appeared taken aback by the question. "I—I don't remember. I probably just said hello."

"Did Arthur say where he was going, who he was meeting?"

"No. I didn't ask. Why would I?"

"Stephen barely knows Arthur," Gretchen cut in.

"Then why don't you tell me how you knew Arthur, Gretchen? Why you exchanged a dozen or so calls with him in the past two weeks?"

Before she could reply, the young woman who had been watching over the sidewalk sale came into the gallery. "Mr. Vale, I need some help out here," she said. "A customer has some questions."

"Excuse me," Stephen said, looking thrilled to leave the conversation.

"Well?" he prodded.

Gretchen gave him an unhappy look and then motioned him toward the office, clearly wanting to get him away from a group of customers who had just entered the gallery.

"Arthur was interested in a local artist by the name of Imogene Rocca," Gretchen said as they moved into the office that had once belonged to his father.

He deliberately kept his gaze on her, refusing to allow himself to be distracted by the memories.

"Imogene had a show here a few weeks ago," Gretchen continued. "Arthur wanted to buy some of her paintings. I arranged for him to have a private viewing, and he became quite interested in a piece in her studio that she had not yet finished. He told her he'd like to buy it as soon as it was done. I was keeping him apprised of the progress."

He frowned, thinking that the unfinished art scenario with this female painter sounded very much like the situation with Marcus Vitelli. "When did Arthur become so interested in unfinished work by young artists?"

"He prided himself on being able to discover new talent."

She was acting as if she had nothing to hide, but he wasn't quite sure he was buying her story. "Why were you so involved? Why not have Arthur make his own contact?"

"I got a cut for being the go-between."

"And that's all you were talking about—nothing else?"

"I don't know what you want me to say. And I really don't like what you said to Stephen. Just because he ran into Arthur in the stairwell doesn't make him guilty. I know you never liked him, but you can't pin a murder on him because of that."

"You're right. I didn't like him. He was an ass to me when I was a kid, especially when my father wasn't looking. But I don't pin crimes on innocent people, so if he's innocent, he has nothing to worry about. You, on the other hand, might want to think hard about whether you're answering my questions truthfully."

"Why would you think I wasn't?" she countered.

"Were you having an affair with Arthur?"

She gasped at his question, her gaze darting to the door.

"Don't worry. Stephen is still outside."

"You're crazy, Flynn. You're trying to get back at me for not lying to protect your father."

"And you're deflecting. Answer the question."

"No. We weren't having an affair. If Juliette told you that, then you have to understand that she's a jealous woman with a history of paranoia."

He wasn't sure he believed her, but he decided to switch gears. "When I saw you at the museum on Friday night, you told me we needed to talk. Why?"

"I just wanted to catch up."

"Gretchen, if you have something you need me to know, tell

me now. I am going to find Arthur's killer, and if you have valuable information, you need to share. Otherwise, you're obstructing justice."

"You're different, Flynn. You're a lot harder, tougher, almost cruel. That's not who you used to be. And it's hard for me to believe you became an agent after how the FBI came for your father."

"My father was a thief, and I'm not a kid anymore. I take my job seriously, and you'd be wise to remember that."

"All right." She took a quick breath. "When I saw you at the event, I was shocked, not just because it has been so many years since our paths crossed, but because I thought I saw your father last Thursday. It was just before closing. I glanced toward the window. It was almost dark outside, but I could see him so clearly."

His gut churned. "Did you go out and talk to him?"

"No. We just stared at each other, and then he walked away. It was unnerving."

"Are you sure it was him?"

"I know it was him. His face was older, and he didn't have a moustache anymore, but his eyes—so blue, just like yours—were exactly the same. Why do you think he would come back here, Flynn? Isn't the FBI still looking for him? Isn't he still a wanted man?"

"Yes, he is. I don't know why he'd come back. Maybe he just wanted to see the gallery he built."

"I'm sure you think that Stephen and I turned your dad in, but we didn't. We were as surprised as anyone when the FBI showed up. We had no idea what your dad's side business involved."

"But you benefited more than anyone by his disappearance. You ended up with this gallery."

"We did, but it took us years to rebuild our reputation, to prove that we were honest art dealers. This is our gallery now. It has no ties to your dad."

"You and Stephen are tied to my dad. As long as you're here, there will always be a connection."

"Have you ever heard from your father? I can't imagine that at some point he didn't reach out to you. He loved you so much."

Her words were like a knife to the gut. "He didn't love me. He left me and my mother. He abandoned us so he could save himself."

"He was terrified of going to prison. He wasn't a man who could be locked up."

"He should have thought of that before he became a thief."

"I know he hurt you. That's why when I saw you, I felt like I should tell you that he might be back in town." She paused. "And the fact that he's here, and now Arthur is dead…it doesn't feel like a coincidence."

"My father never killed anyone."

"That you know of. I admired Sam a lot. He was my mentor, and I thought he was spectacularly good at his job. But I realized after he left that I never knew him. You figured out the same thing. Can either of us really say that he couldn't kill someone?"

"Why would he?" he countered.

"I don't know. But then, I don't know why he did half the things he did. I need to get back to the showroom. It's a busy day."

"Fine, but next time I call, answer the phone or call me back. Otherwise, I might start thinking you still have something to hide."

"That sounds like a threat, Flynn."

"It's a fact," he said harshly.

"I'm not your enemy, Flynn. I'm sorry you seem to think I am."

She led the way out of the office, and he followed, deliberately keeping his gaze focused on her back. She joined a group of customers in the showroom, and he headed outside. Stephen was nowhere in sight, but Callie was leaning against a parking meter, sipping wine from a plastic glass.

"How did it go?" she asked. "You were gone awhile."

"I'll tell you in the car. Let's get out of here." He urged her toward the SUV, eager to put his father's gallery behind him.

Callie followed, dumping her wineglass into a recycle bin. Then she hopped into her seat as he started the engine.

"Before we go," she said, "I think you might be interested in this." She handed him her phone. "Stephen was talking to his sales associate on the sidewalk. Then he got a call and he seemed agitated. He walked down the street, and I followed him. He moved to that car and had a conversation with a person who I think you might recognize."

He stared down at the photo. "That's Gerard Bissette."

"I couldn't get close enough to hear what they were saying, but Stephen seemed upset. I took some pictures, thinking they might be helpful."

"Did they see you?" he asked sharply.

"No. I may not be an agent, but I can stay out of sight when I need to. It probably doesn't even relate to the case, but I figured it wouldn't hurt for you to see this."

He was both impressed and annoyed. "I told you to wander around and have some wine."

"I did have wine. And I did wander around. I also saw what I saw."

"I just hope they didn't see you. This is a dangerous situation, Callie."

She met his gaze. "Flynn, I know that. I know that better than anyone. And they didn't see me. So, get over it. And, by the way, you're welcome."

He handed her back her phone. "Thank you."

"A little late, but okay. Now what happened with Gretchen? Did she tell you anything?"

"She claimed Arthur was interested in a local artist—Imogene Rocca. Like Marcus Vitelli, apparently Arthur was encouraging Imogene to finish a painting that he wanted to buy. Gretchen claims that Arthur fancied himself as someone who could discover new talent."

"He did think a lot about himself," she said dryly.

"She also said she thought she saw my father outside the gallery last week. Seemed to think Arthur's death and my father's reappearance were connected."

"Do you believe her?"

"I honestly don't know. But my father has no ties to Arthur. They never met before he took off and fled the country."

She stared back at him. "But they both knew you. And if your father stole art, and Arthur was buying stolen art, then there are ties all over the place."

He frowned. "You're right. I just wish you weren't."

She gave him a compassionate smile. "I know how you feel. I wish for a lot of things I can never have. But whatever the truth is, you'll deal with it. You'll get through the storm."

He smiled. "We're back to the boat?"

"I was trying to lighten the mood."

"Nice job." He pulled out of his parking spot, eager to put Laguna Beach in the rearview mirror.

CHAPTER FOURTEEN

As THEY DROVE toward the desert town of Palm Springs, Callie decided to get Flynn's mind off his dad. "I read through some of Arthur's trust this morning," she said. "My mom gets a sizeable flat sum payment and the condo in Hawaii. She can also stay in the Pacific Palisades house for one year before it's put up for sale. The proceeds from the sale will go to Arthur's foundation as well as the bulk of his other assets, but the Piquard Museum and other arts organizations will be receiving donations as well. Oh, and Layana's studio was also noted in the trust, which was updated four weeks ago."

"Interesting. And there was no mention of the Palm Springs house?"

"No. And since the trust was updated recently, it wasn't like he just hadn't had a chance to put the house in there. Although, there were a bunch of LLCs listed that I didn't recognize. You should probably take the binder and go through it. I should have brought it with me, but you can get it when you take me home."

"A month ago," he mused. "I wonder what spurred the change."

"I have no idea. I did put in a call to the lawyer. But since it's Sunday, I'm not expecting a return call until tomorrow."

"Will your mother be unhappy with her inheritance?"

"I don't think so. Although, she might be sad to move out of the house. She really loves that place. But it won't be the same without Arthur. There might be too many memories there." She paused, thinking about all the changes headed her mom's way. "Going back to work at the museum might be problematic, too. She met Arthur at the museum, and the fact that he died there...I can't imagine her being able to walk across the grand hall and not see his body on the marble floor."

"That would be difficult."

"I feel like she's going to be lost in her head again. When she gets out of the hospital, she'll probably need to live with me, or I might have to move into the Palisades house until it's sold." That thought depressed her. She'd gotten used to being on her own, to having a life that didn't include her mother. She'd probably have to reduce her hours at the restaurant, too, which wouldn't make the owner happy. She might even have to get another job.

"Hopefully, her doctor will be able to help her get through this," Flynn said quietly.

"I want to believe that; I've just been down this road before."

He gave her a sympathetic smile. "It's a rough road, isn't it?"

"Very rough. Lots of unexpected potholes and surprising curves. But I love her. She's my mom. I can't abandon her. Anyway, let's talk about something else. What did you do this morning?"

"I started my day in the ocean."

"Seriously? You went surfing today? It's cold."

"I had a wetsuit. I do my best thinking on the water."

"Did you catch any waves?"

"A few."

"I'm sure you needed a break. You've been on this investigation nonstop since Friday night."

"That's how we roll when we catch a case. The truth gets more difficult to find as the days pass. By the way, Savannah and Lucas are going through Arthur's house this afternoon to see if there's anything we missed."

"I can't imagine Arthur had more than one hiding place."

"Probably not. But I don't want to leave any stone unturned. I did get some happy personal news this morning."

"Well, don't keep it to yourself," she said. "I wouldn't mind hearing something happy."

"One of my agents, Bree, is pregnant. She hosted a brunch at her house this morning. I thought it was just for her husband's birthday, but it turned out there was a big announcement. We'll have a new addition to our team family in about six months."

"It sounds like your team is close."

"We're a tight group, which is partly because we've known each other since we went through Quantico together."

"Really? That's unusual, isn't it? For a class of FBI trainees to stay together?"

"We were scattered across the country for almost four years, but once I was allowed to build my own team, I went to the people I trusted the most. We all have different skills, and I know how to use those skills to get the job done."

"There's no jealousy from the others that you're the boss now?"

"They're used to it. We were broken into teams at Quantico, and I was one of the leaders."

"That doesn't surprise me. You seem like a natural born leader."

"Damon Wolfe was the leader of a rival team. There were six of them and six of us, and we went head-to-head on a lot of training missions. I hate to admit that they came out on top a lot, but we put a few W's in the win column."

"Is Damon on your team?"

"No. He's in charge of the LA field office. I actually report to him, which is fine with me, because Damon is a straight shooter. No politics. No games. What you see is what you get. And he respects me enough to let me run without trying to pull back on the reins."

"That's a great trait in a boss. So, you and Savannah knew each other at Quantico?"

"Yes."

"She's very pretty. She doesn't look like an agent, although I guess there's no real look, is there?"

"There's kind of a look," he said with a laugh. "And Savannah does not have it. She's a former Miss Georgia. She finished third in the Miss USA pageant, which everyone loves to tease her about."

"She went from beauty queen to the FBI. That's crazy."

"With eight years in the Army in between."

"Now I find her even more interesting."

"She's one of a kind and very good at whatever job I throw her way."

"And the others on your team?"

"Beck is also ex-military. He was my roommate at Quantico, so I probably know him the best. He's intense, very private, and incredibly smart. The other three from my original team are Caitlyn, Jax, and Lucas. In the last few months, I also picked up three from Damon's former team: Bree, Diego, and Wyatt. I'm still trying to get Parisa, but she's in love with a CIA agent, and she's staying in DC for now."

"Are all those people working on Arthur's case?"

"It's just been Lucas and Savannah so far, but Wyatt and Bree will be jumping in tomorrow. Wyatt was on his honeymoon, and Bree was tied up on a kidnapping case yesterday."

"It seems like with all those people, someone should be able to find something. I keep wondering how anyone could have thrown Arthur over that rail without being seen, without there being a fight. Arthur is not a huge guy, but he's not a weakling, either."

"I do know something about that. I can't give you the specifics, but it looks like Arthur was incapacitated before he went over the rail."

"What does that mean?"

"That's all I can say at the moment."

She didn't care for his vague answer. "I thought we were being honest with each other."

"I'm being as honest as I can be without compromising the investigation."

"Because my mother is still a suspect?"

"And because you're not an agent."

"Fine. So incapacitated means he was knocked out in some

way, and it couldn't have been loud because no one heard anything."

He sent a smile in her direction. "Think you've figured it out?"

"I'm close. If Arthur couldn't fight, then his assailant could have been any size or gender."

"Yes."

"But I still think it was a man and not just because I want my mother off the hot seat. I don't believe that even an incapacitated Arthur could have been lifted by a woman high enough to get him over the railing."

"We could be looking for more than one person," he reminded her. "It's possible that someone was hired to take care of Arthur."

She sighed. "True. And the killer probably walked right past us when they left the museum."

"It would have been easy to get lost in the crowd, especially if the perpetrator was someone who was comfortable in the art world. We're going through the security footage before the cameras went out, trying to pinpoint who was in the grand hall against the witness list. But people were coming and going, including yourself."

"I was in the restroom."

"Wiping away your tears after your fight with Arthur."

"Yes. And thinking about getting the hell out of there. I only came because my mom was nervous about the event. Gerard Bissette was a good friend of Arthur's, and she didn't want anything to go wrong. But in the end, everything went wrong. Did you speak to Gerard that night?"

"For a few minutes before he took the stage. Arthur introduced us. I did read his statement, which was taken by Detective Gage, but there was nothing of importance. Gerard was in full view of everyone when Arthur came over the railing."

"Unless he was the person who hired Arthur's killer. You just pointed out that there could be more than one individual involved."

"I'm having trouble eliminating anyone," he admitted.

"Is it interesting that Gerard was in Laguna Beach talking to Stephen?"

"On the face of it, no. He's an artist. Stephen runs a gallery. Although, I'm surprised Gerard didn't come into the gallery."

"And they did seem to be arguing. Maybe you should talk to Gerard."

He smiled at Callie's directive. "Good idea."

She gave him a rueful look. "You probably already thought of it. I just keep thinking we're going to get more answers, but all we get are more questions."

"That's often the way things unfold."

"I'd like them to unfold faster. Then, when my mom is released, she won't have to face any more interrogation. She'll be able to bury Arthur and grieve properly and hopefully find a way to move on. Not that I think that will be easy. I'm sure it will be very difficult, and she'll need as much support as I can give her."

"What about you, Callie? What about your needs?"

"I don't need anything except for my mother to be well."

"I don't think that's true. You've just gotten used to putting your mom first."

"She needs to be first. She needs a lot more than I do. My mom once told me I was like a self-cleaning oven. When things got messy in my life, I cleaned them up on my own. I still do that, and I have a feeling you do, too."

"I do now, but when I was a child, I had parental support. I hate to admit it, but during my childhood, my dad was a good father. We spent a lot of time together."

"What was he like?" she asked curiously.

"He was funny, easygoing, and always smiling. He liked video games and baseball and was the first person who ever took me out on the ocean to surf. He liked to teach me things, especially when it came to art. I started going into his gallery when I was about twelve. At first, I was sweeping floors and taking out the trash, but eventually he got me involved in the business of running a gallery. He wanted me to understand it, to be able to run the place one day. When he traveled to trade shows, he took me with him."

"You really did grow up in that world."

"I did. Of course, I had no idea what he was really doing on some of those trips until his mask was stripped away."

She heard the hardness return to Flynn's voice. The love he'd expressed just a moment ago was now buried in pain.

"Do you miss him, Flynn?"

He gave her a hard look. "I shouldn't."

"But you do."

"Sometimes—when I think about happier days," he reluctantly admitted. "But then I remember how it all ended. He wasn't the person I thought he was."

"But he was there for you when you were a child. Maybe that counts for something."

"It doesn't count for much. He abandoned us to save himself. How could I ever forgive him for that?"

"Maybe you can't." She paused. "Do you think Arthur contacted you because you know art or because you're FBI? Or was he collecting on an old debt—the support he gave you when Olivia died?"

"I've asked myself all those questions. He told me someone was watching him, and there was fear in his voice. He didn't look me up because I was an old friend. He wanted my professional help, and he probably thought he could trust me to keep his confidence."

"But he was taking a risk, if he really was involved in stolen art. Getting you involved was dangerous."

"He must have felt desperate."

"It's strange to think of Arthur as being desperate; I always saw him as this self-assured, overly confident, somewhat self-righteous man. Every aspect of his life was under his control. He ran his court with precision and efficiency and his home the same way. But there was this other side to him. The way Layana spoke of him as this passionate, almost dreamy, art lover, it was like she was talking about someone I had never met. I knew he liked art, but she said that he was obsessed with it, that he needed to be with someone who shared that obsession, that my mom couldn't ever be that person."

"Sounds like she was obsessed with Arthur."

"She definitely was. Her grief was palpable."

"So was her anger in the text she sent to your mother."

She glanced back at Flynn. "Do you think she could have killed Arthur, because he didn't want to leave my mother?"

"It wouldn't be the first time that happened."

"But she wasn't at the party, was she?"

"Her name wasn't on the guest list or the witness list. I checked on that this morning. Although, at the time, I only had her first name. Maybe she was listed under her business name as some of the guests were."

"I don't think she was there. If she had been, she would have thrown herself on Arthur's body. So that means she's not our killer, unless she hired someone to do it for her. I feel like we keep spinning around, only to end up at the same place. Does your job ever drive you crazy?"

"Often," he admitted. "But I like the challenge."

"Let's talk about something else for a while."

"Good idea. What do you do for fun, Callie?"

"I cook."

"That's your job."

"I know, but it's my favorite pastime, too."

"What else do you do?"

"I like to run. I ran a half-marathon last year."

"Then you really like to run," he said, giving her a smile.

"It's a good stress reducer. I also love watching baseball. My dad was a huge Dodgers fan. We had season tickets when I was a kid, and we used to go to the games on the weekends. He'd buy me a Dodger dog and a huge carton of popcorn, and I'd go home happy with a big stomachache."

"My father used to take me to Dodgers' games, too. We might have walked right by each other."

"Probably. Did you play baseball?"

"No, I was basketball and soccer. What about you?"

"I played softball from age six to ten. My dad was my coach. I was pretty good, too. I was the pitcher. I was the only girl who could throw a strike at that age."

"Did you quit after he died?"

"Yes. It wasn't the same without him." Her phone buzzed with an incoming text. "It's Arthur's housekeeper, Lois. She wants to know if she should come in to work tomorrow." She glanced over at him. "The answer should be no, right?"

"Right. We don't need anyone else in the house."

"I'll let her know we'll be in touch, that we're still figuring things out." She typed out her text and hit Send. "I really have to start focusing on the funeral arrangements tomorrow. But I have no idea what Arthur would want, and my mom can't tell me yet. I don't know how I'm going to do it all." She felt an overwhelming rush of anxiety at everything that needed to be done.

Flynn put a hand on her thigh. "Callie, stop. Don't think that far ahead. Nothing has to be done this second."

"It has to be done sometime. I can't keep avoiding it."

"Sometime isn't today. Think about it tomorrow."

"That won't make the problem go away."

"No, but you'll be more prepared to deal with it then. You can't take care of everyone and everything. You're only one person."

"I don't take care of everyone, just my mom."

"You take care of other people, too. Didn't Melissa say you'd helped her move?"

She tipped her head. "I did do that. She's a friend."

"And you take care of your friends."

"That's what friends do."

"Good friends—the ones you can count on."

"I try to be someone my friends can count on."

"So do I." He glanced over at her. "You can count on me, too, Callie."

"Does that mean we're friends?" she asked lightly.

"I don't know. Do you kiss all your friends the way you kissed me?"

"Do you?"

"I asked you first."

"We don't need to talk about kissing," she declared.

"You're right. I'd rather do it than talk about it."

"Just drive, Flynn," she ordered, as his sexy smile made her stomach flutter. She turned her gaze out the window, grateful to see the desert mountains. Only a few more miles to Palm Springs. She couldn't wait. She needed to get out of this car and get her mind off Flynn and back on finding Arthur's killer.

CHAPTER FIFTEEN

CALLIE GAVE him the address for Arthur's house when they got off the freeway. He pulled up in front of a large home near the base of the mountains in Palm Springs ten minutes later. There were only about six homes on this particular block, with plenty of land and shrubbery between them.

As he got out of the car, his gaze swept the area. There were no other cars in sight, no sign of movement inside the house or in the adjacent yards. There was a quiet stillness to the air, not a hint of a breeze or a speck of a cloud, just sunshine and blue skies. He only wished he didn't feel a sense of foreboding, but he did. The fact that Arthur had kept this house hidden away meant something; he needed to find out what.

"This looks luxurious," he said, leading the way to the front door, which was massive in size and surrounded by two long windows with closed shades.

"Only the best for Arthur," Callie replied. "Have you ever been to the condo on Maui? It's beautiful, too. It's on the beach in Wailea. Maybe we should include that on our list of places to search."

He smiled. "I'm betting you'd be happy to go there with me, too."

"Getting away to the islands does sound lovely, but not realistic." She paused, then frowned, her gaze dropping to the gun holstered on his hip and just visible under his brown leather jacket. "Are you expecting trouble?"

"I'm always prepared for trouble, whether I'm expecting it or not."

"Have you ever shot anyone?"

"Yes."

"That must have been strange. I don't know if I could pull the trigger on anyone."

"You could, especially if it was to protect someone else. I have no doubt about that." His gaze moved to the security camera in the corner of the porch. "Do you have access to the cameras here?"

"I don't, and I doubt it's on my mom's phone. She rarely came here."

"That's fine. I can get into it later. Tell me what I'm going to find on the first floor."

"Living room, dining room, then a kitchen and walk-in pantry on one side. On the other side, two bedrooms and baths plus a guest bath, and a small den."

"Second floor?"

"Three bedrooms with attached baths, a laundry room, another family room, and that's it. Are we going in?"

"I am. You wait here."

"Is that one of your orders?" she asked dryly.

He gave her a small smile. "It is. So, please, do it."

"Since you said please..." She put in the door code and then stepped back, her gaze widening as he drew his weapon, then opened the door.

Stepping onto the cool gray tile, his gaze moved across the rooms adjoining the entry, making note of the floor plan, which was exactly as Callie had said. From the entry, a staircase with an ornate iron railing wound its way up to the second floor. He listened for a moment, hearing nothing but the steady click of a large clock on the wall. He walked quickly through the rooms. Nothing was out of place. No dishes on the kitchen counter or in the sink. All of the beds were made in the guest rooms on the main floor. The living room and dining room were impeccably neat.

Jogging up the stairs, he looked through the master bedroom and bath, the two other guest rooms, and the living space, and then came back downstairs. Callie was standing in the doorway, giving him an expectant look. "I'm still technically outside."

"You can come in. The house is empty. It doesn't look like anyone has been here, but you said Arthur was here last Wednesday."

"That's what Layana told me. I'm sure Arthur has a cleaning service that comes in after every visit and perhaps even more frequently. What do we do now?"

He pulled the envelope of photos out of his inside jacket pocket. "To start, let's look for these paintings. I did a little more research this morning, and I was able to determine that they were all stolen, these first two from the museum in Madrid I told you about earlier, these three from a museum in Paris, and the last one from the home of a German billionaire during a burglary in which a diamond was stolen along with the painting."

"Were these thefts recent?"

"Within the last five years, the most recent eight months ago."

He handed her three pictures. "You concentrate on these; I'll take the other three."

They started in the living room where three paintings were on display, none of which matched those displayed in the photos. And upon closer inspection, he could see that they were all copies, good copies, maybe worth a couple thousand each, but they weren't as valuable as those in the house in Pacific Palisades. That didn't surprise him. *Why would Arthur risk leaving priceless art in a vacation home in Palm Springs that was unoccupied half the year?*

In the master bedroom, there was only one painting, and it was also a copy. While he was in the room, he checked the drawers of the nightstand and found a mystery novel and a digital reader as well as some very expensive headphones.

"Is your mom a reader?" he asked.

"That would be Arthur. My mom doesn't have an attention span suited to books. She prefers reality TV."

"Which has nothing to do with reality," he said dryly.

"That's the kind of reality my mom likes—scripted, entertaining, and mostly mindlessly happy."

"Which do you prefer—books or TV?"

"Books. I love suspense novels. Now, I feel like I'm living in one. I just hope that good will triumph over evil as it does in fiction."

"I'm going to work hard to make that happen."

"I know. But this trip is a bit of a letdown. There's nothing here, Flynn. No trace of Arthur bringing his secret lover here. No stolen paintings. No phones or computers."

Her disappointment matched his own. They went back downstairs, and Callie wandered onto the patio. The pool was covered, as were the deck chairs and barbecue. But the grounds were beautifully landscaped with desert-friendly plants and shrubs. A water feature was dry, but apparently cascaded into the pool on warmer days. The back of the house was almost up against a rocky hillside, giving it a very private feel.

Callie lifted her face to the sun. "It feels good out here, cold but nice. Arthur loved the desert air. He said there was something magical about it. The weekend I was here, we spent all our time on this patio, swimming in the pool, barbecuing every meal, and having a lot of drinks. Of course, it was much warmer in September."

"Was anyone else here but you and your mother?"

"No; it was just the three of us." She glanced at him. "What do we do now? Head back to LA? Fly to Maui and check that place out?"

He smiled. "I probably need to stick closer to the crime scene."

"But the paintings could be in Hawaii."

"I'll get someone on Maui to check that out for me." He looked at his watch. "It's four now. We might as well go home."

"I suppose, but if we want to make this trip worth something, we could make a stop before we leave and get one of those gigantic ice cream cones—you know, those big waffle cones that hold like three scoops. There's a place nearby I went to with my mom." She gave him a hopeful look. "It's really good."

He smiled at the sparkle in her eyes. "You're an ice cream girl."

"Guilty. Nothing better than ice cream, even on a cold day in January. It solves so many problems."

"We can stop on the way out. I could eat some ice cream." As his gaze moved around the backyard once more, he couldn't shake the feeling that he was missing something that was right in front of him.

"What's wrong?" Callie asked, giving him a thoughtful look.

"I don't know. My gut says there's something here, but I don't know what it is or where it might be." He paused, thinking about what Callie had said earlier. "You told me that Arthur bought the house six months ago, but that your mother didn't really like coming down here."

"No, she wasn't a fan of the desert. She thought it was boring, but Arthur insisted this would be a great getaway place for them."

"How often would you say they came down?"

"Together? Maybe three times. However, Arthur came down a lot on his own. My mother often ran events at the museum on weekends, so she wasn't as free as he was to make the trip." She gave him a disgruntled look. "This must be his love nest."

"It's a long way to come for an affair when there are plenty of hotels in LA or the surrounding suburbs."

"He's well known in Los Angeles. Maybe he wanted to get farther away."

"Maybe," he muttered. "How did he find this place? Did the idea just come out of the blue? Does he have friends who vacation down here?"

"He brought my mother to a big tennis tournament here last March. Arthur loved tennis."

"I remember. He was a very competitive player; he hated to lose."

"It was after that tournament that he started talking about getting a place down here. He kept saying how the dry air was good for him. He felt like he could breathe better. He must have said that a dozen times, and I couldn't figure out why he needed to be in dry air. It's not like he had a lot of allergies or anything. It's also not like Pacific Palisades is extremely humid, although they are close to the ocean. I guess that might make the air wetter."

His mind began to spin with her words.

Why had Arthur been so consumed with the air quality? And why did all that sound familiar?

His dad had always worried about humidity, too. He was always trying to lower the humidity level in his gallery to protect the art. "You know what else does well in areas with low humidity?" he muttered. "Paintings, especially oil paintings."

Callie gave him a confused look. "But you said the art down here isn't valuable or important."

"It's not."

He turned and strode back into the house.

"What are you thinking?" she asked, following him inside.

"Is there a basement?"

"I don't believe so."

He walked through the kitchen, the laundry room, back into the garage, looking for any entry point to a basement, but he couldn't find anything.

"Where did Arthur spend his time the weekend you were here?" he asked Callie, who had been dogging his steps.

"He was all over—the living room, the patio, his bedroom, the den. Oh, and he sometimes took calls in the bedroom at the end of the hall. He said he got better reception in there."

Flynn jogged quickly down the hall, following his gut like a dog sniffing out drugs. There was something about this house that had been important to Arthur, and his raving about the humidity level made him think the paintings they were looking for were somewhere in the home.

Entering the guest room that Callie had pointed out, he went straight to the closet. There were men's clothes hanging on the rails.

"I'm surprised Arthur kept clothes in this bedroom," Callie murmured. "He always called it the guest room."

"Did anyone sleep in here the weekend you were here?"

"No. We were all upstairs."

He shoved the clothes to one side and looked at a piece of decorative brick tile along the back wall of the closet. *Why the hell would anyone tile the back wall of a closet?* As he pressed his fingers along the tiles, something clicked, and a door in the wall suddenly swung open.

"Oh, my God," Callie murmured, peering over his shoulder. "There's a door."

"And stairs." He moved forward using the light on his phone to see the steps. When he got to the bottom, he saw a light switch and flipped it on.

His heart skipped a beat as Callie gasped in shock.

He'd expected to find a few paintings stashed away, but Arthur had set up what looked like his own private gallery. There were paintings on every wall, with individual lights over them, and in the middle of the room was a round dais upon which one could sit and view the paintings from any angle.

"It's like a museum," she murmured.

"Arthur's own private art world," he said, moving over to the first painting. "This is the Vega." He matched the photograph in his hand to the art on the wall. "And the one over there is a Monet. They're all here—all six of them, all stolen." A knot formed in his throat as his worst fears came true. Just like his father, Arthur was not the man he'd appeared to be. He'd stood for what was right, what was just. He'd punished people for breaking the law. He'd taken righteous delight in sentencing them for their crimes when he was a criminal, too. *What a hypocrite.*

"I'm sorry, Flynn." Callie put a hand on his arm, her eyes filled with understanding and emotion.

"What are you sorry about? You didn't know this was here."

"I'm sorry he disappointed you."

"I should be used to it," he said harshly.

"You never get used to being disappointed by the people you love."

"Who did I love, Callie? Arthur was just an illusion."

He walked away from her, because her kindness was almost too much. As he moved around the room, he saw a large open crate leaning against the wall and inside were two paintings that had yet to be hung. One was by Gerard Bissette. *Was it stolen, too?* He was still thinking about that when he looked at the other smaller oil painting. The sight of it stole what was left of the breath in his chest.

"My God," he murmured, pulling out the painting of what appeared to be a beautiful flower, but he knew better. "Damn. Now I know why Arthur got spooked."

"Why?" Callie asked in confusion.

"Because he got this in his shipment." He held up the painting so she could see it.

"What is it about this painting that would spook Arthur? It's a gorgeous picture of a flower. I don't get it."

"This flower is an atropa belladonna, which is more popularly known as deadly nightshade," he explained. "It appears harmless with its green leaves, shiny blackberries, and reddish-brown flowers that look like little bells. But it's also lethal. It contains a toxin called atropine, which when used medically keeps muscles paralyzed during surgery and regulates heartbeat."

"Okay," she said slowly, as she processed that piece of infor-mation. "And you think this flower has something to do with Arthur's death?"

"There was a broken champagne glass found in the hallway where Arthur went over the rail. It tested positive for traces of atropine."

"You said he was incapacitated. That's why."

"It's believed that Arthur ingested the atropine and suffered paralysis, which would have made it easier for someone to push him over the railing."

"Like a woman."

"Yes," he said, meeting her now troubled gaze. "But there's

more to the story."

"Then please share, because I want to understand."

"The name atropa belladonna means pretty lady. It's also tied to Atropos, one of the three Greek female fates, who were goddesses of destiny, sometimes known as Daughters of the Night."

"We're talking Greek mythology now?"

"Yes. The fates controlled the threads of each mortal's life. It was Atropos who cut the thread of life and brought death."

"How do you know all this, Flynn?"

"Because this is an infamous painting, Callie. It has been used as a calling card, a precursor to at least four known murders that the FBI refers to as the Belladonna murders. When someone receives the painting, they're marked for death."

Her eyes widened. "Are you serious? Arthur was marked for death?"

"I believe he thought so. That's why he contacted me. He must have gotten the painting in the shipment of stolen art—maybe when he came down here on Wednesday. That's why he was upset."

"Why he didn't want to meet with Layana," she put in.

"And why he thought someone was watching him. He wanted me to protect him."

"This all sounds kind of wild."

"I know. But that doesn't mean it isn't true."

"You said there are four known murders. Who were those people?"

"The first was an artist who ran his own gallery in Paris— Rafael Linderman. Not only did he display his own brilliant pieces of art, but every year he chose two or three young and emerging artists to feature. Anyone who got into that gallery became an instant success."

"How did he die?"

"He threw himself out the third-story window of his lover's house on the Rue du Bac, landing on the awning for a chocolate shop, then rolling onto the sidewalk, where he died instantly. That happened five years ago."

"What happened to his lover? Was she killed as well?" Callie asked, an eager light in her eyes.

"No. She had gone out to buy pastries. When she returned, she found him on the sidewalk. She later told the police that he had received a painting by special delivery at his home, two hours earlier, and that he had been very upset by it. He'd told her he'd thought the artist was crazy. When the investigators searched her home, they were unable to find the painting. But they did discover a photo of the painting that was left in its place. There was a message scrawled across the front: *You deserve to be punished.*"

"That's fascinating. What happened next?"

"A year later, an art dealer in Colorado was rock climbing in the Rockies. His harness broke and he fell a hundred feet to his death. His wife told the police that he had gone up to the mountains to meet a friend, but she had no name, and no one was able to discover who else he'd been climbing with. The wife also said he'd been upset by a painting he'd received the day before. He'd showed it to her, and it was a painting of the deadly nightshade. Upon searching the house and the gallery, the painting was not discovered. But they found a similar photo with the same disturbing message."

"Crazy," she murmured. "So the painting shows up, and the person dies. And they always fall. Is that what happened in the other two cases?"

"Yes. The third was three years ago in New York City. An elevator malfunctioned, and Chuck Hernan plunged thirty-seven stories to his death. He was a private collector. He lived in a penthouse on the top floor. His housekeeper said she had seen the painting earlier that day and that Chuck had seemed upset. He'd told her he was leaving town for a business trip. His suitcases were also in the elevator."

"And the fourth?"

"That was about eighteen months ago. It was a woman."

"Interesting—a twist."

He smiled at her rapt gaze. "She ran a gallery in New Orleans. Her assistant took photos of every art piece that was delivered to the gallery. As you might have guessed, the picture had arrived a day earlier."

"How did she die?"

"She was found dead, floating in her swimming pool. The third-floor railing above the pool was broken. It looked like she was shoved over the rail."

"Just like Arthur. And all four were involved with art in some way."

"And in every case the painting disappeared, replaced by the photo."

"Except now." Her gaze moved to the painting. "That's why they broke into Arthur's house last night. They were looking for the painting."

"I think so."

"But the painting was here, in a house no one knew about."

"The home must be in the name of a sham corporation, something that can't be traced to him."

"But it wasn't that big of a secret. I knew about it, and so did my mom. Layana and Moira at the very least knew that Arthur came to Palm Springs. But even if they had come here, they never would have found his secret room. I certainly didn't, and I was here for three days."

"Arthur was clever," he said, feeling a pit of anger and disappointment deep in his soul. "Another liar."

"It sounds like the killer of all these people believes they are handing out a deserved punishment. Why would Arthur have to be punished?"

"He was dealing in stolen art. He was having an affair. Who knows what else he was doing?"

"Well, the murderer has to be someone in the art world, someone who knew the legend. Frankly, it sounds like a mad, evil artist. Maybe Layana is the killer."

"You mean the woman you confronted all by yourself?" he asked pointedly.

"I'm beginning to realize the stupidity of that move."

"Good. Maybe that will stop you from being so impulsive again."

Callie started as her phone buzzed. She pulled it out of her purse. "It's Dr. Clarke. I need to take this."

"Go ahead."

"Hello?" she said. "Hello? Can you hear me?" She frowned, moving around the room. "Hello? Hold on, I'm going to move to another location. There's no reception down here."

"I'll meet you upstairs," he told her. "I want to take a few photos before we go."

She gave a quick nod and hurried upstairs. He turned his gaze back on the painting. He couldn't believe he was holding it in his hands. It looked so innocuous. Its size alone was barely bigger than a laptop. To the ordinary observer, it was just a run-of-the-mill flower painting, but it was so much more.

Positioning his phone, he snapped photos of it as well as the paintings on the walls. He'd have his team secure the house and the art, but he was taking the belladonna painting with him.

As he moved up the steps and through the closet, an uneasy feeling ran down his spine. It was very quiet. He couldn't hear Callie on the phone. *Had she gone outside?*

He took out his gun as he neared the door to the guest room. Setting down the painting, he stepped into the hallway. His heart stopped at the sight of Callie facedown on the floor fifteen feet away.

He rushed forward, but he hadn't taken more than two steps, when he heard someone behind him. He whirled around, gun drawn, but the man was on him before he could fire a shot. He was slammed into the wall, his weapon flying out of his hand and sliding down the slick hallway floor. There was no time to go for it. He needed to disarm his assailant.

He grabbed the man's arm, at the same time knocking his feet out from under him. His weapon clattered as it hit the floor. And then it was hand-to-hand combat, a fight for not only his life but also Callie's. The man was tall and stocky with a ski mask that covered his hair and face, but his eyes were dark and mean.

Blow after blow fell, as they each strove to control the situation. Their fight went into the living room, knocking over chairs and vases. Every time he thought he'd gained the advantage, the man bounced back.

And then Flynn made a critical mistake. He heard Callie moan and call his name. In that split second of distraction, his attacker knocked him against the wall.

His head bounced off the wood and he struggled to stay on his feet, but he was going down.

As soon as he hit the floor, he rolled to one side, getting ready to fight again, but his assailant was running out of the room. He staggered to his feet, then raced down the hall.

When he got to the front of the house, he was just in time to see a gray sedan speed down the street. He couldn't see the license plate, but hopefully Arthur's cameras were working in this house. If not, maybe the car would be caught by another camera in the area.

He ran back into the house to find Callie struggling to sit up, her face white, her eyes glazed with pain. "What—what happened?" She put a hand to the back of her head, then stared at her bloody fingers in horror. "Someone hit me."

He squatted down next to her, pulling out his phone. "Don't move. I'm calling an ambulance."

"I don't need an ambulance. Do I?" She paused in confusion. "Am I dying?"

"No, you are not dying," he told her firmly, praying he was telling the truth. "You can't die. You hear me?"

"My head hurts."

"Don't close your eyes."

Panic ran through him as her eyes closed in spite of his order.

He punched in 911 and told them he needed an ambulance right away. Then he put his arms around her. "You have to stay with me, Callie. I need you to be all right. You're a fighter, babe, and now's the time to fight like hell. Don't quit on me."

He wanted her to open her eyes and tell him she was going to be fine, but she didn't, and a terrifying fear ran through him.

CHAPTER SIXTEEN

CALLIE FLOATED in and out of painful consciousness on the way to the hospital. The pain in her head felt like it was ripping her in two, and when she got to the ER, she could barely speak. Thankfully, she was seen quickly and given something to take the edge off the pain. Then there were doctors and tests and waiting for results. She didn't know how much time had passed, but eventually Flynn showed up in the ER, with worry darkening his beautiful blue eyes.

He was so handsome, so sexy. She probably shouldn't be thinking about that now, but when he smiled at her and put his hand over hers, a rush of warmth ran through her. *She was going to be okay. Flynn was here.* But there was worry in his eyes and that bothered her.

She vaguely remembered him telling her not to die. That she needed to stay with him. That he needed her.

Did he need her? That random thought ran around her confused brain along with the idea that she might need him, too. But she didn't let herself need people, because then they usually needed her to do things for them, and she couldn't take anyone else on. Her mom's needs were consuming enough.

"How are you doing, Callie?" His hand tightened around hers. "Your skin is warmer now."

"I feel better. What happened, Flynn?"

"You were knocked out. The doctor says you have a mild concussion, but no sign of a fracture, so that's good news. Are you in pain?"

"Not as much as I was. Your eye is swollen."

He put a hand to his face. "It's fine."

"You were fighting. I wanted to help you, but I couldn't get up. I'm sorry."

He perched on the side of her bed. "The last thing you need to do is apologize to me. I never should have let you come with me. That was a big mistake."

"I insisted. I wouldn't tell you the address or the code if you didn't let me come."

"I should have figured it out another way."

She could see the guilt in his eyes. "You said I'm going to be okay, so let's not fight about it."

He gave her a small smile. "I don't want to fight with you. I just wish I could take away your pain."

"Whatever the doctor gave me is doing a good job of that. Do you know who attacked us?"

"His face was covered while he was in the house. He dropped his weapon, so we'll trace the gun and see if that gets us a lead. My team is also looking for video footage from security cameras in the area to see if we can locate the car."

"Did he get the painting?"

"No, he ran off before that."

"Because of you. You should feel good about that."

"Good? No way. I shouldn't have taken you there. I shouldn't have let you go upstairs alone. As soon as I saw the painting, I should have realized we were in danger."

"Are you done beating yourself up?"

"Not even close," he said grimly.

"I'm all right, Flynn. Let's just look forward. Where is the painting now?"

He picked up the canvas bag near his feet. "In here. Wyatt and

Savannah are on their way down from LA to get it. I'm not letting it out of my sight until then."

As he picked up the bag and pulled out the painting, a shiver ran down her spine. The flower looked more deadly now than it had before, maybe because she knew the story and because she'd almost been killed. "I think you need to put that down," she said, feeling suddenly afraid. "What if the legend rubs off on you —on us?"

He frowned. "We weren't sent the painting."

"But we have it now. You're holding it. What if whoever touches it, is the next to..." She didn't want to say the word, but it was echoing around in her head.

"I'm not going to die, and neither are you," he said firmly, as he put the painting back into the bag.

"You told me that before. I remember you saying I needed to fight."

"I wasn't sure how badly you were hurt. You closed your eyes, and I couldn't get you to open them." He put his hand back on hers, squeezing her fingers. "You gave me a hell of a scare, Callie."

"I was trying to stay awake, but the pain was so bad; I couldn't keep my eyes open. What did he hit me with?"

"Probably the butt of his gun."

"I guess I'm lucky he didn't shoot me." She paused. "I didn't hear him come into the house. I was trying to hear Dr. Clarke and then I felt someone behind me. I thought it was you. I started to turn around and then I felt this tremendous pain at the back of my head as I fell forward. I don't know how long I was out, but then I saw you and that guy fighting, and I wanted to help, but I couldn't move. I've never had anyone hit me like that before."

"Hopefully, that was the last time it will ever happen."

"That would be fine with me. I guess the house wasn't so secret after all."

His lips tightened and anger entered his gaze. "Or we were followed. I kept an eye out on the way down. I didn't see a tail, but it's possible we led him to the house."

She frowned as Flynn found more things to blame himself for. "I'm the one who messed this up, Flynn. I should have given you the address last night and let you come down with your team. I was just afraid you'd find something on my mom, and I wanted to be there if you did."

"I know. I understood your motivation."

"Ever since you asked me about the accident with my dad, I started wondering if my mom could be capable of murder. She can go a little crazy when it comes to a man. But if the painting is tied to the murder of four other victims over a period of five years in different locations across the country and abroad, she really can't be involved."

"Unless she exposed Arthur's crimes to this mad lunatic and got someone else to go after him. She does work in a museum, and she is very involved in the art world. If the painting and the murder is meant to punish someone for their greed or their illicit activities, then someone had to know about Arthur's private collection or his affair."

Her heart sank at his words. "I guess I still need to worry about her then."

"I don't want you to worry; I just want to be up-front with you. You deserve that."

"But the person who knocked me out, who went after the painting, who is he? How is he tied to this? Why don't you think he's the murderer?"

"He could very well be."

"We know my mother is not orchestrating anything from her hospital room."

"No, she's not doing that."

"My head is starting to hurt again," she said with a sigh.

He gave her a compassionate smile. "Don't worry too much about your mom."

"But you just said—"

"I know. I made a good case for her to still be a person of interest, mostly because I was thinking it through as I was talking, but I could also make a good case for her being innocent. The timing and location of the other murders would make it doubtful, if not outright impossible, that your mother is the serial killer."

"Well, I'm glad you believe that much. My mom cannot be a serial killer. And I don't believe she knows anything about this painting or is involved in Arthur's murder in any way."

"We'll get to the truth, Callie."

"I know. I want to go home, Flynn. The doctor said he would check me out one more time, and if I had someone willing to stay with me tonight, I could be released. I was thinking I could call Melissa or one of my other friends to come over."

"I'll stay with you tonight. We'll go to my place. I have a good security system. You'll be safe there. I'll make sure of it. You might not believe that after what happened today, but—"

"I do believe it," she interrupted. "I trust you, Flynn, and I promise not to play any more games with information. If I know something, I'll tell you."

"Good."

"I just realized I never finished my conversation with Dr. Clarke. I wonder what he thought when I just disappeared on the call."

"He probably thought you didn't have a signal. Did he say anything about your mom before you got hit?"

"He said she was doing better, that she understands Arthur is dead and that she needs to rest and regroup before she goes home. She's not fighting the hospital stay anymore, and he'd like to keep her at least another day or two. He said she'd like to see me tomorrow morning. That's the last thing I heard."

"That's good news."

"It is. I hope she really does want to see me and not because she wants to tell me what a lousy daughter I am for lying to her and putting her in the hospital."

"She probably doesn't even remember how she got there. But the important thing is she's getting better, and you'll be able to see her tomorrow."

"I'm not going to tell her about this. At least my bump is hidden in my hair, and I don't have a big bruise on my face like you."

"You don't think it's sexy?"

"Oh, I do," she admitted, as his blue gaze darkened. "I kind of think everything about you is sexy." She paused. "I shouldn't have said that; I'm going to blame the painkillers, even though I don't think they're that strong."

He smiled. "I feel the same way about you, and I have no painkillers to blame my truth on."

"This is a terrible time—there couldn't be a worse time, I don't think—to, you know, be attracted to each other."

He smiled. "Don't overthink it."

"I'm really good at overthinking. I like to forecast what's going to happen in advance, then I can be ready. I just don't know that any amount of planning would make me ready for you."

His gaze clung to hers. "You are not like any woman I know."

"I hope that's a compliment, and I hope I'm going to remember it tomorrow."

"I'll tell you again if you don't." He got to his feet as the door opened, his wary expression easing as Savannah walked into the room, accompanied by a handsome man with brown hair and dark eyes.

"Is it okay to come in?" Savannah asked, as they paused inside the doorway.

"Yes," Flynn answered, motioning them inside. "Callie, you know Savannah. And this is Wyatt Tanner. He's on my team as well."

"Is everyone on your team extremely good-looking?" she asked.

"It's a requirement," he joked, adding to Wyatt and Savannah, "Callie is enjoying her painkillers."

"Good for you," Savannah said. "I heard you took a rough hit on the head."

"Yes. It was the most pain I've ever felt."

"Sorry about that." Savannah gave her a sympathetic smile and then turned to Flynn. "How are you feeling, Flynn?"

"I'm fine. Just wishing I hadn't let him get away."

"We'll find him," Wyatt said firmly. "Do you have the painting?"

Flynn took the painting out of the bag once more. "It's right here."

"That's it?" Savannah asked, a note of disappointment in her voice. "That's the deadly calling card? It looks like something I'd hang in my kitchen."

Callie laughed at her words, and Savannah sent her a smile.

"I'm not much of an art critic," Savannah said.

"Me, either," she replied. "But the story about that painting is crazy. Are you sure you want to take it? I think it's cursed."

"I'm not worried about curses," she said. "The painting is our best clue to the murderer so far."

"I spoke to Gil in Art Crime," Wyatt put in. "He's sending over all the files on the Belladonna murders, so Savannah and I can get up to speed. I know you've reviewed them before, so I'm guessing there's no clue to the identity of the artist or the owner of the painting?"

Flynn shook his head. "No. There are a lot of rumors, speculation about who could be the mad artist serial killer, but no factual evidence. But someone knows something, and we have to figure out who."

"We'll get on it," Wyatt said. "Are you returning to LA tonight?"

"As soon as Callie is cleared. Thanks for driving down here. I didn't want to put Callie's life at risk again by keeping the painting in my possession."

"Understandable," Wyatt said with a nod.

"The police have sealed off Arthur's house here in Palm Springs, and they're packing up the stolen paintings. They'll be logged into evidence here and then the Art Crime Team will take over the task of getting them back to their rightful owners,"

Savannah said. "I will also look into Layana Vazquez, find out more about their affair."

"You told them about Layana?" Callie asked.

"I texted them everything we know so far while you were having your head scanned," he replied.

"Lucas is checking security footage around the Palm Springs house," Wyatt put in. "As soon as he picks up the car, we should have a lead on your assailant. We're also tracing the gun to see what comes back on that."

"Thanks for doing all that. I know I've taken over both your Sundays."

"It's what we do," Savannah said with a shrug. She turned back to Callie. "I hope you feel better."

"Thanks. I just want this to all be over. I want Arthur's killer caught and my mom to get back to normal." Although, even as she said all that, she couldn't help thinking that when this was over, she would probably never see Flynn again, and that did not make her happy.

"We'll take off now," Wyatt said.

"I'll talk to you later tonight," Flynn said.

As they left, Flynn moved back to the bed.

"You have good people working for you," she commented.

"And with me."

"When you filled them in, did you tell them about your dad being seen outside his former gallery in Laguna Beach?"

"I should have, but I didn't. There are more concrete clues to follow first. Gretchen could have easily been lying." He paused. "Or maybe I'm just telling myself that, because I don't want to go there."

"My brain is really muddled right now, but I know one thing for sure, Flynn."

"What's that?" he asked, meeting her gaze.

"Whatever your dad did, whoever he is, you're not him. You're a good man. And I trust you."

He grabbed her hand once more, his fingers curling around hers, sending a rush of warmth right through her.

"I hope I don't let you down, Callie."

"I hope you don't, either." She paused, thinking that probably wasn't the best thing to say. "I should have said I know you won't, but these drugs are like a truth serum."

He grinned. "Good to know. I'll have to see what other secrets I can get out of you on the way home."

CHAPTER SEVENTEEN

CALLIE SLEPT all the way back to Los Angeles. Flynn spent most of the two-hour drive dividing his gaze between her and the road. Part of him wanted to wake her up, just to make sure she was all right, but the doctor had said it was perfectly fine for her to sleep and that she needed rest to recover. He was grateful she would recover. She'd been lucky. She could have been shot instead of just knocked out. But her assailant probably hadn't wanted to alert him to his presence in the house.

The man had to have seen their car out front, but that hadn't deterred him from entering the property. And they'd made it incredibly easy for him. He realized now that they'd left the patio doors open when they'd stepped outside. The guy hadn't even had to break in.

He shook his head in self-disgust. All this was on him and there was nothing anyone could say that would change his mind.

He'd made a tactical error taking Callie to Palm Springs. He couldn't let that happen again. Although, as much as he needed to push her away, he also needed to protect her. She wasn't just a witness to Arthur's murder anymore; she was also a witness to the attack in Palm Springs. He needed to make sure that no one came after her again, which meant he had to stay close. He just needed to be smarter about it.

As he glanced over at her sweet face, something inside him shifted. He didn't know what it was about her that had gotten so deep under his skin, but he couldn't deny that she was becoming important to him in a way he'd never imagined. He needed to slow it all down, but all he really wanted to do was take her to bed and see how hot the flames could be.

She might even want that, too. But she was injured and on painkillers, and he wouldn't take advantage of that. She trusted him.

Her words rang once more through his head, and her trust touched him. He didn't know if he had earned it after everything that had happened, but he wanted it. And he wanted to trust her, too. So many people had let him down in his life. His father was at the top of that list and now Arthur was on it. He'd put them both on a pedestal of good, and they'd tumbled off, shattering into a thousand broken pieces. Maybe he'd been a fool to put them there in the first place. He needed to be more careful about who he chose to believe in.

But he didn't think he needed to be careful with Callie. He knew her agenda. She wanted to protect her mother, and he could understand why she was so fierce about that. He respected the depth of her love, her willingness to put her own needs aside for someone else. He just hoped they wouldn't come to a point where he would have to choose between getting justice and protecting Callie's mother.

As much as he wanted to lean away from Juliette being involved in Arthur's death, every time he started to move in that direction, something changed. Like the fact that there were only a few people who knew about the house in Palm Springs. Like the fact that Juliette had been missing at the time of Arthur's murder, and that she'd received damning information about her husband having an affair. Like the fact that she had had access to the museum's security systems. She might have even been able to get someone in security to help her out.

On the other hand, he didn't believe she was a serial killer or that she had painted the belladonna. There was no way she had had anything to do with the previous murders.

But the pattern of this particular serial killer was to punish people in the art world. And he was starting to see why someone might have believed that Arthur needed to be punished.

Did the serial killer get information about a potential victim before going after them? Was there always someone else involved? Someone else who had been damaged in some way? The first victim had also been having an affair. *Had his wife wanted him punished? Had she gotten someone to help her do that?*

He still had too many questions to clear Juliette. Hopefully, tomorrow he could talk to her directly. Maybe she would be able to tell him something that would point him in another direction.

And hopefully that direction wouldn't lead to his father.

He was trying not to think about his dad, but two women had mentioned that his father might be back in business—Victoria and Gretchen. And both those women had known his father before he'd vanished into thin air. But Victoria had said her knowledge came from Arthur.

Was it possible Arthur had been buying stolen art from his dad? That seemed impossible to believe. Arthur had seen firsthand how his father's crimes had affected him. *If he'd been involved with his dad, why on earth would Arthur have asked him to come to the museum, to help him?* It didn't make sense. He was missing a piece of the puzzle, something that would tie everything up, but he didn't have it yet, and he didn't know where to find it.

As his exit came into view, he changed lanes, checking his rearview mirror to see if anyone was following them off the freeway. There was one car behind him, but it moved into the left lane, turning in the other direction at the stoplight.

A few blocks later, he pulled into the garage of his two-story townhouse, located in a duplex in Santa Monica, a few blocks from the beach and his office, making it the perfect location. The other side of the duplex was owned by Beck, so he also had the perfect neighbor. They'd put a security system on the entire building, with individual controls for each townhouse. Work rarely followed him home, but occasionally they needed to put a witness or a fellow agent somewhere safe, and his apartment or Beck's apartment could double as a safe house.

As the door shut behind his vehicle, the lights came on in the garage. He put his hand on Callie's leg.

She jerked awake, giving him a startled, fearful look.

"It's okay," he assured her. "We're in my building. You're safe."

"Oh." She straightened in her seat, blinking the daze out of her eyes. "I guess I fell asleep."

"About ten minutes after we left Palm Springs. How do you feel?"

"Kind of groggy, but not too bad."

"Let's go inside." He got out of the car and went around to her side to help her out. "You can lean on me."

She put her hand in his and took a second to get her bearings. Then she squared her shoulders and let out a breath. "I'm okay."

"Good." Despite her assurance, he didn't let go of her hand until they were in the house.

The garage door took them into the hallway outside the kitchen. He led her through the kitchen to the adjoining family room, urging her to take a seat on the brown leather couch.

As she sat down, her gaze moved toward the dark windows. "What time is it?"

"Almost nine." He walked across the room to pull down the shade. The back of the house was completely secure, but he wanted Callie to feel safe. "Are you hungry? Thirsty? Do you want to go to bed? I have a guest room."

"Slow down," she said with a small smile. "I'm still waking up."

"Sorry."

"Why don't you sit?" she suggested.

He opted for the chair adjacent to the couch, rather than sit next to her. She gave him a thoughtful look.

"Everything okay?" she asked.

"It's fine."

"So, this is your place." Her gaze moved around the room. "It's homier than I would have thought."

He shrugged, knowing that he wasn't at all responsible for the colorful rug or the buttery-soft leather furniture or the throw pillows with just the right accent of color. Although, he had picked out the recliner and the TV. "I had some help on the décor," he admitted.

"From who? A girlfriend?"

"No. It was from a friend of my mother's. She's an interior designer. When I bought this place, my mom called her and asked her to make sure I wasn't sleeping on the floor and propping my television up on empty crates. My mother doesn't seem to think I've grown up since I was nineteen and living in my first apartment."

"Which, I'm assuming, had you sleeping on the floor and using crates for tables."

"Possibly," he conceded. "But it didn't bother me. I can sleep anywhere."

"Well, I like this place. It's comfortable."

"And it's safe."

"Even better," she murmured. "Flynn...I think I might have said a few things at the hospital that I shouldn't have. Or maybe I was dreaming. It's all a little foggy in my head."

"You didn't say anything worth worrying about."

"Are you sure?"

"Positive. Your secrets are still intact. Well, except for one. When we got in the car, you did tell me that you backed into a pole at a fast-food restaurant when you were sixteen and told your mother that someone else had hit you. But that was really the only time you lied."

"I can't believe I told you that."

"You were a little loopy. As crimes go, it wasn't all that bad. Although, I'm curious who Rick was."

She flushed at that. "I told you about Rick? Wow, that's embarrassing. What did I say?"

180

"Actually, you didn't tell me, but if it was embarrassing, I'm now curious."

"Rick and I went to the prom my junior year. I thought he was going to be my boyfriend, but it turns out he had his eyes on another girl. My friend Kim and I went to the fast-food restaurant to see if he was cheating on me. And he was. He and this cheerleader were practically devouring each other. I got so angry I couldn't see straight."

"And you backed into a pole."

"I felt like an idiot."

"We've all been there."

"You've had someone cheat on you?"

"Not exactly. Or if they did, I didn't know about it. But I did some stupid, reckless things when I was a teen. I'm probably lucky to have made it through those years. I became especially careless after my father left. I think deep down I wanted him to see that his leaving had really screwed me up. Of course, he didn't see, because he wasn't around. I eventually realized I was only hurting myself."

"At least you figured it out before you did hurt yourself." She paused. "Did Olivia have a good influence on you?"

"She did."

"What was she like?"

"She was…calming. She had a very chill personality. She didn't worry about much. I'm not sure if that came from growing up in a world that was pretty damn good to her. She had everything she wanted and needed. She was secure in her family. She had a lot of friends. She was smart and pretty. She never faced any real adversity. I tell myself that's a good thing, because her life was so short. At least she was happy for the time that she had."

"I thought you said she and Arthur got into it sometimes."

"Occasionally, yes. They argued because he was controlling, and she rebelled by hiding things in her room, like tickets to concerts where he'd told her she couldn't go. But it was just kid stuff. As much as she felt her father had too much power over her, she really looked up to him, as did I. But I don't think he was ever as good as we thought he was."

"Maybe he was good. He might not have gotten involved in stolen art until recently. It could have been just one bad, reckless mistake."

"A mistake that cost him his life."

"But not one that should erase all the good things he did. Until you really know the extent of his crimes, maybe give him the benefit of the doubt."

"If I wasn't investigating his murder, I could do that, but I can't let my feelings for him cloud my judgment or obscure the truth."

As she shivered, he frowned and got up to grab a blanket from the back of the recliner. He came back to the couch and wrapped it around her shoulders.

"Thanks," she said. "I suddenly got a chill."

"What else can I get you?"

"Maybe some coffee."

"I don't have any decaf."

"Good, because I was thinking some caffeine might clear my mind."

"No way. You need to sleep tonight. The doctor said rest is important."

"I just slept in the car."

He smiled at her beautiful defiance. "You're very stubborn. But we're following doctor's orders. You are taking it easy, and I'm going to make you some herbal tea."

"You have herbal tea? Isn't that kind of for sissies?"

He laughed. "Make fun of me all you want. Green tea is good for you. It builds the immune system."

"Coffee is better for kicking ass."

"Well, we're not doing any more ass-kicking tonight. Do you want anything with your tea?"

"What if I said I wanted a kiss?" she asked, a reckless light in her eyes.

"I'd say that would be as bad for you as coffee," he returned, feeling a rush of desire run through him. "No more excitement tonight, Callie."

"I feel wired. I need to burn it off. And since I assume you won't let me go for a run—"

"You assume right."

"Then I need another way to release all this tension, and I can think of a really good one."

He put up a hand, as she leaned into him. "You are not making this easy."

"I'm not trying to," she said with a smile. "I almost died today, Flynn. I feel like savoring how alive I am."

"I get it. I've felt that way before."

"Then why are you resisting?"

"Because I want to protect you."

"From you?"

"And from yourself. I'm making you tea and then you're going to bed—alone."

"You're not as much fun as I thought you'd be," she complained.

"I don't have fun with women who just suffered a concussion. You need to rest." He got to his feet, which required an almost superhuman effort. But he was going to do the right thing tonight.

Tomorrow might be a different story.

Callie woke up Monday morning around nine. As she glanced at the clock on the nightstand, she was surprised she'd slept so late. She was usually an early bird, rising with the sun, getting in a run before a shower, but that wasn't happening today. While she felt immensely better, she still had a small ache in her head, reminding her of yesterday's close call.

As she slid out of bed, she heard Flynn's voice in the kitchen. He appeared to be on the phone. She couldn't hear what he was saying, but there was energy in his voice. Hopefully, he was getting some new leads.

She used the bathroom, making a face at her tangled hair and pale skin. She needed a shower before she could see anyone.

Stripping off the sweats and T-shirt that Flynn had loaned her the night before, she hopped into the shower, letting the warm water ease her aching neck muscles. She'd been hit on the back of the head, but fortunately she'd only had some minor bleeding and hadn't needed stitches. But she still washed her hair with gentle hands, as the bump on her head was quite prominent.

When she moved back into the guest room, she found a bag of clothes next to those she'd stripped off the night before. And they were her clothes. *Where had they come from?* Frowning, she got dressed and then made her way into the kitchen.

Flynn was off the phone and at the stove, flipping pancakes and frying bacon. He wore dark jeans and a navy-blue crew-neck sweater that brought out the blue in his eyes. His blond hair was damp and a bit curly, his cheeks cleanly shaven, his mouth looking oh so sexy as it curved into a welcoming smile that put a knot in her throat. Every time she thought she was imagining how attractive he was, he appeared in the flesh, looking just as handsome in person as he was in her head.

"You're up," he said.

"And you're cooking. I love pancakes."

"Good. I also made coffee." He moved over to the coffeemaker and poured her a mug. "Do you take anything in it?"

"No. I like it strong."

"I figured."

She took a sip and sighed with delight.

"You're easy to please," he said with a laugh. "I have a feeling you might be a coffee addict."

"Guilty. Although, your tea wasn't bad. It put me right out last night, even when I thought I was too hyped up to sleep." She paused as he moved back to the griddle. "Those look good, perfectly golden, just the right size."

"You missed my first batch," he said with a grin.

"Well, no one makes a good first pancake. You have to get the heat of the griddle just right."

"So I've been told. Anyway, these are almost ready."

"How did you get my clothes?" she asked, as she watched him flip the pancakes.

"I went into your apartment early this morning."

"But you don't know the code."

"I watched you put it in the other night."

"Oh. I guess I should have been more careful with an FBI agent looking over my shoulder."

"Sorry, habit." He gave her a smile. "How's your head?"

"Better. I thought I heard you on the phone earlier. Is there any news?"

He slid the pancakes onto a plate and turned off the stove. "Yes."

Her body tightened at his answer. "Good or bad?"

"A little of both. Sit. We'll eat and we'll talk."

She sat down in a chair at the kitchen table as he handed her a plate. "This is the second time you've cooked breakfast for me. I might be getting used to it."

"You shouldn't. I'm almost out of ideas. Eggs and pancakes are the total sum of my breakfast skills."

"Well, you won't starve." She munched on a piece of crispy bacon. "I think you could probably cook a lot more if you wanted to."

"I don't have time."

"So, tell me the news," she said, as he sat down across from her.

"My team located the vehicle our attacker was driving. It was a rental car. The driver was listed as Olin Sergei, a Russian national. We got a photo, but it turns out that the ID was stolen. Sergei died three years ago." He held up his phone. "Do you recognize this guy?"

She gave the picture a good look, but the man with the greasy brown hair, dark eyes, and prominent cheekbones was not familiar. "I've never seen him before. Does this mean we've reached another dead end?"

"No. We caught a break. Lucas was able to isolate the man who dropped off the car and tracked him to another vehicle, a

Jeep also registered to Olin Sergei. Apparently, this guy took over Olin's life. At any rate, the Jeep was driven to the Wickham Hotel in West Hollywood. The cameras picked up our man exiting the fifth-floor elevator. Eventually, we got a room number. That's where the good news ends. Savannah and Wyatt went to the hotel. Our attacker was found dead in his room. He'd been poisoned with the room service breakfast he'd ordered an hour earlier."

She was disappointed and a little terrified by the ending to his story. "Poisoned? Just like Arthur?"

"Yes. My guess is that our attacker was hired to retrieve the painting. When he was unsuccessful, he was eliminated."

"Eliminated," she echoed. "That's a scary word."

"I wouldn't feel too bad for him. He could have killed us both."

"I know. So, whoever hired him took him out."

"Yes."

"What about the person who delivered the room service? Are you looking for him?"

"Unfortunately, that individual was able to avoid showing his face to the camera. Lucas is working on blowing up different angles and checking other cameras, but so far, no luck."

"Wouldn't the hotel know who the waiter was?"

"It wasn't a hotel employee. The man who was supposed to deliver the food was found unconscious in the hallway near the freight elevator. He's awake now, but he never saw who hit him, which is where the trail goes cold."

She poured maple syrup on her pancakes, thinking she needed to eat after that story. "A lot happened while I was asleep. The bad news seems to outweigh the good."

"Not necessarily. The trail may be cold, but at least there's something to follow. Are your pancakes all right?"

She swallowed her first bite. "They're delicious, Flynn. It's nice to have someone cook for me. It doesn't happen very often."

"I was happy to do it. I still feel badly about you getting hurt yesterday."

"I'm pretty sure there's nothing I can say that will change that, but I don't hold you responsible. I made some mistakes, too. I'm going to try to do better."

"You don't have to do better. Finding Arthur's killer is my job. I've already involved you way too much."

"I still want to help, so don't shut me out completely." She could see by the look in his eyes that that was exactly what he intended to do, but she wasn't going to let that happen. However, she needed to think about what he'd told her and to eat, so she concentrated on her breakfast for the next few minutes, as a myriad of thoughts raced through her head. When she was done eating, she said, "If the man who attacked us is dead, and we no longer have the painting, then does that mean we're not in danger anymore?"

"I never like to get too comfortable or overconfident," he replied.

She frowned at his very careful response. "I was hoping for a different answer."

"I think the danger has diminished, but I still want to keep an eye on you, Callie."

"I don't mind that, but I need to go to the hospital this morning to see my mom."

"I'll take you there."

"I'm planning on staying for a while. It could be hours. If she's sleeping, I'm going to wait for her to wake up. I need to talk to her."

"That's fine. I'll drop you off on my way to the office."

"Is it really on the way?"

"It's a short detour. You can call me when you're ready to leave. It doesn't matter when."

"Or I can just call a car and go home."

"That would prevent me from keeping an eye on you," he returned. "Let's play it by ear. There are a lot of balls in the air at the moment. I'd like to see where some of them are landing before I let you out of my sight completely."

She didn't know if Flynn's protectiveness was just due to his strong sense of responsibility or if it was more personal, but it was nice to have someone worry about her for a change. "I guess we can see how the morning goes," she said. "Where's the painting now?"

"It's in a secure room at my office."

"The killer seems to have a way of getting in and out of secure places."

"The painting isn't going anywhere. Don't worry about that."

"What do you think the person will do without his calling card?"

"I don't know. Maybe he'll paint another one—start the game over."

"It is odd that they would deliver the painting, then steal it back. You said they also left a photo when they took the painting, so they wanted credit for the crime."

"It could just be part of their twisted game. Or there could be something identifiable in the painting. I have an art expert coming by later today to take a look."

"I hope they can find some way to identify the artist."

"So do I. I'm also hoping that the killer's frustration in losing the painting will lead to a mistake, something that could break this case wide open before anyone else dies."

"I hope so, too. Your eye looks better today, but I can still see the bruise."

"This is nothing."

"Which means you've probably been hurt a lot worse. Your job is dangerous, isn't it?"

"It can be, but it's worth it."

"You love it, don't you?"

"More than I imagined I would. I started out just wanting to bring my dad down, pay him back for what he did to me and my mother, but it became a lot more. My work hasn't really been about him in years. It's about doing my part to keep people safe. And if I can't keep them safe, I can find out who hurt them and make sure it doesn't happen again."

"I'm impressed."

"I'm not trying to impress you," he said, his blue gaze meeting hers.

"Maybe that's why you're impressive. Your mission is clear in your head, and it's a selfless, generous mission. You put your life on the line for strangers. You probably don't get much credit for anything you do."

"I don't look for credit. In my job, staying in the shadows is a good thing."

"I've noticed that you don't wear a uniform or an FBI jacket. Why is that?"

"My task force operates in a more surreptitious manner. We go undercover a lot. We move through cases in ways that our more public agents cannot. We become whoever we need to be to get a job done."

"That sounds intriguing. Tell me more."

He gave her a speculative look. "Is my job that fascinating, or are you stalling a little, Callie?"

He was really a little too perceptive at times. "I do find your job interesting, but I guess I'm stalling, too. I want to see my mom, but I'm also afraid."

"That she'll hate you for putting her in the hospital?"

"There's that, but it's more that I'm afraid of how she'll be. I don't want to see her lost and confused and sad. I've seen her that way too many times. I want her to be who she was last week, before all this happened."

"I get it. Maybe she will be."

"I doubt it. It always takes time for her to recover, more time than I ever want or expect."

"Who stayed with you the last time, when you were sixteen?"

His question took her back to a very unhappy and lonely time. "I stayed by myself. When concerned health officials asked who I was with, I lied and gave them a neighbor's name or the names of my friends' parents. I was old enough that no one was too concerned. They were worried about my mother more than me."

His expression turned grim. "That's not right."

"I was fine. I could drive by then. I could cook for myself, and I'd always done the shopping and the banking. I knew all the credit card numbers and the passwords. I was perfectly capable of being alone."

"But you were alone and that had to be hard."

"It wasn't easy," she admitted. "But I got through it."

"Were your friends there for you?"

"I tried not to tell anyone. Eventually, it came out. Most of my friends were there for me. Some just wanted to make fun of my mother behind my back. But I survived and my mom got better, and we moved on."

"You're a very strong woman."

"I don't often feel that way," she murmured, not sure why she was revealing so many of her secrets. "I just fake it. It's easier. When people ask you how you're doing, they don't really want to know. They just want to hear you say you're fine. So, I'm fine."

"Well, when I ask, I really want to know. Don't tell me you're fine, if you're not."

"Did I tell you I was fine? I think I've shared a lot of other emotions with you. For some reason, I can't seem to lie to you."

He gave her a faint smile. "You know a lot of my secrets, too. Things I've shared with only a handful of people. We both have something to lose."

"Which makes it easier to trust each other. I thought when you first told me about your dad that that was why you were telling me, so I'd trust you, so I'd talk to you about my mom. You were playing me."

"I did want to get you on my side," he admitted. "But my original intent faded fast after I realized what you were dealing with in terms of your mom's mental health."

"When she tried to jump off the balcony."

"I saw your face and your pain. It was a brutally real moment. While I couldn't say then or even now that your mother had nothing to do with Arthur's death, I knew that you were innocent, and I couldn't play you. I had to hope you'd be willing to cooperate with me because it was the right thing to do and the best way to protect your mother."

"I'm still here."

"But it hasn't been one-sided, Callie," he reminded her. "You were there when I walked into Olivia's room for the first time in fifteen years. I also told you not only about my father's past, but the fact that Gretchen thought she'd seen him outside the gallery. You have as much on me as I have on you. And you could be playing me, too, so that I go easy on your mother."

"I can't deny that that thought did cross my mind early on. There I go, being honest again."

"It's better this way. We both know what each other wants."

"Is it better, Flynn? When we both know that we also want each other?"

He sucked in a quick breath at her words.

"And that's a crazy, ridiculous desire in the midst of all this," she continued. "We are so entangled with each other, and it's not just us, it's our parents, too—my mom, your dad. I worry where this is all going to end up."

"I worry about that, too," he said, his gaze darkening. "But they're not us. We can't be responsible for them."

"It's easier for you to say that. Your dad has been gone more than half your life, but my mom has always been there. Her problems are my problems."

"I understand, but let's not borrow more trouble than we already have. I will find out what happened to Arthur. And then we'll figure out the rest."

"What if you can't find out? This killer seems fairly invincible."

"Failure is not an option."

Looking at his determined jaw, she knew he really believed that. "You call me stubborn, but I think you might have me beat."

"We have a lot in common."

She shivered at that thought, because what they mostly had in common was their passionate lust for each other. Shadows entered Flynn's eyes as their gazes held for a long minute. She was moving into dangerous territory once more, and she had to call a halt. Because she did need to get to the hospital to see her mom.

Pushing back her chair, she stood up and took her plate to the kitchen. "I'll just get my things, and we can go."

"You can leave your clothes here. You can get your stuff later, after we see how today goes."

"Well, I hope it goes better than the last few days," she said, putting her dishes into the dishwasher.

He moved into the kitchen, setting his plate on the counter, and then surprising her by sliding his arms around her waist.

"What—what are you doing?" she asked, her words coming out a little breathlessly.

"I haven't kissed you this morning," he said, a purposeful gleam in his eyes.

"Are we doing that? I thought we were putting all that on hold. And last night is a little hazy, but I'm pretty sure you turned me down quite forcefully."

"Because last night was hazy." His gaze settled on hers. "I didn't want to take advantage of you. Not that you made it easy to say no."

"You were quite the gentleman."

"But today you seem better."

"I am better," she said, feeling a tingle of anticipation. "But don't we have to go?"

"One minute—make that two," he said, as he leaned in for a kiss.

She closed her eyes, savoring the kiss she'd been wanting for what seemed like forever.

And just like the last time, there was an instant spark, a strong, intensely emotional connection. She wanted to stay in Flynn's arms, linger in his kiss, disappear for a while into a beautiful, sexy world of emotion and feeling. But it ended all too quickly; Flynn was moving away.

He gave her a hard look, his jaw tight, as if he was having a difficult time holding himself back.

"I'd like to see you let go," she murmured. "I wonder what that would take."

"Not much," he said shortly. "Let's get out of here before we do something we regret."

"It might be a mistake, Flynn, but I don't think either of us would regret it."

"Well, we're not going to find out."

"Maybe not now, but this thing between us...I don't think it's going away." She grabbed her purse and headed toward the door.

CHAPTER EIGHTEEN

THEY DIDN'T TALK MUCH on the way to the hospital. Callie wasn't sure what Flynn was thinking about—maybe their kiss in the kitchen, or perhaps his mind had already returned to work, to trying to figure out who had killed Arthur and the man in the hotel room.

She needed to get her head together, too, because her mother was going to need her attention, and she had to be ready for whatever was ahead.

As Flynn drove into the hospital parking lot, she said, "You can drop me off at the front door. There's no reason for you to come inside. My mom hasn't been cleared to talk to law enforcement, only to me. Dr. Clarke said he'll make that determination later today."

"I wasn't going to come up to interrogate your mother, although I would like to speak to her when she's well enough to do so. My offer is solely for you—moral support."

She saw the sincerity in his soft smile. "I appreciate that, Flynn. But I'm good. Just drop me off."

"All right." He drove into the circular loading zone in front of the hospital. "Call me or text me when you're done here."

"I will."

"Good luck, Callie."

"Thanks. I know it's foolish, but I'm hoping for a small miracle."

"I hope you get one."

"Thanks. Bye." She got out of the car and closed the door, then headed into the hospital. She took the elevator up to the seventh floor, and then stopped at the nurses' station, which was necessary in order to access her mother's room while she was on a psychiatric hold.

"Perfect timing. She's awake," the nurse told her.

"How is she doing today?"

"Much better. She's making good progress."

Callie was happy to hear that, although progress made it sound like her mom had a lot further to go.

The nurse let her into her mother's room with a reassuring smile. "I'm sure she'll be happy to see you."

"I hope so," she said, as she stepped inside.

Her mom was sitting up in bed, wearing her own nightgown and the robe Callie had brought from the house. That seemed like a long time ago, even though it had only been two days. Her mother's face was very pale, but her eyes were more alert and focused than they had been. Her gaze, however, also expressed disappointment and anger.

Callie's heart sank as she moved next to the bed. "How are you, Mom?"

"It's about time you came to see me, Callie."

"I was here yesterday, but you were sleeping. Didn't the nurse tell you that?"

"No. And I was sleeping because they drugged me."

"You needed to rest. You were hysterical."

"I can't believe you brought me here. You know how much I hate being in the hospital."

"I didn't have a choice. You were not yourself."

"Because my husband died right in front of me."

"I know. It was horrific. You had every right to be upset. I was just worried about you, and I didn't want you to hurt yourself."

"I wouldn't do that."

She wanted to remind her mother that she'd tried to do exactly that, but she didn't know if that would be helpful at this point in her recovery. So, she changed the subject. "How did your session go with Dr. Clarke yesterday?"

"It was all right. He's better than some of the doctors I've had. He actually listens and at least pretends to respect me."

"I know he respects you. He wants to help you. It's difficult for anyone to get through something like this. But I can see you're doing better."

"I don't know how I'm doing. When I first wake up, before I open my eyes, I think everything is normal. I can almost feel Arthur's body next to mine, his breath on my neck, his arms around me. He loved to hold me when we slept." Her mom wrapped her arms around herself. "He said he would miss me if he didn't. God, I miss him now."

It was difficult to see the pain and love in her mother's eyes, not only because Arthur was dead, but because he'd cheated on her.

"But then I come fully awake and I see this bare room," her mother continued. "This place that is not my home. And I'm alone."

"You're not alone. I'm here for you. I'll always be here for you." She put her arms around her mom and gave her a hug. It scared her a little at how thin her mom was. Even before this horrible weekend, she'd been losing weight, a sure sign that she wasn't as happy as she needed to be to keep her mental problems at bay.

"You're a good daughter, Callie. But sometimes you listen to the doctors when you should listen to me."

"You weren't making sense, Mom. And I was worried, because there was an FBI agent in the house. He wanted to talk to you. I didn't think you were in any condition for questions."

"Has he found Arthur's killer?"

"Not yet. But there are a lot of people looking. They want justice for Arthur. You don't have to worry about that."

"Of course they want justice. Arthur was such a good man. And he died so young. I can't believe it, Callie. I'm alone again. I thought it would be years before I'd have to feel like this. It reminds me of when your father died, how lonely the world got."

"It's hard to lose someone you love." She licked her lips, knowing she needed to talk to her mother about some difficult subjects. Seeing how alert and lucid her mother was, she had to assume that Dr. Clarke would give Flynn permission to speak to her as early as this afternoon. "Mom, we have to talk about a few things."

"Like the funeral? Who's planning that? I should be doing it. I hope Moira isn't trying to take over. She can get very territorial when it comes to Arthur. She's just his assistant; I'm his wife."

"Nothing is happening yet. It's early days. There's no rush. Arthur wanted to be cremated. I saw that in his trust."

Her mom's lip trembled. "Is he really dead?"

"I'm sorry. I shouldn't have said it that way. But, yes, he is dead. I'm very sorry. We will talk about his funeral when you're ready and I will help you plan everything. But the most important thing right now is to find the person who killed him. Do you know of anyone who was angry with him or threatening him? Did he talk to you about cases at work or something happening within the art world? Any small detail could be important."

Her mom stared back at her, her gaze contemplative. "Arthur was acting strange all week. He took Wednesday off and went to Palm Springs on a whim. He never does that. And then he wanted to go back again on the weekend. I couldn't understand why he was so insistent about that. He was also on the phone a lot, but he would stop talking when I came into the room. I'm pretty sure he was talking to Gretchen Vale. She was at the museum event. I ran into her in the ladies' room. I actually asked her why she was bothering Arthur with so many calls."

Her mother's words surprised her. "You confronted her about calling Arthur? What did she say?"

"She said she was selling Arthur some paintings and the deal was complicated. But then she gave me a funny look and said that maybe I shouldn't ask questions, because I might not want to know the answers."

"That's odd."

"I thought so, too, but then she was gone. I kept thinking about it, and I wanted to know more, so I went looking for her. I started to think maybe she and Arthur were together, because I didn't see either of them. Victoria told me that Gretchen had asked about the sculpture in the Seville Room, so I went there, but the room was empty. When I came back into the grand hall, I heard screaming. Everyone was running. I didn't know what was going on. And then I saw him on the floor." Tears spilled out of her eyes. "If I'd found him earlier, maybe it wouldn't have happened. Maybe I could have stopped it."

"Or you could have been hurt yourself. Did you see anyone when you were looking for Gretchen and Arthur?"

"I remember people pushing past me to get to the show while I was going the other direction, but I couldn't tell you who those people were. I so focused in on Gretchen and Arthur." Her mom paused. "Why are you asking me so many questions, Callie?"

"Because the FBI is going to ask you, and you need to be clear on your answers."

Her mother's gaze narrowed. "Oh, my God, do you think Gretchen killed him?"

"I have no idea." She'd actually been trying to tell her mother in a subtle way that she needed to protect herself, but, clearly, she'd been too ambiguous.

"Maybe Gretchen wanted an affair, and Arthur refused," her mom speculated. "She was stalking him, harassing him. She couldn't take no for an answer. And when he wouldn't leave me, she killed him."

"That's one possibility," she said, a little alarmed at how her mom had put it together so quickly, almost as if she'd come up with it before. She had a feeling Flynn was going to find the answer practiced, and she didn't want that. "Do you have any other ideas?"

"I don't know. That one seems very strong."

"What about Layana?"

"What?" her mom asked in confusion. "The artist who painted

Arthur's portrait? Why are you asking about her? Was she at the party?"

"No." She paused, wanting to choose her words carefully. She didn't want to set her mom back with evidence of an affair at this point, even though her mother had already convinced herself that Gretchen was a possible threat to her marriage. But there were no facts to support that.

"Callie, why did you ask me about her?"

"Arthur's assistant, Moira, mentioned to the FBI that Arthur had spoken to Layana the week before he died. I was curious, because the portrait was done a long time ago."

"I don't know why he'd speak to her now. Should I be concerned?"

"I'm just trying to piece things together. Help the FBI find some suspects."

Her mother gave her a suspicious look. "What aren't you telling me, Callie?"

There was so much she wasn't telling her mom she had no idea how to answer that question. "I'm just looking for a motive, a reason for someone to want Arthur dead."

"There's something else going on. You're worried. I can see it in your eyes."

"I'm worried about you."

"I know I struggle, and you often have to carry my weight, but I feel better."

"I'm really glad about that."

"But I want to go home. I want to be near Arthur's things. I can't feel him here. It's so sterile."

"You'll be home soon, but it's important for you to be ready to face everything."

"I'll be ready. I'll make sure Arthur has a good memorial service. That's on me."

"I don't just mean you have to be ready to deal with that." She drew in a breath. "You have to be ready to talk to the FBI about where you were when Arthur was killed."

"I just told you where I was."

"Yes, and the answer concerns me."

"Why? Callie, spit it out. Please, just say it."

"You're a suspect, Mom. You were seen on a security camera at the museum having a fight with Arthur fifteen minutes before he was killed, and you were not in the hall when he fell over the railing."

Her mother's eyes widened with each word. "And you think I killed him?"

"I don't, but others are suspicious. The FBI wants to talk to you so they can eliminate you as a suspect."

"Why would I kill the man I love?" she asked in bewilderment.

"They don't know how much you loved him. All they saw was a fight."

"I was just annoyed that he wanted to go back to Palm Springs again. I had this terrible feeling he was using that place to have an affair, because he always wanted to go when I couldn't. I accused him of that, and he said I was crazy. I hate that word. So I left and went to the restroom. I needed a minute."

"I understand. You should say that. I'm just telling you what's coming your way so that you can be prepared."

"I didn't do it, Callie."

She really wanted to believe her mom.

"Do you believe me?" her mother asked. "Please tell me you do."

"I do," she said, desperately hoping she wasn't wrong. "But we still need to prove it."

"How are we going to do that?"

"I'll find a way."

Relief filled her mom's eyes. "You always make me feel better, Callie. I guess it's just the two of us now. Like the old days."

She really hoped it wouldn't be like the old days, but she just smiled and sat down on the edge of the bed. "Do you want me to do your hair and makeup?"

A smile spread across her mom's face. "You know me so well."

She opened her purse and pulled out her makeup bag. "Then let's get started."

Flynn stood at the end of the conference table, a large board behind him displaying the photos of potential suspects. He'd just finished a long briefing at his office with Detectives Gage and Palmer from the LAPD, Damon and two other agents from the LA Field Office, and his team: Savannah, Lucas, Wyatt, and Bree. They'd compared notes, gone over witness statements, and discussed every possible angle and connection currently being explored.

They'd ended just after one, everyone going off to tackle their particular assignment.

The LAPD would continue to focus on Judge Corbyn's work circle: attorneys, clerks, court cases, convictions—anything that would provide a motive for murder. They were also now investigating the homicide at the Wickham hotel. Damon's team was conducting additional, more in-depth interviews with Arthur's neighbors, associates, people who worked at his house, the staff members at his foundation, anyone who had any kind of relationship with the judge. Wyatt and Bree were working with agents from Art Crime to trace the stolen paintings found in Arthur's home, and Lucas was focused on finding the cyber trail. Which left the key art players to Savannah and himself.

As the group dispersed, he glanced back at the board, at the faces on the top of their suspect list: Layana Vazquez, Arthur's alleged mistress and someone he'd left money to in his trust. Gretchen Vale, who had possibly brokered the stolen art purchase, and her husband Stephen. He didn't have Gerard Bissette on the list, although he was still curious about what had transpired between Gerard and Stephen and why they'd had an intense discussion in a car down the street from the gallery. He'd put Marcus Vitelli on the list, because he'd exchanged numerous calls with Arthur and had been under pressure from Arthur to finish a painting or lose a purchase. Because Marcus was on the list, he'd also added Imogene Rocca, the other young artist Arthur had been interested in.

Juliette was next. He hadn't wanted to put her there, but he'd had no choice. They'd gone over the video of her fight with Arthur in the museum again and had also caught her on a security camera heading toward a stairwell moments before the cameras went out. Hopefully, Callie would get some better information from her mother today.

There was one suspect not on the board, someone he'd left off while the LAPD was in the room.

Now, he reached into a file folder on the table and pulled out his father's photo from fifteen years ago, the one the FBI had had on file ever since he disappeared. He tacked it to the board and stared long and hard at his dad's face, at the blue eyes so similar to his own. A range of extreme emotions ran through him. He honestly didn't know what to think.

"I was wondering if you were going to put him on the list," Damon said, joining him by the board. "That's your father, isn't it? He looks like you, especially in the eyes. You don't really think he's involved, do you?"

"His name has come up several times, but I didn't want to distract the police detectives with his name."

"Understood. Maybe his name has come up because people are talking to you—his son. They might want to rattle you, get you thinking about someone else other than themselves."

"That might be true, but I can't deny that there's a possibility he's involved. He's an art thief. He lives in the shadows, but he has to be funding his survival in some way. Finding him, however, has been impossible to date. He has managed to hide himself away for a very long time."

"You sure you don't want to step back from this, Flynn?"

"No. If my father is involved, I would have no problem arresting him."

"I know you believe that. But thinking it and doing it are two different things. You can't forecast how you would feel in that situation, and that bothers me."

"How I would feel?" he echoed. "The man abandoned me and my mother. You think I want to save him?"

Damon stared back at him. "Like I said, I don't think you can predict how you'll feel if you see him again."

"Well, I can predict it. It will be the same anger that I've always felt. And that's all I want to say about it. You can trust me or not—up to you."

"I'll trust you."

"Good. Not that I should have had to say that," he added pointedly.

Damon frowned. "You're right, Flynn. We've all had conflicts of interests come up, myself included. I actually didn't ask the question because I was worried about the case. I'm more concerned about you, and what the potential personal cost might be."

He could see the sincerity in Damon's eyes. "I appreciate that. I don't know what the cost will be, or even if there will be a cost, but I'm not backing down. I'm not walking away. You can take me off the case, but that won't stop me. I will get to the bottom of this and whatever the truth is, I'll deal with it."

"I get it."

"Then let me get back to work."

"Keep in touch."

As Damon left, Savannah came into the room, a questioning gleam in her eyes. "What was that about? You and Damon were having a heated conversation."

"He's concerned about my father presenting a conflict of interest for me. I'm hoping you're not here to say the same thing."

"I wouldn't dream of it."

"Good. What's up? Something new happen in the last few minutes?"

"We just identified your assailant. His real name is Eddie Norman, twenty-seven years old, born in France to an American mother who was studying abroad at the time. They came to the US when he was three. He grew up in LA, dishonorably discharged from the Army four years ago for assault on a senior officer. Since then, he's been working for a paint crew and, according to one of his coworkers, was flashing new cash last week from what he referred to as a side job."

"Is there a connection to any of our suspects?"

"No, but there is a connection to the art world. Before Eddie was born, his mother, Tracy Norman, was an art student in Paris and worked part-time at a gallery called Maison d'art. The gallery has changed owners twice since then. The new owner has never heard of Tracy Norman or her son. I'm trying to track down the previous owners. I don't know if it means anything, but the art connection tells me this information could be relevant."

"I agree. Keep on it."

"I will. I was going to head over to Layana Vazquez's studio this morning to interview her, but Bree said she'd take that over so I can concentrate on Norman."

"That's great. Thanks for helping me keep all the balls in the air."

"No problem. How is Callie doing?"

"She's better. She's with her mom. I'm heading over there now to see if I can speak to Juliette."

"I hope Juliette can tell you something that will prove her innocence."

"I wouldn't mind that," he admitted.

She gave him a knowing look. "Because you have a thing for her daughter."

"I don't have a thing," he said dismissively.

"That's the real conflict of interest for you, Flynn. It's not your dad; it's Callie."

He didn't bother to address her comment, mostly because he had a feeling she might be right.

CHAPTER NINETEEN

CALLIE WAS WAITING outside her mother's room when Flynn walked down the hallway a little before two. She'd been at the hospital for hours. He'd almost been afraid she'd gotten a car and gone back to her apartment on her own. But, eventually, she'd texted and said her mother had been cleared to speak to him.

As he drew near, she gave him a tired smile, and he had to fight the urge to sweep her up into his arms.

"How did it go?" he asked, digging his hands into his pockets.

"We talked for hours. I did her hair and makeup and tried to cheer her up as best I could. We actually had lunch together in the sunroom at the end of the hall. She ate more than I expected. I didn't realize she'd gotten so thin, which is always a sign that she's bothered about something. Anyway, after lunch, we met with Dr. Clarke, and he said she can speak to you, but only for a short time. She's much better, but I'd really appreciate it if you would go easy on her."

"I will do my best."

"I did tell her that she's a suspect. I had to, Flynn."

He wasn't thrilled about that, but he doubted it would matter. "All right. Did she say anything?"

"Yes. After she argued with Arthur about Palm Springs, which was the conversation you saw on the security footage, she went into the restroom to pull herself together. She ran into Gretchen Vale there. My mom was suspicious of all the phone calls between Arthur and Gretchen, so she asked Gretchen about them. Gretchen replied that she was buying art for Arthur, and that it was complicated. But then she paused and told my mom that she might want to stop asking questions, because there was a good chance she wouldn't like the answers."

"That's cryptic, which is consistent with Gretchen. She seems to like to be deliberately vague."

"My mom thought about it and got angry. She decided to follow up with Gretchen, so she went looking for her. That's why she wasn't in the Grand Hall when the event began. She checked out the Seville Room because Victoria had mentioned Gretchen was headed that way, but she wasn't there. When my mom returned to the hall, she heard the screams and saw Arthur on the floor." She paused. "So that explains where she was when the cameras were off and Arthur was pushed over the railing. She wasn't anywhere near the fourth floor."

"All right. Anything else?"

She frowned. "You still don't believe her, Flynn?"

He could see the disappointment in her eyes. "I didn't say I didn't believe her. I'm processing."

"I wish you'd process with a smile on your face."

"Sorry. Did she say anything else?"

"I mentioned Layana's name to her, and she had no reaction beyond wondering why I was asking her about the artist who did Arthur's portrait. I don't think she ever saw the email. She was jealous of Gretchen, not of Layana. Anyway, that's pretty much it. Given that I've already told you everything, maybe you don't need to talk to her?" she asked hopefully.

"I have to play this out, Callie. It's not that I don't trust you."

"I am being honest, Flynn."

"I understand. It's better that it's me than anyone else, right?" he asked lightly.

"I'll answer that after you're done speaking to her."

When they entered the room, he saw Juliette sitting in a chair by the window, wearing a robe over her nightgown with fuzzy slippers on her feet. When she turned her gaze on him, he was actually surprised at how good she looked. Her hair was brushed and there was a hint of pink on her lips and blush on her cheeks. However, she still had a fragile air about her, as if a good strong wind might knock her out of that chair.

"Mom, this is Agent MacKenzie," Callie said. "You met him on Friday night."

"Arthur's old friend," Juliette said. "And Olivia's boyfriend."

"That's me." He took the seat across from Juliette as Callie perched on the end of the bed. "How are you feeling, Mrs. Corbyn?"

"I'm tired and sad—angry." She shrugged. "So many emotions."

"I'm sure they're overwhelming."

"You must think I'm very weak, falling apart the way I did."

"I think you suffered a tragic loss."

"I loved Arthur so much. When we met, it was like the clouds parted, and the warm sun hit me right in the face. I felt awake and alive again. He was an amazing man. He made me feel very cherished…at least, in the beginning. The last few weeks, Arthur was stressed. He couldn't sleep. He worked late. He was always on the phone. He kept saying he needed to go down to Palm Springs, so he could breathe that warm desert air and take a break from the madness of LA."

"Did you know about the room off the guest bedroom downstairs?" he asked, not wanting to waste too much time in case Juliette suddenly decided not to talk.

"What room? The bathroom?"

"No, it was through the closet in the downstairs guest room at the end of the hall. Callie said Arthur used to take calls in there."

"Yes, he did. We didn't always get reception in the rest of the house."

"Well, Callie and I discovered a secret room off that guest bedroom."

"A secret room?" she echoed, bewilderment in her eyes. "I don't understand." She looked at her daughter. "What is he talking about, Callie?"

"Arthur had created a room for art," Callie said. "It was downstairs, in a basement, but it could only be accessed through a hidden panel in the closet wall. Did he ever talk to you about wanting to keep his paintings in a safer location?"

"No. He didn't even want to take his more valuable paintings down there. He said it wasn't safe because we weren't there all the time. He also thought art should be appreciated, not sealed away in some bank vault. I can't believe he would set up a secret room to hide it all away. But maybe that's why he wanted to go down there so often. I had the idea that he might be using the house for an affair with that Gretchen woman. But maybe he really was just buying art."

"Did Arthur ever tell you that he thought someone was watching him?" he asked.

She shook her head, more confusion in her eyes. "No. He never said that. Why? Did Arthur tell you that?"

"He did. He asked me to meet him at the museum Friday night. He said he needed my help, but I never heard what he needed. I think whatever he was worried about was what got him killed."

Juliette stared back at him. "I know that he was upset with that young painter, Marcus Vitelli. Marcus was at the museum last week when Arthur was picking me up. They ran into each other in the hall, and Arthur told Marcus that he wasn't going to continue to support Marcus's work if he didn't finish his painting. Marcus said he was having trouble. He was blocked. Arthur told him real artists paint through the block and their emotions make their work better. Arthur could be impatient at times, especially when he thought someone was just being lazy. Marcus did not appreciate his comments."

"Did anyone else hear this conversation?"

"Do you think I'm making it up?"

"I don't. I just like to have multiple witnesses to corroborate stories. It helps build a case."

"You don't think Marcus killed him, do you?" Juliette asked. "I can't imagine that. Even though Arthur was annoyed with him, he was willing to buy his work."

"I understand."

"I think Victoria might have heard part of their conversation," Juliette continued. "She came into the hall as they were finishing their discussion. I know she told Arthur at some point that Marcus had a great talent and it needed to be nurtured. He couldn't produce on demand. He was a true artist."

"Did Arthur and Marcus talk again after that?" he queried."

"Yes, a few days later. Arthur told me that Marcus was painting again. He was happy about that, and I was relieved, because Victoria is my boss and Arthur is my husband. I didn't want anything to be awkward between the three of us, and I knew Victoria had taken Marcus under her wing." Juliette took a breath, glancing at her daughter, then back at him. "Callie says that I'm a suspect. But I didn't kill Arthur. I loved my husband. And our argument was not that big of a deal. It was just about a trip. I'm not crazy. I'm not a violent person. I wish you could see that."

He could see that Juliette was starting to get agitated.

Callie stood up, obviously thinking the same thing. "I think that's enough, Flynn," she said. "You can talk to my mother again tomorrow. She needs to rest now."

"I am tired," Juliette said. "But I do want to help you find Arthur's killer."

He nodded, thinking that Juliette was nowhere near as easy to read as her daughter. She wavered between weak fragility and stubborn anger. *How far would she have gone if she thought her husband was having an affair?*

And he couldn't forget that Juliette couldn't seem to remember trying to throw herself off the balcony. Maybe she'd blocked out what she'd done to Arthur, too.

Not that he wanted her to be guilty. He didn't. That would hurt Callie, and that's the last thing he wanted. He got to his feet, giving them both a smile. "You should rest," he said. "We'll talk again another time."

"Thank you for being understanding." Juliette's gaze sharpened as it moved between him and Callie. "I must say, you and my daughter seem very friendly. She called you by your first name."

"I've been trying to help Flynn find Arthur's killer, Mom. So that no one has to suspect you for something you didn't do," Callie explained.

"You're always fighting for me," Juliette said, giving her daughter a loving smile. She looked back at Flynn. "Callie is special."

"I think so, too," he agreed, not just because he was talking to her mother, but because he believed it.

"She has taken care of me since she was a little girl," Juliette added. "Whenever life got to be too much, Callie was there. Just like she's here now."

He was glad that Juliette didn't seem to blame Callie for her hospitalization.

"I'll always be here for you, Mom," Callie promised.

"Thank you for your time, Mrs. Corbyn."

"I think you should call me Juliette. After all, you were friends with Arthur, and now you're friends with my daughter."

"Juliette," he said with a nod.

"Mom, I'll call you later and I'll be by tomorrow morning." Callie gave her mom a hug and a kiss on the cheek and then they walked out of the room.

They didn't speak until they had left the hospital. Callie stopped on the sidewalk to take a deep breath. "I hate being in there. I can understand why my mother does, too."

"She seems to be doing well. Are you relieved?"

"Yes and no. I want her to be better, of course, but now she's going to be grilled. Do you still think she's a suspect?"

"I don't want to."

"That's not a good answer," she said, disappointment in her eyes.

"I'd like to go by the museum and speak to Victoria. Maybe she can give us her take on whatever conversation took place between Arthur and Marcus."

"That's a great idea. I'll go with you. Although, it's going to feel weird to be there again, to see the spot where Arthur died."

"I can do it on my own."

"No. I'm going with you, Flynn. I can handle myself. You don't have to worry. I won't fall apart."

"I'm not worried about that. I know how strong you are. I just think you might need a break. I'm sure you've had a rough day."

"Well, we could stop for ice cream on the way. We never did do that yesterday."

"We can do that."

Her sweet smile made him realize that he wanted to give her anything her heart desired. Savannah was right. Callie was a bigger conflict of interest than Arthur or his father. Because he wanted her to be happy. He was starting to want that more than just about anything.

They went to an ice cream parlor a few blocks from the museum, and Callie instantly felt better after she took her first bite of her double scoop of chocolate and mint chip ice cream. Flynn had, of course, felt compelled to outdo her, ordering three scoops with a mix of cookie dough, strawberry, and vanilla ice cream. Apparently, he was not a chocolate fan.

For the twenty minutes it took to eat their ice cream, she felt astonishingly happy. She didn't know what it was about Flynn, because even in the middle of everything that was going on, he could make her laugh. And she could bring out his sexy grin pretty easily, too. There were sparks going off at an amazing rate, but they somehow managed to keep the small table between them.

They didn't talk about the case at all, just chatted about food favorites and people-watched, as they ate their waffle cones down to the last bite.

And then their break was over. As they drove to the museum, the mood between them grew more somber, and when they parked in the lot and made their way through the front doors, her steps slowed.

She was actually a little surprised to see that the museum was open to the public only three days after Arthur's death, but there were people inside, some of them clustered in the grand hall, probably near the spot where Arthur had died.

It turned her stomach to think that some visitors might have come to the museum out of a macabre interest in Arthur's murder rather than their love of art.

Flynn didn't let her linger, his firm hand on the small of her back propelling her toward the hallway leading to the executive offices.

Elaine Monroe, Victoria Waltham's admin, sat at a desk in a small lobby area. Elaine was one of her mom's favorite people, because she was always willing to help anyone out, even if it wasn't technically her job. She was a widow in her late fifties and had been working at the museum for almost two years.

"Callie, hello. How are you?" Elaine asked.

"I'm hanging in there."

"I've been thinking about your mom. We all have," she added, as Shari Watkins, the educational director, stepped out of her office. Shari handled the kids' events at the museum and worked closely with her mom. At twenty-eight, she had an abundance of energy and lots of creative ideas, something her mom loved and respected.

"How is Juliette?" Shari asked, concern in her gaze.

"She's dealing with everything as best she can."

"It felt horrible to come to work this morning," Shari said. "There's a terrible pall over this place. I wish we could have stayed closed for a few more days."

"I was a little surprised the museum reopened so quickly," she admitted.

"Victoria said the board wanted people to be allowed to mourn in the place where Judge Corbyn died," Shari explained.

"I think they also wanted to move past it as quickly as possible," Elaine interjected, a more cynical note in her voice. "Not that they want to diminish the tragedy."

She nodded. "That makes sense. Is Victoria in? We need to speak to her. This is Agent Flynn MacKenzie with the FBI."

"Victoria is in a meeting," Elaine replied. "She should be done shortly if you can wait. I'm sure she wants to talk to you both as well."

"Okay. We're going to stop into my mom's office in the meantime. She wanted me to pick up a few of her personal things. Can you let us know when Victoria is free?"

"Of course."

She led Flynn down the hall, turning right into another corridor where her mom's office was located. In this wing, there were also offices belonging to three museum curators as well as the public relations director. At the far end was the restoration department.

She was just about to open her mother's door when a woman came out of the restroom down the hall. Her waist-length, black hair stopped Callie in her tracks. The woman lifted her gaze, which suddenly filled with alarm.

"Layana," Callie said sharply, her pulse jumping at the sight of Arthur's lover. "What are you doing here?"

"I—I have a meeting."

Layana looked more put together than she had on Sunday, but her face was still pale and there were dark shadows under her eyes.

"Excuse me," Layana said, as she moved to pass them.

"Wait," Flynn ordered.

Layana paused at his commanding tone.

"I'm Agent MacKenzie with the FBI. I'd like to have a word with you, Ms. Vazquez."

"I don't have anything to say. I told Agent Adams that when I spoke to her at my studio an hour ago. I don't understand why you're harassing me."

"This will only take a minute," Flynn said, ignoring her protest. He waved Layana toward her mother's office, and Callie moved inside quickly, Layana reluctantly following.

She stopped in the middle of the room, her arms folded across her chest, her expression defiant. "What do you want?" she asked.

"I understand you were having an affair with Judge Corbyn," Flynn said.

"Yes, but I didn't kill him," Layana replied. "I loved him. You should be talking to Juliette. She's the one who's crazy. She snapped when she found out about us. I told her daughter that yesterday."

Callie wanted to defend her mother, but she could see the warning light in Flynn's eyes, so she turned away, wandering over to the window, drawing deep, calming breaths.

"Where were you Friday night?" Flynn asked.

"I was at home."

"Anyone with you?"

"No. I was alone. I already told the agent this."

"When did you find out Judge Corbyn had died?"

Callie turned back around at that question, wondering at her answer.

"A friend called me to let me know," Layana said.

"Who was the friend?"

"It doesn't matter."

"It matters. Answer the question."

"I don't have to talk to you."

"Actually, you do, and I'd be happy to have you come down to our office if you'd rather be questioned there."

Layana frowned. "It was Kyle Logan."

"What did he say?" Flynn asked.

"He said someone killed Arthur."

"What time was this?"

"I don't remember."

"Try a little harder."

"Probably about nine. He was still at the museum. He said everyone was being questioned."

"So, he called you very soon after Arthur's death. Did he know you were having an affair?"

"He knew that I cared about Arthur. That's all."

Callie didn't believe her, and she didn't think Flynn did, either. If this Kyle Logan knew about the affair, then maybe he knew other stuff, too.

"I have to go. I have a meeting," Layana said. "If you want to talk to me again, you can talk to my lawyer."

"Who's your lawyer?"

"I'll find one," Layana said, moving past Flynn.

"What do you think?" she asked as Layana left the office.

"She's cagey, but whether that's because she was sleeping with a married man, or she's guilty of something worse...who knows?"

"Who's Kyle Logan?"

"He runs a gallery in New York. He took it over for his father. I actually met him years ago at a trade show."

"Have you interviewed him? I haven't heard his name mentioned before."

"He was interviewed after the event. I have not followed up. I haven't had a reason to—until now." As his gaze moved around the office, he added, "Anything look out of place or different in here?"

She followed his gaze. The space was small and crowded with a desk in the center, two filing cabinets on one side and a table laden with boxes of giveaway items that her mother used for special events. On the desk next to her mom's computer was a pile of flyers for the upcoming event on Valentine's Day, an artist's celebration of love, as well as two framed photographs: one of Arthur and her mother, and the other of her mother and herself.

As she walked around the desk, she thought things looked a little messier than usual. A few of the drawers were partly ajar, but since the room had been searched by various people, that was probably to be expected.

Flynn riffled through the boxes on the table while she looked through the drawers, although she didn't know what she was looking for.

"Everything is the same as the last time I was here," she said, drawing his gaze to hers. "I don't know what you think might be here."

"Probably nothing. We've already accessed your mother's work computer, thanks to cooperation from Victoria and the owner of the museum. There was nothing noteworthy in Juliette's work emails, and you've gone through her personal emails, so that was covered."

She frowned. "Victoria gave you permission to go through my mom's computer?"

"Yes. Why wouldn't she?"

"It seems like an invasion of privacy."

"The computer is owned by the museum, not your mother. But there's nothing to be angry about. There wasn't anything there."

"I'm worried because this is my mom's job, and if they think she's a suspect in Arthur's murder, they might fire her. And if she loses her job, too…" She couldn't even think of what that would do to her mom.

"I understand your concern, but it was a necessary step and as soon as we find the real killer, your mother will be in the clear. Since she won't be returning to work for probably at least another week, we have some time."

"I hope so." She picked up the photo of her mother and Arthur, staring at his features for a long minute. He was smiling in the picture, his arms around her mom, and they looked happy. "This was taken on their wedding day. It's difficult to believe that was only a little over a year ago. I was worried about their whirl-wind romance. I thought things were moving way too fast, but I was hoping for the best. I wanted Arthur to love my mom, to always be there for her, but my suspicions were right. I wish they'd been wrong. I wish Arthur had been the man my mom thought he was."

"I wish he'd been that man, too," Flynn said heavily, reminding her that he, too, felt betrayed by Arthur, not because of Arthur's affair with Layana, but because he'd been dealing in stolen art.

"I don't know what my mom will do when she finds out the extent of Arthur's crimes," she muttered. "I foresee a lot of bad days ahead."

"You'll help her get through them—one day at a time," he said pragmatically.

"It feels exhausting to think about."

"Then don't think about it. She won't find out today, so you can push that worry off for at least twenty-four hours."

"Good point." She paused as Victoria entered the room, looking as stylish and beautiful as ever in a body-con black dress that hugged her figure and set off her blonde hair.

"Callie, Agent MacKenzie, I understand you want to speak to me. How is Juliette?" Victoria asked.

"She's dealing with everything," Callie replied.

"I'd love to help. Juliette is more than an employee; she's my friend. And I know how much she adored Arthur. I can't imagine how she's handling this loss. I hope you'll tell her not to worry about her job here. It will be waiting for her when she's ready to return."

"She'll be happy to hear that."

Victoria's gaze turned to Flynn. "Are you making progress toward finding Arthur's killer?"

"We are, but I wanted to ask you a few questions, if you have time."

"I'm happy to make the time. What do you need?"

"First of all, do you know Layana Vazquez?"

"Yes. She's a talented artist, and she did Arthur's portrait. Why do you ask?"

At Victoria's question, Callie stiffened. *Did she want Flynn to reveal Arthur's affair with Layana to her mother's boss? On the other hand, would it be possible to keep it a secret as the investigation continued?*

Flynn shot her a quick, cautioning look, as if to tell her not to jump in. Then he said, "Were Layana and Arthur having a personal relationship?"

"I think Layana had a bit of a crush on Arthur, but I don't know that she or he ever acted on it," Victoria said carefully. "Why?"

Flynn ignored her question. "What about Gretchen Vale? Did Arthur ever speak to you about his relationship with Gretchen?"

"He sometimes bought paintings from Gretchen and Stephen. I know they were friends."

"Juliette was looking for Gretchen right before the exhibition began," Flynn continued. "She mentioned that you told her Gretchen was in the Seville Room."

"Yes. Gretchen wanted to see a sculpture that we had on loan from the British Museum. I must say that Juliette seemed rather upset in that moment and angry with Gretchen about something. She wanted to speak to her right away. I didn't pay much attention, because I was about to get on the stage." She paused, giving Flynn a thoughtful look. "It sounds like you think Arthur was having an affair and that his murder was a crime of passion."

"We're considering all the options," Flynn said vaguely. "Including Marcus Vitelli's relationship with Arthur."

"I told you the other day that they were in communication because Arthur was supporting Marcus's work and was impatient to get his next painting. What more is there to know? If Arthur was hard on Marcus, it was only because he cared about his talent. Marcus knew that. There was no bad blood between them."

"Juliette mentioned they had an argument right here in the hall only a few weeks ago."

"Yes, but Arthur's comments to Marcus fired him up, and he got back to work. Arthur was pleased about that."

"Interesting that you know so much about their relationship. Why is that?"

Was it her imagination or did Victoria hesitate?

"I'm his friend and his mentor," Victoria answered. "I believe in Marcus's talent. I've helped him make connections with galleries and collectors, because he's an amazing artist. However, I shouldn't speak for Marcus. You should talk to him again if you have more concerns. Perhaps there was something going on that I didn't know."

"All right. I'm curious about something else," Flynn continued. "When was the exhibition for Gerard's work set up?"

"Three months ago. It was actually Arthur's idea." She stopped abruptly. "I didn't think about that until just this second. But Arthur suggested it to Juliette, who brought it to me. The museum is a big fan of Gerard's, so, of course, we were happy to host the event. Gerard hadn't done any shows in about eight years. It was quite a coup for the museum to have him, and all that was due to Arthur's relationship with him." Victoria glanced down at her watch. "I hate to cut this short, but I have another meeting. Is there anything else? Or perhaps we can speak again later?"

"Later is fine. Thanks," Flynn said.

"You're more than welcome." Victoria gave her a sympathetic smile. "Please tell your mom I'm just a phone call away, Callie. Whatever she needs. She's such a sweet person, and I know how much she adored Arthur. She must feel terribly lost."

"I'll let her know," she replied.

"Also..." Victoria stopped, her gaze focused on Flynn. "Perhaps we should step outside for a moment."

Callie frowned, wondering why Victoria suddenly needed to speak to Flynn alone.

She wanted Flynn to tell her she could say whatever she needed to say in front of her, but he simply gave a nod and followed her into the hall, closing the door behind him.

Callie moved to the door, opening it slightly, more than a little curious to hear what was happening. She could see that Flynn and Victoria had moved down the hall. Victoria's back was to her, and she thought Flynn could see her, but he didn't seem to care.

"What's this about?" he asked.

"I mentioned to you the other day that I heard your father might be back in the States."

"You said Arthur told you that."

"Well, his name came up again in a conversation I had with Gerard yesterday. Gerard mentioned that your father was a big fan of Paulette Martine and that her most famous painting, *Lady in the Wood,* was stolen from the Kentwell Museum in Boston last week. He mused that perhaps your dad was back in the business of stealing art."

Callie saw the tension tighten Flynn's lips. *Was his father involved?* She couldn't imagine how he would deal with that, especially if his father had killed Arthur, who had been a second father to him.

How horrible would that be?

She was starting to worry about him as much as she was worrying about her mother. But it wasn't her job to protect Flynn, and he'd probably think she was crazy for even thinking she should try.

"Thanks for sharing that," Flynn told Victoria, his tone showing no emotion.

"I thought you should know."

As Victoria left, Flynn came back down the hall. "You heard?"

"Yes. Are you okay, Flynn?"

His hard gaze met hers. "I'm fine."

"You don't look fine."

"Well, I am. Are you ready to go?"

"Absolutely," she said, eager to leave. She needed sunshine and air and distance from this place. She didn't know how her mother was ever going to come back here to work. She would never be able to forget what had happened.

They walked in silence back to the car. As they fastened their seat belts, she said, "What are you thinking about?"

"Everything."

"It was weird that Layana was there."

"Was it? She's an artist at a museum—not that weird."

"I guess not, but her lover died there a few days ago."

"Maybe that's why she came."

"It was also strange that Arthur set up the event that led to his death. That's ironic, isn't it? It almost makes me wonder if Gerard had some part in this. It seems like getting the show to happen could have been part of someone's evil, twisted plan. Plus, Victoria mentions your father again, after a conversation with Gerard. Doesn't it seem like they want you to start looking at your dad?"

"It does," he murmured, glancing over at her. "There's a lot to consider."

"There definitely is," she agreed.

He started the car and pulled out of the lot. They made their way toward the steep, curving road that would take them down to the freeway. They had only made their way around the first curve when the roar of an engine behind them startled her. She turned around in her seat as Flynn checked the rearview mirror.

There was a dark-green museum van bearing down upon them at a ridiculously high rate of speed.

Flynn swore as he sped up.

Callie grabbed the armrest, fear running through her. They were on a narrow winding road with steep drops on her side of the car. Only a small rail provided a buffer from the canyon.

"Hang on," Flynn said tersely as he maneuvered the car around a tight curve.

"Is he trying to run us off the road?" she yelled in panic.

Flynn didn't answer, and she didn't need him to. It was very clear what was happening. She said a silent prayer as the van bumped them from behind, and they bounced off the guard rail. Her heart was beating so hard and fast it was all she could hear besides the deadly screech of tires.

CHAPTER TWENTY

THE VAN HIT THEM AGAIN. Callie bounced forward, the seat belt preventing her from hitting the dashboard, but just barely. Her breath froze in her chest as she saw another narrow turn coming up. If they didn't make the curve, they would fly right off the side of the road.

Flynn increased their speed. She squeezed her eyes shut, anticipating the car crashing through the rail, flying down the hill, turning over and over. It was so real she could see it in her head, but Flynn wasn't going out without a fight. He took the next turn on two wheels, almost throwing her into him.

Her eyes jerked open just in time to see them clear the last curve, and then it was a straight shot to the exit. Once they passed through the gates, they turned right on the frontage road. The van turned left, going in the other direction.

"We made it," Flynn said, a triumphant light in his eyes.

"I don't know how," she said in amazement, as he drove onto the freeway, taking them back down to a reasonable rate of speed. Her heart was beating so fast, she was still gasping for breath.

"Take it easy," he said. "Slow, deep breaths."

"I—I don't know if I can."

"You can do it, Callie. Breathe in—hold—breathe out."

For the next few minutes, he talked her through her breathing. Finally, her heart began to slow down.

"I'm okay now. I don't know how you can be so calm or how you can drive so well."

"I've had a little training, and *little* is an understatement."

"Who do you think was trying to run us off the road? It looked like one of the vans the museum uses."

"It was. I never caught the license plate, but the museum should be able to tell us who has access to their vans."

Her mind raced back to the museum, to the people they'd met with: Layana, Victoria, Elaine Monroe and Shari Watkins. *But who else had been there that they hadn't seen?* There were probably at least twenty-five to thirty more employees who had been somewhere in the building, not to mention the visitors. There could have been a hundred people or more on the grounds, but they wouldn't have had access to a museum van; it had to be an employee who was driving. She wanted to believe that a security camera had caught the image of the driver, but so far whoever they were chasing was very good at staying out of sight.

It took them about thirty minutes to get back to Flynn's townhouse, and it was dusk by the time they pulled into his garage at half past six.

She followed him into the townhouse, waiting by the garage door, as he did a cursory sweep of his home and then waved her inside. They went into the kitchen/family room, with Flynn heading straight for the wet bar.

"Do you want a drink?" he asked.

"Absolutely," she said without hesitation.

"Scotch okay?"

"Anything with a kick to it."

He poured Scotch into two small tumbler glasses and handed her one.

She took a sip, the liquid burning a fiery path down her throat. Along with that blast of heat came a feeling of relief. "That's better. My pulse is still too fast." She sat down at the kitchen table.

Flynn smiled. "It will slow down. I need to call the museum."

"Can you put it on speaker? It will save you from having to answer my questions as soon as you hang up."

"You got it." He set down his glass and picked up his phone. After connecting with the museum, he asked to speak to the director of security, Rand Bentley. A moment later, Rand's voice came over the phone.

"Agent MacKenzie, what can I do for you?"

"I was just at the museum with Callie Harper. When we left, someone driving a museum van tried to run us off the road. I need to know who that was."

"Are you serious?" Rand asked.

"You know I am."

"Hold on. Let me check with the security desk."

As they waited, Flynn picked up his glass of Scotch and took another draught.

Callie sipped her drink as well, silently hoping that for once they'd get something other than a vague response.

A moment later, Rand came back onto the line. "Greg Barkley checked out a van thirty minutes ago. He has not yet returned to the museum."

"What can you tell me about him?"

"One second." Rand took another minute and then said, "He's twenty-six years old and has been employed as a driver at the museum for the past year. He mainly transports pieces between the museum and the airport or the Port of Los Angeles. He lives in Culver City. His last job was driving for Harriman Art Couriers in Beverly Hills."

"I'll take his home address." Flynn jotted down the street and number, then added, "I'll need you to detain him if and when he comes back to the museum."

"Will do."

Flynn ended the call and punched in another number. "Wyatt, it's Flynn. Are you still at the office?"

"Just left. What's up?"

"Someone tried to run Callie and me off the road as we were leaving the Piquard Museum. Security said a driver by the name of

Greg Barkley signed out the van, but he hasn't returned. I have a home address for him. I'd go there myself, but—"

"You need to stay close to Callie," Wyatt said. "I'm on it."

"Take someone with you."

"Will do."

Flynn relayed the address. "Let me know what you find out."

As he set down the phone, Flynn finished his drink and set down the glass. "Wyatt will check out Barkley's house, but my gut tells me that the driver will not be returning."

"Wouldn't that mean he'd be giving up his job, his home? How does he just vanish so quickly? This wasn't planned out. Someone saw us at the museum and wanted to get rid of us. But we were only there an hour or so."

"It was an impulsive decision," he agreed. "I don't think Barkley is the one who made the decision."

"But he's once again tied to art—not only to the museum, but also that other courier service."

Flynn nodded, picking up his phone to send a text.

"Who are you contacting now?"

"Savannah. I'll see what she can dig up on Harriman Art Couriers."

"Do you need to go into the office?" Even as she asked the question, she was hoping he would say no, because her nerves were rattled and she didn't want to be alone.

"No, we'll stay put for the moment."

She took another sip of scotch, relieved by his answer. "Do you think someone paid this man to run us off the road? Or was he operating on his own? He works at the museum. He could have been involved in Arthur's murder. Maybe he saw us there and took it upon himself to try to get rid of us."

"It's possible. This was a good thing."

"Are you serious?" she asked, bewildered by his words. "We could have died. You have no idea the visions of smoke and flames going on in my head."

He smiled. "I was not letting us go over that rail. Since we survived, the good news is that we have another lead to follow. Our perpetrator is getting nervous, making impulsive decisions. Bad decisions can lead to big mistakes. Barkley could be our key to this whole puzzle."

"If he lives. What if he ends up like the guy at the hotel?"

"That would not be good."

She shook her head in bemusement. "I can't believe we're talking so cavalierly about people dying." She got up from the table, feeling too filled with adrenaline to just sit.

"Sorry. I sometimes forget that you're not used to this."

"No, I'm not. What's next, Flynn?"

"We'll wait to see what my team comes up with."

"Waiting doesn't sound very proactive. You don't like it either," she said, noting his nervous energy as he went to pour himself another drink. "You want to be the one kicking down doors and chasing down leads instead of babysitting me."

He set down the bottle and moved across the room to her. He put his hands on her shoulders. "This is exactly where I want to be and where I need to be. Keeping you safe is the most important thing in the world."

She was incredibly touched by his words. "I—I don't know what to say."

"Well, that might be a first," he said lightly.

"You're a nice guy, Flynn."

He winced. "Nice? Ouch."

"It's not a bad thing," she said with a laugh.

"When a woman tells you you're nice, it's usually part of the kiss-off."

"It's not that now."

"Are you sure?"

His hands tightened on her shoulders, and she had a feeling his question went much deeper than what she'd just said. She licked her lips, feeling not only grateful to be alive but also reckless and needy.

Flynn must have seen something in her expression, because desire flared in his beautiful blue eyes. "Callie?"

"You turned me down last night, Flynn."

"You had a concussion."

"I don't anymore."

"We're trying to slow your heart down, not speed it up."

"What if I don't want to slow it down?"

"It's natural to want to blow off steam, but there's always a morning after, Callie. I don't think you're ready for that."

"You don't need to make decisions for me, Flynn. And the way things are going, who knows if we'll even make it to morning?"

"You're safe here. You're safe with me. I will not let anything happen to you."

She had never had someone so determined to protect her. It was mind-blowing and heartwarming and so damned sexy. "Flynn, I don't want to just blow off some steam; I want to seize the moment. The last few days have shown me how fragile and short life can be. I've spent too long putting off things I want, telling myself there will be a better time, a better place. I don't want to do that anymore. I want to live. I want to be happy. I want to be with you. Please don't say no again."

His eyes sparkled as he moved his hands through her hair, cradling her head, pulling her close. "Last chance."

"I don't need a last chance. I need you. I want to see where this can go."

"Then let's find out."

He pushed her back against the wall and took possession of her mouth in a desire-fueled hunger that matched her own. She loved being pressed between Flynn and the wall. She could feel every hard angle of his body, and tingles of anticipation shot through her body, from her head to her toes.

Flynn had made her feel safe, but now he made her feel wild and free to be whoever she wanted to be. No responsibility. No worry about tomorrow. No care for anyone else but Flynn and herself. It was just the two of them on an island of desire, and she opened her mouth to his, tasting the fire on his lips, the Scotch on his tongue. It was a heady feeling. Her body felt weightless. Her head was spinning. And then Flynn's hands slid under her sweater, his hot fingers sending shivers down her spine.

Impatient to touch him, she pulled his shirt up, sliding her hands up his back, and around to his chest, her fingers sliding lower. He groaned with pleasure against her mouth.

"We have to slow down," he said roughly.

"Not now. I want to go fast. I want to fly."

His blue eyes darkened as he kissed her again and then swung her back around so quickly she got dizzy.

"Bedroom," he muttered, kissing her down the hall until they reached his room.

"Your bed isn't made," she said, smiling at the tangled covers.

"I'm glad I didn't bother now," he replied with a grin.

"Me, too." As she leaned forward to kiss him again, he pulled slightly back.

"Hold on. Before we both lose our minds, I need to get a condom." As he moved toward the adjoining bathroom, he said, "Don't move."

She had no intention of moving or leaving. She was exactly where she wanted to be. She pulled off her shirt and slid down her jeans, standing next to his bed in her mismatched white lacy bra and pink panties.

Flynn rushed back into the room, his gaze widening as it raked her body. He dropped two condoms on the nightstand and then ripped his shirt over his head as he moved back to her. His chest was broad, tan, and muscled.

"You're...wow..." she murmured. "I had no idea your clothes were hiding this."

"I was going to say the same thing about you," he said with a sexy grin. He kicked off his jeans, taking his black briefs down at the same time.

She swallowed hard. "I've run out of adjectives."

"I don't need adjectives, babe. I need you. You took my breath away the first minute I saw you, before I knew your name."

"That can't be true," she said automatically, but she wanted to believe him. She wanted to linger in the admiration of his gaze.

"I told you I wouldn't lie to you, Callie. I meant it."

"I meant it, too." She opened her bra and let it slip over her shoulders.

And then his hands were on her breasts, his thumbs sliding across her nipples, sending jolts of desire down her body. He kissed her again, his tongue sliding deep into her mouth as his fingers teased her nipples into hard, needy points. And then he moved his mouth across her cheek, his tongue swirling around the curve of her ear, making her shiver once more.

He licked a path of heat down the side of her neck, taking a tremendously long time to get to where she wanted him to go. Finally, his mouth settled on her breast, and she ran her hands through his thick blond hair, feeling a little weak from the overwhelming rush of desire. "I feel like I could fall," she said.

He lifted his head, meeting her gaze. "I'll catch you."

She believed him in a way she'd never believed anyone else. After her father had died, there had never been anyone to catch her. She'd always had to be in control.

"You can let go," he said, his gaze meeting hers. "You can hang on to me."

"I want you to let go, too."

"Oh, trust me, that won't be a problem." His hands slid to her panties, sliding them down her legs, his fingers slipping into her heat, making her mindless with pleasure.

They moved onto the bed together, and as he covered her body with his, she sighed with happy joy as they came together—skin-to-skin, mouth-to-mouth—her legs wrapping around his, his hardness pressing against her softness. They rolled around in the tangled covers, touching, tasting, teasing, tormenting until the intense heat sent her flying in exactly the way she'd wanted.

And Flynn caught her, just like he'd promised, his arms wrapping around her as they floated back down to earth.

CHAPTER TWENTY-ONE

THEY MADE LOVE TWICE, grabbed a late-night snack around midnight, and then Flynn held Callie in his arms as she slept, as the moon moved low in the sky and slivers of early morning sunlight filled the bedroom. He'd drifted off for a bit himself, but now he found himself wanting her again.

Her body fit perfectly with his. Even now, he could feel their hearts beating in sync. He felt connected to her in every possible way. It was unlike anything he'd ever experienced. It wasn't just sex…it was more. He didn't want to sleep, because he didn't want to miss a second of this, and he felt almost desperate to make the night last as long as possible, to keep the sun from coming up.

He didn't know what today would bring, but he wasn't ready to find out. He wanted to stay in this bed forever, spend as much time as he could getting to know Callie, learning every ticklish spot, every touch that made her sigh. He liked the catch in her breath when he kissed her breasts, the way she said his name when she was mindless with desire, as if only he could make her feel the way she did.

It wasn't one-sided, either. Callie had unlocked something inside him, something he'd put away a very long time ago. It was probably after Olivia died. The pain of losing her coming so closely after his father's betrayal had been too much for him to shoulder. He'd put up a wall and he had never let anyone get past that wall. Until now…

Callie had found her way into his heart without him even realizing it. The off-the-charts chemistry and sex was amazing, but it was the emotional connection that was surprising and, if he was honest, a little terrifying.

Callie shifted in his arms, giving a sleepy smile. "Are you awake? What time is it?"

"Almost seven."

"Too early to get up," she said, snuggling in closer to him, her arm moving around his waist. "I like this, Flynn."

"So do I."

"Last night was pretty spectacular."

"That's a good way to describe it."

"What are you thinking about?" she asked, giving him a thoughtful look.

"Not much."

"We're being honest with each other, remember?"

"Fine. I was thinking about you."

"That's good, because I was dreaming about you," she said. "You were doing things to me that were really amazing."

He laughed. "No need to dream, babe. I'm right here. And I am ready to fulfill every fantasy."

"That might take a long time."

"Who cares?"

She smiled. "I wish I could say not me. I wish we could stay right here and not have to deal with anything else today."

"We have a little time before we have to get up."

"But then we have to get up," she said with a sigh. "And deal with my mom, Arthur's estate, the search for his killer, keeping ourselves alive. At some point, I need to go back to work, too."

"You're making me tired, Callie. Let's go back to your fantasies." As he finished speaking, his stomach gave a noisy rumble.

She laughed. "I think you need food, not fantasy."

"Maybe I could have both. You and a little maple syrup…"

Her cheeks flushed. "That sounds…sticky."

He grinned. "It could be worth it."

"Why don't I make you breakfast instead? It's my turn."

"I don't want you to have to cook."

"Have to cook? I love to cook." She slipped out of his arms, and he felt an instant chill. "Hey, you don't have to get up right now."

She rolled out of bed, taking the top sheet with her, as she draped it around her beautiful naked body. "I'm hungry, too."

"You don't need to cover up," he told her. "I've already seen everything."

"I know, but it's cold."

"My robe is hanging on the back of the bathroom door."

She moved into the bathroom, returning a moment later wearing his gray fleece robe that hung down to her ankles.

"Do you want some help with breakfast?" he asked, loving the look of her well-kissed lips, her sparkling brown eyes and her tangled, silky brown hair. "Or a better idea—come back to bed."

"It's so tempting, Flynn, but I'm going to make you a meal. You rest. You've earned it."

He laughed. "I wouldn't mind earning it again."

"We'll see," she said with a saucy smile as she left the bedroom.

Despite the fact that she'd told him to rest, he knew he wasn't going back to sleep. Instead, he headed into the bathroom to shower and shave. Afterward, he threw on black jeans and a blue knit shirt and moved into the kitchen.

Callie was at the stove, and he immediately crossed the room to kiss her as well as to sneak a peek at what she was cooking.

"What have we got here?" he asked.

"Scrambled egg burritos. I found eggs, tortillas, cheese, salsa, and avocado in your fridge. I assume you like Mexican food."

"I could eat it every day of the week."

"It's almost ready. You smell good," she said, as he moved

behind her, putting his arms around her. "I feel a little underdressed."

"In my opinion, you have too many clothes on," he told her.

"You're distracting me," she said, as he nuzzled her neck.

"And you don't like it?"

"I love it, but I also don't want to burn the eggs."

"Got it." As he stepped back and moved around the counter, his gaze came to rest on a large white envelope on the coffee table in front of the couch. "Did you put that envelope there?"

"What?"

He walked over to the table and picked up the envelope. He knew he had never seen it before.

"Flynn, is something wrong?"

"I think so. Someone has been in the house."

"Are you serious?"

"Yes." He just didn't know how it had happened. His alarm system was still on. There had been no breaches during the night. *Had this envelope been here when they'd come back from the museum?* He'd been so caught up in Callie, maybe he hadn't seen it.

He stared at the envelope for a long minute and then slipped his finger under the flap and opened it. Inside were two pieces of paper. One was a photographic copy of a painting and not just any painting—the belladonna, the deadly nightshade, the calling card of death.

"What is it?" Callie asked, a worried expression on her face as she joined him.

He handed her the picture. "Someone left this in the apartment."

"Is this supposed to be a warning that you're next?"

"I don't think so," he said tightly as he read the scribbled words on the second piece of paper. He couldn't believe it.

"Flynn?" Callie put a hand on his arm. "What does it say?"

He shook his head, unable to say the words.

Callie grabbed the paper out of his hand and read it aloud. "You need my help, Flynn. Meet me this morning at our spot. Dad." She gave him a look filled with both worry and compassion. "Is this really from your father? How did it get here?"

"He must have broken in."

"But how? You have tight security."

"My dad is a master burglar." He blew out a breath, shocked to think his father was not only in town but had been in his apartment, maybe while they'd slept.

"Are you going to meet him?"

"I don't know."

She stared back at him. "You have to, don't you?"

"This could be a trick."

"Or he wants to help you. He's trying to tell you he knows something about the painting. Maybe he knows who painted it."

"That would be my guess, but I don't know if I can trust my father. Let me reword that. I'm *sure* I can't trust my father, if this is even from him. Maybe it's a setup."

"If it was a setup, the note would not have mentioned a specific place known only to you and your father."

"Damn. You're right." He sat down on the couch. "I was not expecting this."

She sat next to him, putting her hand on his leg. "I'll go with you, Flynn."

"No. I can't put you in danger again, Callie."

"Your father isn't a danger to me."

"You don't know that. You don't know anything about him, what he's done, what he's capable of." He pressed his hands against his temples. "I have thought about seeing him a million times. For years, I tried like hell to find him. I used every resource I had to do that, and I never succeeded. Now, he somehow finds a way to break into my home and leave me this note. Why?"

"He said he wants to help you."

"Why would he want to do that? He has ignored me for seventeen years."

"Maybe he hasn't been as far away as you might think."

He looked into her eyes. "You think he's been watching me?"

"He knows where you live. He knows the case you're investigating."

"Because that case is in his world."

"But you've investigated cases in his world before. You said you did it for two years. But this case is about you. You've almost been killed twice."

"I've been in danger many times, almost killed many times."

She frowned. "I really don't like to think about that, but maybe it's also the Arthur connection. Could Arthur have been in touch with your father?"

"At this point, I have no idea. Maybe. Victoria said Arthur had mentioned his name to her."

"What are you going to do?"

"I shouldn't meet him alone. I should set up the meet with at least a few members of my team. I should arrest him, bring him in."

She stared back at him with no judgment but a lot of doubt.

"To do otherwise would be going against everything I stand for," he added.

"Which is why I should go—not with you, by myself," she suggested.

"No way."

"Think about it. I could meet him. I could find out what he has, what he wants. If he came here, he probably knows we're together. You don't think he came in while we were..."

"Who knows? I was more than a little caught up in you, Callie."

"Likewise."

"But he also could have entered earlier, when we were at the museum. I didn't look around this room when we came home. I checked for intruders, not for envelopes sitting on my coffee table."

"He probably came in earlier. I could do this for you, Flynn. I want to do it. I want to help you. This way, you're not put into an impossible position. You don't have to make a moral choice. You just have to tell me where to go."

"I can't let you do that, Callie," he said, incredibly touched by her offer. She had a very big heart and a generous spirit. "It's too much."

"I care about you, Flynn. I think you might know that."

"I care about you, too. That's why you're not going. I'll do it. I'll meet him. There was never really a decision to make. I have to see him. I have to face him. I just don't know who he'll be—the dad I remember from when I was a kid, or the man who packed his bag in the middle of the night and thought no one would see him leave."

"You saw him leave?" she asked with surprise.

"And he saw me. I was asleep, but I heard something. I got up and went into the living room. He was halfway out the door. He paused for one second. Our eyes met. And then the door shut in my face."

"What did you do?"

"I stood there for about five minutes and then I went and opened it. His car was there, but he was gone. I didn't know what all was going on at that moment. I knew he'd been taking a lot of calls. He'd been traveling. And he'd had a big fight with my mother earlier that evening. I found out later that he'd told her he'd done some bad things and the only way to protect her and me was to leave. She'd begged him to stay, to let her help him, but he said there was nothing she could do."

"Oh, Flynn. I'm so sorry. You must have been devastated."

"He could have said something in that one second, but he didn't. He just looked at me, like he was memorizing my face. Maybe I was doing the same thing." He shook his head. "Now, I'm supposed to do what? Forgive him? Accept his help? Arrest him?"

"I don't know. What I do know is that there's a bond between you and your dad. No matter what happened, he's still your father. You still have those memories of him teaching you to surf." She paused. "It's the beach, isn't it? That's where he wants you to go. Can I at least come with you? I can be your backup."

Her eager words brought a smile to his lips. "You're amazing, Callie. But, no, I can't take you there."

"Then maybe you should take Savannah or Wyatt. If this isn't your father, if it's a trap, I don't want you to be alone."

"No. It's him. I have to go on my own. I can't put anyone else on my team in a position where they have to do something that could cost them their job. It's my risk to take."

Disappointment entered her eyes, but she gave him an agreeable nod. "All right. I get it. I can't go, but I can feed you. And I'm not letting you do this on an empty stomach, so come on." She got to her feet and moved into the kitchen.

He took one last look at the note and then took everything over to the kitchen table. As he sat down, his gaze returned to the photo of the painting. If his father knew the artist, then he knew the killer. He could provide the missing clue.

His father had baited the hook with a piece of information that Flynn desperately needed to find Arthur's killer. His dad had always been smart.

Callie brought two plates to the table and sat down. "Eat, Flynn. I think it's going to be a big day."

He set down the picture of the painting and picked up his fork. "I think you're right."

CHAPTER TWENTY-TWO

FLYNN DROVE to Zuma Beach a little before nine on Tuesday morning, feeling as if each mile was taking him back in time. That feeling got worse after he parked in the lot. Because it was midweek, there weren't many cars. Most of the early morning surfers had already gone home, although there were two teenage boys changing out of their wetsuits next to a gray minivan.

Those boys reminded him of himself, of all the days he'd cut school or gone in late with some imaginary excuse because he'd ridden one wave too many. Of course, that had gotten worse after his father left. He'd barely been able to stand being in a classroom, too filled with rage and grief to be able to learn something.

He walked along a small cement wall that edged the parking lot, scanning the wide stretch of sand for any sign of his dad. There were a couple of surfers in the water, but he doubted his father would be one of them. His dad would want this meeting to be on land. It would be easier for him to get away.

He left the parking lot, taking a narrow path toward the fishing pier. As he came up the ramp, he saw there were two fishermen on the pier: one nearby wearing a big canvas sunhat, the other standing at the far end of the pier, wearing a baseball cap with the LA Dodgers insignia.

His gut twisted.

That was his dad. Thirty feet away, his back turned toward him, but he still knew it was him.

He had a second to leave. His father hadn't yet seen him arrive. Or maybe he had.

From his vantage point, his father would have been able to see him drive into the lot and walk along the beach. Perhaps his dad was giving him the chance to run.

But he wasn't his father. He didn't run. He stood his ground. He faced his problems head-on.

He walked purposefully and deliberately to the end of the pier.

His dad turned around when he was only a few feet away.

As their eyes met, he took off his sunglasses. His father did the same.

His heart pounded against his chest. Sam Beringer looked much as he had the last time Flynn had seen him. His blond hair was mostly covered by his cap, so he couldn't see if it had grayed or thinned, but his blue eyes were as sharp as ever.

"Flynn," his father said, stopping there, as if he didn't know what words should come next.

He didn't know, either. He also didn't even know if he could call him Dad. "How did you get into my house?" He wasn't sure why those were the first words to come out of his mouth, but there they were.

"Does it matter? What's important is that you came. I wasn't sure you would."

"Nor was I. What do you want?"

"I want to help you."

"Why?" he asked harshly. "You left me and Mom to fend for ourselves a very long time ago. You know I can arrest you, don't you? If you had my address, I'm sure you're aware that I'm a federal agent."

"And that you spent years trying to find me and put me away. I'm aware," his father returned.

"But I was unsuccessful. You stayed out of sight, out of my reach, until now. Why?"

"Someone wants to kill you, and I don't want that to happen."

"Other people have tried to kill me; I didn't see you around then"

"This is different, Flynn. I can help you now. I can show you how to find Arthur Corbyn's killer."

He sucked in a breath at the mention of Arthur. "How do you know Arthur?"

"I met him years ago, before I ever left Laguna Beach."

He shook his head at that impossible idea. "No way. Arthur didn't know you."

"He did. He came into the gallery several times. I sold him a painting by Veritas, and I helped him hang it in his living room."

He stared at his father in shock. He'd seen that painting a thousand times. He'd sat on the couch right beneath it. Arthur had never admitted to knowing his father, to having bought art from him or his gallery. And Arthur had had plenty of chances to mention that encounter. *Why had he hidden it?*

"Was the painting stolen?" he asked. "Is that why Arthur never told me that he knew you?"

"I told him not to tell you shortly after I realized you were dating his daughter. You were happy, and I thought if you knew that Arthur and I had had dealings together, you would be crushed again."

"So he kept your secret. And you kept his." He felt incredibly disappointed.

"Yes."

"Where did you go after you left Laguna? Where have you been?"

"A lot of places, but I never stopped keeping an eye on you. I've always known where you were, Flynn—what you were doing. I admit I was shocked when you joined the FBI. And when you started searching for me, I realized the depth of the hatred you had for me."

"You're right. I do hate you," he said flatly. "Why am I here? What is this all about?"

His father's jaw tightened, as if he hadn't been expecting such hard honesty. "It's about wanting to do right by Arthur and by you. You're involved with his stepdaughter now."

"Leave Callie out of this."

"She's a beautiful young woman. She makes you smile."

His skin crawled. "You've been watching us?"

"Only from afar. I wasn't in the house last night, if you're worrying about that. I left the envelope for you earlier in the day, but I did see you come home together."

"Cut to the chase. Why did you send me a photo of that painting?"

"Because I realized after you pulled it out of the house in Palm Springs exactly who had killed Arthur."

"How would you know that?"

"I know who the artist is, Flynn."

His breath caught in his chest. "How? No one else in the art world knows—unless, it's you."

"It's not me. I only discovered the information six weeks ago. I've been debating what to do with it."

"Debating? You know the identity of a serial killer, and you don't know what to do about it? I really never knew who you were, did I?"

"I couldn't exactly go to the FBI with my information, could I?"

"Cut to the chase? Who's the artist?"

"Before I tell you, I have some conditions."

"I should have figured," he said shortly. "You never do anything for nothing, do you?"

"I need you to let me go when this is all over. Let me disappear, the way I did before."

Flynn stared at his father for a long minute. "Why would I do that?"

"Because you're my son."

"That doesn't mean anything to me anymore." Despite his harsh words, he wondered if that was really true.

"It means something to me. I never stopped loving you or your mother, Flynn, but I couldn't go to jail. I couldn't survive in a cell.

I'm claustrophobic. I'd have been panicking from the second the doors clanged shut."

"Then maybe you shouldn't have been a thief. You could have run a legitimate art business, but you had to steal, sometimes right out from under someone's nose. What was it that drove you? Money, greed, excitement?"

"All of the above. It was money in the beginning. You know that my father was a painter, but that he died young. I was only fourteen when I had to start taking care of my mom and younger brother. We had no money, no food in the fridge, nothing. We were on the verge of being homeless. Then I went to a party at a rich kid's house and I saw a painting by Laraine Simone and another by Falcon Holt, and I thought how easy it would be to take them and sell them. I knew their worth because I knew art."

"You did it that night?" he asked, wishing he wasn't so interested in his father's history.

"No. I slipped into the house three days later when the family was at my friend's soccer game. The thrill of that theft was amazing. I found a friend of my father's, who ran a gallery, and told him the paintings had belonged to my dad, but we needed money. He felt sorry for me and asked me no questions. He paid me seven thousand dollars for both pieces. I told my mother I had made the money working after school. That paid the rent for the next several months. When that ran out, I looked for more items to steal. I got more daring and bolder the longer I did it. By the time I was in my twenties, I had developed a network of dealers to sell to. But I needed a front, so I opened the gallery."

"Did Mom ever know what you were doing?"

"She had no idea. I'm a very good liar," he said pragmatically. "I'm an even better thief."

"You also apparently have no conscience."

"I was stealing from rich people and selling to other rich people, and those buyers didn't give a damn about the provenance of the art. Their private collections were filled with stolen art. And sometimes I stole back from them, because they could hardly report the crime, not when they'd willingly bought a stolen painting in the first place."

"I don't know what you want me to say. You're a thief and a criminal, but what you did to me and Mom was even worse. You left us with nothing—you, the man who allegedly got into stealing because you wanted to take care of your mom and brother. What about your wife and son? Why didn't we matter? The government froze your assets. We lost the house. We ended up with nothing."

"I know that the first few years were difficult," he admitted. "But I started sending money to your mother as soon as I could."

His jaw dropped at that fact. "You never sent money."

"I made deposits into her banking account every couple of months. They looked like they were coming from the publishing house, who was buying her books."

He stared at his dad in amazement. "She told me a small press bought her books. Did she know you were the press?"

"No. I hired someone else to run the company. He published your mother's books, getting them into print and digital. He inflated the sales and paid her based on really good terms. Of course, he couldn't go too big or it might have drawn attention. I knew the feds were watching her. I assumed she was using some of that money to support you, Flynn."

He shook his head in disbelief. "And she never knew?"

"No."

"Or she didn't want to know," he said, thinking that sounded more likely as he remembered how his mom had told him she'd gotten fortunate in locating a press that could consistently sell her books. It wasn't a ton of money, but it kept her going, and she had helped him pay for his education. After that, he'd been on his own.

"We're not so different, you know," his father continued. "I've followed your career, Flynn. You go undercover, you lie to get what you need, you love the rush of adrenaline that comes from facing down fear."

"But I'm on the right side of the law; you're not."

"I didn't have the same kind of people in my corner that you did. You had Arthur Corbyn to look up to."

"He was just an illusion, too. He was buying stolen art from you before you disappeared and continued afterward. Did he always work through you?"

"No, after I left, he worked through Gretchen."

"So she was dirty this whole time. Stephen, too, I assume."

"They've helped me distribute art throughout the years, yes. It was the least they could do for me. They wouldn't have that gallery if I hadn't started it."

All the pieces were falling into place, except the most important piece. "Who was the artist of the painting?"

"I need your promise first, Flynn."

"My promise could be a lie."

His dad met his gaze. "I don't believe it will be, if you're willing to make it."

"You're asking me to break the law."

"I'm actually just asking you not to enforce it. There's a difference."

"You're splitting hairs."

"I'm offering you a lead that could stop a serial killer. Isn't that worth one look in the other direction? Don't you offer assets similar deals?"

"You're not an asset."

"You could make me one. What's it going to be, Flynn? And think carefully because there are a lot of lives at stake, including yours. Including Callie's."

"I told you not to talk about her."

"But she's in the middle of this. If you want to protect her, then you need to make me a deal."

He'd always known love could make him vulnerable.

Another shock hit his heart.

He was in love with Callie. And he did want to protect her.

But could he really let his father go free?

"I have to get out of here, Callie," Juliette said, a plea in her eyes. "Can't you see I'm better now? Can't you tell Dr. Clarke that?"

Callie sighed. Flynn had dropped her off at the hospital on the way to meet his dad, and she had spent the better part of the last hour trying to keep her mother from asking about her release. She'd done her hair and her nails, talked to her nonstop about things from their past that would make her smile, doing everything she could not to discuss Arthur or his death or her discharge date. But now they were where she hadn't wanted to be, and she couldn't avoid the subject any longer.

"Dr. Clarke thinks you should stay here for a couple more days. It's not that long, Mom."

"That's easy for you to say. I'm the one trapped in here."

"I know it's difficult. But it's important that you get well, that you're stronger before you come home and have to deal with everything."

"But I should be dealing with everything. It's Tuesday. Arthur needs to be buried. What's happening with all that?"

"The medical examiner released Arthur's body to the funeral home yesterday. He was cremated this morning." It felt horrible to say that to her mother, but she had to give her the truth. "As you know, those were his wishes. I read through the trust and spoke to his lawyer, and that's what he wanted."

Distress filled her mother's eyes. "But I wanted to see him one more time."

"I'm sorry, Mom. But Arthur didn't want a viewing. He didn't want anyone looking at his body."

"I'm his wife. He wasn't talking about me."

"It's done. His ashes were placed in a temporary urn. You can pick something else out when you're ready. As for a service, we can set that up for next week if you want."

"That's too long from now."

"It's not, and it's really best to wait. There's a lot going on with the investigation into Arthur's death. You're safer here than anywhere else."

"Why would I be in danger at home, Callie?"

She hesitated, knowing she would have to start filling in some blanks very soon, because her mother was asking more questions and getting more curious by the hour. She didn't want to destroy Arthur in her mom's eyes, but the truth would eventually come out. "It appears that Arthur bought some paintings that were stolen. Those stolen paintings are tied to his death."

"Stolen? Are you sure? Arthur wouldn't do anything illegal, Callie. You have to be wrong."

"I wish I was wrong, but I'm not. Yesterday, Flynn told you about the secret underground room in the Palm Springs house. Well, it's been determined that the paintings being kept there were stolen. That's why Arthur never told you or anyone else about the room. He didn't want you to know what he was up to."

"I can't believe it. It doesn't make sense."

"I know. Arthur didn't seem like the kind of person who would deal in stolen art."

"Was Gretchen involved? Was she his dealer?"

"I'm not sure, but I think she might have been."

"And someone killed him because of these paintings?"

"They're connected; I don't know exactly how. But the investigation is moving quickly, and the best thing we can do is stay out of their way. I know you want justice for Arthur, and this is how we get it."

Her mom let out a sigh. "I suppose you're right. But I could stay at your apartment, Callie."

She couldn't tell her mother she wasn't even staying at her apartment; then she'd have more to be upset about. "You'll only be here another day or two, Mom. And then you'll be ready to deal with the funeral arrangements. You'll need to be strong to get through this."

"I wish I was stronger, Callie. You don't know how much I wish that. But something inside my brain switches off, and I'm filled with anxiety and depression."

"At least you can recognize that now. That's a good step."

"I thought I was doing well until Arthur died. I was doing a good job at work." She stopped abruptly. "I hope I don't lose my job. What have you told Victoria? Does she know I'm in the hospital?"

"She doesn't. No one knows. She told me to reassure you that your job is waiting whenever you feel up to it. But there's no rush."

"I should call her. Do you have my phone?"

"I left it at home," she lied.

"Can I use yours?"

"I think it's better if you wait until you're released."

"I feel like there's more you're not telling me, Callie."

"You need to rest, Mom. That's all you need to do right now."

"I am feeling a little tired."

"Then I'll let you sleep. I need to go into work myself."

Her mother frowned. "I know I don't make things easy on you, honey. I haven't been the best mother. You're always taking care of me instead of the other way around. I try to make it up to you, but then something happens, and I'm back where I started."

She was happy to hear her mother speaking objectively about her mental health issues. That was a good sign. "You're dealing with an illness, Mom, but we're going to get you well and keep you well. I know that Arthur's death is a terrible loss for you, and it won't be easy to get over or move past the tragedy, but I will help you."

"I know you will. You always do." Her mom paused. "Does Flynn still consider me a suspect?"

"No," she said, even though Flynn had never actually said that. But she had to give her mother some good news.

"That's a relief. I have to say, you seem awfully close to him."

She felt herself flushing as memories of her night with Flynn ran through her head. "We've become friends. Let's just leave it at that."

"I'm not sure I can leave it at that, considering the sparkle in your eyes. You like him, don't you?"

"I might," she admitted. "But there's a lot going on."

"There's always a lot going on, Callie. And you usually push love away in favor of all those other things. Maybe you should think about changing that habit. As devastated as I am about

Arthur's death, I can't regret the love we shared the past year and a half. The same was true for your father. We had eleven years together. They weren't always easy, but there was always love. I don't want to see you end up alone."

"I have plenty of time."

"It's easy to say that, but it's not always true. Sometimes time is not your friend. Don't choose work over love. Don't choose me over love."

"Mom—"

"Don't even bother to deny it, Callie. I know I've been a burden. I'm going to try to stop weighing you down; I really will."

"You're not a burden. I love you."

"And I love you, which is why I will do what you ask. I'll stay here until Dr. Clarke says I'm well enough to leave."

"Thank you." She was relieved to see her mom willing to accept the help she needed.

"I think I'm going to sleep for a while. I'm feeling tired."

"I'll check on you later."

"Okay, and if you speak to Victoria, tell her I'll talk to her in a few days. I really want to keep my job, even though I know it will be difficult to go back to the museum after what happened there, but I like what I do. It makes me feel useful and even a little smart."

"You are very smart, Mom, as well as creative, something I'm pretty sure I got from you."

Her mother gave her a tired smile. "I'm just glad you didn't get my depression and anxiety and panic. It's exhausting and over-whelming."

"You're a warrior for fighting as hard as you do."

"You're the warrior. You fight for both of us. But one of these days I would love to be able to take care of you."

"You've done that, and you'll do it again. I have no doubt."

As her mom's eyes closed, she watched her sleep for a long minute, thinking what a beautiful and fragile woman she was. But she wasn't a killer. She hadn't killed her father and she hadn't killed Arthur. She knew that truth deep in her heart. She felt guilty for ever having had those thoughts. But going forward, she could be free of those doubts.

And maybe she'd find a way to choose love, because she'd already found the man she wanted to love.

Smiling to herself, she walked out of the room and headed downstairs. On her way, she texted Flynn that she was ready to leave the hospital. She waited around in the lobby for a few minutes, but she didn't get a text back. *He must be tied up with his dad.* She hoped that was a good sign. But she really didn't want to hang out where she was. She wanted to go home and change clothes. He would be annoyed if she left on her own, but what else was she supposed to do? And was she really still in danger on her own. It seemed like Flynn was the real target.

She waited another ten minutes and then pulled up an app and called for a ride. When the car was only two minutes away, she made her way out front. There were a couple of cars parked in the roundabout, so she moved down the drive, watching her app as the car made its way toward the hospital. While she was waiting, she opened her email on her phone, seeing more messages of condolence and offers to help, but nothing pressing. She was about to check her mom's email when a gray van pulled up right in front of her.

The side door opened, and then she felt someone come up behind her.

She was about to turn when an arm came around her waist, and something sickly sweet was pressed against her nose. It made her dizzy. She couldn't breathe. And then she was picked up and tossed into the van.

She bounced around on the hard floor as the van sped out of the parking lot. She struggled to stay conscious, to figure a way out, but her eyes were closing, and darkness settled all around her.

CHAPTER TWENTY-THREE

FLYNN HAD WALKED the length of the pier and back several times as he considered whether he could make a deal with his father. He wanted to solve Arthur's murder, but his dad was asking a lot. On the other hand, he and Callie had been targets, and while he had no doubt he could protect himself, the longer this went on, the more vulnerable Callie could be. She wouldn't let him watch her twenty-four seven, and what about when her mother came home?

As he returned to his dad, who had actually tossed his fishing line back into the water, he still wasn't sure what he wanted to do.

"You didn't used to take this long to decide anything," his father said. "You were so confident in your decisions."

"When I was young and stupid. You're asking a lot. You know that."

His father pulled his line back up and leaned his rod against the fence. "Do you think I would have come back, shown my face to you, if I didn't have a good reason?"

"I'm not buying that it's because you want to protect me."

"You don't have to buy it, but it's true."

"You want something else. You have another angle. You're always working a hidden agenda. What is it this time?"

"Someone killed my friend. Someone threatened my son and a woman I think is important to him."

"You're calling Arthur your friend?"

"Yes. And I'm not working an angle, Flynn. So, what's it going to be? You want me to walk away with what I know? Or do you want to make a deal?"

He took a deep breath and then slowly let it out. "All right. Who's the artist?"

His father stared back at him. "I have your word you'll let me go?"

"I already said I was agreeing to your terms. Now it's your turn."

"The artist is Victoria Waltham."

His gut tightened at the unexpected answer. "What? Are you serious? How do you know that?"

"Because I saw the painting in her home six weeks ago."

"How did that happen? She wouldn't have just shown it to you."

"I might have been looking around her house without her knowledge."

He raised a brow in amazement. "You stole from Victoria?"

"She had something a client of mine wanted, something Victoria had acquired by not so legal channels."

"You're telling me that Victoria also deals in stolen art. Is anyone legit?"

"Plenty of people are; plenty of people aren't," he said with a shrug. "Victoria is very ambitious. She started out wanting to be a famous artist, but she wasn't any good. I told her a long time ago that she had a brilliant mind for business, and she could be running the art world if she went in that direction. It took her a while to realize I was right. I thought she had given up her art completely, but it turns out that her obsession was still there, just below the surface."

"You're calling her a serial killer—Victoria Waltham, the director of the Piquard Museum, a beautiful, smart, capable woman."

"I know exactly what I'm saying, Flynn. I also know Victoria better than you do."

"Just because the painting was in her house doesn't mean she painted it."

"I considered that, but after Arthur died in her museum, the same way those other people died, I knew it was her."

He wrestled with the idea his father was trying to sell him. He'd never liked Victoria, but she had a very successful career, and he was still trying to figure out a motive. "Does Victoria know you saw the painting?"

"I didn't take it or remove it, but she guessed I stole her painting by Jovani. Arthur told me she asked him about me a few days before his death."

"You talked to Arthur last week?"

"Yes. On Tuesday. He called me again on Thursday, but I wasn't available. Next thing I knew, he was dead."

"So, you didn't know he got the belladonna painting."

"Not until you were in Palm Springs, and I saw you carry it out of the house."

"I can't believe you were there, and I didn't see you. Were you also there when someone tried to kill me?"

"No. When I arrived, I saw a guy run out of the house and jump into his car. I heard the sirens a moment later. I wish I'd gotten there sooner."

"How did you get there at all? Did Arthur tell you about his secret art stash?"

"Yes, I knew about it. And I had a feeling you'd end up down there." He paused. "I know Victoria didn't kill Arthur herself, but I believe she's the artist of the belladonna painting. The question is —what do you believe?"

"I have no idea."

"I have nothing to gain by pointing the finger at Victoria, Flynn. In fact, I could have said nothing instead of putting myself in jeopardy, but I want to honor my friend and protect you."

"I need a way to tie that painting to Victoria besides your word."

"An x-ray would tell us a lot about the painting, including whether or not she painted over another piece, something that might have had a signature. I'm assuming the bureau will have someone conducting those tests."

"Yes, but it will take time."

"Time you don't have." His dad paused, a thoughtful look on his face. "I have to say that something feels off about this murder. It's not as precise or as clean as the others."

"No, it's not," he agreed. "I reviewed those files again yesterday. The crimes were perfect—no clues, no traces of evidence anywhere. She could be losing her touch. Or she didn't know Arthur took the painting to Palm Springs, to his underground bunker. She thought she'd be able to retrieve it from his house after he died." Flynn paused as his phone buzzed. He didn't recognize the number for the incoming text.

But the photo made his heart stop. Callie was lying on a floor on her side, her hands tied behind her back, her eyes closed. The message said: *She's not dead yet. If you want her back, bring the belladonna painting to the Hollister Sculpture on Mulholland Drive at noon. Come alone. Otherwise, she dies.*

"Oh, my God," he murmured, staring in horror at her picture. *She was supposed to be at the hospital with her mother. She was supposed to be safe.* He never should have left her alone, not even for a second.

"What is it?" his father asked.

"Callie has been kidnapped. They want to trade her for the painting." He had to fight the fear racing through his bloodstream. There was no time for emotion. "I'm supposed to hand it off at noon." He glanced at his watch. It was ten. He had a little time, but not much.

"You can't do that. The painting is the only way to prove Victoria's guilt. It's your leverage."

"I don't need you to tell me how to do my job." He paced around in a circle, his brain whirring with options, all of them bad. He couldn't play this out to the kidnapper's demands. There was no guarantee Callie would be let go or kept alive, even if he did turn over the painting. He had to find another way.

"Can I make a suggestion?" his father asked.

"No." He blew out an angry breath. "Yes."

"We find her before the meet."

"That's great," he said sarcastically. "I didn't think of that. Got any idea where she is?"

"Let me look at the photo again."

He handed his father his phone. "It has to be a place Victoria has access to. But it wouldn't be her home. I don't think it's the museum. Damn! It could be anywhere." He felt more overwhelmed than he'd ever felt in his life, because the victim, the person in trouble was Callie.

He couldn't stand the thought of her being hurt, and in the photo she appeared to be unconscious. He prayed she was still breathing.

"There's something about the pattern of light falling across Callie's face," his dad muttered. "I can't see the window above her, but I'd venture a guess that it's stained glass, patterned in some way."

He stared at his dad in amazement. "You think she's in a church?"

"No, I don't. See that by mark by her foot? It's the frame of a painting." His father handed him back his phone.

He hadn't even noticed the tiny black square at the bottom of the picture. "How can you tell it's a frame?"

"Because I'm good at details, especially when I'm looking at a room."

"Casing a house, you mean."

His father shrugged. "We all get our skills somewhere. The floor is stone, but it's also stained. The splotch of blue by her head looks like old paint to me. The wall is aged." His dad paused, his expression thoughtful.

"I don't have time for this. I need to go to my office, get my team."

"Wait a second, Flynn. I know where she is. There's a warehouse in downtown LA. It was originally a stained-glass artists' co-op, but it was converted into a warehouse about ten years ago. The space is now used by museums, galleries, and dealers to store art being transported through the Los Angeles area. It's not expensive art. Most of it is worth nothing, although occasionally there are pieces of interest."

He stared at his father in suspicion. "It's amazing that you can tell me exactly where Callie is based on some light pattern and a dark square. Maybe you wanted to be here when I got the text so you could send me in the wrong direction. This could be a setup."

His father gave him a disappointed look. "You're very cynical. I guess that's my fault."

"You guess?" He shook his head. "I'm done with this conversation and I'm done with you. I need to find Callie."

"Then you're not done with me. I once broke into this warehouse. I know all the doors, all the windows, all the inside specs. As I mentioned, the security system is minimal. I doubt Victoria will have more than a few people with her. All the previous murders were done with a very small footprint. I can help you get Callie back, Flynn."

"I have a team I can call in."

"You don't need a team. You just need me."

"I don't need you," he said automatically, even though at this moment, he probably did need him.

"You can hate me later. Let's go."

"Fine. But you better keep up, because I'm not slowing down for you."

He jogged down the pier to his car, his father right on his heels.

As he started the engine, he couldn't help thinking that the last time they'd driven together had been when he was sixteen and practicing for his driver's test. A hell of a lot had happened since then.

Could he really trust the information his father was giving him?

He didn't think he had a choice. If he didn't act on it, Callie could die. If he did act on it, and it was wrong, she could die, too.

He had to rescue her before the swap, catch her kidnapper unaware. It was his best chance to get her back alive.

His gut churned at the thought of losing her. He couldn't let that happen. She had a whole life to live. She had so many things to do, so many dreams, and he wanted to share in each and every one of them. They'd only just found each other. This couldn't be the end. It just couldn't be.

"We'll get your girl back," his dad said.

"You better be right about this." As he got onto the freeway, he texted the kidnapper back, agreeing to turn over the painting.

Then he punched in Savannah's number and filled her in on the details of the meet, asking her to get a team in position at the installation on Mulholland. While she wanted to send backup to the warehouse he was headed to, he didn't have time to wait for anyone. They'd be at least twenty minutes behind him, and every minute counted. If Callie wasn't in the warehouse, then he could still get to Mulholland in time for the swap.

"Good idea," his dad said as he hung up. "Make it look like you're going ahead with the meet."

"I don't need your approval, nor do I want it."

"Got it. But can I just say—"

"No. Don't say anything."

"I'm proud of you, Flynn. You've grown up to be a good man."

"Someone had to balance out your sins."

"Is that why you joined the FBI?"

"I don't know why I'm even talking to you."

"Because we're here—together."

"For now," he said. "But not forever."

"No," his father agreed. "A long time ago, I made a terrible choice that made forever impossible."

"But you don't regret it, do you?"

"I regret hurting you and your mother, but I had to run. I wouldn't have survived in jail. I would have rather died. Maybe you would have had more respect for me if I'd killed myself."

His jaw tightened. "Don't play the martyr. You're a criminal.

You knew what you were doing every step of the way. You chose to play with danger, and it was never just about the money."

"You're right. I'm an adrenaline junkie. I like the thrill as much as anything. It makes me feel alive, powerful, and in control. You're not so different from me, Flynn."

He didn't want to believe he was anything like his father, but there was a small part of him that thought he might be.

"Is there anything else you want to ask me, Flynn? Because once we get to the warehouse, things are going to happen fast, and you're going to let me walk away at the end, right?"

"We made a deal," he said tersely. "Unlike you, I keep my promises. Even though it could cost me my job."

"No one knows we're together, do they?"

He almost wished he could say he'd already reported his father to the bureau. But they were past the point of lying. "Callie knows. She's the only one."

"You trusted her enough to tell her about me?"

"Yes."

"She must be important. Did you know her before Arthur was killed?"

"No, I didn't. But now I feel like I've known her forever."

"I felt that way about your mother."

"Until you left her."

"She had a better life without me. She wouldn't have moved back to England. She wouldn't have written her books. She would have been trapped in a life waiting for me to get out, to come back. She wouldn't have left me. It wasn't in her to do that."

"Now, you want to pretend you were selfless?"

"No. I was selfish. I never should have married her or had a baby with her, because I was living in a house of cards, and they all fell down. My only excuse was love. I was blinded by it. I wanted to have the family that I'd always dreamed of."

"But you also wanted to be a thief."

"Yes," he admitted. "I know I've disappointed you, Flynn."

"Disappointment doesn't begin to cover how I feel about you."

"I understand. I can never make it up to you. But I can help you stop a serial killer. I can help you get justice for Arthur, and I can help you save the woman you're falling in love with. That's why I came out of the shadows."

"Or you could be lying about everything."

"I could be, but I'm not. I wish you could believe me."

"I wish I could, too."

CHAPTER TWENTY-FOUR

CALLIE OPENED HER EYES, blinking in confusion, as her brain tried to process where she was, what was happening. Everything was fuzzy. Her head didn't hurt, but her vision was blurry. As she tried to reach for her eyes to rub the sleep out of them, she realized her hands were tied behind her back. She was half-lying, half-sitting on a cold stone floor, and in front of her were stacks of crates and a couple of paintings propped against the wall. The room was small, no more than ten by ten, with a tall window with diamond-paned glass that held specks of green and coral.

It was strange to see such a pretty window in what amounted to a large closet or storage area. *Where the hell was she?*

She didn't remember that kind of window on the museum building or at the gallery where Flynn had gone to meet Gretchen, but she was in some place connected to art. She just wished she knew how she'd gotten here.

She remembered standing outside the hospital, waiting for her car, when someone had grabbed her and pressed something against her nose so she couldn't breathe. Then she'd been shoved into a van. *Had she seen her kidnappers?* She didn't think so, but there had to have been two of them—the driver and the one who had come up behind her.

She sat up, her gaze taking in as many details as she could. Along with the high window that would be difficult to reach, there was one door. She managed to get to her feet and walk over to the door. She turned around so she could wrap her hand around the knob and try to open it, but the knob didn't move; it was locked.

She looked for some other way out. There was a good-sized ceiling vent, but how would she get up there with nothing to stand on, and her hands tied behind her back?

Fear started to take hold as she realized the seriousness of her predicament, which was followed by questions. *Why had someone wanted to kidnap her? What did they think she knew? How had they known she was at the hospital? Why did they want her alive when other people had already been killed?*

She could only come up with one answer. Someone wanted to use her for something. *To get to her mother? To get to Flynn?*

But how would kidnapping her gain anyone anything? She wasn't rich and Arthur's money was tied up. Even if her mother wasn't in the hospital, she probably couldn't get her hands on much.

If it wasn't about money, then it had to be about something else…

The painting. Of course! It had to be about the painting. Flynn had taken it from the house in Palm Springs. It was in a secure location. If the killer was desperate to get it back, then they needed leverage, and she was it.

She wondered if Flynn already knew she was gone. He'd be going out of his mind, blaming himself for leaving her on her own. But she was the idiot who had decided she wasn't in danger, who thought she could just call a car and go home.

She drew in an angry breath, but she told herself to focus, think.

That brought her mind to Flynn's father. *How was he tied into all this? Had his father's sudden reappearance been a way to separate Flynn and herself?*

She looked around for her bag, but it was nowhere in sight. Obviously, the kidnappers had not wanted to leave her with a phone. But maybe Flynn could trace her phone and figure out where she was, unless her phone had been tossed out along the way. That was probably the case.

Her heart was pounding against her chest, and she felt close to panic, because the truth was hitting her in the face. *She might be leverage now, but what about later? What about when the kidnappers got what they wanted? Would she be able to survive?*

She had to find a way to save herself. She had her mom to take care of. She had a life she wanted to live. And she wasn't going down without a fight.

She slowly twisted her hands and wrists, flattening out her fingers, so that the tie would loosen. After a few minutes, she felt a bit more space, but her skin was already starting to sting from the friction. She had to get free before anything swelled up. She tried to make herself as calm as possible, closing her eyes and using yoga mantras to loosen her muscles, to release her tension, to make herself as small and flexible as possible. She would turn herself into a boneless mass.

Pulling one hand up and the other down, a twist of the wrist one way, then the other, and to her shock and amazement, one hand came free. She pulled the tie off her other arm and shook her arms out, feeling an amazing wave of relief. At least she had her hands. *Now what?*

She could possibly break one of the frames apart, use the jagged edge as a weapon. But it wouldn't do much against a gun.

Her gaze moved to the ceiling once more, then over to the window. There was a small sill on the window, wide enough to stand on. She might be able to reach the vent from there. *But how could she get up on the sill?*

There were a couple of crates in the room. She dragged them over to the window, putting one on top of the other. Standing on the highest one, she could put her hands on the window. She tried pressing down and jumping, but she couldn't land herself high enough. She got down, digging through the pile of stuff in the corner of the room, feeling a bit more triumphant as she found three cans of paint. She placed them on her makeshift ladder and managed to get her knee onto the windowsill. She pulled herself up from there, using the window lever for support.

A bit more maneuvering, and she got herself into a squatting position. Bracing her hand against the window, she slowly stood up and now she was close enough to the ceiling to push the vent open. The square space was about three-feet wide, plenty big enough for her to crawl through. But it took all the courage she had to release the window and grab the edges of the vent, swinging her legs into the air.

For a moment, she thought she was going to fall, but somehow she managed to hang on and pull herself up into the vented crawl space. She was really grateful now for the bootcamp she'd taken last summer.

Her eyes took a second to adjust to the dim light, but through the crawlspace she could see a shimmer of light. She scooted along on her hands and knees, having to squeeze herself through narrow passageways and around large ducts. As she reached another vent, she looked down, seeing a hallway below her.

There was no one in sight. She carefully pulled the cover off and then she lowered her body out of the vent, dropping the last few feet to the floor. She winced as she hit the ground, hoping that no one had heard her land. Thankfully, there were large canvases leaning across the railing in front of her, blocking her from the view below.

As she looked around, she realized she was in a warehouse. In front of her was a corridor with an open rail looking out over the main floor of the building. At the end of the hall was another stairway. She wondered if the building was in use. The floors were thick with dust. There was loose plaster and sheets of drywall stacked against the wall a short distance from her. There were more empty crates and a couple of folding chairs farther down the corridor, near what appeared to be an office door.

What she didn't see was an exit.

Turning around, she saw a water fountain, another door—which she suspected might lead to the storage room she'd just been in—and at that end of the hall was another stairwell. She needed to get down to the ground level.

Before she could move, she heard voices coming from the floor below. She ducked behind the two large canvases, hoping no one was coming up the stairs.

"What the hell are you doing here?" a man asked, not just anger in his voice, but also shock.

Callie stiffened at his words, realizing someone was standing on the first floor, very near to where she was. But whatever was happening now was not part of this man's plan. Maybe Flynn had found her. But the voice that followed was female.

"I knew you were going to do something stupid," she replied. "It's been one mistake after another. You're not only going to destroy yourself; you're going to take me down with you, and I can't allow that."

Callie's heart leapt into her throat. She knew that voice. It belonged to Victoria Waltham. *Was she in on this?* It seemed unimaginable.

"How did you find me?" the man asked.

"After security reported that Flynn and Callie were almost run off the road yesterday by a museum van, I realized your desperation was getting the better of you. I didn't call you to tell you about their visit so you could do something stupid. But you got on the phone ten seconds later and got your pal Greg involved. Now this? I can't believe you've kidnapped Callie. Are you crazy? Where is she?"

"She's locked away. She's fine. I'm going to use her to get the painting back."

"You never should have lost my painting in the first place," Victoria said sharply.

Callie took in a breath at her words. *Victoria was the artist and the serial killer?* But she was a museum director. She was beautiful and successful. She had everything. *Why would she have done any of it?*

"You've made a mess of everything, Marcus," Victoria continued. "I never should have told you about the painting. I never should have trusted you. And how you could believe that you could be me is unimaginable."

"Is it unimaginable—Mother? You don't think I inherited anything from you?"

Her heart skipped a beat, and she had to bite back a gasp. *Marcus was Victoria's son?*

But Victoria had told her mother several times how she'd missed having children, but she'd always put her career first. Apparently, not always. She'd had a son. A son who was now in his twenties. And Victoria had celebrated her fortieth birthday a few months ago. She had to have been a teenager at the time of his birth.

"I've got this under control," Marcus continued. "MacKenzie will trade the painting for Callie's life. You said yourself that he clearly has feelings for her. In a few hours, the painting will be back in your control."

"They could have already used the painting to figure out my identity, you idiot. They'll be able to pin all the murders on me. Or maybe that's what you want. You want me to go down for Arthur's death, too."

It didn't sound like Victoria had killed Arthur, which meant Marcus had done it. *But why had Marcus wanted to kill his benefactor?*

Callie crept forward, peeking through the rail.

Marcus and Victoria were standing in the middle of a large open space, surrounded by tables and chairs, easels and canvases, shelves of paints and materials. It looked like it had once been used for art classes. But like everything else in the building, the space had the air of abandonment and disrepair.

"We're both going free, Mother," Marcus said. "I have it all planned out." He lifted his chin and squared his shoulders, giving his mother a cocky look.

They didn't appear to be related in any way. Marcus was dark and handsome. Victoria was blonde and beautiful and didn't look anywhere near old enough to be this man's mother.

"Even if Flynn gives you the painting, he's had it long enough to have it examined," Victoria said. "He'll be able to find my initials through an x-ray. He'll believe I killed Arthur. And he'll hunt me to the ends of the earth."

"He might not have had time to x-ray it."

"What about Callie?"

"She hasn't seen me. She knows nothing. We'll drop her off somewhere."

"She'll be a loose end. I don't like loose ends, Marcus. I also don't like people who betray me. I shared the painting with you because you're my son. I wanted us to have a relationship. But you used me to cover your ass, to kill Arthur and pin it on me. At first, I thought I could help you, but you're out of control. You won't listen. You won't learn. I'm done."

Callie was stunned once more when Victoria pulled out a small black revolver, aiming it at her son.

Marcus put up a hand in shock. "What are you doing? You can't kill me."

"I can kill you and save Callie. I'll be the hero. You'll be the murderer."

"But the painting will point to you. You just said that," he reminded his mother, a desperate note in his voice.

"Not if I say the painting was always yours, that you painted it and used my initials to set me up. You did it to pay me back for giving you up for adoption all those years ago. And they'll understand that the murders started five years ago, when you were nineteen, when you found out you were adopted. I'll help them make the connection. I'll help them see that you were determined to hurt me, the mother who abandoned you. There will be records from your psychiatrist."

"I saw a psychiatrist once."

"There will be many visits, Marcus. You will be seen as a mentally ill man who painted his madness and used that painting as a calling card for death. I almost hate to let you take the glory of my legend, but it's something I have to do. The evil must be punished. Did you learn nothing from my story? Did I not tell you before that people who cross me, who abuse their power, who betray trust, who take what isn't theirs must fall from their high horse, must shatter themselves on the ground of humbleness?"

As Victoria's voice rose with passion and madness, terror ran through Callie. She didn't know what to do. She didn't know how to get past them and out of the building. If Victoria killed Marcus, she'd come for her next. She'd just said she hated loose ends. Although, she'd also said she could be seen as the hero, so maybe there was a chance she wouldn't die. But it was hard to believe that with the crazy scene unfolding below. She wanted to run. *But what if she drew their attention?* She had to stay put, wait for her chance.

"You're truly insane," Marcus said. "I'm your son. You'd be killing a part of yourself."

"A part I gave away a long time ago. While I may be insane, I'm not stupid. I don't get caught. Not ever. It's my superpower. And I won't lose it because of you."

"You don't have to kill me. We can make this work. I'll get the painting back. Or I'll confess to everything. I'll keep you out of it."

He was begging for his life, but Callie didn't think Victoria was listening.

"It's too late, Marcus. I know what I have to do."

Callie held her breath, wondering if she was about to see Victoria kill her own son, when a door slammed. Both Victoria and Marcus turned in the direction of that sound. A man was hauled into the room by another man. She didn't recognize either one of them. One was young and stocky, wearing ripped jeans and a denim jacket over a T-shirt. The other was much older—maybe in his sixties—with blond hair and a lean build.

As he turned toward the light, she saw his strikingly light eyes, and she was reminded of Flynn. Suddenly she knew exactly who this man was: Flynn's father—Sam Beringer.

Did that mean that Flynn was close by?

She was almost afraid that was true. She didn't want him to walk into a trap to rescue her, and she was afraid that was exactly what was about to happen.

Flynn moved quietly into the warehouse. His father had deliberately gotten caught by the guard standing outside and had been taken into the building. The door had been left open, and it had been easy to slip in behind them. He moved toward the sound of voices, straining to hear Callie's voice, to know that she was alive.

Sliding behind a pallet of boxes, his gaze quickly swept the room, assessing the situation. He wasn't completely surprised to see Marcus Vitelli standing in front of Victoria, who had a gun in her hand. He'd always thought there was something between them.

There was no sign of Callie. She had to be stashed away somewhere in the building. He wanted to look for her, but he needed to deal with this dangerous group first.

"Found this guy outside," the guard said.

"Get back out there, Greg. Make sure he didn't bring his FBI son with him," Victoria ordered.

"Don't go anywhere," Marcus said. "She's crazy. She's going to kill us all."

"I'm not going to kill you, Greg," Victoria said, an evil sneer in her voice. "But these two—maybe. I don't think you want to be here for that, do you? Go outside and make sure no one else comes in."

Greg hesitated. The young guy was clearly over his head.

"Don't move," Marcus ordered.

"Dude, this is not what I agreed to," Greg said, as he jogged toward the exit, leaving Marcus and Sam alone with Victoria.

He was happy to see Greg go. One less man to deal with. He'd track him down later. He'd pay for trying to run him and Callie off the road.

He moved around the perimeter, searching for the best position to take a shot.

"You don't have to kill me, Victoria," his father said. "I came here because I want in on the action. I can help you. I know what's going on."

"No, you don't," she said.

"Oh, but I do. I saw the painting in your house when I stole the Jovani from you."

"I had a feeling that was you."

"As soon as I saw the belladonna, I knew you were the serial killer. It made perfect sense. You loved to paint flowers, and you were desperate for recognition of your talent. Is that why you killed those people, because they couldn't see how good you were?"

"It was one of my reasons," she admitted. "Especially with Rafael; he was so disdainful. He never thought I could be famous, but he was wrong, and he helped bring me fame."

"Then why hide in the shadows?" his father asked.

"I'm not in the shadows. I'm exactly where I want to be, or I was, until this idiot came into my life."

As she glared at Marcus, Flynn realized he was wrong about them. They weren't together. They were in opposition.

"Well, my silence can be bought," his father continued. "You know that. We are two of a kind. We do what it takes to survive."

He found himself admiring his dad's cool.

Was it an act? Or was this a scene he'd played out before?

Pulling out his phone, he texted Savannah his location, asking her to send backup, but to keep it quiet. No sirens. No police. Not until he had located Callie and gotten her to a safe location.

"Or I could just kill you, Sam," Victoria said. "No one would care—least of all, your son."

"That's true. But why create more problems for yourself? You need an ally. This man isn't up to your standards, is he?"

As his father spoke, Flynn saw Marcus start inching his way backward, as if he were trying to escape notice. But Victoria suddenly swung her gun in his direction. "Where do you think you're going?"

"Mother, please."

Marcus was Victoria's son? Now he was shocked. He'd thought they were lovers. He had been way off base.

"Don't call me that. You're too stupid, too inept to be my son."

Victoria turned her gaze on Sam. "You did it, didn't you, Sam? You figured everything out and you told Flynn about me."

"I haven't told him a thing. Why would I? He would arrest me and put me in jail for the rest of my life."

"Then why are you here?"

"Because Arthur was a valuable client, and I'm going to need to find a way to replace that income stream. I'm surprised you had him killed before you knew where he'd put the painting. That was sloppy."

"It wasn't me. It was my son. Marcus thought he could copy me, solve his problems with Arthur by using my painting, my calling card. And now he's going to pay. But first I have to deal with you. I'm not interested in your deal. I think you're working with your son. But when he gets here, you'll both be dead."

Even from the shadows, Flynn could see the murderous intent in her eyes. He took aim, about to pull the trigger, when something flew through the air, hitting Victoria square in the chest. She stumbled and fired, the blast taking Marcus down.

Sam rushed Victoria, wrestling for the gun. It went off a second time, and his father fell to the ground.

He finally had a clean shot, and he took it, but the bullet only grazed Victoria's shoulder as she took off on a dead run.

He ran after her, shoving tables and chairs out of his way.

As she headed for the stairwell, she fired shots at him. Their gun battle continued as they both raced up the steps. When they reached the top floor, Victoria ran out of hallway. She was trapped, and she knew it. Blood was gushing from her arm. As she lifted her weapon, her hand was shaking. He didn't think she had the strength to pull the trigger, so he stepped out from behind the sheets of drywall that he'd ducked behind. "Drop it."

"Stay back," she warned.

"It's over, Victoria. You're going to prison for murdering five people."

"Four. Marcus killed Arthur. I had no idea he was going to kill him. Or that he would use me to do it. My son has no original ideas."

"I can't believe he's your son. Why did you keep it a secret?"

"Because I thought I could help him more if no one knew of our connection. But he betrayed me. And he wasn't just a bad killer, he was a bad artist. He fooled even me at first, but then I realized what he was doing."

"What was he doing?"

"Copying obscure artists who had real talent and selling the work as his own. Arthur found out and vowed to destroy him. I told Marcus I would take care of it, but he wouldn't listen. He had to kill using my legendary painting, only he completely screwed it up. He lost my painting. And then I found out he'd kidnapped Callie. It was the last straw."

"So you came here to stop him?" he challenged.

"No. I came here to kill him," she said bluntly.

"Your own son?"

"I gave him away when I was sixteen. I couldn't allow that baby to ruin my life. I had big plans for myself. But when Marcus found me, I thought maybe I'd been wrong to turn away from him all those years ago. He was my flesh and blood. But I wasn't wrong. He was always going to be my downfall. Now, I have to kill myself. Or you can do it. You can shoot me. It would make for a dramatic exit from this world. I could appreciate the art of that."

He shook his head, seeing the mad light in her eyes. "How did you hide your mental issues for so long?"

"People see what they want to see. And I was always very good at my job."

"Why did you do it, Victoria? Why did you kill all those people?"

"They threatened my power in one way or another, so they had to go. I'm in charge. They needed to know that. They needed to fall from the heights of their glory. I should have killed your father after he broke into my house, but I wasn't sure he'd seen the painting, and I never dreamed he'd risk his life of freedom to turn me in. But he always had a weakness for you. You were his one regret."

"It's over, Victoria. Drop the gun."

She did as he asked, but then she turned toward the railing.

He started forward a second too late.

She hurled herself over the rail, falling to the cement floor below like a broken rag doll.

As he looked at the scene below, he was reminded of the view from the top floor of the museum when Arthur had fallen to his death.

Victoria had wanted to die in the same artistic way as her previous victims.

He couldn't say he was sorry. Now he had to find Callie.

He jogged down the stairs. When he hit the second landing, he saw Callie running toward him. She threw herself into his arms, and he held on tight.

"I thought she was going to kill you," she said.

He closed his eyes for a split second, relief flooding through him that she was all right. Then he looked at her, wanting to make sure she wasn't hurt. "I was afraid for you, too, Callie. Where did you come from?"

"I was hiding. I got out of the storage room, but then everyone came in, and I didn't know where to go."

He nodded. "We'll talk about it all, but we need to get downstairs. I have to check on my father and make sure Marcus can't hurt anyone else."

She nodded and followed him down to the first floor. Marcus was bleeding and lying crippled on the floor, his leg shattered, and his eyes dazed with pain.

His father was also bleeding, but his arm wound didn't look too bad, and his dad was still on his feet.

"Are you all right?" he asked his father.

"I'll live." His dad offered Callie a smile. "I'm glad you're alive. My son was very worried about you, Callie, so worried he even let me help him."

"Thank you for that."

"Oh, and nice throw. You ever play softball?"

"A long time ago. I was trying to knock the gun out of her hand, but I missed."

"Not by much. I wish I could get to know you, but I can't." His dad turned away from Callie to give him a look filled with pain and sadness. "Good-bye, Flynn. Take care of yourself."

He nodded, feeling a tightness in his chest. His dad walked up to him, put his hand on his shoulder, and then headed toward the far side of the warehouse.

Flynn didn't see where he went after that as the sound of footsteps coming through the front door made him grab for Callie and push her behind him. He raised his gun once more, until he heard Savannah's voice. He blew out a breath of relief as Savannah and Wyatt walked into the room.

"You okay, Flynn?" Savannah asked.

"I'm fine. Did you get the guy outside?"

"We didn't see anyone," she replied. "He must have taken off."

"Probably when Marcus got shot." He tipped his head toward the man on the floor.

"I'll call for an ambulance," she said, taking out her phone.

"Looks like we have one survivor and one deceased," Wyatt said, squatting down by Victoria's body. "Beautiful woman."

"Beautiful but deadly," he said. "Victoria was the serial killer. Marcus is her son. Apparently, she gave him up when she was a teenager, and he found her a few years ago. He's the one who killed Arthur. He thought if he copied his mother's method of murder, he'd get away with it or be able to blame it on her."

Savannah grabbed a moving blanket off a nearby crate and pressed it against Marcus's wound.

Marcus groaned with pain, but he was fading in and out of consciousness.

A siren lit up the air, and a moment later, the police and paramedics responded to the scene.

As the room filled with personnel, Flynn put his arm around Callie's shoulder. She gazed up at him with her heart in her eyes.

"I knew you'd come for me," she said. "But I was afraid you'd be walking into a trap."

"I had luck on my side."

"And your father."

"Yeah, him, too. Did you know that they were going to trade you for the painting?"

She nodded. "I heard. They grabbed me at the hospital while I was waiting for a car."

"I told you I would come and get you."

"You didn't answer my text. I was just going to go home and change clothes. It was stupid. I'm sorry."

"Don't apologize. I'm just glad you're not hurt. They sent me a photo of you lying passed out on the floor. I didn't even know if you were breathing."

Her gaze filled with dark shadows. "I didn't know they did that. They shoved me into a van, put something against my nose, so I'd pass out. When I woke up, I was in a storage room with my hands zip-tied behind my back. I didn't know where anyone was. I managed to get free and I climbed up to the ceiling and went through the air vent."

He looked at her in astonishment. "You did what?"

"I was actually pretty amazed at myself," she said proudly. "I crawled through the duct, and then I dropped down onto the second-floor hallway from another vent. I was hidden behind the canvases up there." She tipped her head to the massive paintings upstairs. "I heard voices and I stayed out of sight. I couldn't believe it was Victoria or that Marcus was her son. She was furious with him. She said he was going to ruin her. And then your dad got hauled into the room. I thought you had to be somewhere close by, but I didn't know, and I was afraid of what you'd walk into. When she looked like she was going to shoot your dad, I threw a wrench at her. Then shots were going off and people were falling. I didn't know what to do. But you were there. You were going after Victoria. You were shooting at each other. I wanted to help, but I didn't want to distract you."

"I'm glad you didn't try."

"I thought you were going to shoot her."

"I wanted to. But she wanted it as well, and I couldn't give her what she wanted."

"So, she killed herself." Callie glanced over at her body. "She died just like Arthur, but she didn't kill him."

"No. But she killed other people. She got what she deserved. She always wanted to be famous."

"Well, I think she might be after all this." She blew out a breath. "It's over, isn't it?"

"I think so, yes."

"And my mom..."

"Is no longer a suspect," he said with a smile.

She smiled back at him and gave him another hug. But that wasn't enough. He didn't care that his team was standing nearby. He gave her a long kiss before letting her go.

"That's to keep me going until later," he murmured. "I have work to do here. I'm going to have Savannah take you to my place, okay?"

"I can go home."

"Not yet. Just let me take care of you a while longer."

"All right. But Flynn...what should I say when they ask who was here?"

"Tell the truth."

She met his gaze. "About everything and everyone?"

His lips tightened. "I don't want you to lie."

"You let him go, Flynn."

"We made a deal. He would help me get you back, and I would let him walk. He said he came out of the shadows to save me."

"He tried, Flynn. He threw himself on Victoria. He took a bullet for you." She paused. "I didn't see him leave."

"Me, either. One minute he was there..."

"And the next minute he was gone," she finished.

He nodded. "That's the way I remember it."

"Flynn?" Savannah interrupted. "Damon is on his way over."

"Good."

"Wyatt is going to the hospital, to make sure Marcus is put under guard until we can get his statement. How can I help?"

"Could you take Callie to my apartment? She can give her statement to you."

"Sure."

He let Callie go. "I'll see you soon."

"Thanks for saving my life again."

"You had a hand in that yourself. You really are a fighter, Callie."

"So are you."

It was difficult to let her out of his sight. But he had a job to do. And he intended to make sure that Marcus paid for everything that he'd done.

CHAPTER TWENTY-FIVE

CALLIE AND SAVANNAH spent the next few hours together at Flynn's apartment. Savannah took her official statement, expressing some surprise at the fact that Flynn's father had been on the scene, but Flynn had told her to tell the truth, so she did. She rationalized that she wasn't really lying about how Sam had disappeared, because she hadn't seen him leave the building. He'd just disappeared out of sight.

After she was done with her story, Savannah filled her in on how Flynn had received a text demanding an exchange—the painting for her—but that he'd somehow figured out where she was from the photo. Neither of them knew exactly how Flynn had determined where she was being held, but Callie had a pretty good idea that Sam's knowledge had played a role.

"I still can't believe Flynn saw his father after so many years," Savannah said, as they settled back against the couch. "And anything you say from now on is off the record."

"I wasn't lying before."

"Good to know. How did Sam and Flynn end up together?"

"You'll have to ask him that."

Savannah smiled. "Okay, then I'll ask you another question."

"I have a feeling I'm not going to like this one any better," she said, seeing the gleam in Savannah's eyes.

"There's something going on between you and Flynn. That was quite a kiss at the warehouse."

"We've gotten close," she admitted. "But…"

"There's a *but*?"

"Everything has been moving so fast. This isn't my real life. I don't get kidnapped or dodge bullets or get hit over the head. I don't chase bad guys. I'm a chef. I cook for people. I live a very ordinary life. I can't see Flynn involved with anyone ordinary. Not that I should even be thinking that way. Because we just had a… fling." She found herself feeling way too emotional at the end of that statement. "Do you want something to eat? I'm starving. I can find something to cook for us."

"I wouldn't say no to food."

"Although, you don't have to stay with me. I don't need a babysitter."

"Hey, you just offered free food. I'm in," Savannah said with a grin, as she followed her into the kitchen.

She opened Flynn's fridge, happy to find steaks and vegetables. "We're in luck. I can definitely do something with this."

As she set the ingredients on the counter, Savannah poured herself another mug of coffee. "I'm actually surprised Flynn has food in the house. I took him for more of a takeout guy."

"He makes a good breakfast," she said, as she found some herbs to rub on the steaks. Then she grabbed a knife and started cutting up vegetables.

Savannah laughed. "Interesting that you would know that."

She gave a shrug, then added, "Flynn told me that you met at Quantico."

"Yes, we had one of the best classes at the academy. Of course, that's my very biased opinion. Every class probably feels that way. But we formed a tight bond. Now wherever we are, whatever we're doing, we try to help each other out."

"It must be nice to know that there's always someone who will have your back." She hadn't really had that in her life. She'd usually been the one who had some else's back. "Flynn said you were a beauty queen and an ex-soldier. I find that fascinating."

"My journey through life has been filled with twists and turns."

Savannah didn't elaborate, and Callie couldn't help thinking there was definitely more to Savannah's story, but she didn't seem inclined to share.

"How is your mother?" Savannah asked, changing the subject.

"Oh, wow." She set down the knife she'd been about to use on some red, juicy tomatoes. "I probably should call her and tell her what's happening."

"Why don't you wait until Flynn gets back, until we know the whole story?"

"I think I know it already, but I can wait. My mom and I had a good talk this morning, and I'm glad she's tucked away. I'm sure the press will have a field day with all this. My mom is going to have to deal with the fact that Arthur was engaged in criminal activities and that he most likely had an affair with the woman who painted his portrait. He's not the honest, ethical judge everyone thought he was. Nor was he a particularly good husband."

"It's hard when the people you love disappoint you in such a profound way."

"Yes, it is," she agreed, seeing more shadows in Savannah's eyes.

"But your mother will have you to help her get through it."

"She will. I'm just afraid of how difficult that path will be. Anyway..." She picked up the knife and finished slicing the tomatoes. Then she put a skillet on the stove to cook the steaks. It felt good to be back in the kitchen. This was her world, where she was comfortable, confident, and happy.

As Savannah excused herself to take a call, she cooked the steaks, hoping Flynn would make it home soon.

It felt both right and wrong to think of Flynn's townhouse as home. It was his home, not hers. And tomorrow their lives would go back to their individual realities. She would have to deal with her mom, return to work, figure out how they were going to bury

Arthur, and Flynn would probably be wrapping up the case against Marcus and getting involved in whatever he was going to do next.

Frowning, she decided not to think about all that now. She wanted to just appreciate the fact that she was alive and safe, and that Arthur's horrible, tragic murder had been solved.

She'd just slid the steaks onto a platter to rest when she heard the garage door open, and a minute later, Flynn walked into the room.

Her heart soared with giddy excitement, and she found herself running into his embrace. She threw her arms around his neck as they kissed. She didn't want to let him go. Maybe tomorrow she would have to, but that was tomorrow.

Savannah's deliberate throat clearing finally broke them apart.

She gave Savannah an embarrassed smile. "Sorry."

"Please don't apologize," Savannah said, smiling at Flynn. "Everything okay?"

"It will be. Thanks for staying with Callie."

"No problem. I have her statement, and I will write it up tomorrow. It sounds like you had quite a day, Flynn."

"You could say that. By the way, it smells really good in here."

"That's because Callie has been cooking," Savannah said.

"I made dinner for all of us. It's actually ready."

"Good. I'm starving," he replied.

"Actually, I'm not going to stay," Savannah said.

"But you said you were hungry," she protested.

"You don't have to run," Flynn put in.

"I think the two of you need time together, and I have some of my own personal business to attend to. I'll talk to you tomorrow." Savannah smiled at Callie. "It was nice getting to know you better. I'm really glad you're all right."

"Thanks." As Savannah left the kitchen, she turned to Flynn. "Are you ready to eat?"

"In a second. How are you doing?"

"I'm fine. But I'm curious as to what's been happening. Is Marcus going to live?"

"He had surgery on his leg. His kneecap was shattered. But he will survive, and he will go to prison. He didn't do much talking on the way to the hospital, but there will be many more interviews to come."

"I told Savannah everything that I heard Marcus and Victoria say to each other, but there are still some blanks, like who adopted Marcus, how did he find out Victoria was his mother, and what was he really doing with Arthur? She implied that he was a fraud and that Arthur found out, but I didn't understand exactly what that meant."

"She told me that Marcus copied someone else's work, that he never had an original idea. He couldn't even kill someone in his own way. He had to use her method of murder."

"She was crazy. I could hear it in her voice. I could see it in her eyes. But she hid it so well for so long, maybe her whole life. My mother thought she was a great person, not that she's necessarily the best judge of character. But look how far Victoria rose in the art world. She was running one of the biggest museums in the world. She held the career of artists in her hands with her connections to gallery owners and art dealers. She had a lot of power."

"I think that's what it was about for her. She wanted power even more than money. But the money allowed her to do what she wanted. And anyone who got in her way went down."

"I never thought I would say this about anyone, but I am so glad she's dead. She was pure evil. I just hope Marcus never goes free, because I think he might be the same."

"Only not nearly as good at getting away with anything. We might not have ever caught her if it hadn't been for his bumbling mistakes and copycat crime." He took a breath. "Did you talk to your mom yet?"

"No. I'll see her in the morning. I want to tell her everything in person."

"Everything?" he queried, a gleam in his eyes.

"I don't think I can keep the truth from her. It's going to come out, right? Every last sordid detail."

"I would expect so. There will be a trial. The investigation into Arthur's life will reveal every secret."

"That's what I think as well. I'd rather my mom know all that while she's in close contact with her doctor. Speaking of parents…I did tell Savannah that Sam was at the warehouse, that he tried to get the gun away from Victoria, and that he might have saved our lives, but in the chaos that followed, I never saw him leave. She didn't press for anything else."

"No, she wouldn't. Others might. But I said the same thing."

"It's true. I never saw him leave the building." She gave him a thoughtful look. "How do you feel about it, Flynn? Are you angry with yourself for letting him go?"

"I made him a deal. Your life for his freedom. It was worth it."

"How did you even know where I was?"

"That was my father. On the photo Marcus sent, my dad recognized the pattern of light falling over your body as coming from a stained-glass window. He put that together with the edge of a frame by your foot and guessed you were in a former art co-op that had been used for stained-glass art classes and later as a warehouse. Apparently, my father had actually broken into the building several years ago to retrieve a painting that was in transport."

"That's…lucky," she said slowly, in search of the right word.

He gave her a cynical smile. "I guess you could say that. It seemed too easy to me. I thought he might be part of it all, luring me into a trap, so that I couldn't rescue you."

"I can see why you'd think that."

"But he was persuasive, and my back was against the wall. I had less than two hours to find you before the meet, and the best time for me to get you out safely was before that. I had to take a leap of faith."

"You trusted him. That must have been extremely difficult."

"I didn't have another option. I had to save you."

Her heart swelled with love at his words. "I wanted to save you, too, Flynn. I probably messed things up when I threw that wrench. You were about to take her down. I'm responsible for Marcus and your dad getting shot."

"Who cares about Marcus? And my dad's injury was nothing. You had no idea I was in the building. You did what you needed to do. You created a distraction, which gave everyone a chance to escape, including yourself. I'm more than a little impressed. I guess that softball you played came in handy."

"I can thank my dad for that. I never knew it was a skill that could save my life."

Flynn moved forward, sliding his arms around her waist, pulling her up against his chest. She let her head rest on his shoulder for a long minute, as he kissed the top of her head, and they just held each other.

In the circle of his arms, she felt loved, protected, safe from everything, and right now, that's exactly what she needed. She had no idea what tomorrow would bring. Actually, she was afraid of what tomorrow might bring—not in terms of the case or her mom but with Flynn. She'd fallen for him hard and fast, but it was during an adrenaline-fueled situation where they'd been spending every second together.

"Callie, stop thinking," he said.

She lifted her head. "How do you know I'm thinking?"

"Because you stiffened. What are you worrying about?"

"Nothing," she lied. "Everything is good now. We should eat dinner." She slipped out of his arms, determined not to think about the future just yet. She still had tonight, and tomorrow could wait a little longer.

Flynn drove to his office on Wednesday morning in a bad mood. He shouldn't have been surprised Callie was gone when he woke up. In retrospect, she'd been saying goodbye to him all night. They'd made love with passion and tenderness and so much feeling that he'd felt like he'd ridden a rollercoaster upside down and backward, until he was physically and emotionally spent but also amazingly content.

He'd slept dreamlessly, not waking up until after nine, when his phone had started buzzing with texts. That's when he'd seen the empty side of the bed, when he'd heard the intense quiet that he'd always liked about his home...until this morning.

She hadn't left a note, either. But the few things she'd had at his place were gone. She must have called a car to take her home.

He'd wanted to drive her there, maybe take her to see her mom. But it was too late now.

Maybe it was just as well. He had a ton of work to do to wrap up the case.

But, somehow, he didn't think work would take his mind off Callie. There was too much he still wanted to say to her. Everything felt upended, and he didn't like it.

A small voice inside his head reminded him that he was usually the one who left before the other person was ready, but that didn't make him feel any better.

When he arrived at his building, he pulled into the underground lot, and then headed upstairs.

He was surprised to see Beckett in his office. The ex-Army Ranger was seated in front of his computer, looking decidedly weary, his dark eyes bloodshot, his cheeks scruffy, and his skin pale. He'd been out of touch for almost a week and while Flynn appreciated his dedication to work and his undercover assignment, now he was worried. "You look like shit," he said.

"I feel that way, too," Beck replied. "I've been up for seventy-two hours straight, but it was worth it. We caught the traffickers on Highway 5 outside of Sacramento. Ten young women are now back with their families."

"Good work." He knew how hard Beck and Jax had been working on bringing down a trafficking ring that operated between San Diego, Los Angeles and San Francisco. "I didn't realize you and Jax were that close."

"We caught a break. Jax is tying up the loose ends. He'll be back later today." Beck sat back in his chair. "I hear there's been a lot of excitement around here."

"I filled him in," Savannah interjected as she came into the office holding a mug of coffee in one hand and a protein bar in the other. "Not the part about you and Callie, but, you know, the rest of it," she added with a mischievous smile.

Beck raised an eyebrow. "Now that sounds like the part I'm most interested in, Flynn."

"Nothing to say," he replied tersely, kind of wishing there was something to say, which was unusual for him. "I need to get down to the hospital. I just wanted to check in here first. I've been a little out of touch the last few days."

"We're still operating like a well-oiled machine," Savannah said. "Bree and Wyatt are meeting with someone at Vector Air. One of Wyatt's buddies from Novastar is now at Vector and wants to talk to him about a potential problem with a Chinese investor. Caitlyn is still in DC with her family. I'm not sure what Diego is up to, but Lucas is digging into Marcus Vitelli's life to see if we can fill in some of the blanks. By the way, Damon asked that you check in at his office after you see Marcus, and I'd like to tag along to your interview with Vitelli, if you don't mind."

"Absolutely. Get some sleep, Beck."

"I plan on it," Beck replied. "I'll catch up with you later."

As they headed down to the garage, Savannah said, "Sorry, Flynn."

"What are you apologizing for?" he asked, as he flipped the locks on his SUV.

"That crack about Callie. I knew I'd struck a nerve when you got all serious. You never get quiet like that—not about women anyway."

He got into the car, thinking about her comment. "It's fine. I'm just tired."

"For what it's worth, I like her."

He gave her a smile. "I like her, too."

"So, what are you going to do about it?"

"I have no idea. I've always flown solo. It's what I do best. I also have no idea what she wants."

"Maybe you should find out."

"Maybe." But as he drove onto the freeway, he started thinking that Callie leaving without a word had already told him all he needed to know. "By the way, thanks for keeping things running at the office. I appreciate your support and your backup."

"No problem. That's what we do for each other. One of these days, I'll need your backup, and you'll be there for me."

"I will."

"Callie told me about your dad showing up. That must have been something."

"I can't even describe how it felt to see him again, to talk to him. It almost seems surreal to me."

"He came out of the dark to help you. That's something."

"It doesn't make up for everything he did. But it is something. And he did help me find Callie. He was the one who figured out where she was being held."

"And he was the reason you didn't want me or Wyatt to come there, not until it was almost too late."

"I didn't want to put you in a difficult position," he admitted.

"Because one of us might have actually seen him leave or tried to stop him. I get it, Flynn. Damon gets it, too. But since you and Callie both mentioned your father's name in your statements, I suspect you're going to get some flak from the higher-ups."

"Probably, but I'll deal with whatever happens."

"You had to do what you had to do," she murmured. "Sometimes the lines are blurry."

"More often than not," he agreed. Hearing something in her tone, he glanced over at her. There was a contemplative expression in her eyes. "Everything all right with you?"

"Oh, it's fine, just some personal stuff."

"If you ever want to talk..."

"I know, but not now. Let's focus on Mr. Vitelli."

At her words, his mind moved to Marcus. He had a lot of questions for Victoria's son. Hopefully, he'd finally get some answers.

CHAPTER TWENTY-SIX

WHEN THEY ARRIVED at the hospital, they found a security guard posted outside Marcus's room. They showed their badges and entered the room. Marcus was in bed, one leg casted and propped up on a pillow on the bed. His left arm was shackled to the rail.

He gave them a tired, defeated look. "I already said everything."

"Then you'll say it again," he returned. "This is Agent Kane."

"I know. I talked to her at the museum last Friday."

"After you shoved Arthur over the railing."

Marcus stared back at him. "You still have to prove that."

"That won't be difficult now. You made a lot of mistakes Marcus, and your pal Greg is already talking. Oh, yes, we found him and he's under arrest for attempted murder. He wants to save himself, as I'm sure you do. The list of charges against you will be quite long before we're done. It might get shorter if you're willing to talk about your mother."

"My mother," he spat out. "She tried to kill me. You saw how crazy she was. She's the person responsible for all this."

"When did you find out you were adopted?"

"Six years ago, when I was eighteen. My adoptive mother was very sick. She confessed that I was adopted right before she died. I found Victoria about eight months later. She said she was happy to see me, but I could never tell anyone about our relationship. If I honored her request, she would help me get my art career going."

"Which she did. You were an instant success."

"She helped me sell my first painting," he admitted. "She also arranged for Judge Corbyn to become my benefactor. But he was putting a lot of pressure on me. I couldn't paint fast enough for him. He threatened to withhold money if I didn't produce."

"Victoria said you were a fraud. You were copying other people's work."

"Only a few times when I was blocked, and I needed cash," he said defensively. "I didn't think Arthur would figure it out, but he did, and he threatened to destroy me."

"So you killed him."

"I didn't say that," he muttered, still trying to hang on to some defense.

"How did you know about the belladonna painting? When did your mother tell you she was a serial killer?"

"Six months ago. She was drunk, and she wanted to show me some of her work. She pulled out the painting, and I, of course, knew the legend. But I didn't really know the ins and outs of it until she started talking. I was impressed and terrified. She said she had only killed people who deserved to be punished. Each one had not only wronged her, but they'd wronged someone else. She had the power to make them pay, so she did."

"Did she tell you the specific reasons?"

"I remember the first one. She wanted to get Rafael's endorsement, his patronage, so she'd shown him her painting, the belladonna. He told her she was an amateur and she would never be good or famous. Her anger simmered for years. She plotted the best way to take him down and then she found out he was cheating on his wife. He was a pig; that's what she told me. She sent him the painting with a note that she was coming for him. Two hours later, he was dead. She got her revenge and the painting back."

"And the others?" Savannah asked.

"I don't remember the details. I'm in a lot of pain."

"So you decided to copy her when you went after Arthur. How did you set that up?" he asked.

"Why should I tell you?"

"Because I'm the only one who can help you."

"Why would you help me?"

He shrugged. "Maybe I appreciate the fact that you had a criminal for a mother."

Marcus met his gaze. "Like your father?"

"Exactly. Tell me what happened. How did you set Arthur Corbyn up?"

Marcus hesitated and then said, "I stole the painting from my mother, and I sent it to Arthur's house."

"What day was that?"

"Wednesday morning. I wanted him to sweat, to wonder what might be coming. On Friday afternoon, I texted him a note to meet me at the museum, on the top floor hallway, just as the exhibition was starting. I told him that I would keep his secret of buying stolen paintings if he showed up. When Arthur arrived, I had a waiter hand him a glass of champagne while he was waiting. He drank it all the way down, and when I walked down the hall, he could see the truth in my eyes. But he couldn't move. I loosened his belt, so it would look like he'd been having sex with someone. Then I shoved him over the railing."

"What about the security cameras? Who hacked into the system?"

"A hacker who goes by the name Dreambuster. I don't know who he is. I bought his services on the internet. I actually used Arthur's money to buy the hack."

"He tripped the cameras at Arthur's house as well?"

"Yes."

"How was Eddie Norman involved?"

"He was someone I knew would do anything needed for a little cash. I sent him to get the painting back, but he couldn't find it in the judge's house."

"How did he find the Palm Springs home?"

"He followed you and Callie. We hoped you'd lead us to the painting."

Marcus's answer made him grimace with disgust that he'd allowed that to happen. "When Eddie didn't get the painting, you killed him."

"Actually, I didn't. That was my mother. She was on to me, and when she realized her painting was missing, she knew I'd taken it and she guessed that I'd killed Arthur. She was furious that I hadn't gotten it back and when Eddie failed, he became a loose end."

"Then your next move was to kidnap Callie."

"I thought my mother might kill me if I didn't get the painting back. It was the only way I knew how to do it." Marcus gave him a questioning look. "How did you find the warehouse?"

"My father identified it by the picture you took."

"There was nothing identifiable in that photo."

"The light through the stained glass made a pattern on the floor. There was a picture frame in one corner. Those are the details a true artist might notice, or a master art thief who had been in the building before."

Marcus shook his head. "I didn't see that coming."

"You didn't see a lot of things coming."

"But you're going to help me, right? You said we're the same—children of criminals."

"We're not the same. I don't cheat or lie or kill. That's all on you, Marcus." He paused. "Actually, we do have one thing in common. We can both lie to get what we want. I'm not going to help you. The courts will decide how you pay for your crimes."

"I can turn on you. I can tell everyone that your father was there," Marcus said desperately.

"They already know, Marcus. You have nothing left to barter."

"It's not like Arthur was a saint. He was buying stolen art through the Vales' gallery. Arthur was a criminal, too. I didn't kill a good person."

"Save your story for the jury. And in the meantime, get yourself a good lawyer. You're going to need it."

He tipped his head to Savannah and they walked out of the room.

Pausing in the hall, she said, "Well, that was quite a story. All the puzzle pieces finally fell into place."

"He might have gotten away with it if he hadn't used his mother's painting, if she hadn't gotten angry with him. That's when he got careless. In some ways, they took each other out."

"Good riddance to both of them. And nice work on getting him to talk."

He shrugged. "It won't hold up in court, but knowing what we do, we can build a good case. I'm sure Greg Barkley will be happy to make a deal and throw Marcus under the bus. Same with Gretchen and Stephen Vale. They'd rather own up to theft than murder. And we'll see if Lucas can find the hacker named Dreambuster."

"We're going to be busy for a while."

"We are," he agreed, as they headed for the elevator. But maybe busy was just what he needed to take his mind off Callie.

"I hope you have good news for me, Callie," Juliette said.

She walked over to the small table where her mother was seated. Taking the chair across from her, she said, "I have very good news."

"I'm going home?"

"Actually, I don't know about that yet. The nurse said Dr. Clarke would be in this afternoon to make that decision."

Her mom's face fell. "I'm tired of waiting for him. I want to go home."

"I know. But let me tell you the news. They found Arthur's killer."

"They did? Who was it?"

"It was Marcus Vitelli."

Her mom blinked in surprise. "Marcus? But Arthur was

helping Marcus. He was his benefactor. Victoria will be shocked. She thought he was amazing and brilliant and talented."

"Victoria knew what Arthur did, Mom, maybe not right away, but eventually."

"How would she know?"

"Because Marcus wasn't just Victoria's protégé—he was her son."

Her mom's jaw dropped. "I don't understand. She didn't have children, and certainly not one that old."

"Marcus was twenty-four. Victoria had him when she was sixteen. She gave him up so she could have the career she wanted. He tracked her down when he was in his late teens. I don't know all the details, but Victoria gave him opportunities to get ahead."

"I can't believe this. Is Marcus under arrest? What about Victoria?"

"Marcus is under arrest. As for Victoria, it's a long story, Mom, and I don't want to get into it all now, but she was also a killer. She committed murder several times in her life."

"This is nuts," her mom said, shock in her eyes. "She's a museum director."

"She was that, but she was also mentally ill. There was a big confrontation yesterday. Marcus ended up shot, and Victoria is dead."

Her mother put a hand to her mouth, her eyes wide with surprise. "She's dead? Who killed her?"

"She committed suicide. She knew that she was going to be caught."

"This is unbelievable, Callie. And people say I'm the crazy one."

"You're not crazy, but Victoria was."

"Well, I guess if she was that bad of a person, I shouldn't be sad or upset about her death. I just think of all the lunches we shared as friends. I never would have guessed she was hiding a secret life or that she even had the capability to kill anyone."

"She was very good at putting on a front." She drew in a breath. "I'm afraid thatArthur had secrets as well."

"The stolen art. His name will be ruined, won't it?"

"I think so. The press will be hounding you for interviews. It's not going to be easy, Mom. Especially not while Marcus's trial is going on. Other things may come out that could be hurtful. You need to prepare yourself."

Her mother stared back at her. "You're choosing your words very carefully. What else am I going to find out, Callie?"

She really didn't want to answer, but what choice did she have? "Arthur had an affair with Layana Vazquez."

"The portrait artist? That's why you were asking me about her the other day. She's a child. How could he sleep with her?"

"She's not a child. She's in her thirties."

"And he was in his sixties. I was right about my suspicions. I thought it was Gretchen..." Her mom stopped abruptly. "Was he sleeping with her, too?"

"Not that I know of. I believe she was selling him the stolen art."

"Well, I guess I wasn't being paranoid."

She was a little surprised and relieved that her mother hadn't burst into tears or collapsed in a heap of despair. "Your instincts were right. I'm sorry I didn't offer you more support in that regard."

"I've been wrong before, and you knew that. You probably also didn't want me to find out the truth. You always try to protect me."

"I do try, but sometimes I can't. I can't change what Arthur did. I can only help you move forward. And I hope you can find a way to do that, because he isn't worth losing the rest of your life over. Maybe that sounds harsh, but it's the way I feel. I don't care about him anymore. I care about you. I want you to be healthy and happy. You deserve that. I know you loved Arthur and I think he loved you, too, but he's gone."

Her mom slowly nodded. "I do deserve to be happy. Dr. Clarke and I have been talking a lot about my issues with self-esteem, my inability to forgive myself for your father's death, for not being a better mother to you. I have so much guilt, Callie. I hope I can make it up to you some day."

"If you're happy, you will have made it up to me."

"Then I guess I'll have to try really hard to get there. Thank you for being honest with me, for treating me with respect."

"You're more than welcome." She blew out a breath, feeling like she'd gotten the worst behind her. "I can come back this afternoon if Dr. Clarke discharges you. I can take you to my apartment. You can stay there as long as you want."

"You only have one bedroom."

"I'll sleep on the couch; it's not a big deal."

"No. I'm going home. To my house."

"It will only be your house for a year, Mom. The trust specifies after that time, it has to be sold."

"Then I have a year. I'm going to take it. That will give me time to figure out where I want to be and what I want to do." She paused. "I wonder who will get Victoria's job."

"I have no idea."

"Well, I'll find out soon enough. Hopefully it will be someone I like. Because I enjoy that job. And maybe I'm being overconfident about my ability to walk back into that building after what happened, but I'm going to try. I can't keep running away inside my head, because, frankly, that's an even scarier place to be at times."

She was blown away by how rational her mother was being. She could hardly believe this was the same woman she had brought in five days earlier. "You really are doing so well, Mom. I'm proud of you."

"I'm proud of me, too. Now, tell me what's happening with that very attractive FBI agent?"

"Oh, that's a story for another day," she said with a sigh.

"Or we could all just spend some time together, so I can get to know him, and he can get to know me when I'm not hysterical."

"I'm not planning to spend any more time with him."

"Why not? Don't tell me you're going to push him away like you've done with everyone else?"

"I haven't done that with everyone else."

"Of course, you have. You never allow yourself to get too close to a man. When things get serious, you run away. I'm sure I'm partly to blame for your lack of commitment. But I can't change that—only you can."

"I can commit. I've been in the same job for five years."

"Because it gives you the security to take care of me."

"That's not the only reason."

"And you haven't introduced me to a boyfriend in almost two years. You always say you haven't met the right man, but I think you hold back because you just don't have it in you to take care of anyone else. I'm already too big of a burden. And, by the way, I told Dr. Clarke that, and he could see my point."

"You and Dr. Clarke have been talking about me?"

"Yes, about our relationship—how you became the mom, and I became the daughter. But that has to switch back. You have to live your life."

"Well, maybe there's some truth to what you say, but Flynn and I aren't a couple. It was just a fling in a whirlwind of adrenaline and danger. Now we go back to our real lives, and they don't sync up. Anyway, that's enough of that." She got to her feet. "I'll check in with you later."

"Okay. But Callie…"

She paused at the door. "What?"

"Love is a wonderful thing, no matter how long it lasts. Don't turn your back on it."

Her mother's words rang through her head all the way back to her car. She sat in the driver's seat for a long few minutes, thinking not only about how wise and self-aware her mother had suddenly become but also about Flynn.

Had she been a coward to leave without a good-bye? Last night had been so incredibly amazing. She'd never felt so happy.

But Flynn didn't love her. And she didn't love him. It was just sex—fabulous, over-the-top, break-your-heart kind of sex.

Tears pooled in her eyes. She was a terrible liar. She was mad about Flynn, which was why she hadn't said good-bye. Because she was afraid she wouldn't be able to get the word out. And maybe she hadn't wanted to hear him say good-bye, either.

CHAPTER TWENTY-SEVEN

THREE DAYS HAD PASSED since he'd seen Callie, and it felt like a lifetime. Flynn paddled through the ocean on Sunday morning, wondering how he would get through another twenty-four hours. He'd kept busy wrapping up Arthur's case, but most of that was done. Come tomorrow, it would be time to move on to something new. He was more than ready to do that, but he wasn't ready to face the fact that Callie was no longer in his life.

He'd picked up the phone to text her or call her a bunch of times. But he kept coming back to the fact that she hadn't said good-bye, that she hadn't reached out to him. She'd just disappeared, like so many other people in his life.

Frowning at that reminder, he concentrated on picking a wave, on letting the ocean chase away his pain. It felt good to get up on the surfboard, to battle the sea, to ride to victory, but he still couldn't shake the melancholy that had settled over his soul.

He paddled out to the break, keeping his distance from the other surfers as he waited for his next run. But the ocean had settled down. The waves not coming as fast or as big. The wind had died, too. It was almost eerily calm.

He sat on his board, dragging his hand through the water as another surfer came toward him. There was something familiar about him, but it wasn't until he was five feet away that he realized it was his father. He was truly stunned.

"I thought you'd be back in Europe by now." His gaze moved to his dad's injured arm, but it was covered by the sleeve of his wetsuit.

"I wanted to see you one more time."

"How did you know I'd be here?"

"Because it's where you come on Sunday mornings, unless a woman keeps you occupied elsewhere. But it seems like you've lost your woman."

He gave his father a dark look. "Have you been following me again?"

"I like to keep an eye on you."

"You almost got me fired."

"Almost?"

"No one wanted to come down on me too hard since I'd just brought them not only Arthur's killer but a serial killer," he admitted.

"I was hoping that was the way it would play out."

"What are you really doing here?"

His dad gave him a long look. "I don't know. I should have left. I told myself to go a dozen times. I just wanted to tell you how sorry I was. I'm not sure I ever said that. I tried to explain myself. I tried to make you understand. But I don't think I actually apologized."

"Sorry doesn't mean anything."

"I figured it wouldn't, but I had to say it at least once. Will you tell your mother you saw me?"

"She's happy now, Dad. She has moved on. I don't think she needs to know any more than she already does." The more he'd thought about his dad's publishing company scheme, the more he'd come to think that his mom had known his dad was behind it all along. Maybe he'd ask her one day, or perhaps he wouldn't. He didn't need to screw up her life by bringing up the past.

"You're a fine man, Flynn. That's not due to me, but I want you to know I'm proud of you."

"I don't care," he said automatically.

His father nodded. "All right. I just have one more thing to say."

"Somehow, I doubt that," he said dryly.

His father smiled, and in that moment, the years in-between, the anger and the pain, faded away. He was with his dad again, someone he'd looked up to, the person who'd first brought him to the ocean and taught him how to surf.

"We had some good times when you were young, especially out here," his father said, obviously going down the same memory lane.

"It felt like it was just the two of us," he murmured. "It was our thing."

"Every time I go into the water, wherever I am in the world, I think about you, Flynn. I hope you can have a happy life, a better life than I ever had. I hope you won't hide yourself from love, from people who could hurt you if you open your heart up to them. That would be my worst legacy to you."

"I'll live my life on my own terms. I won't make my choices because of anything you did."

"Good. One last ride together?"

He should have said no, but when his father started paddling, so did he. They stood up on their boards within seconds of each other and rode the wave all the way into the shore.

When he hit the ground, he jogged out of the water, with his surfboard under his arm.

And this time, he was the one who didn't look back.

—————

Sunday night, Flynn drove to Callie's apartment a little past eight. He felt more nervous than he'd ever felt in his life. He could face down a bullet or a bomb. He could freefall from a skyscraper. He could jump out of a plane. But facing love...that was absolutely terrifying.

Callie's car was in her garage, and her lights were on. That was a good sign. He knew Juliette had been discharged from the hospital and had gone home a few days ago. Savannah had stopped by to speak to her and had reported that she was doing very well, and that Arthur's funeral was scheduled for next Tuesday. He probably should have waited until after that to speak to Callie, but after talking to his dad, he'd wondered if he was waiting because he had a good reason or because he was a coward.

After his father had left, after Olivia had died, he'd never allowed himself to deal in the word *love*. He'd lusted after women. He'd liked and respected previous girlfriends. He'd felt fondness and affection. He'd cared about them. But using the word love had not been part of his vocabulary. He'd never let himself go there, until Callie.

They might not have spoken of love, but they'd definitely shared it. They'd opened themselves up to each other in every possible way. They'd been honest. They'd been vulnerable. They'd trusted each other, even when they had no reason to.

She was the one. And he was damned if he was going to be too afraid to accept that, to act on it. He'd lived his life being fearless with everything but love. Now he was going to walk up to the edge of that cliff, and he'd either survive, or it would be a hell of a ride on the way down. But he wouldn't regret what he hadn't done.

Striding up to her door, he punched her buzzer with an impatient hand.

Her voice came over the speaker. "Hello?" she asked on a wary note.

"It's Flynn. Can I come up?"

She hesitated. "All right." She hit the buzzer.

He moved into the building before she had a chance to change her mind. He jogged up the stairs, and when he got to her door, she was waiting for him. She was dressed for a night at home, lounging leggings and a fuzzy, soft purple sweatshirt. Her brown hair fell loose about her shoulders. Her cheeks were flushed, her eyes sparkling, her lips slightly parted, and he wanted so much to kiss her. But first…

He handed her the bouquet of red roses he'd picked up on his way over.

"This is probably cheesy," he said. "But what the hell. I'm going all in."

"What does that mean?"

"It means I don't want this to end, Callie."

"You haven't called me in days."

"And you didn't say good-bye after the incredible night we had together."

"I wasn't sure I could," she admitted. "But I knew I should. What we had was fueled by adrenaline, danger, and passion. It wasn't real life. I'm actually pretty boring in real life."

"There's no way that's true."

"It is true. I work a lot."

"So do I."

"I just feed people. I don't solve crimes or save the world."

"Who cares about our jobs?"

"I have my mom, who can sometimes be a full-time job."

"I have people I care about, too. None of that matters. We go together, Callie." He put his arms around her, crushing the flowers between them. He pushed her back into her apartment, kicking the door shut.

"Ow," she yelped. "These roses have thorns."

"Sorry," he said with a laugh, taking the bouquet out of her hands and tossing it onto the couch. "We'll get to those later." He lowered his head and took the kiss he'd been hungering for.

She kissed him back for a long minute, then broke away with a breathless smile. "This is crazy, Flynn."

"Isn't that what love is?"

Her gaze darkened. "You're going there? You're using the L word?"

"I'm already there, babe."

"It's so fast. How can we fall in love in a week?"

"I don't know, but it happened. Can you tell me I'm wrong?"

"I don't want to tell you that. I want to believe it. But I'm scared. I usually push people away long before I feel like this."

He smiled into her eyes. "So do I. And maybe that's why I didn't call you."

"And maybe that's why I didn't say good-bye."

Her eyes grew a little misty, and his heart squeezed tight with emotion. "We can be scared together," he said.

"You're not afraid of anything, Flynn."

"I wish that were true, but I've kept my heart under wraps for a long time. I don't want to do that anymore. I don't want to screw up the best thing that's ever happened to me. I don't care if it's fast or it's crazy; I just know it's right. We can slow down. We can try to be rational, but we're going to get to the same place. I know it. I have no doubts." He realized how true his words were as he finally said them out loud.

"You're being so sweet. You're going to make me cry."

"I want to make you happy. I want to take some of the weight off your shoulders. You will never have to choose between your mother and me. I'll be right there with you, whatever happens, whatever you need."

"It can be a lot, Flynn. She's doing great now, but who knows how long that will last? She might have to live with me."

"Then she can live with us. I know better than anyone how important family is. I respect your fight, your loyalty. You have a tremendously big heart, Callie Harper, and if you're willing to give me even a piece of it, I would be forever happy."

"Oh, my God, that's the most incredible thing anyone has ever said to me."

"I meant every word. I want to be the person in your life you can count on, the one who'll hold you up when you feel like you can't stand. I want to share everything, the good, the bad, and the boring."

She gave him a sweet smile. "I want that, too, Flynn. I love the way you protect me, fight for me, stand by me. I also love the way you take care of your friends, how your team is your family. And I love that you could forgive your father enough to save my life."

"Forgive might be a big word, but I've let go of some of my anger toward him. I believe I can finally move on in my life."

"Will your dad go free? Did you get into trouble? I've been wanting to ask you so many things."

"I'll fill you in on everything. Bottom line, my dad is still a free man and the bureau is happy that we solved several murders, including Arthur's, so we're good."

"I'm so glad you didn't have to lose your job for him. That would have been too much."

"No. Because he helped me save you, and that's the only thing that mattered then and now."

"Do you really think we can make this work, Flynn?"

He smiled. "We are two of the most stubborn and determined people I know."

"Well, that's true," she said with a laugh.

"Then I have something important to ask you."

"What's that?" she asked, a breathless note in her voice.

"Will you go on a date with me?"

Her eyes filled with happiness. "I will. But not tonight. Tonight, I just want to be with you and only you."

"That sounds perfect," he said, feeling an overwhelming rush of love. "Can we start now?"

She tightened her arms around his neck and looked deep into his eyes. "I think we've already started."

"I agree. Let's keep it going."

"Forever," she murmured. "I've always been afraid of that word, but now I like it."

"I like it, too, as long as forever includes you."

# # #

Want more thrilling romantic suspense?

Savannah's story is up next in CRITICAL DOUBT!

Have you missed any of the OFF THE GRID: FBI SERIES?

ABOUT THE AUTHOR

Barbara Freethy is a #1 New York Times Bestselling Author of 68 novels ranging from contemporary romance to romantic suspense and women's fiction. With over 14 million copies sold, twenty-three of Barbara's books have appeared on the New York Times and USA Today Bestseller Lists, including SUMMER SECRETS which hit #1 on the New York Times and DON'T SAY A WORD, which spent 12 weeks on the list!

Known for her emotional and compelling stories of love, family, mystery and romance, Barbara enjoys writing about ordinary people caught up in extraordinary adventures.

She is currently writing two ongoing series: The romantic suspense series OFF THE GRID: FBI SERIES and the contemporary romance series WHISPER LAKE.

Printed in Great Britain
by Amazon

32887306R00184